Visibility Zero

Visibility Zero

by

BERNARD PALMER
Author, *Parson John, Storm Winds*, etc.

ZONDERVAN PUBLISHING HOUSE
Grand Rapids, Michigan

Eight Forty-seven Ottawa Ave.
Grand Rapids, Michigan

This novel could not possibly have been written without the active assistance and technical information given by Staff Sergeant Roger Dale Palmer, ball turret gunner on a B-17, who is now stationed "somewhere in England." He has received the Air Medal with three oak leaf clusters, and the Distinguished Flying Cross.

DEDICATION

This book is respectfully dedicated to the men and boys of Phelps County, Nebraska — many of whom I know personally — who have left farms, small towns and schools to flock to answer the call of the air force for personnel.

They have no desire to kill or maim, and get no morbid satisfaction from watching an enemy crash to his death. They kill because there is no other way to keep the oppressor's heel from American soil. They bomb cities because planes or tanks or guns are made there — matériel that one day would wreak havoc among American troops. And they strafe troop transports and communication lines to keep those enemies from spilling American blood.

Theirs is no easy task; living in the stinking tropics of the Solomons or the cold and desolation of the Aleutians; going continuously into hostile skies, braving ack-ack and fighter planes without complaint.

This book is not intended to be an authoritative treatise on the war or aerial warfare. Such a task is better left to posterity. Rather, this is the story of those who fly. You all know them — the boys who live around the corner or up the street from you. They feel the giddy, bewildering, unstable pace of the times with its confused standards. They know the tense excitement of bombing missions and the unceasing, gnawing desolation of fear. Life for them is stripped of gaudy trimmings. They see it as it is with all of its uncertainties. And many of them see, for the first time, *their* need of the Lord Jesus.

CHAPTER 1

Gray, icy fog was everywhere. It dripped from the eaves of buzzing hangars and squished underfoot in the grass along the narrow, flare-lined runways that stretched hazily into the infinity of space. Motors made muffled and eerie sounds, and British lorries, moving in an unending stream towards town, loomed up suddenly and faded away, their blackout lights pricking pin holes in the opaque curtain before them.

The meteorologist told of headwinds across the channel and of rain and poor visibility over target areas. Flight officers and commanders conferred, and the big Lancasters and Sterlings of the RAF wheeled into position. Ground crews returned to the warmth and light of their barracks, and fliers filed reluctantly out of the alert rooms where they had been briefing for the evening attack. Their objectives would have to await a more favorable night. It was not fit weather for flying.

In the American base close by, mechanics were swarming over the group of B-17's which had returned from a mission over occupied France just before the fog rolled in. It had been a rough afternoon and the big planes bore silent testimony of the flak and fighter opposition. Great jagged holes were blasted in the tail assemblies and the skin of the planes was riddled and curled by cannon fire. Wing sections were damaged and motors impaired before the group came limping home. Now the ground crews were sweating to put them into serviceable condition once

9

more; they were repairing each damaged part and adjusting each motor with the accuracy and skill of a watchmaker. Lives depended upon their work on the ground, and they proceeded painstakingly, testing each section and tuning each motor until an exacting crew chief gave it a "Roger." All their ability went into the ship, and then they waited, and hoped, and prayed that she would come winging back.

Some of the planes had not come back. Their battle-scarred wreckage had rested on the floor of the storm-tossed channel or had been cremated beside the target they had set out to bomb. Others had felt the sting of flak and cannon. They had felt them steal away their power and foul their controls with jarring blows. These weary planes had stumbled on as best they could, lagging far behind their flights and losing altitude. It was for these that the ground crews waited. Still clustered in little knots between the landing strips, they tried to talk about other things, but always drifted back to the subject of planes and men and sounds of familiar motors. The wind had lifted the fog somewhat and it began to rain. But the dim outline of the field was still visible. The field lights were still on, and flares still marked the landing strips in the vain hope of guiding a wounded bomber back to her haven.

The chaplain was still at the base — he always was when some of his boys were out — drifting from one tense group to another, encouraging his men with a reassuring smile, word or pat on the back. He had been stationed at the field since the first contingent of American airmen joined the RAF after Pearl Harbor, and a little piece of his heart had gone up with every plane. He knew and shared the anxiety of the ground crews who waited like a mother for her only child. He rejoiced when a big bomber circled the base and landed, and he sorrowed when a plane was reported lost.

Stories were beginning to filter through as to the fate of some of the big Fortresses. The pilot of the *Cherokee Bell* saw *Poor Willie* crash in flames, and had counted at least five parachutes billowed white against the green terrain. The navigator of an unidentified B-17 saw another hit by cannon fire and explode in the air. No parachutes had fluttered from it. And the men in the two remaining planes in flight five had grim word for the mechanics who were waiting for the *Terrier*.

She was hit by flak her first run over the target area. The number three motor was silenced, and a gaping hole was blown in her belly just aft of the bomb bays. How many were killed or injured no one knew. She completed her run and turned with them, fighting to keep her place, when a pair of Focke Wulfs dove on her, raking her unmercifully. One enemy fighter did not pull out of his screaming dive as the tail gunner caught him.

The flight pulled into a tight protective V, and dared the enemy plane to make another run. He caught the challenge, weighed the possibilities as he cruised along just out of gun range, then dipped his wings and veered off to find less formidable prey. Few fighter pilots would run the gauntlet of Fortress fire in an attempt to break the formation. They were at their best picking up cripples and stragglers.

The *Terrier's* crew battled valiantly to keep abreast of the flight, but she continued to lose both altitude and speed. The number two motor tore itself loose from its moorings before the co-pilot feathered the prop.

The other two pilots insisted upon staying with her to screen her from fighter attack, but Madden was adamant. He was the senior officer in the flight. The crew had to admit the logic of his order. The *Terrier* was cumbersome and unwieldy with two of her power plants gone and a wing flap control all but cut in two. There was considerable question as to whether she would reach the base of operations, excluding the ever-present possibility of fighter planes pouncing out of the sun. The three bombers waddling along just fast enough to keep in the air would be like ducks on the water to speedy Focke Wulfs. And they were still five hundred miles inside an enemy territory that bristled with fighters and ack-ack. It was better to lose one bomber than to risk losing three. Reluctantly, the other two had left her to her fate.

The ground crew took the news silently, with tight lips, and, perhaps, some misty eyes. They all had friends aboard the *Terrier*, for they had played "nursemaid" to their "baby" for weeks.

The chaplain came and stood silently among them; beads of rain dotted his weathered face and soaked through his light coat, chilling him. It would have been pleasant to go into operations headquarters or one of the hangars where it was warm and light, but his boys needed him. They were comforted knowing that he was there, ready with a prayer or a word of encouragement. He sensed their dependence upon him and the Master, and he thanked the Lord for it. It gave him opportunities for presenting the Gospel that were often lacking at home.

There was a faint hum of motors in the distance, a mere suggestion of sound that was snatched away instantaneously by a jealous wind. Men looked from one to another quickly, wondering whether it had really been a plane or was merely a fantasy, born of hope. Faces that had lit up expectantly at the sound tensed once more. Conversation that had been cut off suddenly began again, desultory and uninteresting. Everyone was listening beyond the sound of voice for the deep-throated roar of the *Terrier*.

In a moment the sound returned, a slowly crescendoing roar that came from the east, somewhere in the cloud banks above the arc of lights that was the airfield. They waited; suppressed emotions charged the air as the men strained to see into the darkness.

The plane was coming in low, and the sound was steadily growing louder. But it was not the full, vibrant hum of a four-motored B-17. It was high pitched and thinner, like a B-25 or one of the British Mediums, or perhaps an injured Fortress with half her power plants blasted to uselessness.

"It's the *Terrier*," someone said hopefully. The words were half question, half statement of fact.

"Thank God." The voice was hushed and humbly grateful.

The remaining motors were limping badly, and the plane was still swallowed by clouds towards the channel. She faltered an instant, and the men stood breathlessly until the laboring motors began to purr again, after missing only a stroke or two.

The big Fortress exploded suddenly out of the mist and darkness — so suddenly that the men gasped.

It was the *Terrier*, and it was obvious, even from the ground, that she had taken a terrific pounding.

She came in over the hangars like a gaunt brown ghost and dipped sharply towards the ground. An involuntary cry sprang from the lips of her ground crew, and a prayer arose from the chaplain's heart. Those in the path of the disabled craft scurried for cover. After fighting through five hundred miles of bristling enemy territory she was going to crash at her base of operations! But the pilot eased back — carefully, for fear of severing his already crippled controls, and the plane responded.

The *Terrier* shuddered from one wing tip to the other as she leveled off, with wheels almost touching the spongy, rain-soaked ground between the runways. Madden opened the throttle and coaxed an additional ounce of power from the protesting motors and climbed in order to come in up-wind and on a landing strip. He made a clumsy turn, skimming the tree-tops, and went into a steep glide. The big Fortress bounded into the air like a frightened rabbit, in spite of its thirty-two tons, and smacked the concrete strip a second time, crumpling the landing gear. With that she careened off the runway, plowed a furrow in the grass with a wing tip and finally nosed over.

An ambulance and a fire truck had been waiting on the edge of the field and they screamed out towards the wrecked plane even before it came to a stop. Every man at that end of the base raced towards the wreckage. Often the difference of a second or two meant the difference between life and death. A little gasoline from one of the big tanks had only to drip on a hot motor to turn the ship into a raging inferno.

The men in the *Terrier* were fortunate in that respect, for, although the plane was badly damaged, there was no fire. By the time the ambulance arrived the crew was beginning to climb out of the B-17. They climbed out wearily, men who had waited and fought and prayed to the point of exhaustion. Chaplain Davies began to count them as he ran, just as he counted the planes in returning formations, fearfully and thankfully. There were five — six — seven. The medical detachment went into the wreckage. Three of the *Terrier's* crew must still be inside.

The ground men clustered about the plane, marveling that even a pilot like Madden had been able to bring it back. To them he was the most skilled pilot in the group, and *almost* the best at the base.

"It must have been a rough afternoon, sir," the crew chief said to Captain Madden.

"Yes, Sergeant, it was that. And I'm afraid we didn't do your airplane any good, either."

Sergeant Byler surveyed it cryptically. "I wouldn't want to fly in that thing, sir. It leaks."

The pilot's face twisted into a crooked, infectious grin, more like his twenty-four years than the grim cut of his jaw and his grey-flecked hair. The last thirty-seven weeks had been thirty-seven years to him.

Sergeant Byler, a veteran mechanic from the last war, was glad to see "his boys" laugh. It eased the tension. "Maybe it'll keep some of these grease monkeys out of mischief for a couple of days, sir," said Byler.

"I think it will — if you put it in order," Rex replied doubtfully.

"Oh, we'll do that, sir, if we have to jack up one prop and drive a new plane under it."

Rex turned to his crew. "Let's go over to intelligence and get the report off our chests."

They obeyed mechanically. It was impossible to brush death one moment, seeing buddies die, and then laugh lightheartedly the next. But for the grace of God any one of them might be lying back there in the *Terrier*. And they had to go out again, and again, and again — playing with death, tempting it.

A flier could not allow himself to think, and yet how could he help it when his most intense desire was to live? Even the veterans had times of abject terror, when life was the most important thing in the world. Christian men and boys turned to their God, finding the ever-present Lord Jesus a source of strength and courage, but the others could only turn, in hopelessness and despair, to themselves.

The fliers filed into the little frame building that served "intelligence" as an office and stood about the long, narrow table in the center of the room, still bundled in their heavy flying togs. Several officers were waiting to complete the history of the night's operations.

The major asked them to be seated. Informality was the rule at the base, and not a few straight-laced West Pointers would have been rudely shocked to see the officers fraternizing with enlisted men. But form and military convention had little place at this base of operations where enlisted men and officers alike were flying and fighting and dying hourly.

Major Apel surveyed them carefully, searching each taut, sallow face, looking into the eyes that reflected some of the horror they had seen. Sympathy lurked behind his military manner. He had talked with many crews in just that same situation, had seen them fighting for self-control while they waited to tell their stories.

"Let me congratulate you and your crew, Captain," he began. "You've done a fine job in bringing back your plane. We'd almost given you up for lost."

"Thank you, sir."

The major looked at him and smiled. "Was that for the commendation or for giving you up?" he asked. Then he turned to the business at hand. "I understand that you had some nasty going, Captain Madden."

"It was pretty hot, sir. They almost had our number."

"The other boys had quite a tussle with fighters. I suppose you saw your share of them, too."

Briefly, haltingly, for the memories were still white-hot in his mind, Rex Madden related what had happened. He told about the fighter opposition and the ack-ack batteries they had encountered.

Major Apel was particularly interested in the increased numbers of fighters and the new antiaircraft batteries.

"Jerry must be beginning to smart a little," he observed, "or he wouldn't be shifting so much stuff from Russia."

When the bomber pilot told of their own injuries the intelligence officer sobered noticeably. He told how a direct hit in the radio compartment had killed Staff Sergeant Hemingsford and Sergeant Johnson. At the mention of Johnson, young Georgie Stebbins winced. He was only nineteen and Mitt Johnson had been his pal. They had enlisted together, trained together and had contrived to be assigned to the same bomber. Together they had manned the waist guns, Stebbins as assistant engineer and Johnson as armorer.

Rex went on with his story. A cannon shell had

splintered, ripping into the nose and seriously wounding Lieutenant Meyers, the bombardier. Navigator Norgren narrowly missed being killed when a fragment raced past his head and tore through the top of the plane, tearing a jagged hole as big as his fist.

Major Apel sat quietly, asking a question now and then and making comments as the story unfolded. The other crew members supplied details until the account was complete.

"Well, I guess that's all, boys," the major said as he gathered up his notes and handed them to an attaché. "You'd better turn in now and get some sleep. You've had a big day."

Georgie Stebbins was still sitting stiffly in the chair as the men arose to go. He was staring at the blank wall before him, struggling to control his nerves. His hands were clasped so tightly that the veins stood out, and cold beads of sweat dotted his face.

"Boy, this is big time, ain't it?" he mumbled incoherently. "Nobody here plays for fun. No, sir, this is for keeps." His lower lip was quivering and he strove to stem the flow of words. The men about him watched, tight lipped and sorrowing. They understood just how he felt. "No, sir, this is for keeps — this is for keeps."

With that he threw himself across the table and began to sob — long, dry, heart-rending sobs that tore at their souls. One of the men went to call Chaplain Davies, who had sensed he would be needed and was standing just outside the door. He talked with the young soldier a moment, until the sobbing ceased, and then helped him to his feet and brought him to the barracks. The slim shoulder was still trembling under his arm.

Major Apel stood there silently until he and the captain, Rex Madden, were alone.

"Was this his first mission, Captain?"

Rex stared out at the darkened field, going back to a day when another flier, a pilot, had come back from his first tough journey over a target area. The memories were heart-searing.

"Yes, sir," he replied.

CHAPTER 2

Rex Madden walked slowly back to the officers' quarters, dragging his feet through the thick wet carpet of grass. The field lights were off now and the landing flares had been snuffed out, to be lighted again another night when other bombers would come wandering home through the fog.

The planes not yet reported in would have, long since, run out of fuel; so they must be considered lost. The barracks and officers' quarters were shrouded in darkness, but not all of the men would be asleep. Some would still be fighting — fighting bitter, heart-searing memories. They joked and laughed and fought by day, and battled with terror by night.

Captain Madden's straight, broad shoulders sagged forward and he held his cap carelessly in one hand as though he lacked the strength to lift it to his head. With his face streaked and dirty, and his whiskers bristling, he looked more like his father shuffling home after a hard day at the mill than the dapper, well dressed young lieutenant who had landed in England months before. Excitement and fear had pumped their stimuli into his blood, and he had felt no trace of weariness during the perilous flight home. But now, after the interview with intelligence, the dikes which had held back the fatigue burst under the weight of it, and weariness came pouring out, flooding his soul.

There would be letters to write in the morning. How he dreaded that ordeal! Letters to mothers, wives or sweethearts telling them that their world had been broken in two. With a few short words and empty phrases he would try to lighten their burden. It was easier when Rex knew the flier had been a disciple of the Lord Jesus, for then he could write of the promises of God. But if the dead man had scoffed at Christ, as so many did, the task was doubly difficult. There was then no hope, no words of encouragement he could give except the time-worn phrase "He died a soldier." With all its wealth of meaning and honor that phrase is empty and hollow indeed to a mother who has lost her only son.

There had been many letters in the past weeks. There was Bartlett, Sims and Ronnquist of his first crew. And a little Jew with a German name he could never pronounce. He had been a tail gunner replacement and had gone out on only a couple of missions. There were others, too, whom it hurt to remember — splendid, fun-loving comrades who seemed to be too young and brave and manly to die.

He stopped momentarily at the door to the officers' quarters. There was a voice at his elbow. "Is that you, Rex?"

"Yes," he replied hesitantly. It sounded like Gaslin, his co-pilot, but in the darkness he couldn't be sure.

"I've been waiting for you." He swallowed hard. "I couldn't sleep."

It was Gaslin. He hadn't been with the crew long, and this had been his first bloody mission. Rex leaned against the door casing and tried to make out his companion's face in the shadows.

"What's on your mind?"

"It's Dixie. Have you heard how he is?"

The thought of Dixie stopped him short. He had not really remembered his bombardier until that very moment. What Mitt Johnson had been to Georgie Stebbins, Dixie Meyers was to Rex. They were buddies, and had been since that first day when they were given their wings and put into the same crew. They had been together constantly.

It was strange that he had forgotten about Dixie, and yet, there is no explaining what a man will or will not do under stress of battle. To be sure he had made the report about Lieutenant Meyers to intelligence, but that was mechanical — an inanimate thing void of emotion. It had been related in the same expressionless voice in which he had told about the damaged motors and the deaths of two men in his crew.

In that instant the soldier became a man again and he felt an overwhelming impulse to find out about his bombardier and friend. Why, he did not even know if Dixie was alive! Fright clutched at his heart as he remembered that Norgren had been pessimistic in his report over the interphone after the hit. A piece of shrapnel had almost severed the bombardier's arm and he had lost considerable blood before the navigator had applied a tourniquet and forced him to swallow a sulfa pill. Now the whole picture came rushing back to him.

Deliberately he forced every trace of emotion from his voice before he spoke. "I haven't heard a word yet."

"I thought maybe you'd go over to the hospital with me to find out," Gaslin suggested. "You know your way around here a lot better than I do."

"Let's go."

They turned and walked side by side over to the base hospital, a rambling one-story building set apart from the others and clearly marked with big red crosses on the roof. They were supposed to protect it from bombing when Jerry came over.

"That was tough about Johnson and Hemji, wasn't it?"

Rex did not answer at once.

Gaslin repeated the question.

"It was that." Suddenly he became angry with his co-pilot. Sure, it was tough about Johnson and Hemingsford. It was tough about all of them, but a fellow couldn't think about that if he wanted to hold down his berth and keep flying.

At the hospital a gruff, dour head nurse met them in the corridor. "It's after visiting hours," she snapped before they had an opportunity to speak.

"May we see Miss Patterson, please?"

The stubby little first lieutenant drew herself up haughtily and glared at Rex as if he did not realize what a heresy he had committed in asking to see one of the nurses in the middle of the night. He smiled a little. This particular supervisor had a wide reputation for grumpiness, but the men liked her in spite of it. She looked like Napoleon barring the door.

"Miss Patterson is on duty and very busy. You may see her any time after hours."

"I know she's busy," he conceded, "and we're sorry to bother you. We only wanted to find out how the last patient that was brought in this evening was getting along. Perhaps you could tell us." When she looked at him quizzically he added. "He was on that

bombing mission this afternoon. I was piloting and
Lieutenant Gaslin, here, was the co-pilot."

"I see." She softened a little, but her manner served
warning that her generosity was not to be abused.
"If you'll just wait a moment." She whisked efficiently down the long hallway and into the room at
the end, her starched skirts rustling. In a moment she
was back. "Were you inquiring about Lieutenant
Meyers?"

"Yes, that's him," Gaslin blurted eagerly.

"I got the right one then," she said, scanning the
chart. "Hmm. This doesn't look too good. He had
lost a lot of blood when they brought him in, and
there's a notation here to watch for signs of infection.
They gave him a transfusion immediately and have
one scheduled for ten in the morning. He's awfully
weak, but he's resting quite well now."

"Will he lose his arm?" the co-pilot ventured.

"We are interested in saving his life first, Lieutenant. Then we will worry about his arm."

"Thank you," said Rex, turning to go.

"Oh, Captain?"

"Yes?"

"We'll do all we can for him, sir. You both can be
sure of that."

They were walking in silence across the field. The
nurse had given them news of Dixie, but as Rex
mulled it over he could see that she had told them
nothing except the fact that his chum was seriously
injured. And that much he had known already.
There was a satisfaction in the knowledge that Dixie
was at a hospital where he would receive the best care
in the world in spite of over-efficient nurses. It would
probably be several days before the bombardier would

be out of danger, and in the meantime there was nothing to do but to watch and wait and pray.

Gaslin grasped him by the shoulder, jerking him out of his thoughts. "Captain," he said in a strange, taut voice. "How do you manage to carry on as you do? There's your best friend, dying for all you know, and you go calmly back to your bed as though nothing has happened. What are you made of? Stone?"

"No, Don," Rex replied. "I'm just as worried as you are. Right now all I can think about is Dixie and how he'll get along."

"But what keeps you from showing it? Why, I can hardly control my nerves tonight, and you're as cool as ever. Have you always been like this?"

They were at their quarters now and Rex sat down on a top step, crossing his legs and dropping his cap over one knee. Don Gaslin squatted in front of him.

"I think I've been more upset than you'll ever be," Rex told him. "But would you really like to know what has given me self-control?"

"Of course I would. I'd give anything for it."

"That isn't enough, Don. The question is: Are you willing to give *everything*?" He leaned forward and pressed a small oblong khaki book into the co-pilot's hand. The latter knew what it was by the feel of it. "The answer is here. Read this Testament every day; when we're in the air and when we're on the ground. Follow its teachings and *accept* its Christ. Confess your sins and pray! That is my way of going on missions repeatedly regardless of what happens."

"I know about the prayer meetings your crew holds before going upstairs." He could have added that he had loitered, purposely, in the briefing room to escape that prayer meeting only this afternoon. He was new in the squadron and the other boys had lost no time in telling him about the type of plane to which he had been assigned.

"I can truthfully say," Rex went on, "that if it weren't for the grace of the Lord Jesus I would not be flying today. I'd be at home and out of the army; probably a disgrace to myself and the squadron as well."

Lieutenant Gaslin fingered the Book meditatively before following his captain into the long narrow building. Prayer meetings and fighting sounded incongruously silly, but when you put it that way . . .

The next morning Rex was up and over to the hospital by the time Mildred Patterson came off duty. She was a pretty girl, even in the drab uniform of an army nurse. It was small wonder that Dixie Meyers had fallen in love with her. Half the patients on her floor dreamed of her at night. Dixie had met her in the States, and Rex could never decide whether it was coincidence or clever contriving that stationed them at the same base. If it had been anyone else, Rex would have said that a second lieutenant could not pull enough strings to get a favorite nurse assigned to his base. But Dixie Meyers had never heard of the word *impossible*. So the question still remained.

Patty's dark hair had been caught up hurriedly and pinned. It was supposed to stay in place, but it poked out from under her cap in an alarmingly feminine and unmilitary fashion. Her eyes were usually dancing, but this morning as she came out of the hospital, they were drab and lifeless.

"Good morning, Captain."

"Hello, Patts." He fell in beside her. "How's our favorite patient this morning?"

She tried to speak, but could only shake her head. The tears were brimming. In a moment she gulped them down and managed, "There's no change, Rex, except that he's a little weaker."

"I'm going to write his mother and I thought I'd find out before I did."

"Thanks," she smiled. "That'll save me from writing to her until . . . until we know for sure."

"I suppose the War Department will send her a cable in a day or two."

She nodded, and Rex squeezed her arm in sympathy. There were no words for the occasion.

The letters to Johnson's and Hemingsford's parents were comparatively easy to write, but he dreaded the one to Mrs. Meyers. Perhaps that was the reason he left it until the last. Mrs. Meyers' husband had been killed at Belleau Wood in the other war without ever seeing his son, and now Dixie was wounded and might be taken from her.

Rex reached for another V-mail blank and filled his pen with black ink, for Mrs. Meyers' eyes were tired eyes.

Dear Mrs. Meyers:

The War Department has undoubtedly informed you that Lee has been seriously wounded. I can't begin to express my sympathy to you. He has been more than a friend to me: he's been a brother.

He is getting special care as he was put on Patty's floor and she is taking care of him. All of us are praying for his recovery.

I know that you will be pleased to know that Lee has been active in bringing many of his companions to

Jesus Christ — including myself. His great spiritual fortitude has been his richest blessing. He is confident of his Lord and Saviour.

Sincerely,
REX

Before folding it he read it over a third time. Why did letters sound so cold and formal? Why could he not express the feelings in his heart?

It was towards evening and the letter had already gone when an enlisted man came in with word of Dixie. After the second transfusion he had rallied instantly and was getting stronger. The doctors expressed confidence that he was on the way to recovery.

Rex was surprised to learn that the Napoleonesque supervisor had sent word over to him as soon as she came on duty.

CHAPTER 3

The necessity of writing to Mrs. Meyers brought back memories of training days when he and Dixie and the rest of the *Terrier's* first crew were assigned to duty together. It was years ago instead of months, if time be measured by events. Half of that group were dead, and two others were in the hospital, probably never to fly again. Only Trout, Rogers and himself were left. They had never expected anything like that while making operational flights back in the States. Theirs was a charmed crew in a charmed plane, destined to go sailing blithely through flak and fighter opposition without mishap. But it was not long until their faith in their own select invincibility was shattered. Bill Jordan saw to that.

The climax of Rex's early training came the night he was assigned to a combat crew at the crew-forming base out of Cheyenne. He had spent seven long arduous months in training, studying mathematics, learning motors and flying under heartless instructors who discharged a man at the first indication of weakness. They had to be heartless, for the cadets would some day be turned loose with a quarter of a million dollars' worth of airplane and an incalculable sum in men. But that did not make it any easier for Rex, wondering whether he would still be at the field. Those wings meant a great deal to him.

He made it easier than he had ever dreamed possible, and then he was sent to Cheyenne where nine other men, as eager as he, were assigned to fly with him.

29

Captain Doyle, who was just home from duty in the Solomons, introduced them to each other.

"There's one thing you birds want to remember," he said. "There isn't any such thing as rank in the air corps. All the brass and saluting stay on the ground. A Jap or Jerry slug'll kill a major just as quick as a buck private, and if one man on the plane lays down, it isn't safe for any of the rest to be in the air. Suppose one gunner quits. It leaves a pretty good hunk of airplane open to attack and makes it a lot riskier to complete a mission.

"That's why the air corps doesn't tell you who to fly with, or when. If you've got a hunch you ought to stay on the ground, that's your privilege; and if there's a member of your crew you don't like, you don't have to fly with him." He paused a moment while they mulled over his words. "You guys are going to be eating and living and fighting together from now on, so you'd better be getting acquainted."

In the days to come they were to feel a bond forged about them, and between them, to weld them into a single fighting force. They were to stand by one another with far greater loyalty than they had ever felt for their fraternity brothers in college. If one of them got into an argument he would immediately have nine firm supporters. And if another had trouble with his girl, nine kibitzers would be available.

However, for the present the conversation was reluctant and stiff. Other crews were talking animatedly in the long barnlike structure, but the ten men who were to fly the *Terrier* stood about awkwardly, looking one another over and making sporadic halfhearted attempts at conversation. Sentences dangled in the air, unsupported by interest or con-

tinuity, and fragments of speech trailed off into
nothingness. The situation was becoming embarrass-
ing.

Lieutenant Meyers, a gangling farm hand turned
bombardier, stood with his hands on his hips and ap-
praised Rex Madden with exaggerated severity.

"So you're the guy who's going to drive for me?"
he mused, his slow drawl accentuating each syllable.

"What do you mean, drive for you? I'm the pilot.
I'm going to be the boss of this airplane crew."

"Ah-ah-ah," he shook his finger at Rex. "You remember what the captain said. You got to play nice
with us."

They all laughed a little at that and some of the
stiffness disappeared. Meyers shoved his cap back on
his head in a very nonmilitary manner, to expose a
sheaf of curly blond hair. He was warming up on
Rex and the crew loved it.

"Besides, I'm your bombardier, Mr. Airplane
Chauffeur. You got to be extra special nice to me or
I won't drop any eggs where you want 'em."

"And I'm liable to warm me a bombardier right in
the seat of the britches with a two by four," Rex
bantered, "if he tries that."

The bombardier scratched his head speculatively,
"You know, fellows, I don't think this guy knows
much about airplanes. He don't look much like a
flier to me."

"Come to think of it, he doesn't," the co-pilot put
in.

"Nope. His ears aren't big enough."

"My mom warned me about guys like him. She
said, 'Now Lee Allen Meyers, don't you let them put
you in no flying machine 'less you're sure the man

who's runnin' it knows how.' I'm going to take her advice."

"You don't suppose they made a mistake at the training field?" the radio operator said. "They're turning out pilots awful fast. Maybe it's like automobiles. Every once in awhile up turns a lemon."

"And you think we might've got the lemon, is that it, Sergeant?"

"Could be."

"Just wait till I get you guys up there with me," Rex said, laughing. "I'll show you whether I can fly or not."

"And by that time it might be too late," Meyers countered with mock sincerity. "What do you say we make him fly first? Maybe the CO would loan us an *old* B-17 so's the loss wouldn't be so big, just in case— There isn't any use of wasting a good airplane and ten good men just to find out if a pilot knows the score."

"Now you're talkin'."

"It's all right with me. I'll fly her blindfolded with my hands tied if that'll make you feel any better."

"You just fly her, Lieutenant. We'll ride in her."

"I'll bet you're from Georgia or Texas or Arkansas," Rex said, mocking his dialect.

"You aren't even close," he contradicted. "I'm a Swede from Minnesota."

"With that accent?"

"Okay, Yankee, I'm from Alabama."

"Now that's more like it. Come on, Dixie, let's treat the boys to a coke."

They got their own trim, olive drab "baby" to pamper and coax and abuse. She was an old plane that had seen her share of combat and had retired to

quieter climes; but they could not have loved her
more if they had put her together rivet by rivet, and
tightened each nut themselves.

After a few leisurely, exploratory flights, during
which the boys began to apply theory to actual experience, the training began. They were flying daily,
from Cheyenne to Amarillo to Spokane to Los
Angeles and back again. They sped across the desert
on simulated bombing runs, dropping live hundred-
pounders among the wooden practice bombs and
navigating by instruments and dead reckoning over
unknown terrain. Then they flew out over the ocean
some six or seven hundred miles to an infinitesimal
heap of sand that thrust itself a bare twenty feet
above the ocean level, there to land, refuel and return.
Operations kept a constant check on the plane by·
radio, but Eddie Zorn plotted the course alone and
hit it right on the nose. That was the proof of a good
navigator. The crew cheered him as they circled the
landing strip.

They turned north to battle snow flurries and south
for thunder storms and high winds. In combat they
would be operating in bad weather as well as good,
and they had to learn to ride out storms and get the
feel of their plane as she bucked headwinds. It meant
something quite apart from bombing and war to sense
the smooth, delicate, irresistible response of the B-17,
even in nasty weather. As the young crew piled up
the hours, their confidence in the big ship grew. It
was an exhilarating thrill to be in the air in her. They
all felt it.

The time not spent in flying was devoted to
mechanics and the lecture room. Every member of
the crew had two jobs which he had to learn thor-

oughly. Intelligence brought in men who had flown in combat over enemy territory and had acquired priceless knowledge concerning Jap and Jerry fighting planes and ack-ack. They reported the latest patterns of attack used by the enemy, and the methods that had been worked out to counteract each new trick.

A Captain Smith, slight, bronzed and prematurely gray, told of living three months in the hills of France with peasants and townspeople who risked their very lives to shelter him. Even the children knew of his presence and kept it secret. A Lieutenant Carmichael told of escaping an Italian prison camp and making his way to Switzerland and freedom. After each lecture the boys were better able to take care of themselves.

The crew expected furloughs when they completed the second phase of their training, but had to be content with three-day passes instead. Only the assistant engineer, who was near his home town, was able to visit his family. The rest went up into the mountains to a spot where a nameless stream spilled out of Bear Lake, tumbling downward in a series of rapids.

Some thoughtful mountaineer had built a pair of cabins beside the lake, anticipating, perhaps, a tourist rush that did not come. The road he had hewn into the side of the hill was overgrown with brush, and the cabins were in poor repair; but, amply fortified with netting, the little shelters did keep out the mosquitoes. And the fishing was good.

For three glorious days Rex, Dixie and the crew forgot about planes and missions and bombs. They even forgot to be homesick, and the one thought that was weighing upon their minds was gone for a time. The second phase of their training was completed.

The third would be over in a whirl of operational flights and they would be ready for a new B-17 with the latest improvements, the routine shakedown and then — overseas.

The second evening they learned that Dixie Meyers was *different* from most of them. They were sitting about a campfire swapping yarns and singing when he got out his accordion and began to play. It was a small box and his big hands seemed to swallow the keyboard as he gripped it.

In the west the sun was coasting cloudlessly behind distant hills, splashing gold and shadows on the cliffs. The wind was teasing pine needles in the trees above and they whispered their protestations. Now and again little ripples would go skittering across the water. It was getting colder, and one by one the boys slipped into their leather flying jackets and moved closer to the fire.

Dixie began playing softly, old haunting melodies that blended into the serenity of the evening. He drifted from song to song, singing snatches of them and humming when he did not know the words. Several others joined him, their subdued voices mingling in obligato to his rich full tenor. When he stopped playing they talked quietly of home and sweethearts and pleasant things.

"Let's sing another, shall we, Dixie?" Rex asked after several moments of silence.

"All right." He adjusted his accordion and sounded a chord with hushed feeling. His voice thrilled with love and devotion to the words. The soft accordion accompaniment was so soft as to be indistinguishable in itself. Yet it was there, lending color and harmony and beauty to the song.

I come to the garden alone,
While the dew is still on the roses;
And the voice I hear, falling on my ear,
The Son of God discloses.

And He walks with me, and He talks with me,
And He tells me I am His own,
And the joy we share as we tarry there,
None other has ever known.

He speaks, and the sound of His voice
Is so sweet the birds hush their singing,
And the melody that He gave to me,
Within my heart is ringing . . .

The boys looked from one to another, startled by the sudden change of tempo. It had been quiet before, but now the silence, except for Dixie's gentle tenor, took on new majesty. The patch of grass and the campfire became a hallowed place, a chapel with trees for walls and the starlit sky for a roof.

It seemed that the Holy Spirit had descended to lend reverence and peace to the little group. When Dixie finished singing, the boys sat without talking, awed by the strange new feeling that had come over them. Some of them knew little of Christ Jesus, and yet they felt the glory of His Presence.

After a minute or two Bill Jordan got to his feet noisily. "I think I'll go out and have a smoke," he said.

Time slid silently by. The wind stirred sleeping trees and fanned the dying embers of the fire. From a distant crag came the haunting howl of a wolf.

"I've always liked 'In the Garden'" Rogers said quietly, his tones matching the evening's sacred mood. "It's been my mother's favorite. She always sings it when she's troubled about something."

"The words do have a lot of consolation," Dixie agreed. "Isn't it wonderful to know that we have the privilege of walking with Him?"

"It sort of makes a fellow think, doesn't it?"

"You know I used to refuse to go to church with my girl," the radio operator observed. "But here I sit listening to you guys and loving it. It's hard to believe there's even a war on anywhere in the world, it's so peaceful here. Why do you suppose God lets things get into such a mess, anyway?"

There was a long silence.

"I don't think it's God; I think it's us," young Rogers replied. "Hatred and greed and sin have caused this war, just like all the rest. It's man who's to be blamed, not God."

A shooting star streamed across the heavens and vanished; their eyes followed its flaming path.

"Looks just like a tracer, doesn't it?"

"I wonder if they'll seem that harmless and pretty when Jerry starts arcing them up at us?"

"We ought to know before long." Dixie's eyes wandered over the group, resting on each tanned face. "I wonder how many of us will come back?"

They stirred momentarily, jarred back to the immediate present by his words. If anyone else had talked in such a manner they would have hooted him down, but this was Dixie. His warm quick smile and his understanding had made him one of the most beloved in the crew. His reputation among them gave weight and dignity to his words.

"It isn't pleasant to think about, I know, but it's something we've all had on our minds for weeks. While we've been sitting here, warmed by the very Presence of Jesus, I've been wondering how many of us are prepared for the things we're going to have to face."

"Of course we're prepared, Dixie," Rex cut in. "We've been in various kinds of training more than a year already, and we've still got one phase to complete. We'll be ready."

"Yes, we'll be prepared physically, and as mentally ready as possible, but will we be prepared *spiritually*? Will the Lord Jesus Christ mean anything to us?"

Bill Jordan had sauntered back to the circle and was leaning against a tree. He would have spoken tauntingly, but no one gave him attention. Their interest had been captured by Dixie.

"Without thinking of Him and His power to save and watch over me, I'm terrified at the thought of flying over Germany," he went on. "We're going to need Christ *over there* more than we've ever needed Him before. I don't think it's out of keeping for each one of us to search our hearts tonight. If there isn't a place for Jesus in your hearts, then make one for Him. Confess your sins and let Him show you the way of salvation."

He picked up his accordion and played the hymn through again, restrained and meaningful, and sang the chorus.

"Let's have 'The Old Rugged Cross' before we turn in," Bob Trout suggested.

The entire crew, with the exception of Jordan, sang as much of the song as they knew. When it was finished they got to their feet, kicked sand over the last red coals of the fire and trooped silently into the cabins. The evening had made a profound impression upon them.

At the door of his cabin Bill Jordan stopped and

called to Dixie, "Good night, Reverend." His voice
was mocking and edged with sarcasm.

"Lay off that, Bill," Trout ordered, out of the
darkness.

"I suppose you like to be preached to?"

"What I like or don't like is my business. You
just lay off of Dixie."

The next morning the crew paired off and went
fishing. Dixie and Rex were together as usual,
walking downstream to a trout pool they had discovered the day before. They had taken a number of
fish, and the rises had been frequent and vicious
enough to bring them back.

The trout were as wary as they were bellicose and
it took a deal of fishing to fool them. Dixie was standing close to the shore, shivering in his waders for the
water was cold, and Rex was near the middle of the
stream.

"I didn't know you were planning to go into the
ministry," Rex said by way of opening conversation.

Dixie snap-cast a royal coachman out into the clear
cold pool and twitched it tantalizingly, his arms
poised for the strike. "I'm not," he replied. "I've
never even considered going into the ministry. What
kind of a fly are you using?"

"Silver doctor." He was standing knee-deep in the
stream, adjusting his leader. "But I thought . . .
last night . . . "

Dixie laid aside his rod and sat down on a boulder.
"No, I haven't even thought of being a minister.
Why?"

"I guess I was taking it for granted after the
things you said."

"I only said the things that were in my heart. I

know what believing in Jesus Christ has done for me, and I know some of these youngsters are going to need Him when the going gets tough. That's the reason I spoke as I did."

"I can understand that," Rex replied, in a tone that revealed quite plainly that he did not understand at all. "But I've been wondering whether it's good for the crew or not. Bill Jordan took offense last night, and I'm afraid he won't forget it very easy. He's quite a hothead."

"I'm sorry about that, Rex. I didn't want to offend anyone."

"I know you well enough to know that. But we can't have any ill feeling in the crew, even if it is all one-sided." He was finding it difficult to put his thoughts into words. He did not want to hurt Dixie, but he was the skipper of the crew, and they could not have trouble. "Maybe we'd better kind of drop the subject of religion while he's around. How about it?"

"Anything you say," Dixie said soberly. "But I wish it were possible to get him to realize what he's shutting out of his life. I think he must have been under conviction last night or he wouldn't have been so irritable."

Now that he had said what he felt impelled to say, Rex Madden directed the subject to other channels. Dixie's vibrant living faith annoyed him almost as much as it had Jordan, but not for the same reason. It pointed to the shocking contrast between the way Dixie Meyers was living the Christian life and the way Rex was living it.

Rex had believed himself to be a Christian since he had become a member of church. He had acquired a working knowledge of the Scriptures and salvation. He knew the meaning of being "born again." Then he settled down to living an exemplary virtuous life that had earned the commendation of the mothers in his home town and his own unspoken but nonetheless evident self-approval.

To Rex, being a Christian had never meant speaking out for the kingdom as Dixie had done the night before. His Christianity seldom concerned itself with others. It had been definitely a personal affair. It had hurt to have Dixie, by his actions, point so glaringly at the holes in his armor.

That evening they packed their bags and went back to the base for the third and final phase of their training.

CHAPTER 4

During the next few weeks they were in the air every day, flying singly and in formation, doing high-level bombing, and diving low to skim whitecaps with the big ship's belly as they skip-bombed.

Skip-bombing was one thing for a fighter plane, or even the heavier B-25 Medium, and quite another for the four-motored thirty-two-ton Fortress designed for high altitude operation. But under fire it proved as successful as it was dangerous, so it was given an important place in the curriculum of crews who might see action against surface craft.

Of all the tasks they had to perform that was the most breath-taking. The squadron came in at high altitude, drawing enemy fire and keeping attention, as long as possible, from the lone plane that was plummeting out of the sky for the kill. The crew, except for the ball turret gunner, would be at their regular battle stations, with nerves taut and breath coming in short quick gasps. The ball turret gunner would be straddling the open bomb bay to kick out the bomb at precisely the right instant. The crew laughed at the way Rogers sweat before going to his post, but none of them envied him his job. It was enough to feel the heavy plane hurtling down towards the water, and to see the ship that had been selected as a target loom up suddenly before their eyes. Although they trusted Rex to pull out in time, they all breathed a bit easier when it was over.

Every phase of the training was intensified a dozenfold and carried out as nearly as possible under actual war conditions. They went into alert rooms to be briefed for missions, there to remain until the hour to take off. They flew under sealed orders, not knowing their destination until they reached an altitude of five or ten or fifteen thousand feet and opened their orders.

Whenever they came in at the base a ground crew swarmed over their plane, tuning it to minute perfection. It was always ready at any time to fly for an hour or as long as the gasoline in the tanks held out, depending upon the occasion. The crew might fly to Alaska, Miami or circle the field twice and land. They never knew what to expect when they climbed into their plane.

Before each flight the doctor examined them. Even a cold can have serious consequences in high altitudes. A trace of alcohol was enough to upset the most physically perfect flyer. Even the heaviest drinkers in their squadron soon learned, from being ordered to stay on the ground, that abstinence went with flying at thirty thousand feet.

The crew took on a new seriousness as they realized that the day was nearing when they would head out over an ocean for the "big show." Rumors were rife at the bases where they landed. Somebody heard they were being sent to Alaska, and another had inside information that they would be based in Greenland on patrol. And a third soldier, who claimed to have been the crew chief for General Marshall's personal plane when it was at the base a short time before, said that he had on absolute authority — the name was missing, but he left no doubt as to who the authority was

— that all the B-17 crews were to be ordered back to training in some new and terrible type of bombing. The grapevine had it that they were going to England, North Africa, Egypt, Australia and the Aleutians, in that order. At first the boys repeated every story breathlessly, their spirits soaring or falling, according to the location of their supposed destination, but they soon learned to correctly evaluate the rumors. Only a select few knew the actual destination of individual planes and they were not given to careless talking.

Dixie Meyers heeded Rex's request and said nothing to the young tail gunner regarding spiritual things, but the situation did not ease. Time only aggravated it.

Bill Jordan looked down upon the Southern boy disdainfully, as if being a Christian pointed to a serious flaw of character. It was obvious that he felt himself above and beyond Dixie's radiant faith in the Lord Jesus. Although Meyers outranked him, rating a gold bar to his own three stripes, he never missed an opportunity to insult him. On the ground he persisted in ridiculing the bombardier, and in the air he made slurring remarks into the interphone.

"Tail gunner to bombardier, tail gunner to bombardier, go, ahead, bombardier," he said into the throat mike.

"Bombardier to tail gunner. Go ahead, tail gunner."

"How about it, Dixie, are you going to pray for all those little Huns and Japs you drop your bombs on?"

"Of course I will, Bill. And you might like to know that I'm praying for you, too. I'm praying

that you will confess your sins and come to the Lord
Jesus on your knees."

That ended the conversation, for Bill switched off
his interphone. Later in the week they were all sitting in a café in Salt Lake City on one of their rare
evenings off when Bill, his ribald voice carrying to
the surrounding tables in the crowded café, opened
the subject again.

"Tell me, Dixie," he asked, leaning forward in his
chair importantly, "how do you live with yourself?
Dropping bombs in the daytime and praying at night.
Is it 'Let not thy right hand know what thy left hand
doeth'?"

The crew would have risen as one to silence him,
but Dixie seemed capable of handling the situation
alone. Rex started to interfere, but changed his mind.
After all, Bill was asking for it.

If he was expecting his bombardier to pounce upon
the tail gunner verbally, he was wrong. Dixie spoke
with the sincerity of one who assumes the sincerity of
his companion. His voice was not loud and boister-
ous, but he, too, spoke clearly enough to permit those
at the tables close by to hear what he had to say.

"To my way of thinking there isn't any contradic-
tion between being a bombardier and a Christian,
Bill," he replied. "We didn't start this war, and we
didn't start the bombing of cities. You and I and the
rest of the crew aren't going to get any fun out of
killing. It's just a job that's got to be done — a
messy, dirty job that's ruthless because all fighting
for survival is ruthless. Every time we drop a bomb
on a Jerry factory or ammunition dump, we're con-
tributing just that much to the shortening of the war.
And whenever we destroy a submarine we're remov-

ing one more menace to American shipping and American lives.

"You asked me the other day if I was going to pray for the victims of my bombs. Of course I am. I'm going to pray that my bombs may hit their targets and spare innocent women and children. I'm going to pray that the bombs I drop will wreak great havoc among enemy war industries so that all free people may worship their God in safety and peace again."

His argument left Bill Jordan unconvinced, for he had not opened the subject to be convinced of anything, but only to ridicule. However, the force of Dixie's convictions left the arrogant little tail gunner without words to continue the attack.

Presently dinner was over and the crew scattered for the evening. When Rex and Dixie were alone the pilot said, "I'm going to have Bill taken out of our crew, Dixie. He's a trouble maker and a hothead. This affair tonight was too much. I wouldn't have blamed you if you'd knocked that nose of his clear down his throat."

The bombardier smiled slightly. "It's not as bad as all that. If he gets any fun out of riding me, he's welcome to it. He doesn't bother me."

"Just the same I don't like it. I'm going to have him moved."

"I wish you wouldn't, Rex. He can't get me mad at him, but he's going to think I caused him to be removed from the crew. I wouldn't want that."

After considerable persuasion Rex decided to let Bill stay.

The next morning before dawn they were called into the alert room and briefed for a trip to the

Kearney Air Base, a new field just completed on the Platte River between Cheyenne and Omaha. All forty-five planes were on the line, their tarps taken off and their engines warmed; great prehistoric monsters of the air squatting uncomfortably along the runways, as though they sensed their uselessness upon the ground and were impatient to be away. Looking at the rows of somber, olive drab planes, one was profoundly impressed by the huge tails. The fins rose from the sleek fuselage like hills rising out of nowhere on the flat, level desert, or like a row of cottonwoods standing proudly alone, and in a line along a prairie fence. They were spectacularly impressive, the first thing one saw and the last thing he forgot about the Flying Fortresses.

One by one the big ships caught the signal, taxied down the runway and took off, circling the field. Then they maneuvered into formation in groups of three and headed out across the mountains, the mighty tattoo of a hundred and eighty motors presaging their coming.

The meteorologist predicted cross-winds and rain with considerable electricity in the mountain region around Yellowstone, and he warned of dust storms on the plains beyond. But the time had passed when they became upset at the weather.

The air was rough and the swirling clouds gave evidence that the storm predicted might not be long in overtaking them. They were flying high through opaque cloud curtains to avoid the mountains, and the navigator was charting the course without the benefit of landmarks. That, also, had become routine, for church steeples and creeks have a tendency to blur into the terrain at twenty or thirty thousand feet.

The navigator in the flight commander's plane was doing the work, but Eddie Zorn followed through for the practice it afforded.

The crescendoing cross-wind was pushing and clawing at a forty-degree angle and it became increasingly difficult to hold the planes together and on their course. Under orders the planes began to spread out, each allowing itself more space in the formation. The danger of a collision at close quarters was infinitely greater in a storm.

Lightning was cleaving the heavens with a blinding flash to wreak its vengeance on some unsuspecting spot below, and the darkness was deepening rapidly. Rex Madden's crew could scarcely make out the wing tips of the planes at either side. The big craft was being tossed and rolled by the winds like a toy boat in the gutter.

"Flight commander to all planes! Flight commander to all planes! Disperse and proceed to nearest airfield."

"Roger," they chorused.

"And may God go with you."

"What're we going to do, Rex?" The voice was tense and hysterical on the interphone. "What're we going to do?"

"Pilot to tail gunner! Go ahead, tail gunner!"

"Go ahead, pilot." The panic was still there, suppressed but breathless. A word of sympathy or assurance might provide the spark.

"Is that the way you were taught to use the interphone?"

A hesitant "N-no, sir." The "sir" was not required, but Rex's forcefulness commanded it.

"Then don't go bellowing into your mike like a scared calf. Use it in regulation manner."

There was no answer.

"Roger?"

Reluctantly, "Roger."

Rex was already switching his attention to other things. The rest of the group had been swallowed by darkness as they fanned out in the perilous search for a haven, and Rex's ship was left alone. He was glad to know that Eddie Zorn was sitting up front at the navigator's table. On trips like this the navigator's ability to pick up their exact position in the sea of indigo and guide them safely to a landing strip could mean the difference between life and death to all of them.

"Pilot to navigator. Pilot to navigator. Come in, Eddie."

"Navigator to pilot. Come in, Rex."

"Where's the nearest airfield, kiddo?"

"Mileston, Montana." He had been anticipating such an action by the flight commander, and had already made the necessary calculations. "It's west and north of here, but we'll have a tail wind."

"O.K., you give me the course and we'll go home to mama."

"Roger."

They negotiated a turn and rode with the wind, their tired engines coasting. It seemed that the fury of the storm lessened as soon as they ceased battling it and turned about. The strain was less on the plane and men alike. They began to joke a little over the interphone, kidding one another and singing snatches of songs. However, they noticeably avoided any mention of Bill Jordan's near hysteria. His voice, usually so prominent, was scarcely heard at all, and then it was strained and unnatural.

As they neared the base Rex called the radio operator. "Come on there, fellow, you've got work to do. Identify us and get some landing instructions."

"Boy, I'm glad to hear them kind words. An hour ago I was wondering if I'd ever hear them again." In a moment he was back. "She's dead as a pickled catfish, Rex."

"Can you fix it?"

"Give me fifteen minutes and I'll tell you."

Rex looked at his gas gauge. The engines had really been sucking up the fuel during the storm. He had been watching the gauges for a hundred miles, calculating and hoping and calculating again. The co-pilot saw it too, and their eyes met questioningly. He would have told the crew, but with Jordan on the verge of hysteria he decided against it. Now they were nearing the field and it did not matter.

"We've got about fine minutes' gasoline to spare. It looks like we'll have to drop in unannounced and surprise them."

"Anything, anything," the radio operator said with mock resignation. "Just so we get both feet on the ground again."

They dropped out of the clouds and circled the base two or three times, getting the lay of the runways. There were several long ones suitable for bombers, but they were blocked with planes.

"It looks like one of the baby ones for us," he muttered under his breath. "Everybody at crash stations. Susan hasn't used such a little stall before." He turned and began to glide downward. "Here we go!"

The wheels touched lightly on the ground and the

tail settled back as daintily as a swallow descending to her nest. The crew relaxed, but only momentarily.

"Look out!" the co-pilot shouted.

"Grab the brakes!"

The landing strip was rapidly running out, and at the end a cliff sliced down a hundred and fifty feet. There was a screech as the emergency brakes locked; the plane careened and went up on its nose, sheering two props and damaging the superstructure. The crew crawled out, shaken but uninjured.

It took two days to put the big craft back into flying condition. New parts were flown in by plane from Denver and mechanics worked long hours repairing it.

Other planes in the group had not fared so well. One had been struck by lightning and burned in the air, and another crashed into a mountainside, and all the crew were killed. The Fortresses were spread over a five-hundred-mile circle, scattered like chaff by the wind.

Rex communicated with Salt Lake City immediately and was ordered to leave for Kearney as soon as the plane was repaired.

For two days the crew relaxed and enjoyed themselves. They slept and ate without thought of time. They had been putting in stiff hours since their little jaunt into the mountains before the third phase began, and they were nearly exhausted.

Rex sought out Bill Jordan the morning after they landed and apologized for being so rough with him.

"You know I didn't mean what I said, Bill," he told him. "But you sounded kind of excited and I wanted to make you so mad at me you'd forget the storm for awhile."

"That's all right." But his tones lacked their former confidence. His eyes were listless and his face pallid and drawn. He was still visibly shaken.

The pilot watched him carefully, not liking what he saw. The fellows had been talking about Bill the night before. They all knew what had happened and were concerned about him. It reflected upon the entire crew to have a man dismissed for lack of courage, and above anything else, they wanted to prevent that.

"What's he going to do when we go overseas?" the armorer asked.

"We've got to have a gun in that tail we can depend on. Why, it might be curtains for the whole flight if he'd go to pieces on a mission." And that was no exaggeration, for the flights were arranged in groups of three so that each gunner could cover a segment of the skies. One gun out left the entire flight vulnerable from that position.

"He's just a kid," Rex put in. "He'll come out of it once he gets a little seasoning under fire."

"I wouldn't be too sure of that."

And so the conversation went. There seemed to be no solution, only concern.

It was Rogers who suggested that Dixie talk with him.

"I've tried to," he protested, "but you know how he acts to me. I wouldn't be able to get near him at all."

"I wish you'd talk to him anyway," the ball turret gunner insisted. "I know what he needs, and so do you."

Dixie nodded. "I know what we *all* need."

"And you're the only one who knows enough about it. I'll go with you if you want me to."

The rest of the crew agreed heartily. Even those

who were definitely not Christians could see Bill
Jordan's need for Jesus, although they could not see
their own.

Dixie prayed long about the arrogant tail gunner.
The task of talking to him of Christ had to be done
delicately. It would not do to force the discussion, or
begin while others were present; if he did, he would
be finished before he began. He would have to pry in
at the corners of the door with which Bill Jordan had
shut out the Lord. He would have to pique his interest and gain his attention so that he would hear him
out. So he prayed and watched and waited.

CHAPTER 5

Rex thought they would get away Monday evening, but the crew chief had not finished the repairs.

"We've still got a little more to do on her, sir," he told Rex. "The oil pressure's weak on number four, and I don't like the way number one's new prop is adjusted. But the boys are working on her and she'll be gassed and warmed up and ready to go any time you want her after four in the morning."

"Thank you, Sergeant. We'll be out at four." He turned to Dixie. "Well, it looks like we don't go upstairs tonight."

"That's all right with me. I can use a little sleep."

Back at operations the officer in charge said, "I was just going to look you up, Lieutenant. Do you need a little ballast on your trip tomorrow?"

"I don't know. Why?"

"I thought you might have room in your bomb bay for about a hundred and seventy pounds of army nurse. She's going to Kearney too, so I took the liberty of telling her you'd give her a lift."

"You bet we will. I'll have the engineer put her name on the flight list." He thought a moment. "Did you say she weighed a hundred and seven pounds or a hundred and seventy?"

The officer laughed. "She's married, fat and forty, so you can put the old charm back in moth balls."

"That's just my luck. The last woman who rode with us was a skinny old spinster who persisted in calling me the driver and the co-pilot my helper; and

54

him with brand new gold bars. You should have heard him rave!"

The next morning at four, Lieutenant Mildred Patterson was shivering in the darkness outside operations, waiting for the crew. Down on the line the big motors were idling and the crew chief was checking the action of the troublesome oil line and the faulty prop.

When the boys came out of the little office the nurse stepped up to Dixie, who happened to be the closest to her.

"A-are you with the crew of the plane that's going to Kearney?" A nurse was supposed to carry rank equal to that of commissioned male officers, but she had not yet learned to assume it.

"Yes, ma'am. I sure am."

The others stopped and crowded close, trying to make out her features in the dim light.

"I'm Lieutenant Patterson. Operations told me they were sure I could ride with you. I'm being transferred to the Kearney Base."

Rex elbowed his way to the front. Even in the darkness he could see that operations had been deliberately deceiving him. He knew that she must be beautiful from the sound of her voice.

"I don't believe it."

She drew herself up to his shoulder and stared into his eyes. Her voice was sharp and indignant. "I have my papers right here, Lieutenant. And I'm not used to being told I've lied."

"Oh, I didn't mean that. The fellow at operations who talked to you told me you were married, fat and forty. I don't believe it."

When the laughter died away she said coldly and

impersonally, "You still haven't told me whether I may ride with you or not."

"Well, that depends. What's it worth to you?"

"I didn't know the army was allowing its pilots to haul passengers for hire. It must be something new."

"No, they just let us take a little bribe now and then to get a name put on the flight list by the engineer. Like your having dinner with me this evening, for example."

"If the engineer is the one who puts my name on the flight list, perhaps I should have dinner with him."

"Now you're talking, Miss," Bob Trout put in. "This lug doesn't know how to treat a lady."

"Oh, you wouldn't like going with him," Rex continued, ignoring his engineer. "He eats garlic and dunks his bread in his coffee. Besides, he's got a girl who just sits home and cries every time somebody tells her that her 'flying Casanova' has had dinner with another girl."

Trout opened his mouth to deny it vehemently, but Dixie took over before he could say a word.

"Why don't you just put both of these guys on ice, Lieutenant?" he asked. "Besides, if you tell one of them you'll have dinner with him now you might be sorry before evening comes." He took her by the arm and began to lead her towards the plane. "Now if you want a *good* seat in this B-17 you can get up in the bombardier's compartment with me. We sit right out front where you can see everything. You wouldn't believe it, but the whole airplane was built just for the bombardier's compartment . . . " They passed out of hearing of the rest of the crew.

"I wouldn't have believed it if I hadn't seen it,"

Rogers breathed admiringly. "Fat chance any of the rest of us've got as long as he's around."

They got into the plane and Rex took off into a stiff west wind and circled to ride with it over the hills. Flying at dawn, with motors adjusted to such precision they would respond to a feather on the controls, he felt a sense of strength that did not come to him on the ground. He was beyond the reach of man. Nothing could touch him or the plane he flew.

The crew chief had done an excellent job on the B-17 and they cruised along at two hundred miles an hour, just below the altitude that would force their guest to use oxygen.

Patty was delighted with the trip. (Dixie was calling her that before they had taxied to the end of the runway.) It was the first time she had been in a B-17 or anything half its size, and it seemed to her that the bombardier was right when he said that the whole airplane was built around his compartment.

The world stretched out beneath them, a mottled hodgepodge of color and shadows in the early sun. Lilliputian towns pushed up from the green forests to establish minute claims on the hills. The sordidness and dirt were hid from such heights and they looked fresh and clean and beautiful. Silvered threads twisted down the mountainsides to form silvered rope in the valley.

"Oh, it's marvelous!" Patty murmured.

Dixie was silent. While she was engrossed in the scene below he studied her carefully. There was no doubt that she was a newly appointed army nurse, just out of school somewhere and going to her first post. There was a stiff uneasy newness about her uniform, and her cap lacked the jaunty confidence time acquires.

There was also a freshness about her; the clean wholesome look of the girl who lived next door or up the street from home. She was not classically beautiful, he decided. But her attractiveness was all the more captivating for it. That deep-throated laugh and the smile in her eyes welled from a happy soul.

"I notice, Lieutenant," he smiled, "that you've got the pocket of your blouse unbuttoned. Regulations, you know."

She blushed and fumbled with the pocket flap. "I'm afraid I'm going to be court-martialed before I learn all the regulations."

"They couldn't court-martial the prettiest nurse in the army. Why, there'd be a revolution."

"Oh, go along with you."

"I'll bet you picked up that phrase from your grandmother. Mine used to say that every time I teased her."

Patty nodded, smiling.

"But to get back to that pocket. I'll bet you've got either cigarettes or a Testament in it?"

"And why not both?"

"I don't think they go together very well, do you?"

She laughed. "It's my Testament, Mr. Detective. I was reading it before going to bed last night."

"I thought so. I could see it in your face."

"That I was reading it before I went to bed last night?"

"No, that you placed your trust in the Lord."

"I didn't know it showed."

"But it does. Everything you are or have been

shows in your face — sorrow, worry, sin, faith. You can't hide it."

"You're a philosopher as well as a bombardier, aren't you?"

He would have answered, but there was a voice on the interphone. "Pilot to bombardier. Pilot to bombardier. Go ahead, bombardier."

"Bombardier to pilot, go ahead, Rex."

"If you interfere with my date tonight I'll grind you to a pulp."

Dixie looked over at his companion and grinned. "I haven't taken care of that matter yet, Lieutenant Madden, but I'll do so immediately. I'll call you as soon as there is anything to report."

Without turning off the interphone he said, "I'll bet I could find a swell little café in Kearney if I had you to help me hunt for it. Do you think that could be arranged, Patty?"

"You double-crossing Irishman!" came over the interphone. "I'll get even with you! I'll . . . "

"Thanks, Dixie," Mildred Patterson replied. "I'd like to, but I really feel obligated to go with that Lieutenant Madden, or whatever his name is. After all, he did get me a ride, and I've enjoyed it so very much."

"But you'd rather go with me, wouldn't you?"

Her eyes were teasing him. "I've never been with him, so how would I know?"

"I can tell you right now you wouldn't like him. He . . . "

Everyone was talking over the interphone at once.

"And I thought we were pals," Madden moaned. "Just listen to him, and after all I've done for him too. He ought to be lynched . . . And you will be when I get my hands on you, Dixie Meyers!" he promised darkly.

"Give it to him, Rex, pour it on."

"Too bad you can't go up there and protect your interests with that Dixie terror on the loose," someone chortled from his post.

"That's all right, Dixie," Bob Trout put in. "Hold your ground, don't let him scare you. Why, he knifed me the same as you're doing to him, so what's he got to squawk about? Take her away from him. I'm for you!"

Dixie Meyers muffled his throat mike with his hand. There were some things a fellow did not want even his friends to hear.

"You know, Patty, Rex is just kidding about all of this. Why, he didn't even get a good look at you this morning before we took off. I'll bet he wouldn't recognize you if he met you on the street."

She turned, smiling. "You put up a convincing argument, Lieutenant. Do you always double-cross your friends?"

"I reserve that for special occasions," he replied, "when there's a pretty girl like you involved." He could see she was weakening and he pressed his slight advantage. "Besides, this might be the only night we'll be at Kearney. I think we'll be there longer, but we're getting 'hot' and they don't leave us at one place very long. If you don't go into town with me tonight we might never see each other again." Dixie stopped short. "There is a town close to this base, isn't there?"

Patty thought a moment. "I think there must be. I've got a girl friend who's going to school in a

Kearney, Nebraska. The base must be quite close to have the same name."

"That settles it," he announced. "You call the girl friend for Rex, and you go with me."

"I'm not sure I can locate her," she protested. I haven't heard from her in months. She really isn't my girl friend; I just know her a little. She might be home on a vacation, or she may not have even come back last fall."

But Dixie would hear no excuses, and ᴀe planned gleefully for their date.

As soon as they landed and crawled out of the plane he grabbed Patty's bags and shuttled her away from the crew towards the hospital where she was to report for duty.

"I'll see you at supper, young lady," Rex called after her.

"Don't count on it," she said.

Rex thought it strange that Dixie gave in so easily when he announced that he was taking their passenger to dinner.

The bombardier had answered very resignedly, "She's calling a girl friend now. We'll meet you at the PX about four-thirty, after you make your report."

It was as simple as that, and Rex had not suspected a thing, even when he walked into the PX and approached Dixie and the two girls. One was Miss Patterson, trim and efficient in her uniform, and the other a very attractive young blonde who was wearing a cool white dress to bring out the brown of her eyes.

Dixie came forward to meet him, with the little blonde in tow. "Miss Banks, I want you to meet

Lieutenant Rex Madden, the best pilot in the 85 Bomber Group."

Then he saw what was happening, but by that time it was too late. Dixie and Miss Patterson had fallen in behind him and Wilma Banks, and the four of them walked over to the bus stop. Not that he minded it at all, for the blonde was beautiful. On the contrary, he was glad it happened, for she was different from any girl he had ever met.

He had never known anyone quite like her, so sweet and innocent, and so utterly charming. When he teased her a little her eyes grew wide, as though tears trembled there, while she studied his face to see if he meant what he was saying. Her heart was as tender as that of his big springer spaniel at home. Old Jake had looked at him with much that same hurt, hopeful expression in his eyes when he donned his hunting clothes and, just in fun, ordered the dog to the house.

"I'm not the one who was supposed to be with you," she told him seriously. "I hope you don't mind."

"Mind? Why, of course not," he said, meaning it. "I'd a lot rather be with you than Mildred Patterson."

"Oh, I didn't mean her." In her seriousness she did not catch the implication. "You see, Miss Patterson called the dormitory for Beulah Johnson and I answered the telephone. Beulah was gone, so Miss Patterson told me who she was and asked me if I'd like to go out with a handsome young officer for dinner. I don't usually go out on blind dates, but I'd heard Beulah speak of Mildred Patterson, and with her recommendation and all — well," she gave an embarrassed little laugh, "here I am."

Rex squeezed her arm in answer. It made him feel

good to know that she did not make it a practice of blind dating, and that she felt obligated to explain her presence to him.

He did not know when he first decided he had fallen in love with her. It may have been as he walked across the rough floor of the PX to meet her for the first time, or it could have been the evening they went for a boat ride on the reservoir north of town. Or perhaps when they walked hand in hand up and down the broad tree-lined streets and talked of many things. He did not know when or why, but only that he felt he could not live without her.

There were little indications that she returned his love, for instance, the night, some two weeks later, when he told her about the new planes.

"We got a little surprise today, Wilma," he said casually. But it wasn't a casual thing to him, and the importance he gave it was reflected in his voice despite his efforts to keep it down. "They gave us a new B-17, just off the assembly line. It's got *everything* —or will have when they get through with her at the base. Believe me, we're really getting 'hot.' "

She tried to be brave about it. "What does that mean?"

Rex smiled tolerantly at her ignorance. "A 'hot' squadron is one that's about ready to go over after a little of this action we've been training so long to get."

"I don't want to hear about it, Rex," she said softly, her voice catching with emotion. "I can't stand to think of your going away."

"But, honey, we're going in the safest plane in the world. Why the B-17 *can't* be shot out of the air. It's safer than your rocking chair at home. You don't need to worry about me."

"You will come back to me, won't you?"

"Of course I will."

She turned, and he kissed her tenderly, lingering, as if it might be the last time as well as the first.

CHAPTER 6

It was evident to everyone at the base that the laughing, grim young men who made up the 85 Bomber Group were soon to be transferred overseas. New clothing was issued to them in quantities: gabardine coveralls; fur-lined flying suits with an arrangement of zippers that permitted the wearer to shed it in the air in case he should be forced to bail out over water; poleroid sun glasses with unbreakable lenses — the best money could obtain, for Jerry fighters like to hide in the sun and pounce down upon unsuspecting bombers; and new leather flying jackets as soft as the skin on a baby's cheek and as tough as the armor on the fuselage of their favorite planes. Anything fliers could want or need was issued freely. If something should happen to them "over there," it would not be because of lack of equipment or preparation.

The magnificent new B-17's had nearly finished the shakedown flights, and Dixie had yet to contact Bill Jordan. He had been watching for the opportunity, and once or twice would have attempted to talk with him, but he seemed more inaccessible than ever, his dark eyes flashing defiance whenever the bombardier approached. He sensed Dixie's motives and resented them.

The crew was growing increasingly concerned about their tail gunner. He had associated freely with them before, joining in the fun and seeking companionship for infrequent sorties into town, but now he was taciturn and preferred to be alone.

Shadowed crescents crept into the hollows above his cheek bones, darkening his pallid face; and the marks of strange emotions could be seen on his narrow lips and in the corners of his eyes. They all knew those emotions well, for they fought against them constantly — worry, futility, indecision, homesickness, the overwhelming desire to exist and, worst of all, fear.

Fear can be an uncontrollable, ugly thing, stampeding reason and crushing self-respect. It can seize minds and paralyze muscles until man becomes a cringing, helpless creature. It can gnaw at courage with an insatiable appetite, once man gives in to it and begins to think about himself and the immediate, unpredictable future. That was what worried the crew. They feared that Bill was beginning to think and to brood.

The bombardier had almost given up trying to contact him, when they met quite unexpectedly in a café on Central Avenue one evening. At least it was unexpected to Dixie. He tired of army food and had come to town for a steak that tasted like a steak.

Mildred Patterson had planned to come in with him, but she was forced to remain on duty for an unscheduled appendectomy. So the bombardier came in alone.

He saw Jordan when the latter first entered the café, standing to one side of the doorway, scanning the tables and booths; and he was surprised when the gunner made his way over to the booth where he was sitting.

"Hello, Dixie," he said casually. "Are you alone?"

He nodded and replied, "I was just wanting company. Won't you sit down?"

The conversation was disconnected and strained. Their many slurring remarks and the bitter derision could not be put aside in a moment. They ate in comparative silence and were dawdling over their coffee when Bill said suddenly, "Dixie, I've got to talk to some one!" All bravado was gone and his voice was hushed and tense.

Dixie looked at him sympathetically.

"What's the matter with me?" he demanded. "The boys are afraid of me. They're afraid of what I'll do when we get overseas."

"If they're concerned, it's because they like you, I'm sure."

"Or maybe they want someone else in the tail gun. Is that it?" But before the bombardier could speak he hurried on, the words tumbling over themselves in haste, as though they had been too long suppressed. "Do they talk about you like that? Do they get together in huddles and then shut up when you come along?"

Dixie reached for his check. "Let's go out for a walk, Bill, where we can talk without interruption."

The distraught gunner followed him outside, and they walked west and north towards the park.

"Oh, Heavenly Father," Dixie prayed silently, "Help me to show him the Way."

They stopped in an empty corner of the park and sat down at a picnic table.

"What's wrong with me?" Bill asked again as soon as they were seated.

"Well," Dixie began, choosing his words as carefully as a mechanic chooses the tools to assemble a

motor, "the boys are concerned about you, that's true.
They don't want another tail gunner or they'd ask
for one. We don't have to fly with anyone we don't
want to fly with, you know. They're afraid, from the
way you've been acting since we've been getting
'hot,' that you'll crack up when the going's tough."

He expected Jordan to speak loudly in denial, but
instead he clasped his hands so tightly together that
the finger tips showed white. "I'm scared, Dixie,"
he choked. "I'm scared to death."

"There's not a thing I can do for you, Bill," Dixie
answered. "I can't even help myself. But there is
One to whom we both can turn." He took a thin limp
leather Bible from his jacket and thumbed through
it to the book of Isaiah: *Fear thou not; for I am with
thee: be not dismayed; for I am thy God: I will
strengthen thee; yea, I will help thee; yea, I will up-
hold thee with the right hand of my righteousness
. . . For I the Lord thy God will hold thy right
hand, saying unto thee, Fear not; I will help thee.*

"I wish I could believe that," Bill Jordan said fervently.

"You can," Dixie replied. "When I think of going into combat alone I get weak with fear. But the
knowledge that the Lord Jesus is with me constantly
— that I am His, and that my life is in His hands —
permits me to go anywhere with the blessed assurance
that God *is* watching over me."

"It must be wonderful to have faith like that."

"It's wonderful to have a Christ like that, Bill.
And the best part of it is that it's ours for the asking.
It can't be bought with church membership or earned
by good works. It's a gift from God, given freely
to any who sincerely and honestly seek it."

Dixie hesitated, studying the tail gunner's face. Turmoil was reflected there.

"I want to believe that God — that somebody's watching over me — but I don't. I'm afraid I don't follow you at all."

"It's really very simple. You have only to search your heart, confess your sins and accept Jesus Christ as your personal Saviour." He could almost feel Bill Jordan bristle. And then he knew that Jordan had truly been under conviction that night on the mountain. That had been the thing which had caused the antagonism. He could not endure the feeling of guilt which Dixie's words aroused. "The Lord Jesus died on Calvary that we might have eternal life if only we believe on Him."

"I just wanted a little advice and help," he said belligerently, getting up from the table and walking away. "I didn't want to be preached at."

"None of us do, Bill, because we don't like to be told that we've been living in sin. But the Word of God tells us that it's true."

"Well, you can have my share."

He began to walk rapidly up the street towards town. Dixie fell in beside him. If only he could do or say something to break down the barrier Bill had erected against the Lord! If only he could get the *right* quotation from Scripture, or say the *right* word to show his companion the Truth. But the tail gunner was already shutting his heart against Christ, and each step he took without speaking to Dixie placed another bar on the door. Uptown he stopped before the USO.

"I'm sorry I unburdened to you, Dixie. I feel a lot better now," but his eyes belied his words before they were spoken. "I haven't heard from home in quite awhile and I was kind of low. I'll be all right."

"I wish you would let *God* help you, Bill."

He laughed shortly. "Maybe I will, some day — when I get too old to have fun any more." Then he added seriously, "You won't say anything to the crew about this, will you?"

"I won't tell anyone except Rex, Bill, and I think he ought to know. But I can vouch for him. He'll never say a word to them about it."

Rex was disturbed by what Dixie told him. He had been so engrossed in Wilma that he had thought but little of his crew. Of all the crew he was the only one who had not noticed Bill's strange conduct during the past two or three weeks.

"I'm sorry to hear that about the kid," he said. "I was in hopes the whole bunch could stay together. Do you think he'll fizz out on us?

"Frankly, I don't know. He's not in very good shape. And I couldn't get near him at all. As soon as I mentioned Christ and following Him, he froze up."

"That's too bad." Rex thought a moment. "I believe you used the wrong approach on him. If he'd been kind of the type like — well like you, all that religious stuff would have been O.K. It might even have done him some good. But he isn't, and he shed everything you said. Now, if I'd been talking with him, I'd have taken him all over our new plane. I'd have shown him how strong it's made, how well every position's armored, how safe it is. That would have been my idea of the way to buck up Bill Jordan."

"There are B-17's shot down, you know."

"Yes, but not these new ones," he grinned proudly,

"with **Rex** Madden at the controls and *his* crew manning the guns."

"You can have faith in that plane if you want to," Dixie said. "But as for me, I'll put my trust in the Lord."

* * *

Although Dixie and Mildred Patterson did not rush breathtakingly into love, as did Rex and Wilma, their friendship deepened with each successive day. Patty questioned his sincerity at first — or pretended to — and laughingly called Dixie's attention to his approach at their first meeting. It infuriated him until he realized she was only doing it to hear his vehement denials.

There was a definite source of pleasure and satisfaction to them in their mutual love for Jesus. He forged a bond about them and between them, enhancing the attraction they felt to one another, and giving depth and spiritual fiber to their affections.

Dixie had been reared in a Christian home, and had learned to follow Jesus so slowly and naturally that he could not put his finger upon the exact date at which he was "born again." By the time he was accepted into full church membership he knew the fundamentals of the Christian's faith and accepted them all without reservation. The prayers and teaching of his mother and pastor had borne fruit, almost before they realized it themselves. One day his young mind had been grasping feebly at the Truth and the next it had such understanding as to amaze them.

But Mildred, who had also been reared in a Christian home, had only lately come to Him. In the church which her parents attended, she accepted

Christ on the Sunday before she left for her army post. Then she came face to face with reality for the first time; she realized her sinfulness; she realized that she was stepping into an unknown and unpredictable future; she realized that life resolved itself into one simple, unchangeable fundamental, the saving grace of the Lord Jesus.

Although Dixie and Mildred had come to the Saviour by different paths, they both arrived at the same destination. They were Christians, saints, whose sins had been washed away by the blood of Christ.

They enjoyed each other's company immensely, looking forward to the brief, uncertain moments to be snatched hastily at odd times between their busy schedules, and dreading the torturing hours when they were apart.

Neither of them spoke of love, but it was there, the stronger for restraint. There was no need for caresses when the caress lingered in her eyes. There was no need for words when quickening heartbeats spoke so well.

They felt the surging unrest and hurry of the times, and eagerly wanted to live to the fullest in the days or hours that might already be rapidly running out for them. They wanted to *live*, just as Rex and Wilma did. They talked of marriage casually, of the responsibilities and joys of building a home, inserting exploratory little phrases into the conversation to feel out each other's opinions about marriage built on uncertainties. Without ever having spoken of the matter openly, they both decided that, whatever might be right for others, it would be better for them to await calmer days.

CHAPTER 7

It seemed that Dixie's talk with Bill Jordan produced results after all. The young tail gunner was less morose and seemed to mingle with the crew a little better, although it was impossible to tell whether this was the result of forced bravado or genuine self-control. At any rate, the boys began to feel better about him. Perhaps their imaginations had caused them to think he was upset about going into combat. But Dixie was still concerned about him, for he was positive that this change was in his head and not his heart.

He wanted to seek Bill Jordan out and talk with him earnestly and seriously about following Jesus. He had sensed the impact which his words were making on the gunner. He had seen conviction stamped upon the lean white face when he turned away, and sensed that Bill was on the threshold of yielding. But that was not enough. Unless he took the final step and confessed his sins in penitence, accepting the cleansing of the blood of Christ, previous efforts were futile. For that reason Dixie sought another opportunity to talk with him.

None was available.

The gunner was cordial enough when they met casually on the street or at the field, or when in a crowd together, but he refused to remain alone with Dixie. He avoided him studiously, as if he feared him and the things he would say.

Rex had a talk with Bill shortly after Dixie's unsuccessful effort and he was quite pleased with the result.

"Have you noticed a change in our problem child?" he asked one evening when he and Dixie were alone.

"A little," the bombardier admitted.

"I had quite a talk with him. I told you that you were handling him the wrong way. Why, I took the fear right out of him when I showed him the plane and how invulnerable we are. Don't worry about Bill. We aren't going to have any more trouble with him."

"I hope you're right," he replied doubtfully.

The base at Kearney was filled with rumors that seemed to be fairly well authenticated. The grapevine had it that another group of B-17's would be in to be fitted for combat in about ten days. New wingtip tanks had been coming up by the truckload for a week and warehouses were being crammed with spare parts. The group commander sent his wife back to California to live with her mother. It all added up to the fact that the 85th Bombardment Group would be out of Kearney and on its way before the new flight of planes arrived.

The entire group had been expertly trained and the feeling of fitness and ability had made every man eager. Even Bill Jordan caught the excitement. He boasted proudly to gunners in other crews that their squadron leader was a twenty-two-year-old lieutenant colonel of the famous 19th Bombardment Squadron that did such heroic work in the Pacific. He bragged about the *Terrier*, her pilot, her navigator and even her bombardier — although something in his conscience pricked at the thought of Dixie. The latter represented an unpleasant experience, a nightmare of fear swallowed by excitement, and he did not like to be reminded of it.

Rex Madden thrilled with anticipation while making last-minute check-ups and going over plans with other pilots. It was a big task to transport forty-four four-engine bombers across the ocean, and it required much careful planning.

But his heart ached at the thought of leaving Wilma. Something about her had seized him forcibly until it threatened to drive all else from his mind. Both of them had known that parting was inevitable. They talked about it laughingly and with a seeming lack of feeling, but that did not make it any easier when the time came for him to tell her that this was it; that at best they had only a few short hours to be together.

"I might not get to leave the post again," he told her, the first evening of his week-end leave. "When we go back Monday morning we aren't even allowed to make a phone call out, until we leave."

"Are you going to miss me?" she asked, winking to keep the tears from her eyes. He must not see her crying now.

"You're the only thing that makes it hard for me to leave," he said huskily. "I want to go over there, but I want to be with you too."

"I'm glad," she smiled. "I want to be missed just a little." A long while later she asked, "Do—do you know where you're to be sent?"

He nodded hesitantly. "It's hard not to tell you, Wilma dear."

"I know — regulations." She strove to keep the bitterness from her voice.

She moved closer to him on the davenport, nestling

contentedly into the crook of his protecting arm.

"I wish we could stay like this always, and not ever have to think about your going away."

"Do you think you could be happy with me — always?"

"Of course, darling."

"Are you sure enough of it to marry me tomorrow?" He had said it. He had not intended to ask her to marry him tomorrow. He had not even intended to propose to her at all. He had told himself often enough that he would not marry until the fighting stopped and the smoke cleared away. But he had proposed to her, and at that instant he knew he wanted to marry her more than he wanted anything else in the world.

"B-b-but, Rex," she protested. "I don't know what to say. We've only been acquainted such a short time. I don't know anything about you, and you don't know anything about me. I want to be *sure* when I marry."

"We know enough about each other to know that we're in love. What else matters? We've got to work fast and live fast, Wilma," he said fervently. "We're living on a volcano. Any minute it's liable to go off and destroy one of us. Don't you see — if I don't come back, we will have had one week-end of happiness anyway."

"Rex, don't talk like that." Tears trickled into the corners of her mouth. She threw her arms about his neck suddenly and pressed her cheek against his. "Don't ever talk about not coming back! I couldn't stand it!"

"Of course I'm coming back," he said reassuringly. "But there's always that remote possibility. Why,

after a few months they'll probably send me home as
an instructor somewhere. They're always doing that.
Then we could rent a little apartment and be together."

Wilma Banks needed no urging to marry the handsome young pilot. She would have rather had her
father and Rex's parents at the wedding, but there
was no time for that. A week-end is tragically short
for a honeymoon.

They were married early the next morning at the
parsonage. Rex routed out the county judge at six-
thirty and talked him into going down to make out a
license.

"Why can't you soldiers decide to be married at a
decent hour?" he grumbled good-naturedly, pulling
out the marriage license book. "You couldn't have
waited two and a half hours and let a man get his
sleep out, now could you?"

"We're terribly sorry," Wilma apologized, radiant
as only a girl can be on her wedding day. "But Rex
is shipping out soon, and we only have this week-end."

"O.K., I guess we can fix you out this time," he
said amiably.

Rex wanted to have him marry them at the court-
house, but Wilma demurred.

"I wouldn't even feel as though I were married,"
she told him, "unless a minister married us."

"That's all right with me, honey. Anything you
say."

Dixie and Patty met them at the parsonage at
eight. It had taken some string-pulling to get her off
duty, for the head nurse was particularly unromantic.
She could not understand why anyone would want to

get married in the first place, let alone go to a wedding.

"I'm making allowances this time," she snapped, "because you're leaving us soon. If you were assigned here permanently we would have to abide explicitly by the rules."

Reverend Kernan, a strong-faced young minister with a vise grip, invited them into the quiet of his living room.

"Before we begin the ceremony I want to ask you some very pointed questions. Betty," he called to his wife, "would you please entertain this other young couple in the kitchen for a few moments? . . . Thank you."

When they were gone he turned once more to Rex and Wilma. "A lot of soldiers come to me to be married, and I like to marry them. The Lord instituted marriage because He saw that it wasn't good for man to be alone. But we've got to be very careful that the sacred vows we take are premeditated and final. I have no desire to feed the divorce mills with marriages that should never have been consummated."

They sat there uneasily. Rex felt a wave of doubt engulf him while she listened fearfully, afraid that the minister might refuse to perform the ceremony.

"How long have you young folks known each other?"

"About three and a half weeks."

"Hmm," he eyed them thoughtfully. "That's not very long. Are you positive you love each other?"

They nodded.

"I'll bet you're shipping out soon," he said to Rex.

"That's right, sir."

"Do you plan to be true to her?"

Rex nodded affirmatively, his face tense.

"And you, Miss. It's hard for a young girl to put aside going out with other young men after being married such a short time before her husband leaves. Do you plan to remain true to him?"

"Oh, yes, I do."

The minister smiled at her positive, eager answer.

"It's a great responsibility for a minister to be called upon to marry young folks under these conditions. I'll tell you what I'm going to do. I'm going over to my study in the church for about fifteen minutes. I want you to talk over what I've said, and pray over it. If you still want me to marry you when I return I'll do so gladly."

Doubt was chilling Rex's heart. Did he really love Wilma? Or was it only infatuation born of unrest and an unpredictable future? Was it fair to her to tie her down when he might never return?

But the doubt was dispelled when he looked into her starry eyes. Even if he did not love her at all he would have felt obligated to marry her. She was so happy and so beautiful he could not have done anything to shatter her happiness.

When the fifteen minutes had nearly passed he asked softly, "Do you still want to get married?"

"Of course I do, darling."

They borrowed a car from a sympathetic brother officer and spent a deliriously happy honeymoon at Grand Island and Hastings. Precious golden minutes slipped by silently, and with inexorable swiftness. Before they could bring themselves to realize it their brief respite from reality was over and they were separating.

Their good-byes were poignant and sad. Wilma sobbed passionately as she clung to his blouse. It pained him to leave her.

Chapter 8

A certain tenseness emanating from the command enveloped the crews Monday and spread to the mechanics who had been working constantly on the planes when they were on the ground. Truckloads of gasoline were wheeled onto the field and gas tanks were crammed with 100 octane fuel, the kind demanded by the powerful motors of war planes. Equipment was stored aboard with care, and special mechanics inspected the engines thoroughly. There was no doubt that they were moving.

Rumors were thick. And, as usual, they meant nothing at all. On only one thing did they agree: that something big was afoot.

Patty and Dixie met for the last time at the Kearney Base after hours Monday evening. He waited for her at the hospital and they went over to the PX together for a coke. The building was crowded with loud-talking crews and Dixie could find no place at all for the things he wanted to say.

"Let's see if we can't find a little privacy," he suggested, steering her away from the counter.

"Do you have any ideas?"

"No, but we can find something better than this."

They found a jeep pulled up beside one of the hangars. It was just what they had been looking for. Dixie ushered Patty into the back seat and climbed in beside her. She seemed more beautiful than ever to him. The rich tan of her face and arms accentuated the starched whiteness of her uniform.

"I just want to sit and look at you," he told her, "so I can remember exactly how you look sitting there."

"After you see all those pretty little foreign girls you probably won't even want to remember me."

"You know better than that." His voice was harsh.

She nodded, smiling. "I'm sorry, Dixie. I shouldn't tease this evening."

"It might be a long time before we get to see each other again. Will you wait for me?"

"I'll wait for you as long as it takes, Dixie."

"It sounds good to hear you say that."

"May God take care of you," she said prayerfully, "and send you back safely to me."

"It's wonderful to be able to trust in the Lord, isn't it?"

"I don't know how anyone who doesn't can stand up under the things that're happening today."

"Neither do I, but there're a good many who try to go it alone." There was a short silence and his face grew even more serious. "When you're saying your prayers, would you pray for me?"

"Why of course, Dixie, I always do."

"I know. You pray for me to come back safe and well, like Mother does, but there's something that's more important to me than that." He was speaking as one who had been thinking long and deeply. "Would you pray that God may give me the courage and strength to do my job regardless of what happens?"

She reached for his hand and squeezed it tenderly. He smiled weakly in return.

"I can't bear to think of what will be happening or where I'll be in six months — or six weeks for that matter." Lines deepened about his eyes as he went on. He had always seemed so brave and able to care for himself that this new mood was startling. "I must be the biggest coward on the plane. The only way I can carry on is to live from day to day."

She must have been looking at him queerly for he hastened to add, "No, I don't mean 'eat, drink and be merry for tomorrow we die.' But whenever I get up in the morning I pray that the Lord may go with me through every minute of the day, protecting me and giving me courage to carry on just for the hours that lie directly ahead. It's all up to Him, for I don't have any strength of my own that's even worthy of the name."

"I think that's a beautiful way of living, Dixie," she replied, "and I'll be praying for you constantly."

"Thank you, darling." He leaned over and kissed her lightly on the lips. She clung to him with tears fighting their way to the corners of her eyes.

"I don't *want* you to go, Dixie."

"And I don't want to go either, Patts. But we've got to."

"I know."

"I suppose you'll be shipping out soon too."

"I wasn't going to tell you unless you asked because I didn't want to worry you, but we were alerted yesterday. I don't know whether it means anything or not. Some of the girls say they've done it several times before."

"Yes, that's been happening right along. I've been alerted a dozen times when we didn't go any place."

"It doesn't matter, I guess. I'm as ready to go now as I'll ever be."

"I wish all the boys in our crew could say that."

"Why? What do you mean?"

"There's Bill Jordan, and maybe Rex. I haven't made up my mind about him. But we shouldn't be spending our last evening together talking about them."

"If there's any way I can help — "

"I would appreciate it if you'd include them in your prayers — that they might find Jesus before it's too late."

He took her back to quarters about ten minutes before the lights went out and kissed her good-bye. It did not seem possible that before they saw each other again the war would likely be over.

The crews were routed out and briefed at four o'clock Tuesday morning. Most of them did not have to be awakened, as they were positive Tuesday would be the day, whether they were sent to Australia, England or Timbuctoo. And they were lying awake eagerly waiting for the morning. Only Jordan seemed disturbed, and his restless tossing in bed could have been due to excitement. The very air was alive with it.

"You men probably know," the operations officer began when they were all packed into the long, narrow room, "that this is no ordinary routine flight. This is it — the thing you've all been training for. I may as well tell you now that you won't be stopping in New York longer than it takes to gas up and check the motors. You know, without my telling you, that there's to be no letters, telegrams or long distance phone calls. You can all cable your folks and sweethearts when you reach your base." He paused, looking over the grim, drawn faces. "The next time you take off your shoes you'll be in *England*."

The word rippled through the group of men as

their destination was announced. Enthusiasm was running high.

"You'll fly to the designated base along the Atlantic Coast as a group, and there split into squadrons. The pilots have their instructions and the navigators have their maps. Are there any questions?"

"Do we carry ammunition, sir?" an eager young aerial gunner asked. He was a private, and not long out of gunnery school. Expectancy was stamped on his face.

"Yes, soldier, that pea shooter of yours will be bursting with shells."

"Thank you, sir. I wouldn't want to be up in no airplane over there without 'em."

"We wouldn't want you up there without 'em either," the officer laughed, "and I wish you good hunting when you use them."

"Thank you, sir."

There were no more questions.

"I almost forgot to tell you the most important part of the trip." His manner indicated that he had not forgotten at all, but was saving the information for the climax. "You are carrying passengers."

"Passengers, sir?" one of the squadron leaders exclaimed.

"Yes, Major, passengers. And don't sound so horrified. I know it's irregular, but these army nurses are needed in England, and you men can get them there quicker than any other way."

The room buzzed. Nurses. And they thought they were leaving the feminine sex behind for the duration. Crews eyed their pilot officers guardedly with threats unspoken if they failed to get one of the passengers assigned to their ship.

"There's about seventy-five of them and the group commander will assign them to the planes. That's all, boys. Godspeed."

Dixie punched Rex in the back and grinned as they went out of the long tar-paper covered building and down to their planes.

"I'll bet Patts is in that bunch," he chortled. "They were alerted Sunday. This couldn't happen again in a million years!"

She was one of the nurses selected to go, along with others that came in by train Monday night, but Dixie did not see her until after they landed at the base in England.

Rex was a little nervous and excited at first, but two hours in the thin high clouds calmed him. Wilma would be in school by now, trying to study French or English Composition or whatever she studied between ten and eleven. He tried to picture her sitting at her desk, pulling nervously at her blonde curls as she strove to keep her thoughts from him; but he could not call her to mind. It was surprising how quickly the image had disappeared.

The nurses on the *Terrier* were not particularly attractive, but they wandered about the big B-17 asking questions and joking with the crew in a way that made the hours roll.

The B-17's were on the ground three hours in New York and nine on the tip of Newfoundland where they were grounded because of strong headwinds. By the time they reached that isolated spot the excitement had worn off somewhat and they all went into the barracks and got five or six hours of rest.

Several nurses were left behind at the far northern base where a stove had exploded in a barracks a day or two before, killing seven and seriously burning forty or fifty more. The nursing staff was pitifully inadequate to take care of the regular patients as well as the victims of the explosion. The tired, pain-twisted looks of gratitude that the injured gave them fully repaid the nurses for their hard years of training, and the arduous duty they were accepting.

The remainder of the flight was uneventful. But for the determined faces and swift efficiency of the men — duties were dispatched with a snap and interest not readily apparent during training — it would have seemed a routine training flight, like the one to the little island in the Pacific or to Henderson Field at Pearl Harbor.

The navigator in the squadron leader's plane charted the course, but the others kept a constant check on position. Now that they were actually heading into combat, their work would become increasingly important. It added purpose to efficiency.

Two hundred miles out of Iceland an RAF patrol plane, one of America's Catalina flying boats, met them and escorted them in. Another picked them up over the rockbound coast and flew with them for approximately a hundred miles towards England. The crew was made up of grinning young men who waved and gesticulated as they flew along. There was a certain feeling of kinship between the RAF and the American Air Force that brought them very close together. The rivalry was friendly and based upon a keen appreciation of the other's ability.

As the B-17's approached Britain a fog rolled in and they had to pick out the flare-lighted field with instruments. But, even in the fog, all found the base and landed without difficulty.

The American boys already based there swarmed about the men, questioning them eagerly. They asked, with a touch of homesickness poorly disguised in their voices, of home and friends. They wanted to know what things were like back in the States, what rationing was doing to the people, whether the sacrifices they were making were being appreciated. They asked if anyone knew what became of this or that friend who was in one of the schools with them. Many met boys with whom they had trained, and, even though they had been mere acquaintances, the distance from home welded them together, and they met with the happiness and enthusiasm of long separated brothers.

While the veterans wanted to know of the States, the men of the 85th Bombardment Group were eager to learn of England. They wanted to find out about the country and the people.

Dixie was probably the only single man not interested in English girls, and why should he be when the prettiest nurse in the whole American Army was waiting for him somewhere in that maze of buildings.

Chapter 9

For three weeks or more the new group of bombers were sent up only on patrol flights and short exploratory hops to get the crews acclimated, as much as possible, to England's obstinate weather.

Mechanics were assigned to individual planes and allowed to become familiar with the one placed under their care. A car mechanic could be slipshod and careless, but the mechanic who worked on the bombers that were to fly over enemy territory had to be constantly alert, and a perfectionist in his trade. Fully as much responsibility rested on every turn of the wrench as with the pilot who would take the Fortress into battle.

The crews spent those first few weeks getting acquainted with England and finding it different than they ever imagined. Most of them had thought the average Englishman to be a cross between a cockney and an English bull pup, but they found him very similar to the average American. They were a little aloof, perhaps, and spoke with an accent, but were courteous and kind and human.

Dixie, Patts and Rex rented bicycles and peddled down narrow country lanes and through picturesque English villages that looked as though they had been transplanted from illustrations in old folk tales of England. They stopped to visit with shopkeepers, farmers and laboring men and women who worked in the big factories that had been dispersed the length and breadth of the island fortress. Inevitably the sub-

ject turned to war. Many of them had lost husbands
and brothers, even children, and had ceased to count
the bombings. Yet their bitterness was slight. They
agreed with the Americans that cities must be bombed
without mercy, but they made no pretense of enjoying it.

"I know what it's like to hide in shelters and cellars
when Jerry was coming over every night," one
wizened old lady told them when she learned the boys
were part of a bomber crew. "And I can't help but
feel sorry for them as is going through it now. Not
that I'm wantin' it stopped till Jerry's brought to his
knees, mind you," she added hastily, "but I think the
good Lord's going to remember who started bombing cities first, come Judgment Day."

The faith of some of the English people was
astounding to Rex and gave Dixie Meyers and Patty
further testimony of the power of Christ in time of
trouble. They visited a church that had been hit
directly by a high-explosive bomb. A section of the
roof was blown off and a big hole gaped in the stone
wall to one side of the choir loft. But those simple
English villagers had cleared away the rubble, erected
a new pulpit where the old one stood and still wor-
shiped their God in the same church on Sunday morning.

"You can't beat a people with faith in God like
that," Dixie remarked reverently, as he saw evidences
of their belief in the Lord Jesus.

"That might be," Rex replied laconically. "But
they didn't drive off Jerry with prayers. They used
Spitfires and ack-ack."

"I'm not so sure that God didn't have a lot to do
with it," Dixie told him.

Patty cast a quick sidelong glance at the bombardier and he knew that she was remembering his request to pray for the pilot. She thought of Bill Jordan too, whom she had never met.

Back at the base the big bombers were being made ready for their first real trip over enemy territory. They had edged over the coast of France and poked timidly into Holland, but this time they were being loaded with bombs to be sent on their first important mission.

Bill had been drawing within himself once more, and that harassed restless look came into his eyes again, but the rest of the crew, flushed with the excitement of a new strange land, noticed little difference in his actions. He would come down from the barracks, for at this particular base the carefully camouflaged barracks buildings and hospital adjoined the field, and watch the mechanics working on the *Terrier*.

Big planes would take off bravely, heroically into the sun, to come straggling back past midday, empty of their destructive loads, but often bullet-ridden and coughing. There were occasional empty places in the neat formations where a plane had been blasted to the earth or so badly crippled that it had been left to crash or struggle on alone.

Bill Jordan saw all of that as he watched them work on the plane. Those giant chariots of the sky which he had learned to call B-17's were only mortal things. Antiaircraft and cannon fire could destroy them, with all their armor plate and high altitude. Enemy fighters could sting them hard, with shells ripping through the fuselage to get at the crew. The

B-17's were not invincible! They could be brought down!

Bill saw them remove a man from the tail gun of a crippled Fortress — or, what was left of him. A twenty-millimeter cannon shell exploded in his face, tearing the upper half of his body away. A neat sympathetic note would be dispatched to his mother, telling her that her son had been killed in action, but ignoring the information that they had to glean his identity from his dog tags.

Bill's face blanched and his stomach bunched tightly above his belt and turned over. If that plane had been the *Terrier*, and it could have been, *he* would have been the one they were taking out of the tail.

They were alerted and briefed for a ten A.M. flight over Antwerp. It was the first mission for all of them and they were nervous and jumpy while they waited. Intelligence did not add to their peace of mind.

"You'll fly in regular formation in step-down flights of three. You've all been over this before, in practice, so there's no need to go into a lot of detail. If one plane is aborted the other two in the flight are to return to the base with her. There's one thing more to keep in mind. You've had your targets pointed out to you. When you get over the target area drop those eggs and get for home. Don't hang around to watch the fireworks because Jerry'll be on your tail every minute of the way back. You'll run into plenty of ack-ack along here." He indicated the spots on the big map hanging to one side of the table against the wall. "And fighters most of the way home," he added.

They emptied their pockets of all personal belongings and took an escape kit instead. It contained the latest cloth maps available of the territory over which they were to fly, Dutch and French currency, a steel hacksaw blade, a knife and emergency rations. It was a bit sobering to take those items along, for it emphasized the possibility of being forced to parachute onto enemy soil.

They split into groups, talking about everything but the one subject that was in all their minds, while waiting for the orders to leave.

Bob Trout and Rogers were sitting together and Rex and Dixie were standing in one corner aside from the rest.

"I got a V-mail letter from Wilma today," Rex said without interest.

"That's great. I'll bet you were glad to hear from her."

"I don't know," he replied, running his fingers through his stubby brown hair. "I guess I ought to be."

Before Dixie could answer, the word they had been waiting for came.

"O.K., fellows. You know your targets and you've got your bombs. It's time to go. God bless you."

They went out of the building hurriedly, brushing past the chaplain who had been waiting to see them off.

The motors were warmed up, and one by one the big planes roared down the runway and climbed into the air. They formed into flights of three and moved towards the coast, climbing steadily. At ten thousand feet, in accord with army regulations, the pilots adjusted their oxygen masks, and at twenty-two thousand the planes leveled off, cruising directly towards the target. Lone raiders might succeed in slipping in undetected, but it was almost useless for a group of B-17's or Liberators or Sterlings to attempt to reach the target without the enemy being aware of their presence. The big British saturation bombers depended upon darkness rather than surprise, and the Americans relied on their armor and bristling cannon and machine guns for safety.

The men tried to occupy their minds with routine matters; gunners checked their guns and the navigator calculated their position time after time, estimating mentally the number of minutes it would take to reach the target. The boys in the power-driven turrets tested them carefully, whirling rapidly to draw a bead on an imaginary foe, and Dixie, with an unspoken prayer on his lips, dry-bombed his way out to sea.

England stretched below them, an orderly patchwork of color in squares and angles, and beyond the rocky coast lay the channel.

"Take a good look at her," someone said. "It might be the last time we'll ever see her."

"Whoever that was, shut up!" Rex snapped into the interphone. "I took this airplane off the ground, and I'll put her back on her own base under her own power. Just remember that."

He could not let them dwell on such things.

Wilma's letter had been left at the base, together with Rex's billfold and other personal belongings, but it kept running through his mind as if he were still reading it. He had received it without visible interest and read it through a second time and yet a third, but it had not awakened his heart as it should have.

But, if he was beginning to question the wisdom of

their marriage he was alone in his doubt. There was none reflected in her letter.

"It still seems like a gloriously happy dream," she had written. "But it's true, which makes it all the more wonderful. I didn't realize love could come so swiftly. One moment we didn't know each other at all and the next we were in love. Daddy was furious at first, but when he saw how it is between us he realized it was all right. V-mail gives so little room to write the things I want to write, I'm going to send you a regular airmail tomorrow. So good-bye for now, darling."

She was such an innocent, helpless child, and so utterly dependent upon him that he could not bring himself to voice to her the doubts that were, of late, prying in at the corners of his mind.

The *Terrier* lurched a little and Rex looked quickly at the co-pilot. It was too sharp and light to be an air pocket.

"What was that?"

"It felt like it was in the tail."

"Pilot to tail gunner. Pilot to tail gunner. Come in, tail gunner."

There was no answer.

"Come in, tail gunner . . . Come in, tail gunner . . ."

"I can't get Bill to answer," he said to the co-pilot. "Take over for a minute. I'm going back to see what's wrong." With that he took a walk-around bottle of oxygen and snapped it to his mask.

"What's up?" the radio operator asked as he went through the radio compartment.

Rex shook his head and continued along the catwalk to the tail gunner's position.

He could scarcely believe what he saw! The parachute was still in place and the oxygen mask was laying beside the gun handles. The catch on the tail door was unfastened. But there was no one there!

His first thought was that Bill had left his post to go forward, but that would not account for the oxygen mask or the ship's sudden lurch as though it had been lightened in the tail. He might have fallen out, but that scarcely seemed possible.

Then the truth came to him. Bill hadn't fallen out. He had forced the door open with almost superhuman strength against the slip stream of the propellers, and *jumped* out. He had been terrified by the thought of going into combat and chose the only way he could escape it without undergoing the jibes and disdain of his companions.

Rex rushed back along the catwalk to his seat in the plane and switched on his radio to command. He had to contact the squadron leader at once.

"538 to Colonel Mowry. 538 to Colonel Mowry."

"Colonel Mowry to 538. Come in, 538."

"This is Lieutenant Madden." The words were tumbling in their haste. "Our tail gunner has just committed suicide by jumping out, sir!"

"Suicide! Are you positive, Lieutenant?"

"Yes, sir. We felt a slight lurch and when I could not contact him on the interphone I went back to investigate. His parachute and his oxygen mask are still in the plane. *But he's gone!*"

"That's too bad, Lieutenant, a regrettable accident. I'm ordering your flight back to base. Report to operations as soon as you get down."

"Roger."

In a moment the colonel's voice was heard ordering flight three to return to the base.

The crew was stunned to hear of Bill Jordan's fate. They began to remember little things that should have indicated his mental condition. They had noted them once, but when he seemed better they supposed it to be merely a case of excitement-spawned nervousness that was over and done with.

The first hypnosis of shock lasted until they were on the ground and reported to operations and intelligence. Then the rush of sympathy and regret flooded their hearts. The officers were gentle, but probing with their questions and they were not satisfied until Bill Jordan's complete history was in the records. But the boy's parents would never learn of it. They would hear only that their son, William, was killed in action.

Rex Madden choked twice when he made the report, but his superiors were kind enough to pretend they did not notice.

The crew sat around in silence, each one blaming himself in varying degrees for not seeing what was happening to the tail gunner and trying to prevent it. Rex was probably the worst, for he saw the fallacy of the arguments he had presented to Bill. He knew, as though the distracted gunner had told him himself, that the shock of seeing the invulnerable B-17's come in shot to pieces had something to do with the accident. Bill put all of his faith in the plane with its cannon and machine guns, which theoretically protect every position in the ship. He trusted the plane in which he flew until he saw what could happen, what might happen to it on that very flight. And it had been too much for his distracted nerves.

Dixie Meyers took out his Testament. This time Rex welcomed it. Perhaps it had something for him. Perhaps there was something there that would lift the icy fingers of grief from his heart. Bob Trout coughed nervously, and the navigator blotted a tear from the corner of his eye with a forefinger.

. . . *And I will pray the Father, and he shall give you another Comforter, that he may abide with you forever* . . .

When Dixie finished reading from the fourteenth chapter of John they all felt better.

Operations wisely grounded the plane for several days and gave the crew leaves to see London. When they returned a new tail gunner would be assigned to them and they would take their regular place in the squadron, but it seemed advisable to give them a rest.

CHAPTER 10

Those few days in town did a great deal to bring the shaken crew back to normal. One of the boys, an enlisted man and quite young, could be heard sobbing quietly into his pillow at night, and Rex and Eddie Zorn looked as if they had not been asleep.

Dixie Meyers was bothered too, but for an entirely different reason. If he had talked with Bill Jordan just once more, if he had not allowed the rebuff to so injure his pride that he would not mention Christ to him again, if he had not given up so easily at the first sign of opposition, Bill might have been alive today rejoicing in the assurance of salvation. On his knees that night Dixie vowed tearfully to God that he would never stop speaking to one whom the Lord had laid upon his heart. How many others had been lost because he refused to tell them of Jesus and His saving grace he did not know. The thought was terrifying in its implications.

By the end of the week the crew had control of themselves once more and were ready to fly again, which was gratifying to operations. Such incidents at the beginning of combat duty could well ruin all of them — which would mean an appalling waste of money and time. It had been said that infantry divisions could be held on the front against their will by machine guns trained on their backs. But not airmen. They fly willingly or not at all.

Rex answered Wilma's letter immediately, for he knew she would be counting the days until she heard

99

from him. He tried to match her enthusiasm and expression of love, but his efforts sounded hollow and empty — almost as empty as his heart.

Patty, Dixie and Rex went in to London together. It was at Mildred Patterson's insistence that they took Rex with them.

"He looks so lonesome," she told Dixie. "Let's take him along."

"I'd sure like to. He doesn't pal around with the other fellows very much. I'm afraid he feels his marriage is tying him down."

"Oh, that's too bad. But I suppose he does get terribly lonesome."

Rex liked being with them. He enjoyed sharing their companionship and fun, jostling along odd little streets and eating in out of the way cafés where more often than not the food was bad. They missed the Nebraska eggs and thick steaks which they had enjoyed in comparative abundance, even during rationing, and they longed for the ever-present fried chicken on the Nebraska menus. But such a small item as food could scarcely dull their enthusiasm for the evening.

They joked with waitresses, heckled cashiers goodnaturedly as they struggled with pounds, shillings and pence, and laughed gaily with the crowd in the parks. It was almost like being in the States again, Rex found himself thinking. If only he had a companion too. In spite of their attempts to include him in the fun and his real enjoyment of being with them, he felt somewhat left out — a hanger-on who had been invited out of pity.

It had been that way ever since he married Wilma. She was not there to go out with him, and yet she effectively blocked his finding enjoyment and the pleasure of taking new girls to dinner and going out like the rest of the crew. She was tied down too, but it was different with him. He was not among friends or relatives and his time of leisure was short. *It was not fair.*

His face must have reflected bitterness for Patty asked, "Why so glum, Rex? A penny for your thoughts. Or should I say a shilling?"

"A shilling, penny or counterfeit franc, you'd still be getting cheated. I was just thinking of a terrible mistake I'm afraid I've made."

Dixie seized the conversation nimbly before Rex could go on or Mildred could ask questions. There are some things that are better left unsaid, that will smolder on unspoken and perhaps die away; but once uttered aloud they take on added importance and weight. Dixie knew what Rex had been going to say. He had seen it growing in his eyes all evening, every time he looked at Mildred and saw how happy they were together. Lonesomeness will do strange things to a man.

"Well, it won't be any worse in the morning. I'll remind you to worry about it, beginning right at ten."

"O.K., O.K., I guess it doesn't matter much anyway," he said with forced cheerfulness. There's nothing I can do about it."

"Where do we go now?"

"I think *our* young lady ought to decide. After all, she's paying her third of the expenses, isn't she?"

"Not so's I've noticed," Dixie replied. "But those army nurses make enough money. I think she ought to."

"Maybe we ought to charge her for showing her

London. It's worth something to drag her around, you know."

"Well, I like that. And to think I turned down a perfectly good proposal from a soldier in Ward B only this afternoon!"

"By the way, most of those nurses we brought over were scattered all over England. Which one of you pulled the strings to get you stationed at our base, Miss Mildred Patterson?"

"We'll never tell, will we, Dixie?"

He only grinned.

"Whatever you did, it must have been good."

They stayed in London three days, visiting Westminster Abbey, St. Paul's Cathedral, Commons, everything that was suggested to them, until buildings began to blend into one another. Historic spots became as meaningless as so many toy blocks, and museums and art galleries served only to drug their sensibilities. Memory would one day separate the jumble until they could recall with pleasure the things which they had witnessed. But, by the time they had returned to the air base, they had looked until they were tired of looking.

The new tail gunner reported to Rex the morning they returned to the base. He was short and rather fat, with a ruddy complexion which gave concrete evidence of twenty years on an Iowa farm. He was good-natured and steady, with little imagination — just the kind of man for the tail of a B-17.

Their first mission after the leaves went off smoothly. They were briefed before dawn and sent with the squadron to bomb harbor installations at Dunkerque and Calais. It was a short flight that encountered a minimum of opposition and helped to bolster the faltering confidence of the *Terrier* and her crew.

While they were waiting in the cold damp morning air Rogers said to Dixie, almost timidly, for he was uncertain of the reaction of the other fellows, "I'd like to have a word of prayer before we take off, wouldn't you?"

Bob Trout and Eddie Zorn nodded quickly, and the new boy from Iowa voiced his agreement. They all knelt in the wet grass, except Rex, and he turned away. He did not want to parade his faith before the men of the other planes. Besides, they were all watching now, probably laughing at the crew of the *Terrier*.

"Oh, Heavenly Father," Dixie prayed, "Thou knowest the kind of a mission we are going on. Thou knowest that innocent men and women and children are going to be killed, even though our bombs hit their targets. We would ask Thy forgiveness, O Lord, for the things we have to do. And we would pray for those whose lives will be taken. May their number be small, and may those who die know Thee and Thy way of salvation.

"We would ask Thee to bless each member of the crew. Watch over us and care for us as we go through the valley of the shadow of death. Search our hearts, O God. If there be one among us who has not given his life completely to Thee, we would ask that he come to Thee now, while there is yet time. In Jesus' Name, Amen."

Then they got to their feet and clambered into the plane. The tension seemed to be gone as they checked equipment and made ready to take off. There was none of the tense nervousness of the other mission. They were confident, relaxed and unafraid.

The prayer bothered Rex as he piloted the big craft into the clouds and above them. At first the spectacle at the field annoyed him. He was concerned about what the others would think and say. But that had been supplanted with something more. He felt that prayer pointed right at him, knifing through his smug complacency to point at the sin in his life. But he was a Christian, he told himself doggedly. He went to church and repeated the Apostles' Creed. He had been baptized as a child. Why, then, did conviction plague his soul?

It became a regular practice with the crew of the *Terrier* to hold prayer meetings before each mission. Sometimes Rex joined them, kneeling self-consciously at the outer rim of the little group. Gradually the entire crew, with the exception of Rex, took part in the prayers. He wanted to pray but the words clung to the roof of his mouth and refused to be forced out.

The boys were quite surprised to find themselves admired — not ridiculed — by the other crews. Now and then, before a particularly dangerous mission, other fliers or whole crews joined them in their sessions of prayer. They discovered that, far from making them weaklings, a strong, prayer-based faith in Christ made them work harder and fight better.

Dixie tried to talk with Rex several times, but got the same quick answer. "I am a Christian, Dixie," he would protest in a way that precluded further conversation.

But there was something in Rex's manner that brought doubts to Dixie's mind. They were little things that all fitted together: his obvious dislike of the prayer services and his reluctance to join; his complete confidence in the plane they flew and in his own ability; his sporadic church attendance. The bombardier prayed often for Rex. Something fundamental was lacking in his faith.

As the number of mission symbols grew on the side of the plane week after week, and the *Terrier* continued to come back unscathed, she began to earn the reputation of a "lucky" ship. Not a member of her crew had been injured. Not a bullet had marred her dull olive drab skin.

Pride welled within Rex as the reputation grew. He was the pilot of a lucky ship. The *Terrier* could not be hurt. As his confidence in his own ability crescendoed, the conviction that had been developing in his heart during every talk with Dixie subsided.

The stream of letters from Wilma continued. She spoke of her love for him, and of her growing faith in the Lord Jesus. She had drifted away from the church in her college years, but now that he was in mortal danger day and night she came to realize how great was her need for Him. She spoke of what she had missed in those years of indifference and backsliding, and how full and happy her life was now.

"I know everything's going to be all right," she wrote. "Now that I have both you and *Christ*."

That letter contained a picture of her, her blonde hair pushed back from her face and her large brown eyes sparkling. It brought back memories.

He answered her dutifully, but if his letters sounded insincere it was not for lack of trying. He wanted desperately to love her, but now that he was away from her and the spell of infatuation, doubt was turning to certainty. He was bewildered. He wanted to do the right thing. He wanted to go back and make a home for her, loving her as much as she loved him, but how could he when he did not even know her? Their courtship had been measured in hours and minutes; their marriage was the result of hasty thinking.

Her letters began to hint of something important, a "surprise," she called it. She wrote asking for his parents' address in Kansas City. She was going south for a few weeks and wanted to stop and visit with them.

He had never thought that they might want to get together, his mother and Wilma, although they spoke often of wanting to meet. He cabled the address to her immediately, and in about ten days he got an answer, a V-mail letter written in a painstakingly beautiful hand. She had written small to get it all on the page, and he borrowed Dixie's magnifying glass to read it. Her letters were always beautifully written, each word formed perfectly, and paragraphed with neat precision.

Darling,

I am writing to you now because I am going to visit your family and I want to be the first to tell you. I haven't written before, because I didn't want to worry you. You have enough on your mind without thinking about me. But you musn't worry one little minute.

Rex darling, we are going to have a baby! I hope it's a boy — as brave and as strong and as fine as his daddy. I'll be praying for the three of us every minute . . .

A baby. Rex's face blanched and he read the letter over again. Dixie sat down beside him.

"What's the matter? Bad news?"

Without speaking Rex handed him the letter.

"Why, that's splendid," he exclaimed. "We haven't had a father on our plane yet. Wait till the rest of the fellows hear about this . . . I hope it's a boy."

His enthusiasm died away as he looked at Rex's downcast face. "Don't you want children, Rex?"

"Of course I do." There was a long silence. "But I always planned on *loving* their mother."

CHAPTER 11

Rex waited a few days before answering Wilma's letter. The baby should make a difference to him. He had always dreamed of having a little boy of his own some day — one who would look up to him and try to pattern his life after his. Whenever he took a fishing trip he thought how pleasant it would be to have a boy of eight or ten or twelve along to keep him company.

But the news that he was going to be a father only served to confuse him more. At times he was positive he did not love Wilma. Then again, when he would get out her picture to look at it, or one of her old letters to read again, he did not know. Those smiling dark eyes haunted him, and he could almost hear her laugh. After the first letter or two, when she began to write with breathless interest of the things that were happening at home, when she told of amusing little incidents, he found himself looking forward keenly to hearing from her. Her letters were like a breath of cool fresh air on a stifling afternoon.

He missed her, that was true; but perhaps he was lonesome and wanted company. Regardless of whether or not he regretted their marriage, he respected the vows he had taken to be true to her. Perhaps what he felt was only a natural longing for feminine companionship. A fellow could get *so* tired of being around men day after day. He envied Dixie and all the others who had dates during their nights off.

He must have thought something of her once, but was it enough to form a foundation for a marriage? Or was it only a memory? Now that he was away from her he felt the tremendous pull of uncertainty and the pressure of the times. Probably neither one would have been serious under ordinary circumstances. Surely he would not have been so eager to rush blindly into marriage. He would have taken enough time to be certain he loved her.

Now the situation was complicated a hundredfold. He felt keenly his responsibility to both Wilma and the child. He could not desert her now.

But could there be any happiness for a little fellow in a loveless home? Questions tumbled and rolled without answer through his mind. What should he do? What was right?

Rex wanted to talk the matter out; to sit down with some interested listener and pour out the confusion and tangled emotions of his heart. He needed help in straightening his thoughts and adding insight to his judgment. Ordinarily he would have gone to Dixie, for he had always respected his utter honesty and straight thinking. But this would only give the bombardier another opportunity to preach at him. And Rex had had his fill of preaching.

He found himself recalling passages of Scripture which Dixie quoted during some of their more serious talks, which occurred at times when Rex could not get away from him without appearing rude. Dixie had been tactful in his approaches, and he made Christianity attractive. His voice thrilled as he spoke of the love of Jesus. It did not sound emotional or maudlin when he spoke of it, but rather it became the most practical thing in the world. Christianity was not a Sunday emotion to be displayed at funerals and church; it was a practical Way of Life.

Rex had always imagined himself a Christian until the quiet-spoken Southerner joined his crew and showed them Christianity at work. It meant something in *his* life. Doubt began to cast a shadow over the pilot's mind, even as separation was casting doubt over his love for Wilma.

That evening he wrote a letter to his mother, saying all of the things he would have liked to have told Dixie.

" . . . and, Mom," he wrote, "why don't you ask her to come and stay with you until after the baby's born? I feel an awful responsibility for that poor kid, and the baby too. It would probably have been better if I had never met her . . . "

After mailing it he felt better. Mom would know what to do.

The *Terrier* took part in several unimportant and uneventful sorties over enemy territory during the next month. All of the planes in the squadron came through unscathed, and the ground crews began complaining good-naturedly of having nothing to do. But there was something big brewing. Intelligence was putting in long hours poring over maps and the latest reports from Germany, and the top officers in operations were unusually preoccupied and grim. Colonel Brighton and his aide made half a dozen mysterious trips to London, and after each there was an important conference at the base.

Rex heard from his mother the day the flight orders for the big mission were posted on the bulletin board. In a conspicuous place outside the interrogation room a board was mounted where they posted the orders for the coming twenty-four-hour period, together with the numbers of the planes to take part and the time of briefing. The pilot had stopped before the board to search for the *Terrier's* serial number when Sergeant Ellson, the tail gunner from Iowa, approached him with the letter.

"This came for you this morning, sir. Lieutenant Zorn asked me to take it to you."

"Thank you, Sergeant. I see we're listed for the big show tomorrow."

"Yes, sir," he grinned. "It looks like everything but the hangars'll be over Kiel in the morning."

"I'm going to be counting on you to keep Jerry off the back of my neck."

"I'll do my best, sir. I'm right proud to be flying with the *Terrier*. She's a lucky ship."

"That's right. She's a regular homing pigeon."

When the sergeant went back to the barracks Rex opened the letter. It had been ten days since he had heard from Wilma and a month since his mother had written. The opportunity to move in with his parents had been made her. Her own mother was dead and she had felt the need for an older, sympathetic woman to whom she could turn for advice. Mrs. Madden and Wilma became fast friends, and Rex's mother insisted that she stay, at least until after the baby was born.

"You couldn't have married a girl who would fit in with our family better," his mother wrote. "We've already come to love her as our own flesh and blood, and she adores you . . . In writing about her you sounded confused, son. I can't tell you what to do, but you want to remember that we're living in unstable times and most of the world has a false set of standards. Look to the future and set your mind upon doing the will of God . . . He can bring love for her to your heart, my boy, even as He brings salvation to those of us who will accept it.

" . . . The best advice I can give you is to pray without ceasing . . . Your father and I will remember your problems in our morning worship . . . "

Even his mother preached at him. He put the letter aside, but its contents plagued him through the day. He had the growing conviction that all was not right with his faith.

They were briefed at three-thirty the following morning. Every plane that was able to leave the base was going to take part in the raid, the largest the Americans had ever carried out alone.

Dixie went on sick call the night before with a cold, and so a replacement bombardier was filling in. The rest of the boys laughingly accused the Southerner of pulling a "fast one" to get to spend the day with Mildred Patterson, to which he readily agreed.

"Yes, sir, when you guys are up in that old airplane you can remember I'll be right here in this comfortable little bed with the prettiest nurse in the army to hold my hand."

"I'll bet nobody else on the floor gets any attention out of one Miss Patterson while you're here."

"Not if I can help it," he admitted cheerfully. "I take a lot of carin' for, believe me."

Rex would have felt a little better with his regular bombardier at the bomb sight. They were used to working together and on a raid like this teamwork counted. But a man *could not* fly with a cold.

"This isn't an ordinary mission," the officer who was briefing them said. "We've been planning it for weeks, and there's more just like it to follow, only bigger. We're going over Kiel by groups and we're going to give that submarine base everything we've got. The red flak'll be thick enough to walk on and the aim'll be good. Jerry's going to protect his submarine docks and yards with the best ack-ack available and enough of them to throw up a curtain of steel. Going in we'll probably stir up every fighter plane in the area, and we'll have to battle them on the way out."

He showed the crews the points of heaviest ack-ack and the location of enemy fighter nests along their route. There was no guesswork involved. Secret service agents risked their lives to make that information available, and it was accurate.

"This whole venture depends upon split second timing. It's up to the navigator to keep you on the course selected, and the pilot must see that the time schedule is strictly maintained. Ten or fifteen minutes off can upset the whole mission.

"And you new men remember that if a Jerry fighter flies alongside of you let him go. He can't hurt you with his stingers pointed the other way. We're sending you on a bombing mission, not to see how many fighters can be destroyed. And you may need every round of ammunition you've got before you get back to the base." He stopped and looked about the crowd of men.

"I think we've covered everything. Are there any questions?"

A minute or two passed and no one spoke.

"If there are no questions, let's go."

The planes climbed to eight thousand feet and headed up the North Sea. As they neared the target they would go up to twenty thousand. They were to stay out of sight of land going over, cut across the thin waist of Denmark and swoop down upon Kiel from the southwest.

It was bad flying weather, with headwinds and fog over the water. At times they could not make out the planes flying alongside of them. Rex wished Eddie Zorn was plotting the course — not that he did not trust the squadron leader's navigator, but he had *seen* Eddie work under adverse conditions in the States. He knew what he could do.

Regardless of conditions over the North Sea the meteorologist had assured operations that the weather over the target would be favorable, with good visibility, the prerequisite of precision bombing. Clouds and rain along the way would only help to conceal the mission.

The first planes had already reached the target and completed their bombing runs when the *Terrier's* group arrived. And Jerry was wide awake. A few fires had been started at widely separated points and smoke was billowing into the clear, still air. Flak cascaded upwards, seeking the heavy bombers, even before they reached the target area. There was a veritable wall of it. Black puffs showed in the air about them as ack-ack exploded uncomfortably near. Intelligence had been right. Kiel was well protected.

Fighters were climbing rapidly to the right, acting as if they were intent upon braving their own heavy flak in order to get at the Fortresses before they dropped their loads.

"Hang on, fellows!" Rex yelled exultantly into the interphone. "Here we go!"

The big B-17's went into their bombing runs in a

step-down formation at twenty-one thousand feet.
The bombardier in the squadron leader's plane was
directing the bombing and the *Terrier's* substitute
bombardier was sitting tensely at his earphones waiting for the order to drop his eggs.

"Look at that flak," an unidentified speaker exclaimed into the interphone. "Walk on it? Why, you
could drive a jeep on it. Yes, sir, you could drive a
jeep on it. You could drive a jeep on it." And nobody thought it sounded strange at all.

An ack-ack shell exploded just under the wing of
the *Terrier* as they approached the target, and ripped
away a section of the flap. The big plane rocked
violently. Rex fought her back to an even keel, and
the bombardier cried, "Bomb's away!"

The salvos dropped easily from the ship and
angled, nose down, towards the target, screaming
their warning as they neared the ground.

It was the first time a plane Rex was piloting had
been hit in combat and it frightened him. He had
been depending, more than he realized, upon the
"good luck" of the *Terrier*. He had an almost overwhelming impulse to leave the formation and make a
run for it alone, forgetting the safety of his men, the
flight, everything except an uncontrollable will to
exist.

Before he had time to calculate the damage done
someone yelled into the interphone: "There's a
Yellownose coming in at ten o'clock!"

"And an ME 109 at seven o'clock," came from the
other side of the plane.

Their machine guns chattered as the gunners set
the cross lines of their Sperry gun sights on the enemy
craft. The motions were the same as those in practice,

and it was hard to believe that the flashes from the Jerry fighters were actually bullets aimed at them.

The first plane veered away with smoke showing about his motor cowling after a short cannon burst that did no harm, but the Messerschmidt kept boring in, his cannon shells crashing through the skin of the *Terrier.* The big ship rocked and quivered with each new hit. The number four motor conked out and Rex feathered the prop to keep from tearing the engine loose from its moorings. It had only been a few seconds since they entered their bombing run but the B-17 was a shambles. The co-pilot was slumped in his seat and the waist gunners were sprawled on the floor, their guns forever stilled. Rex could only imagine what had happened to the stocky Iowa lad who had been manning the tail gun. It was impossible to contact any of the crew on the interphone. That must have been damaged too.

The flight had salvoed its bombs and limped out to sea to lick its wounds before starting back. The group had scattered, leaving each flight to get back to base as best they could.

"Flight leader to 925. Come in, 925."

"925 to flight leader. Come in, flight leader."

"How badly are you damaged, Mike?"

"Just a little flak in the skin. I don't think it'll cause us any trouble; but I've got a couple of badly injured boys in the crew."

"That's tough. But you think you can make it all right?"

"Yes, sir. I could fly this baby around the world if the gas held out."

"That is all."

"Roger."

It was the *Terrier's* turn next. The flight leader called her numbers and Rex answered, his voice trembling.

"What did they do to you, Madden?"

"We took quite a pounding, sir. Half the crew's dead."

"Never mind that now," he said impatiently. "What's the shape of the plane? Can you make it?"

"I'm not sure." He looked at the gas tanks and tested the controls carefully. "Number four conked out, a section of the right wing flap's blown away and the hydraulic controls are damaged. I'll have to have a man check them to see how bad. But the gas is O.K. and the other controls seem to be working all right."

"Whew. Boy, they really pasted you, didn't they?" In a moment he went on. "We're all set to head for home. I'm going to go back across Denmark and pray that Jerry's pea shooters are busy somewhere else. You were the worst hit in the flight, Rex, but we'll stay with you for awhile at least. Try to keep your speed up and maintain as much altitude as possible. That could be the deciding factor for you."

"Roger."

"And may God bless you and your crew, Madden."

That from a flight leader who had never been to church, to Rex's knowledge.

The engineer found two bad leaks in the hydraulic lines and wallowed in greasy, slimy fluid to tape them. Rex tried the controls cautiously, holding his breath. They worked, but it would take pampering to make them hold all the way home.

They ignored the ever-present danger of fighter opposition, heading across Denmark and directly for

England. The altimeter drifted slowly downward as their speed fell off. It was impossible to keep the heavy plane at high altitude with three motors.

The wind that had been against them on the way over was friendly now, and the crippled Fortress rode on its back, thankful for the assistance. It would need everything to get them safely down again.

The rest of the flight stayed with the *Terrier*, risking their own lives in doing so, for they knew that packs of Focke Wulfs and Messerschmidts would be scouring the skylanes for stragglers. Medals were not given for such heroism as that. The airmen shrugged it aside as routine. Its very frequency made it commonplace.

Rex's mind was stunned by what he saw on the *Terrier* — *his Terrier* — *the lucky ship.* He was flying by instinct alone, with only the most frenzied will to live keeping him at the arduous task of nursing the controls, watching air speed and fighting to keep altitude.

After what seemed an aeon of flying they reached the rocky storm-swept coast of England and safety. Rex dropped onto the first available base and his companions circled the field, waved their congratulations and flew on.

Chapter 12

Rex flashed the "wounded aboard" signal as he came in over the field, and an ambulance was waiting for them on the landing strip. Before the big propellers stopped turning a medical detachment swarmed into the plane to administer first aid. Their task was to wait for just such emergencies, which happened oftener than any of them liked.

The interior of the B-17 was not a pleasant sight. The blood of dying men was spilled in dark blotches on the floor, and their lifeless bodies were slumped grotesquely at battle stations — shapes of flesh that looked but little like the men they once were.

Trout, Benton, the bombardier who had filled in at Dixie's post, Rogers and Rex were the only uninjured men in the crew. Eddie Zorn had caught a piece of shrapnel in his arm when a twenty-millimeter cannon shell crashed through the bulletproof glass. The radio operator had stopped a machine gun bullet with his hip. But both of them had stayed by their guns until the enemy had been driven off, and then they had gone back to their jobs, to work doggedly, until they reached the ground.

It did not seem possible that those carefree boys who had so eagerly left the alert room could have gone so quickly. But they were. Their lives had been spilled out in a brief, furious battle against men whom they had never seen, let alone learned to hate. Hatred was for those back home. They could smear yellow paint on the homes of German Americans and thump

119

their chests with patriotic self-righteousness. But it was enough for the bombing crews to hate the ideology the enemy represented and do the job they were trained to do.

After caring for the wounded, the medical detachment began to remove the others. There would be a grave-digging detail before dark, and, as the mists began to fold over the burial ground, a short prayer service would be held by the chaplain. And four new men would be called for from replacement to fill out the crew again. It was ever thus. Without voiced regret or outward sorrow new men filled the thinning ranks and carried on as though they had been there all the time. That is the way wars are fought.

Bob Trout, Benton and Rogers crawled out of the door and slid quietly to the ground. They expected Rex to follow, for the pilot, like the captain of a ship, is always the last to leave. But instead he remained seated behind the controls, staring, dazed and unseeing, at the floor.

A sergeant with the medical detachment tapped him on the shoulder. "Are you all right, sir?"

"I-I don't know. I guess so."

"Hadn't you better get out, sir?"

There was no answer and he repeated the question.

"Look at her," Rex said bitterly, as though he had just found voice. "She's a lucky ship. A regular homing pigeon. You can't hurt the *Terrier*. She's *lucky*." His face twitched convulsively and his lips were quivering under the attempt to stem the flow of words. "I told them I took her up and I was going to bring her back again. I brought her back all right, but I didn't bring them with her." Hysteria was lurking just below the surface.

"Hadn't you better get out now, sir?" the sergeant repeated softly. "Your buddies are waiting for you."

"Ellson's gone. Bartlett's gone." All of the strain of the past few hours was released at once now that he was on the ground, and he felt the soul-twisting shock of reality. He was just realizing the consequences of their mission over Kiel. "And so are Sims and Ronnquist. Sims was a waist gunner," he continued in an unnatural monotone. "He stood right back there. And now he's gone. That's where my buddies are. *They're all dead!*"

The sergeant grasped him tenderly by the shoulders and guided him to his feet. "You ought to go in and get a cup of coffee, sir. You've had a pretty tough time of it."

Two men on the ground outside the door helped him down.

In the interrogation room some time later he tried to add his version of the raid to those of his three living companions, but he could not. He tried to command his tongue, and tell a logical story in a calm, subdued voice, but he repeated the same things again and again. His tortured mind snatched fragments of events and churned them about until he was unable to recall what he had said and what he had not.

The men who were listening watched with pity as he strove to control himself and the meaningless flow of words. They knew what he was going through. One of their number had gone through it himself. All of them had seen men who had not been able to master it; whose minds refused to come under control again. They had to be sent back to the States and discharged, of no use to the air force, and of very little use to themselves.

After a few minutes intelligence saw that Rex was unable to give a coherent account of what had happened. He was taken over to the hospital, put to bed and quieted with morphine.

When he was gone, one of the aides turned to the officer in charge. "Will that boy ever fly again, sir?"

The officer shook his head. "I wish I could answer that. The only way we can be certain is to put him in a plane again."

"I'm no doctor, but I would have sworn he was insane. I've never seen a man act so strangely."

"You'll see a lot of strange things before you've been over here very long, Captain," he smiled. "This boy wasn't himself tonight, but that doesn't mean he's mentally unhinged. You want to remember he's been through a lot the past five or six hours. Four men in his crew were killed, and the pilot always feels responsible for his crew. He's been through a lot and he's seen a lot — almost more than one man can stand. I suppose you could call this a form of shell shock."

"But to get over it so he could fly a plane in combat again," the captain said doubtfully. "It just doesn't seem possible."

"That's true enough. And maybe he can't. I'll admit the odds are against him. But if he can conquer this and gain enough control over himself to go out on another mission he'll come out of it a better pilot. Whatever happens now is up to him."

They notified the *Terrier's* base of operations of the location of the plane, the extent of damage and injury to the crew. Word came back for the uninjured fliers to remain with their plane until it was determined whether or not it was reparable.

Rex got up late the next morning after a drug-

induced rest. The nurse thought he should be kept in
bed for another day or two, but the doctor examined
him thoroughly and pronounced him physically fit. It
would be better for him to get out among the boys
where he could get his mind off the ordeal of the day
before, rather than to lie in bed and think. He left the
hospital and joined his crew — or what was left of it
— to eat dinner.

Although he was quiet and more composed, he was
still suffering from nervous shock. The words were
slow in coming when anyone questioned him and his
voice was dull and lifeless. At the long table in the
mess hall he scarcely heard the voices of those about
him. He was flying the *Terrier* again, hearing those
awful groans and feeling the big plane quiver as it
was hit. He remembered hearing his co-pilot cry out
softly between clenched teeth and slump forward with
blood staining the back of his flying suit.

He went over the battle continuously, from the
first exhilarating moment of the bombing run until
they followed the flight leader out to sea.

Ellson must have been hit first, or the Messerschmidt *could not* have gotten in at such an angle.
There was no blind spot on the *Terrier* from that
direction — or from any direction, for that matter.
And Trout in the top turret must have been concen-
trating on the other plane. Sims probably got it a
split second later, leaving the whole side of the plane
unprotected. If only he could have sneaked into a
cloud bank! It was strange, but he could not even
remember whether there had been any clouds or not.
If only he had moved in to close the V so that the
crews of the other two planes could have helped fight
off the Jerry!

He could not bring himself to accept the fact that the *Terrier* was anything but invulnerable, and so it must have been something he had done or failed to do that caused the debacle. He went over the scene again and tried to find the cause.

Rex and his comrades walked over to visit the injured members of the crew, both of whom were responding to treatment. The doctors had removed the bullet from the radio operator's hip and had treated the wound on the navigator's arm. Both of them were talking about the time they could be released from the hospital. Rex felt somewhat better after leaving them.

The other three boys understood how it was with Rex and they did their best to keep his mind from himself and the men who had been killed. All of them felt the loss, but they did not have the shattered illusion of invincibility to battle nor the responsibility for the crew.

They wished that Dixie could have come with them, for he and Rex were close friends. They felt that he might be able to do something to ease the pilot's tortured mind.

Rogers was the least affected of any of them. When they marveled at his self-control he seemed surprised. He had not noticed that he was different from the others, but they had noticed it. He had the same qualities of composure that marked Dixie's life. They envied him.

A Boeing specialist from London flew in that afternoon to look over the *Terrier* and determine whether or not it could be made to fly. A year before a plane damaged in such a manner would have been condemned and wrecked for salvage, but the "bomber doctors" had improved their technique a thousandfold in wresting damaged planes from the junk heaps.

Civilian employees of the factory that built the B-17 went into the battlefields all over the world to repair the big planes and make them fly again. Where they lacked tools they used a screwdriver and a pair of pliers, and where they lacked parts they made them or took them off another plane with similar mechanism. There were many Flying Fortresses operating in the Middle East which were patched with parts taken from captured German or Italian planes. Given a dozen army-trained mechanics and a little time, these mechanics could put most any plane back in good repair unless it was burned or a pile of wreckage.

The specialist went over the big B-17 hurriedly, but with the practiced eye of an expert, noting the parts that could be repaired and those that would have to be replaced. The skin could be patched very well with aluminum taken from wreckage and the tail assembly could be repaired. There was a condemned Fortress at a field near by which would provide bulletproof glass to put in the bombardier's compartment, and the line for the hydraulic controls. Only a new number four motor would be needed and they had those in the hangar at the field.

"I'll have her flying in a week," the specialist informed the crew chief who had been assigned to him, "if you can get me a good bunch of men."

"I can have as many as you want," he said proudly. "We've got some good mechanics at this field."

They went to work on the plane immediately. Rex and the boys watched them tear away the bullet-riddled skin and put in smooth aluminum patches.

The work was as carefully done as it was speedy. Other mechanics had brought a heavy hoist up over number four and in a matter of hours had removed the old motor, mounted a new one and had it adjusted perfectly. The Boeing man was all over the plane. One minute he would be supervising the work on the tail and the next he would have his hands plunged in grease up to his elbows as he helped swing the big engine into line.

The CO suggested that the crew go fishing up into the mountains of Scotland while they waited for their plane.

"It's the best trout fishing in the country," he explained. "A lot of the boys from here have been getting swell catches."

They were interested, but Rex could not bring himself to think of fishing. The time was rapidly approaching when he would have to get into that plane, start the motors and take off into the wind. The very thought chilled him. Trout and Benton decided they could not go and leave him alone, and Rogers readily agreed.

The expert had overestimated the time required to put the big plane into flying trim by two days. A proud crew chief informed him that his boys would be done by noon the next day, just five days after they had started work on her.

"Didn't I tell you I had the best mechanics in the business?" he asked. He did not mention the fact that he and three volunteers had been working an extra five or six hours a day to get it finished.

The next morning the riddled crew of the *Terrier* got their things together and were ready to leave when the plane was finished. Only a co-pilot was sent along with the four members of the crew. Operations was still dubious about Rex's ability to handle the big B-17 after his nerve-wracking experience.

Sweat rolled down his face as he got into the pilot's seat. He *had* to get the plane off the ground. They started the motors one by one, and the big Fortress moved slowly up to the runway. Rex was tense at the controls and the boys sensed the things that were going through his mind. Rogers and Trout were praying silently for him to conquer the fear that threatened to ruin him as a pilot.

At the signal from the flight control tower Rex opened the throttle and the plane began to roar down the runway. His face was set in a grim hard line.

"This is the time," he told himself. His future career hinged upon the moment. It was just a simple thing. Let the plane gather speed, tucking air below the wings as she gained momentum. And then ease back on the controls. It was easy as that. He had done it a thousand times, on snow-swept plains and dangerously short mountain runways where the down draft is liable to dash one into a mountainside if he is not watchful. He had flown in wind and rain and fog. This was merely routine. Any cadet with a dozen hours in a B-17 could do it easily. Just get up speed and slowly move the controls. The plane would do the rest. But thoughts of the dead in his old crew blotted his vision and hysteria began to attack reason. He had been responsible for the deaths of those men. He could never fly again. *He could never fly again!*

He cut the throttle and applied the brakes slowly as though something had frozen his will to fly. He sat there trembling.

The control tower began to clamor for information. The plane had been recently overhauled and such action indicated trouble.

Bob Trout patted Rex on the shoulder and the co-pilot looked back at the engineer and nodded understandingly.

"I'm sorry, sir," he said into the radio. "It was just a false start. There's nothing wrong."

Such an explanation would scarcely satisfy operations and he knew that he would have to answer a host of questions when the crew landed at their destination.

They wheeled the *Terrier* back to the end of the runway and took off easily. She flew as smoothly as she ever did. To handle her no one would have known she had been riddled in battle, although she still showed evidence of the ordeal.

When they were in the air and out of sight of the base the co-pilot turned to Rex. "Won't you take over now, Lieutenant?

"I-I couldn't." His face was still ashen.

"Of course you can." The co-pilot got up. "Go ahead and fly her. I'm going to go back and have a look at the tail."

Rex could not fly the *Terrier*. He would crash and kill them all. He had only to throw in the automatic pilot and let it hold her on the course until the co-pilot returned. That was what his fear commanded him to do. He leaned forward, and in so doing moved the right rudder. The plane veered slightly to one side. He straightened quickly, startled at the movement of the ship. It *would* respond to his touch. That fact seemed almost incredible.

Gingerly he took the controls. He tried the rudders and pulled back on the wheel speculatively. The

Terrier lifted her nose like an Irish setter pointing partridges. He pushed forward and she angled gracefully down. There was no sluggish hesitation or faltering. She behaved like the queen she was. A little confidence came back to him, and a bit of the thrill of commanding the giant craft. He hitched himself straighter in the seat and relaxed as he handled the controls.

Bob Trout, watching breathlessly from the spot behind him, grinned. The ruse had worked.

Rex was flying again.

CHAPTER 13

Dixie was out of the hospital and waiting at the field to welcome them when they landed. He had heard that the crew had been badly handled and was anxious to see who had been spared. It was gratifying to learn that the man who had been sent in his place had come back safely. And he thanked God that Rex had not been taken in his unbelief.

Rex was loathe to talk about what had happened. He did not feel the awful fear or the dread of flying that he had before, but he could not dwell on the horrible nightmare over Kiel without feeling his stomach tighten into a knot.

He had been counting on a letter from Wilma when he got back to the base, but there was none. He was more disappointed than he would have admitted, even to himself.

"It's getting time for that boy to arrive," he told Dixie. "I can't understand why they haven't written to me or something."

There was a long silence. Then Dixie said, "I thought you didn't love her."

The phrase slapped Rex hard. He got up from the chair and walked over to the window and back again.

"I'm so mixed up, Dixie, that I don't know what I want, or why," he said. "One day I think I can never love her regardless of what happens. But I get to looking forward to her letters and worry like everything when I don't hear from her." He sat down and crossed his legs.

He did not hear from her the next day, and the next they were slated for an important mission. The new members of the crew were introduced and shown the plane. They had been thoroughly trained at home and were ready and eager for their tasks. That their predecessors had been killed in a raid made no difference to them.

The flight orders slated the briefing for an hour before dawn. It was to be a small raid and highly secret. Their destination was not to be revealed until they reached the briefing room.

Dixie had been talking with Rogers and Trout enough to learn what had happened to Rex after the Kiel raid. He seemed calm enough now as they talked of common things, but how would he act over a target area? Would he be able to hold his course firm and true? Or would he falter when the flak got thick? And, more important than all the rest, was he to gamble with death again without the assurance of salvation? Dixie prayed long about his friend that night. He *had* to talk with him.

He made the opportunity the next morning before the briefing. Rex had not slept well either and they both were up in the chill night air. Rex, too, was wondering what he would do over the target area. With grim determination he resolved to hold straight to the course. He was bigger than the things which had happened to him. He was stronger than Jerry flak. They could shoot up his plane and kill his men but he would still come boring in. The one false note lay in the whiteness about his lips and the tremor in his hands.

Dixie opened the barracks door and stepped out into the fog beside Rex.

"You're up early, Dixie."

They could just make out each other's features in the darkness.

"Yeh, I couldn't sleep very well last night. I seldom do before a mission."

"I couldn't before this one." His voice was taut and he strained to keep it calm.

"The boys were telling me you had a rough time over Kiel. You shouldn't feel responsible for those fellows' lives. You were doing your duty and they were doing theirs. It's just part of the horror of war."

"I keep telling myself it wasn't my fault, but then I see them lying there in the plane with blood all around them. Dixie," he said suddenly, "how do you stay so composed? Nothing seems to bother you."

Dixie thanked God for presenting him with the opportunity to talk to Rex. The pilot was *asking* for help this time, for he already knew that the bombardier attributed his serenity to his faith in God.

"It's nothing I can do for myself. It comes from putting my whole trust in the Lord Jesus. Without Him I'd be much worse than Bill Jordan ever was, I know. We can't trust ourselves and our weapons in something like this. Don't you see that this thing is too big for us? Don't you feel the need for His guidance and help?"

Rex hesitated momentarily, and Dixie waited, watching the effect of his words.

"I've felt the need of someone, or something, Dixie, that would give me back the confidence I've had in myself, but I don't think I ever really defined it as God. I don't know just what I did expect. It's been rather vague."

"Jesus Christ has what I needed, and He has what you need, but He won't give you confidence in yourself. He'll give you confidence in Him." Rex sat down on the step and Dixie sat down beside him. He talked in low tones, but enthusiasm colored his words. "The Lord has laid it on my heart to talk with you, Rex. I guess you know I've tried it before, but you'd never really felt the need for Him and I couldn't begin to get you interested. Now you do feel that you need Him. What happened over Kiel has shown you that you were trusting in sands instead of rock. There's one answer, and only one, to the fears that're torturing your soul. Confess your sins and accept Christ as your personal Saviour."

"But I do believe." Impatience crept into his tone. "I am a Christian."

"Do you believe enough to place Him first in your life? Do you believe enough to cast your sins upon Him and let Him wash you clean? Do you believe enough to give yourself entirely and completely to Him. *Do you believe enough, Rex?*"

There was a long silence. Rex Madden knew what Dixie was thinking. He had been thinking the same thing about himself. He was seeing the sin in his life — the smug, complacent sin that rested upon his vague belief that he was a Christian and thereby above and beyond such things as confessing sins and asking forgiveness.

"Will you show me the way, Dixie?" he asked, his voice soft and charged with emotion.

"*Christ* is the Way. If you would have salvation, confess your sins with the prayer of the sinner, 'God, be merciful unto me.' Ask for His strength and courage and peace."

Dixie opened his Bible to the fourteenth chapter of John and read quietly: *Jesus saith unto him, I am the way, the truth, and the life: no man cometh unto the Father, but by me."*

That verse seemed to open the floodgates of Rex's heart. Without moving from the steps he bowed his head and began to pour out his soul to the Lord. Once Dixie was about to suggest that they kneel, but something stayed him. A wrong word or an inopportune suggestion might well destroy all that was being accomplished.

As Rex prayed, softly and vibrantly, his turbulent heart stilled. It was as the Southerner had said; with the confession of sins and the acceptance of Christ as his Master the load he had been carrying slipped away. Peace and happiness came to him, and with them, courage. He knew then that, regardless of what happened in the future, he would never fear flying again. *Someone* would ride beside him, guiding him and helping him. Christ would guide as he piloted his plane.

He prayed, not for safety for himself, but that he might adequately discharge his duties regardless of the odds against him.

Some minutes later he got to his feet a bit unsteadily. At that moment one of the crew came out to where they were.

"Oh, there you are. I thought I'd have to hunt for you," he said to Rex. "We're going in to be briefed now."

"Thanks."

The officers in charge of the briefing were unusually grim.

"This is a light raid, if we measure it by the number of planes that will take part, but it's an exceedingly important mission. We're only sending over two squadrons, and so you can see the responsibility that rests upon each plane. There's no need in my telling you it's dangerous. But this time, in view of the small number of planes taking part, all flights are to continue to the target. If any of you are aborted on the way over you'll have to get home as best you can alone. The rest of your flight can't be spared from the mission."

When they were filing out of the room after the briefing one of the officers called Dixie aside.

"How's Madden, Lieutenant?"

"I think he'll be all right, sir."

"The co-pilot who helped bring the plane here reported that Madden was afraid to take her off."

"I wasn't there, sir, but that's what I understood. He was just a little upset after the Kiel affair. He's all right now."

"Are you sure of it?"

"Yes, sir."

"Sure enough to fly with him?

"That's right, sir. I'd fly with him anywhere."

"Does the rest of the crew know what happened to his nerves?

"Yes, sir, and they're all willing to go with him."

"Thank you, Lieutenant. We've been concerned about him since we got the report from the base where he landed, and the additional report of the co-pilot. I shall want a detailed report of what happens on this mission from your co-pilot. I've talked to you about this because I understand that you're Madden's best friend and would most likely know his condition better than anyone else."

"I don't think you need worry at all, sir."

As they were climbing into the *Terrier* a private came running up. "Is Lieutenant Madden here?" he asked breathlessly.

"I'm Madden." Rex turned and stepped towards him.

Rex took it hastily. It was from his mother, and had been mailed two weeks before.

"There was a cablegram for you too, sir, but I didn't bring it with me."

"Why not?" Rex shouted at him. A cablegram could only mean that the baby was born.

"I would have had to wait for it, sir, and there wasn't time."

Rex started to retort sharply, but the co-pilot called from the plane, "They're about ready for us, Madden."

There wasn't time to go after the cablegram. He knew it was about Wilma. It had to be. And he would have to wait for five or six or seven hours to find out what it said.

When they had taken off and fallen into formation Rex turned the controls to his co-pilot while he read the letter from his mother.

. . . Wilma asked me not to write to you, but I had to, son, in case things should go wrong. She hasn't been well, in spite of what she's been writing to you . . . I'd feel so much better if you were here. She loves you so much . . .

Rex choked. He could not read any more. As the shackles of sin slipped from him a few moments before, just outside the officers' quarters, so did his doubt about loving Wilma disappear now that her life was in jeopardy. For weeks and months doubt had piled upon doubt. Every attractive girl he saw made him sorry that he was bound by matrimony to be true to a girl he scarcely knew. Every time he saw Dixie and Patts together, or one of the other fellows with a little English girl, he had longed to be in their places. Lonesomeness had dwarfed his affection for Wilma and had magnified his desire to seek other feminine companionship. Even the knowledge that they were to be parents had not changed the situation. But now the rude shock of learning that she was risking death brought him sharply to his senses. Now that her life was hanging in the balances he knew he loved her. The confusion and bewilderment of the past few weeks was gone.

He did not know whether he had always loved her and was just realizing it, or whether he was just beginning to fall in love. But it did not matter. There was no doubt in his mind or heart. He loved her deeply.

Word was waiting for him back at the base, but the hours seemed to stretch into days before they landed again.

The raid went over nicely and the *Terrier* was fortunate to bring her crew back without a scratch. They picked up a little flak and a temperamental motor that had to be coaxed all the way home, but those were little things. Rex urged the big plane on as fast as he could, itching to leave the formation and dash back to the base to get the cablegram.

It might contain news of the birth of their child, or it might . . . He dare not think of the other possibility.

Finally the flight arrived back at the base, and Rex hurried to get his cablegram. It was from his mother.

Baby son born Tuesday. Both doing nicely.

The tears sneaked from under his eyelashes as he read.

"Thank God," he breathed softly. "Thank God."

CHAPTER 14

The following days passed smoothly for Rex. He had gone through his great trial and had come out with a new faith in the Lord Jesus. Not that there were not rough missions. At times when he was over the target area and the flak was blasting holes in the air about the *Terrier*, he was so frightened he felt it would be impossible for him to work the controls. But, like Dixie, he had a Source of strength that never failed him. Whenever the going was toughest, there was always a prayer on his lips.

Their plane was shot up now and again over Europe. Men were killed and new ones were sent from replacement to fill out the crew, but never again did Rex have to battle within himself to control his mind. That battle had been fought and won by Christ Jesus.

He found renewed comfort in the letters from Wilma, and his love for her increased as the days went by. She wrote often, telling him about the little fellow who looked like him. But he did not believe it. All little babies he had ever seen looked like no one at all, excepting another baby. But it flattered him just the same. She promised to send a picture as soon as she could get it taken and he could scarcely wait to see him.

* * *

Gaslin, the co-pilot on the mission on which Dixie was wounded, had marveled at Rex Madden's control. And Georgie Stebbins, whose buddy had been killed, and who was fighting against hysteria, grasped eagerly at the faith which Rex possessed.

"All of us are afraid, Georgie," he said sympathetically. "I went through just what you're going through now, not so long ago. And Dixie Meyers showed me how to lick it." Briefly he told the young aerial gunner what had happened to him. And as he spoke of Christ and His saving grace the boy's face relaxed its taut, strained look and became calm once more. "If we try to fight fear ourselves we're licked before we start. I tried it; so I know. The Lord Jesus alone can give us strength to carry on."

Together they knelt on the barracks floor. Men coming and going in the long narrow building hushed their talking and stepped quietly past. One day they might have laughed, but they could not do that when one of the men was a buddy who had lost his best friend, and the other a veteran captain who wore the Distinguished Flying Cross and an oak leaf cluster on his blouse.

"You have only to accept Him as your personal Saviour, Georgie, confessing your sins and praying for forgiveness. Then you can pray for strength and the courage to go on. He's not only the Christ of the weak and homeless. *He's the Christ of fighting men.*"

GLOSSARY OF AERONAUTICAL AND MILITARY TERMS

Aborted — to be forced to return to the base of operations by mechanical difficulties before reaching the target area.

Ack-ack — antiaircraft guns.

Alert — state of preparedness before going on a mission or before going overseas. When a company or crew is alerted they are on a moment's call and cannot leave the camp or communicate with anyone on the outside.

Alert room — room where pilots and crews are briefed for missions.

Altimeter — instrument for measuring altitude.

Barracks — enlisted men's quarters.

Base — airfield where ground crews, operations, intelligence offices, flying crews, etc., are stationed.

Base of operations — generally same as above.

B-17 — Boeing Flying Fortress.

Bomb bay — portion of the airplane where bombs are carried.

Bombing run — a steady, level trip over the target area, in high level precision bombing, during which the bombardier directs the flight.

Conked — a term generally used in referring to a motor silenced by enemy action, although it can refer to any mechanical difficulty that causes an engine to quit in the air.

Control tower — tower on the airfield used to control the landing and taking off of planes.

Crew — in a B-17, 10 men: pilot, co-pilot, navigator-gunner, bombardier-gunner, engineer-upper turrent gunner, 2nd engineer-waist gunner, armorer-waist gunner (checks ammunition, arms, bombs, etc), radio operator, 2nd radio operator-ball turret gunner, tail gunner.

Feathering the prop — changing the pitch of the propeller.

Fighter at ten o'clock — an example of the method used for pointing out quickly the direction from which an enemy plane is approaching. Lay a watch down face up, imagining that twelve o'clock is on the nose, three on the right wing, six on the tail and nine on the left wing. Hence a fighter coming in at ten o'clock would be approaching the plane at an angle just ahead of the left wing.

Flight orders — orders given for the conducting of a flight, course to follow, speed, landing points, etc.

Flak — fragments of antiaircraft shells.

Formation — an established flying order for several planes, one of the most successful of which is a V or combination of V's.

Focke Wulf — a very formidable German fighting plane, often called Yellownose by Allied airmen.

Group — several squadrons of planes.

Hot — a term used in describing a crew or crews about ready to go overseas.

Intelligence — portion of the army that provides information regarding targets, antiaircraft placements, dispersal of fighter strength, etc. A part of their information is gleaned from returning crews, but a great deal of it comes from daring undercover agents working in the occupied countries and even in Germany.

Interrogation room — room where returning fliers are quizzed by intelligence.

Interphone — communication system linking crew members together.

Messerschmidt — German fighter plane.

Mission — major operation against an enemy target, usually with a large number of planes.

Operations — much the same as headquarters in a ground army. With the aid of intelligence they plan missions, sorties, etc.

Operational flights — training flights designed to give fliers training in every type of flying and under every condition they are likely to encounter in combat.

Precision bombing — high altitude daylight raids in good visibility, for which the Flying Fortress was originally designed. The use of the famous Norden bomb sights making such risky raids worth while.

PX — post exchange.

Replacements or Replacement Center — base that supplies crew members to replace those injured or killed.

Roger — O.K. or "I understand." Used extensively in interphone conversations.

Salvo — to drop all the bombs in the plane at one time.

Shrapnel — slivers of high explosive shell or bomb.

Skin — thin aluminum covering on the plane.

Skip-bombing — a highly dangerous type of bombing in which the plane dives down within twenty or thirty feet of the water to drop the bombs, thus causing it to "skip" into the ship in the unarmored side just below the water line. It is an American maneuver, developed in the Australian theater and proved highly successful against surface craft in the battle of the Bismarck Sea.

Squadron — nine planes.

Sorties — minor operations against enemy installations, strafing, etc.

Throat mike — microphone that fastens about the throat, used with interphone.

Tokios — extra wing tanks.

Walk around bottle — bottle of oxygen to snap to oxygen mask when wearer wants to move from one section of the plane to the other, beyond the reach of the oxygen hose.

The Quick
Red Fox

Books by JOHN D. MacDONALD

All These Condemned
April Evil
Area of Suspicion
Ballroom of the Skies
The Beach Girls
Border Town Girl
The Brass Cupcake
A Bullet for Cinderella
Cancel All Our Vows
Clemmie
Contrary Pleasure
The Crossroads
Cry Hard, Cry Fast
The Damned
Dead Low Tide
Deadly Welcome
Death Trap
The Deceivers
The Drowner
The Empty Trap
The End of the Night
End of the Tiger and Other
   Stories
The Executioners

A Flash of Green
The Girl, the Gold
   Watch & Everything
The House Guests
Judge Me Not
A Key to the Suite
The Last One Left
A Man of Affairs
Murder for the Bride
Murder in the Wind
The Neon Jungle
No Deadly Drug
On the Run
One Monday We Killed
   Them All
The Only Girl in the Game
Please Write for Details
The Price of Murder
S*E*V*E*N
Slam the Big Door
Soft Touch
Where Is Janice Gantry?
Wine of the Dreamers
You Live Once

The Travis McGee Series

The Deep Blue Good-by
Nightmare in Pink
A Purple Place for Dying
The Quick Red Fox
A Deadly Shade of Gold
Bright Orange for the
   Shroud
Darker Than Amber

One Fearful Yellow Eye
Pale Gray for Guilt
The Girl in the
   Plain Brown Wrapper
Dress Her in Indigo
The Long Lavender Look
A Tan and Sandy Silence
The Scarlet Ruse

The Turquoise Lament

The Quick Red Fox

by John D. MacDonald

J. B. Lippincott Company
Philadelphia and New York

Printed in the United States of America

First Hardbound edition 1974
Fourth Printing

U.S. Library of Congress Cataloging in Publication Data

MacDonald, John Dann, birth date
  The quick red fox.

  I. Title.
PZ3.M14439Qi6 [PS3563.A28]   813'.5'4   73–16074
ISBN–0–397–01015–X

For Salamah's younger sibling

One

A BIG NOISY WIND out of the northeast, full of a February chill, herded the tourists off the afternoon beach, driving them to cover, complaining bitterly. It picked up gray slabs of the Atlantic and smacked them down on the public beach across the highway from Bahia Mar. It rattled loose sand across the windshields of the traffic, came into the cramped acres of docks and boat basin, snapped the burgees and went *hoooo* in the spiderwebs of rigging and tuna towers. Fort Lauderdale was a dead loss for the tourists that Saturday afternoon. They would have been more comfortable back in Scranton.

I was cozied up in the big lounge of the *Busted Flush*, my houseboat moored at Slip F-18. My electric heat was turned to high-high. I was stretched out on the big yellow couch and clad in ratty old wool slacks and an old Norm Thompson flannel shirt, faded to a sky blue over the treasured years.

A few days earlier I had junked my old speakers in favor of a pair of AR-3s, and had bracket-mounted them on the far wall. The Scott tuner was locked into WAEZ in Miami, and the Fisher amplifier was driving the new speakers very handsomely. They were broadcasting that Columbia recording of Bernstein conducting the Shostakovich *Fifth*, one hell of a big bold heroic piece of music, and I had the gain high enough to do it justice. You could shut your eyes and float on it.

Skeeter was across the room, hunched over her drawing board. She was wearing gray corduroy coveralls, too big for her. All her clothes always seem too big for her. She is thirty, I think, and looks eighteen. She has cobweb-blond hair, constantly adrift, a Raggedy Ann face, and a narrow graceful immature figure. She is not very well organized, but she makes a pretty fair living doing illustrations for children's books under the pseudonym of Annamara. My friend Meyer found her on the beach a year or so ago. That hairy, ugly, charming fellow can walk down a beach and collect rare people the way anyone else might pick up a left-handed whelk.

She worked with the top of her tongue sticking out of the corner of her mouth. She was doing line drawings of a dissolute field mouse named Quimby. She was working at my place because they had repainted her apartment three blocks away, and the smell made her nauseous, and she had a deadline to meet. Once upon a time, when I had been feeling shattered by the loss of someone very dear to me, we had drifted sideways into a brief affair. We had found we weren't very good for each other on that kind of basis. We seemed to bring out a talent in each other for chipping away at the weak points. The infighting got a bit bloody, and though we felt obligated to pretend otherwise, it was a relief to both of us to call it off and find our way into a casual and offhandedly affectionate friendship.

At the big parts of the music she would use her drawing pen to help Bernstein conduct, and then go back to mouse work. She had uncovered an unexpected talent for making Navy grog, and I had a mild and pleasant glow from the ones she had fixed me. She had made her own weaker. Quimby demanded her sober attentions.

Into the resonant blare of the music came the frail little overpowered *bing-bong* of my bell. I have a button board affixed to a dock post, and a chain across the dock end of my small gangplank.

I got up and went and took a look. It was a tall girl out there, a tall girl in a severe dark suit, with a purse that managed to give the same impression as a briefcase. She stood erect, pretending there was no wind at all. She looked as if she might be going around enrolling people in a business school. As I peered out at her, she punched the button again. There was no hesitancy about her.

I went out onto the rear deck and up the broad short slant of gangplank to face her across the chain. Her survey of me looked inclusive, and I couldn't tell if she registered approval or disapproval. I get both kinds. I am extra big. I have been out in the weather. I look lazy and am. In the words of a Texas chick one time, I look as if I had been there and back.

She had black hair, short and crisply curly. She had vivid dark eyes, heavy black brows, a rather long face, high flat cheekbones and a ski-jump nose. The mouth saved the face from austerity. It was full and broad and nicely modeled. She looked fashionable, competent and humorless.

"Mr. Travis McGee?" she asked. She had a furry contralto.

"Himself."

"I am Dana Holtzer. I couldn't reach you by phone."

"It's turned off, Miss Holtzer."

"I would like to talk to you about a very personal matter."

Sometimes it does happen that way. She had a money look. No jewelry. Earned money. She looked handsomely employed, and she didn't look as if she was in any kind of jam. An emissary for somebody who was. Had she come along a couple of months sooner, I could not have cared less. But the kitty was dwindling. I was soon going to have to cast about for some profitable little problem. It is nice when they come walking up and save you the trouble of looking.

But caution is always essential. "Are you sure you're talking to the right guy?"

"Walter Lowery in San Francisco mentioned your name."

"What do you know? How is old Walt?"

"All right, I expect." She frowned. "He said to say he misses playing chess with you."

So it was all right. Walt and I never played chess in our lives. Not against each other, at least. But that was the identification tag, if he ever sent anybody along. There are the nosy ones, and the troublemakers, and the cuties, and the official investigators. It is good to have a way to weed the doubtful ones out.

"So come in out of the wind," I said, unhooking the chain, rehooking it after she had eased by me. She was long-waisted, with sturdy shapely calves, moving with the grace many women with that kind of build have. Her back was flat and erect, her carriage good.

I opened the door and ushered her into the blast of music. Skeeter gave her an absentminded glance, a vague smile, and continued her work. I left the music on and took Miss Holtzer on through the lounge and past the galley to the little dining booth. I closed the door from the lounge to the galley corridor.

"Coffee? Drink?"

"Nothing, thank you," she said, sliding into the booth.

I poured a mug of coffee for myself and sat opposite her. "I'm not interested in every little thing that comes along," I said.

"We're aware of that, Mr. McGee."

"You do know how I operate."

"I think so. At least, I know what Mr. Lowery said about it. If something has been taken from someone, and there is no way to get it back legally, you will make an effort to get it back—for half its value. Is that correct?"

"I have to know the circumstances."

"Of course, But I would rather have . . . the other party explain it all to you."

"So would I. Send him around."

"It's a woman. I work for her."

"Send her around."

"That's impossible, Mr. McGee. I have to take you to her."

"Sorry. If she's in enough trouble to need me, she's in enough trouble to come ask me herself, Miss Holtzer."

"But you don't understand. Really. She just *couldn't* come here. She would have talked to you if I could have gotten you on the phone. I work for . . . Lysa Dean."

I knew what she meant. That face was too distinctive, even in the darkest sunglasses in town. She wouldn't want to come on such a private mission with a police escort. And if she came alone, the boobs would recognize her at a hundred paces and come clotting around, pressing in as close as they could, standing and staring at her with that curious fixed, damp, silly smile, America's accolade to the celebrity. Ten big movies, four fairly messy marriages, one television-series fiasco and a few high-paid guest spots had made her a household face. Liz Taylor, Barbra

Streisand and Doris Day would take the same stomping among the star-dazed common folk. The public is an untrustworthy animal.

"I can't imagine Lysa Dean in a situation where she thinks she'd need me."

I thought I saw a little glimmer of distaste on the rather somber face of Miss Efficiency. "She'd like to talk to you about it."

"Let me see. Walter did a script for her once upon a time."

"They've been friends ever since."

"Would you say her problem fits into the way I operate?"

She frowned. "I think so. I don't know all the details."

"Aren't you in her confidence?"

"On most things. But as I said, I don't know *all* the details of this. It's been a personal kind of thing. But it is . . . something she wants to get back. And it's valuable to her."

"I can't promise anything. But I'll listen to her. When?"

"Now, if you could manage it, Mr. McGee." The symphony ended. I got up and went and turned the set off. When I came back Miss Holtzer said, "We'd rather you didn't mention this to anyone. Even her name."

"I was just going to run out and tell a few friends."

"I'm sorry. I've gotten so used to trying to protect her. She's beginning a promo for *Winds of Chance*, starting Monday. The world premiere will be next Saturday night in eight Miami theaters. We came early hoping for a chance to see you. She's staying at the house of a friend now. She'll move over to the hotel penthouse on the beach tomorrow evening. She'll have a full schedule, starting Monday."

"Have you worked for her very long?"

"Two years. A little over two years. Why?"

"I wondered what you call yourself."

"Personal secretary."

"She tote a big staff around?"

"Not really. On the road like this there's just me and her personal maid, her hairdresser and the man from the agency. Really, I would rather you asked her the questions. Could you . . . get ready to go see her?"

"In Miami?"

"Yes. I have a car waiting, Mr. McGee. If . . . I could make a call?"

I took her into the master stateroom. The phone extension is in a compartment in the headboard. She looked up the number in a black leather notebook from her big purse. She dialed the operator and made it a credit-card call. "Mary Catherine?" she said. "Please tell her that our friend is coming back with me. . . . No, that's all. . . . Pretty soon now. Thank you, dear."

She stood up and looked around the room. I could not tell if the huge bed repelled her or amused her. I was tempted to explain it. It startled me that I should want to tell her that it had been part of the furnishings when I had won the craft in a long poker siege in Palm Beach. The man wanted another advance to stay in the game, this last time putting up his Brazilian mistress as collateral, under the plausible assumption that she too went with the boat, but his friends saved me the delicate problem of refusal by leading him gently away from the game.

Miss Holtzer did not look particularly austere. She just looked as if she might put people in handy categories.

She decided she would pour herself some coffee while

15

I changed, if that was permitted. I put on the very infrequent necktie and a fairly heavy suit. When we went back into the lounge, Skeeter said, "Hey, both of you look at this lousy mouse a minute."

She showed us the drawing just completed. "This is when Quimby finds out for sure he's really a mouse. That cat just told him. He's crushed. He thought he was a real small pedigreed dog. But I think maybe he looks more scared than crushed. When you look at it, is it as if he's scared of the cat?"

"It's absolutely charming!" Dana Holtzer said. "What a horrid thing, really, to find out that all along you've been a mouse."

"Quimby can't adjust," Skeeter said.

They smiled nicely at each other. "Dana Holtzer, Mary Keith—known as Skeeter. We have to run. Skeet, make sure you lock up if I don't get back before you go."

"Sure. What's bugging him is all that trouble learning to bark."

"Forage if you get hungry."

But she was back at work, insulated and intent. Miss Holtzer and I headed into the wind, toward the parking areas. She said, "That's a dear strange girl, and very talented. Is she a special friend?"

"They've just painted her apartment so I told her she could work on the boat. She has a deadline."

Within another three steps, Miss Holtzer had tucked the escaping loose ends of personality back into her executive secretary shell. I had a memory of how pleasure in the mouse had brought her alive, younger and surprisingly more vivid. But it was not in her manner or habit to give anything away. She would do her job, reserved, armored, efficient. She was not being paid to react to people, or to show her own reactions, if any.

A glittering black Chrysler limousine was waiting, tended by a middle-aged man in dove-gray uniform with silver buttons. He touched his cap and opened the door for us. He looked like a television U.S. Senator. And he had that uncanny ability of the skilled chauffeur to drift a big car through traffic with such rhythm that the bunglings of other drivers seemed like an untidy and unimportant mirage.

"Miss Dean's car?" I asked.

"Oh, no. It belongs to the people where we're staying."

"When did you get in?"

"Yesterday."

"Incognito?"

"Yes."

"That's a good trick."

"Chartered airplane," she said.

There was glass between us and the barbered neck of the skilled driver. Her face was turned away from me, looking placidly out at the gray day.

"Miss Holtzer."

"Yes?" she said, turning with polite query.

"I'd like to know if I am right or wrong. I get this impression of quiet disapproval."

I thought I saw a flicker of bleak amusement. "Is that sort of thing so important to you, Mr. McGee?"

"I've never thought so."

"Mr. McGee, in the past two years I've been sent on so many curious errands, I would have become quite worn out if I'd tried to make value judgments about them."

"Then you avoid having opinions?"

"Except where it is expected of me. She pays for opinions, Mr. McGee. Legal opinions, tax opinions, artistic opinions. She listens and makes up her own mind.

She doesn't particularly care for volunteer opinions."

"And the job pays well?"

"It compensates me for what I do."

"I guess I better give up."

With an almost imperceptible shrug, she turned again to look out her window, presenting me with the nice modeling of the strong line of her throat, the neatness of an ear set into a casualness of cropped black curls, a fringe of black lashes visible beyond the smooth line of her cheek, a faint and unobtrusive and understated fragrance of mild perfume.

Two

THE HOUSE was on a private island, over a small causeway from one of the main causeways between Miami and Miami Beach. A gardener swung the ornate gate open for us. We turned into a winding crunch of gravel between lush and carefully tailored jungle, rounded a buttress of pink and white stucco, parked in a small walled area by a garden.

It seemed to be a back stairway. Miss Dana Holtzer led me up half a flight and into a shadowed hallway. I sat on a Babylonian throne under a black gleam of hanging armor. There was no sound in the house. None. She came back, hatless and purseless, and beckoned to me with all the gravity of a head nurse. I followed her down a paneled and carpeted corridor. She rapped on a fortress door, pushed it open for me and stood aside, saying, "She'll be with you in a moment."

She closed the door and left me alone in what seemed to be a guest suite. I was in a long room with a high ceiling. Plum carpet. Paneling. Seven arched windows along one wall, high narrow windows with leaded panes, deep sills. Black Spanish furniture. The center portion of the room was sunken. At one elevated end was a canopied bed. At the other end was an elevated portion with a conversational grouping of furniture around a small slate fireplace. The sunken portion was furnished in rather formal fashion. On the bed level there were two doorways. One, ajar, opened into a dressing room area. I could see pieces of matched luggage in there. The other door was closed, and I could hear an almost inaudible whisper of running water.

Though the draperies of all the windows were pulled aside, the room was not particularly bright. I went to a window. Tropical trees shaded it. Looking down, I could see patches of shaded green lawn. Off to the left, through foliage, I could see one bright corner of a white swimming pool.

The bathroom door opened suddenly and Lysa Dean came out. She was not smaller than I had expected because I was prepared for a woman smaller than she had looked to me on the VistaVision screen, in living color, in close-up, each slanty gray-green eye as large as a Volkswagen sedan. She came across the bedroom elevation and down the three steps toward me. She made the absolute most of those three steps. She wore flat sandals with gold straps. She wore fawn-colored pants in a fine weave. They fitted as tightly as pants, or paint, or a tattoo, could fit. She wore a strange furry blouse, with a big scooped neck and three-quarter sleeves. It looked as if Skeeter's Quimby and a couple of hundred of his relatives had contributed their pale belly fur to this creation. Around her slender throat was knotted a narrow loose kerchief of green silk precisely matching the single jewel she wore, an emerald as big as a sugar cube on the little finger of her left hand.

She came swiftly toward me, hand outstretched, her smile full of the warm delight of a woman welcoming the returning lover. "So good of you to come!" she said in her light, breathy, personal voice. As I took her hand she turned slightly so as to face the bright and shadowed daylight. It is the most cruel light a woman can accept. Her hand was small and dry and warm, a trusting little animal as intimate as her voice.

They have the distinctive occupational tricks. A lot of expressive business with mouth and eyebrows, animation with gestures.

I could remember, quite vividly, a long conversation with a stunt man named Fedder. Arthritis had forced him out of the business.

"Don't let anybody tell you they're not worth the effort," he had said. "A lot of them aren't. You got to look close to see which type. They all have to be damned good-looking and well-built. So suppose you get a chance at one who's a pretty good little actress. Let it go. The thing there, they sublimate. That's a word I learned once. They take all that steam and they shove it into their work and there isn't enough left over for bed. Now suppose you got one *thinks* she's a hell of an actress, but she's a ham. You skip her too. She'll take all that ham to bed with you and be so damn busy watching herself her heart won't be in it. The ones to wait for, and go a long way out of your way to get, they're the ones that plain started off with such damn good glands they don't have to do any acting. The camera picks up how good they'd be. Man, they can't rest from tracking it down and trying it out. The next one is always going to be the biggest and best yet. They've got what you call a real strong interest."

I had the feeling Fedder would approve of this one. I had not expected her to have such a genuine flavor of youthfulness. By every way I could measure it, she had to be about thirty-three. Yet she was a young girl, and not in any forced way. She had the slimness, the clear-eyed look of enormous vitality, the fine-grained and flawless skin, the heavy swing of burnished hair. Her impact, so carefully measured it seemed unaffected, was of a kind of innocence aware. A gamin sparkle, hinting at a delicious capacity for naughtiness.

But I had known enough of them to know that this was but one role. The enticing woman who is not in the industry will have five or six faces to wear. One like this would have dozens, and this was the one she had momentarily selected for me.

She had the showbiz trick of close-range conversation. Normal people keep their faces a yard apart. Eight inches is the focal distance on the Coast. Eight inches keeps you aware of the girl-breath heat against your chin, and the upthrust breast bud an inch and a half from your chest.

"Any friend of Walt's . . ." I said inanely.

"I treasure that man." She backed away a quarter step to give me a cock of the head and an urchin appraisal. "He said you were big, but he didn't say how huge, Travis. Trav? He called you Trav, I think. I'm Lee to my friends. Dear Trav, he told me you were big and rough-looking and sour and sometimes dangerous, but he did not tell me you are so terribly attractive."

"A veritable doll," I said.

"It's so wonderful of you to agree to help me."

"I haven't."

She was quite motionless for a thoughtful second, her smile in place. The capped teeth gleamed, between moistness. Green of iris speckled amber near the pupil. Delicate geometry of the hairs of red-gold brows. Fantasy length of the darker lashes. Faintest of fuzz on her upper lip. It was an unusual and grotesquely familiar face, the features slightly sharp, extremely sensuous, unmistakable. With her head slightly bowed, looking up at me through her lashes, the gold-red weight of hair at the right side of her face had swung slightly forward. Suddenly I knew what she reminded me of. A vixen. A quick red fox. I had seen one in heat long ago on an Adirondack morning in spring, pacing along well in front of the dog fox with a very alert and springy movement, tail curled high, turning to see if he still followed, tongue lolling from between her doggy grin.

She turned abruptly away, walking toward the elevated part of the room where the chairs and fireplace were. "But you will help me," she said in a small voice.

I followed her. She sat on a small couch and pulled her legs up. She took a cigarette from a table box. I held the light for her. She huffed smoke from the delicate oval nostrils of the slightly pointed nose, and as I sat in a big chair half facing the couch she smiled across at me. "You are refreshing, Trav McGee."

"How am I managing that, Lee?"

Her shrug and laugh were self-deprecatory. "You don't say what I always hear. I loved you in this. I adored you in that. I see every picture you make. You look better off the screen than on, actually. You know what I mean."

"I'll go through all that when I ask for the autograph."

"You know, you are sour, aren't you? Or are you afraid of seeming to be impressed? Or don't you give a damn? It's a little unsettling, dear."

"Your Miss Holtzer unsettled me the same way."

"Dana is a gem. When she reacts, she lets you know it."

I shrugged. "I loved you in this. I adored you in that. You look just fine in person."

Again she was motionless. It was an odd feeling to be so close to her. It made me aware of the uncounted millions of men all over the world who had stared at her image, coveted her, lusted after her, mentally stripped her and plundered those silky little loins. I wondered how many secret, solitary orgasms had been engineered with her in mind. The unmeasurable scope and intensity of all that vast and anonymous wanting gave her a curious physical impact. True, she had spent years being starved, pummeled, flexed, rubbed, plucked, burnished, perfumed and trained into the absolute peak of lovely physical condition. Without a chromium ego and a savage will she could not have endured it so long. But one could also believe that, as sex symbol, she also carried sex to an ultimate otherwise unknown—providing ecstasies unimaginable, greater heats, deeper spasms, longer agonies than mortal woman could know. And this, of course, was the nonsense a man must guard himself against. Her physical confidence, approaching arrogance, would lead the unwary to believe it.

"Excuse me, please," she said politely, and hurried the length of the room, toward the dressing room. A girlish graceful haste, forever eighteen. She came back with a large manila envelope and put it on the table beside the cigarette box.

"That big chest down there is a bar. If you want to fix yourself anything, I would like some of the sherry. Just half a glass, please."

As I walked to the bar, she raised her voice and said, "It is so terribly difficult to know where to start, dear. You don't seem to make it any easier for me."

"Just tell me the problem. You told Walt, didn't you?"

"Just some of it. But I would guess you want to . . . know all of it."

"If I'm to help you."

As I carried the drinks toward her, she said, "Celebrity! If all the ones who'd like to be one could only know what it means. You become such a target, actually. Slimy schemes to fasten themselves onto you for the free ride. You cannot make a single careless move."

This was a new pose. She sipped her wine. I sat down. The suffering celebrity. Public responsibility.

She gave me a sad smile. "It isn't worth it, you know. But you have to get into it as far as I am to realize it isn't worth it. And then it's too late. You can't get out. They still follow Garbo. How long since she made a picture? A thousand years, at least. Oh, there have been some satisfactions, of course. But the things I really treasure—contentment, friendships, peace of mind, marriage—none of those things could survive all the rest of it. There is a terrible loneliness, Trav. Like being on top of a mountain, alone."

"They pay you for it."

"And they pay very well indeed. I've had good advice. I have quite a lot of money. Of course, it is invested in a lot of things, but if I should take it all out, it would be quite a large sum. That's why I did try to . . . buy my way out of trouble."

"Blackmail?"

She put her glass aside and got up quickly, pacing about in an agitated way. "Can you see how valuable it is to me . . . how *essential* to have a little time when I can be myself? Like here with you now. We can talk like two people. I don't have to pose with you. I have to forget sometimes that I am Lysa Dean, and just be plain Lee Schontz from Dayton, Ohio, the fireman's daughter. Sixteen-ten Madison Street." She whirled and stopped with a leg-warmth against my knee. "You can understand that basic human need, can't you?"

"You can't live up to the public image at all times."

"*Thank* you for understanding!"

This was another role. I guessed it was a speech out of an old movie, edited to fit the present need.

"And when I do . . . forget, that's when I'm most vulnerable."

"Sure."

"I *so* want you to try to understand me. I'm not really very complex, Trav. I am the same as everyone. I have times when I feel desperate and self-destructive. I have times when I do foolish things. There are times when I do not give a damn what happens to me."

"Sure."

She reached and drew her fingertips across my cheek and whirled away and sat on the couch again. "I know you're not a prude. I can sense that. This has to be as if I'm talking to my doctor or my lawyer. But I do feel so terribly shy about this."

"What happened?"

She sighed and made a rueful face. "A man happened to me. Of course. He was a very exciting chap. Exciting to me, at least. It happened a year ago last July, over eighteen months ago. We'd just finished shooting *Jack and the Game*. I was literally exhausted, but I went off with Carl. Carl Abelle. He had a ski school. We'd never had a chance to really be alone. He found a place for us. An absolutely fantastic little house. Do you know California? It was just below Point Sur, and clinging to the rock by its fingernails. Friends of his named Chipmann own it. They were in Switzerland. They have another house there. It was just the two of us . . ."

Her voice trailed off into uncertainty.

"Yes?"

"Trav, I am under the most terrible disciplines most of the time. I do work very hard."

26

"So when you let go, you let go?"

"More than most, I guess. Just a little time of not watching every ounce and every quarter inch, every blemish and drink and calorie and bruise . . . God damn it, to be a woman for a change. Fry eggs, let my hair go, get stoned, have a ball. I'm naturally a very passionate woman. But I keep it all under control. Until a time like that a year and a half ago. With Carl. That's what I try to do. Get away like that, with a certain kind of man. Then everything that's been saved up . . ."

"Birds and bees. I didn't think you went into a convent when you had time off, Miss Dean. I don't follow this routine."

"It's just to explain how things happened. It was such a very *private* place. Carl would drive off to buy food and liquor. There were steps cut into the stone, down to a little beach way way down that you couldn't use at high tide. There was a terrace on the ocean side, twenty feet square, about. It was a little offset so you could get morning sun too. A low broad wall around it. And a great stack of weatherproofed sun mattresses and pillows in all kinds of colors. We'd arranged it so we could have three weeks alone. Maybe that was too long. I guess it was. We were marvelously right for each other, in a purely physical way. We knew that before we went there, of course. Except on a ski slope or in bed, Carl isn't very stimulating. It was very intense for about a week, I guess. Day and night all mixed up. Eat when you're hungry, sleep when you're sleepy. When the edge was gone, we both started drinking more. And we spent more and more time on the terrace in the sun. I knew I was getting too brown, but I was too lazy and relaxed to give a damn. I was drinking a lot of vodka. Hot sun and vodka kept me in a sort of permanent daze. We'd make love there in the sun, all slow and sweaty

27

and, I don't know, remote somehow. The thing is, we felt so *private*. You'd see a boat way out, or an airplane far away, or hear a truck sometimes on the highway. The phone was cut off. I had a little radio. You have to understand that nothing seemed important, absolutely nothing at all. Do you understand that, Trav?"

"I've been there."

"Anyway—it must have been just about at the end of two weeks—we needed things and Carl drove to town to get them. He left in the early afternoon sometime. And he was gone so long I began to get damned annoyed at him. I belted the vodka pretty good, so by the time he did come back, I was getting kind of sloppy and confused. He came skidding back into the driveway with two cars following him, and the whole drunken bunch came marching into the house bellowing some goddam German skiing song. Five fellows and three girls. He'd known one of the girls up at the Valley. He ran into them in town, and had drinks with them, and decided we should have a house party. They damned near fell over when they saw who his girl was. They'd brought tons of food and beer and liquor and cigarettes from town. I was sore at him, but I thought that as soon as they had recognized me the damage was done, if any, and the hell with it: I guess I was getting bored with Carl and I lost my sense of caution. They were swingers, every one. The girls were darling. The fellows were fun. I guess there's no good way to avoid telling you all, dear. It was a very scrambled evening, all things considered, and by late afternoon the next day the last holdout, the girl they called Whippy, she got tight enough to let Sonny peel her out of her swimsuit and get her into the fun and games on the terrace. It just seemed to be a crazy time for everybody, and nobody seemed to care much, and you saw everything and did everything through a kind of sleepy crazy haze so that in my memory it's all jumbled up. It was the first and last time I was ever in a situation like that. It's sort of standard practice on the Riviera, with those car-light signals and horn signals to get recruits and all. It didn't offend me. In some ways it was very exciting. But it was just too dangerous for anybody in my position. And I hadn't *wanted* it to happen. Carl brought them back to the house and it just went on from there, and lasted—oh, four days, I guess. When I got back to Brentwood it took me *weeks* to get back in shape. It all seemed like a dream. Then one day toward the end of August I got a big envelope in the mail. There were twelve photographs in it. Eight-by-ten glossies. There is a great deal of difference between remembering something and seeing it . . . like that. Seeing yourself . . . God! I flipped my lunch."

"It came by mail?"

"Yes. To my home. God only knows how Dana didn't get to it first. There was a note with it. I saved it. I put it in my wall safe. Here it is."

She took it out of the envelope and handed it to me. It was done with a carbon ribbon on an electric machine, with several strikeovers.

"Save the envelope?"

"Not that one. It was mailed at the main post office in Los Angeles. Not special or anything like that. Not even marked Personal on the outside. The address was typed with the same type as that note. No return address. Go on. Read it."

It read as follows:

Lysa, dear: You are practical. You know how the industry makes book. So you have no choice, of course. I have ten complete sets of the enclosed and a good idea of how to distribute them. I recommend the investment. Installment plan, ducks. Ten thousand in used hundreds each time. Wrap in plain white paper. Tie securely. Each Sunday night starting a week from next Sunday, you or your dark secretarial type takes a drive. At midnight, precisely, pull into the Narana Kai Drive-in at Topanga Beach. Order something, then walk alone, with the packet in plain view, over to the public pavilion. Walk to the far edge of the concrete, next to the public phone booths. A phone will begin to ring. Count the rings carefully. Wait and it will ring again the same number of times. Go back to your car. Leave the drive-in at exactly twelve-thirty. Take note of the exact mileage on your speedometer. If it says, for example, eight and six tenths and the phone rang seven times, when the mileage ends in five and six tenths (simple addition, dear), be ready. You will be heading west on 101. Be over in the right lane, your right window open, packet in your little right hand. Look for a light ahead and off to the right. Slow to thirty-five and get just as far right as you can. When you see a little green light blink twice, toss the packet out onto the shoulder immediately. If it blinks red twice, take the money home and come back the following Sunday. Each time you will receive the negative of one picture and all the prints made from that negative. They will come in the mail. If all goes well, and if you have no clever and silly ideas, we should be through with this whole affair in twelve weeks.

"So damned complicated," she said.

"Actually pretty shrewd. Two people could manage it with very little risk. One at the drive-in and pavilion to check you or Miss Holtzer out, then, after you've heard the rings, phone up the road for his buddy to get into place at the designated spot. He gets a chance to see that nobody is hiding in your car. He follows you out of the lot, tails you until it looks safe, then passes you and gets there first and gives a headlight signal to his buddy to use the green lens on the flashlight. Not bad at all. Very difficult to trap them. What went wrong?"

"Nothing. At least not then. I paid. One night there was a red light. I don't know why. It took thirteen weeks. I got the stuff in the mail. The worst ones came toward the last. Dana made the deliveries. Her nerves are better than mine, I guess."

"Maybe you should have sent word you weren't in the market."

She jumped to her feet, flushing. "Don't be dull, McGee. Close to seven million went into *Winds of Chance*. Risk money. The character who wrote that note knows this industry. He knew how I had to jump. It isn't like the old days, where you could count on studio protection. Each picture is a separate packaging operation. There are just about ten men these days who can put the really big packages together. If each one of them got a set of those prints, why should they take any future chances on me? Those pictures are poisonous. What's a hundred and twenty thousand compared to my potential? I liquidated some holdings that weren't doing so good, and took my tax loss, and paid off. Don't tell *me* what I should have done!'"

It was a good act and I had to admire it. "How can I help you if all you give me is a smoke screen?"

"What the *hell* do you mean!" she shouted.

"All the industry cares about is money in the bank. Your name on a picture puts money in the bank. The days are long gone when you had to be a dear little but-

tercup all the way. In our culture there is going to be
no huge concerted public censure to drive you out of
business. If you get a little rancid, the PR people have
you endow a dog shelter, and all America loves you.
Drop the act."

The faked indignation was turned off in an instant.
She sat again, looked at me with sullen speculation.
"Smart-ass," she said.

"What is it, then, that made you pay off?"

"A few little things. A while back I swung my weight
around too much. It delayed the wrap-up and bumped
the budget, and some people decided maybe they didn't
want to work with me. But I smartened up and settled
down. I could read what it said on the wall. You know,
like Monroe and Brando. But it left them edgy. Also,
there've been a couple of little things from time to time.
Not as bad as those pictures, but . . . along that line. It
just didn't seem to be the right time to make them feel
any more insecure."

"And?"

"Boy, you really want everything, don't you?"

"I've learned that it helps."

"I have a very dear friend. He's very devout and very
conservative and he owns great big vulgar hunks of California and Hawaii. If he can get the right paper signed by
the Vatican and get loose, I'll never have to take any crap
from anybody again as long as I live. And one of those
sets of prints would have gone to one man who would
have felt obligated to give my friend a look at them. And
that would have torn it."

"So those are the real stakes?"

She moistened her lips. "Under community property, one half of about eighty million, honey. I am his
dear faithful little darlin'. It made the whole thing a lot

more . . . chancy. Otherwise I would have borrowed some muscle from an old buddy in Vegas and turned them loose on this clown photographer. They'd be smart enough to handle that, but they're not smart enough to handle what I need now. Actually, if Mr. X had no knowledge of my friend, and how long it takes to bull something through that Vatican crowd, he made a very stupid pitch. But with my friend in the background, there was just too much chance it might backfire. Before you bet, you count what's in the pot. All my potential plus my friend's heavy purse. So I paid off."

"And hoped that was the end of it. And it wasn't. Incidentally, can he clear you with his church?"

"I was never married in his faith, so nothing counts. I get a clean bill. By the way, McGee, Dana doesn't know a thing about my plans for my friend."

I asked her how she thought the pictures had been taken. "It had to be a long lens," she said. "You can see the flattening and foreshortening effect. Off to the left, south of the house, I remember a little rocky ridge higher than the house with some knotty little trees clinging to it. It had to be from there. The angles match. But he had to be part mountain goat, and it had to be a tremendous lens."

"Is there any clue at all in that letter itself, any hint that's made you think of a specific person?"

"No. I read it over and over. He's been around the industry in some connection, and I think he tried to sound as if he knew me, but he calls me Lysa instead of Lee. That could be a cover-up, of course. And it has a phony kind of limey slant to it, calling me ducks."

"What size were the negatives?"

"Little. Like so." She indicated a 35mm frame size.

"You checked them against the prints each time?"

"Sure did. But in a lot of cases the prints were just an enlargement of part of the negative, even less than half sometimes."

"So you were all paid up well over a year ago. And you thought it was over. When was the next contact?"

"Two months ago. Less than that. Early in January. An old friend, trying to make a comeback, was opening at The Sands in Vegas, and a bunch of us were rallying around to give him a good sendoff. It was in the papers that we were all going to be there. Dana was with me. We had a suite at the Desert Inn. Somebody left this envelope for me at the desk at The Sands. I guess they thought I was staying there. They sent it over. Dana got it. I was just waking up from a nap. She came in with the damnedest expression on her face and handed it to me. She had opened it. It was another set of the pictures. There wasn't any return address. The desk had no idea who had left it off. Dana wanted to quit right then and there. She is a strange gal. I had to explain the whole thing the way I explained it to you, Trav. She knew right away that it was the same thing that had cost me all the money. She still wanted to quit. I had to beg her to stay. Our relationship hasn't been the same since she saw the pictures. I don't blame her. I'd still hate to lose her. This is the envelope. You can see how it was addressed. Somebody just cut my name off the front of a fan magazine, something like that. Here is the note that was with it."

It was quite different. Individual words and letters had been cut from newsprint and newspaper stock and pasted to cheap yellow copy paper. It said: "Shameless whore of Babylon you will be cut down by the sord of decency and money will not save your dirty life this time but you better have money ready you whore of evil I will come to you and you will no the truth and I will set you free."

She hugged herself. "That one just scares the hell out of me, Trav. It's kind of sick and crazy and terrible. It just isn't the same person. It can't be."

"So you went and saw Walter?"

"No. I just got more and more jittery the more I thought of it. I'm still shook. I was at a big party at the Springs and I got a little stoned and made a scene and dear Walt was there and he took me for a walk. I hung onto him and cried like a baby and told him my troubles. He said maybe you would help. I guess you can say something was stolen from me. My privacy or something. And somebody wants to steal my career or maybe my life. I don't know. I've been carrying cash around with me. In thousand-dollar bills. Fifty of them. I don't expect you to get back what I paid. But if you could, you could keep half. And if you can get that nut off me, you can have the money I'm carrying around."

"Are the pictures in that envelope?"

"Yes. But do you have to see them?"

"Yes."

"I was afraid of that. I am not going to let you see them until you say you'll try to help me. Every time I think of that note I feel like a scared kid."

"It's a very cold trail, Lee."

"Walter said you are clever and tough and lucky, and he said being lucky is the most important." She gave me an odd look. "I have this feeling that my luck is running out, darling."

"How many people know about this?"

"The four of us, dear. You and Dana and me and Walter. But you know more than the other two. Not another soul. I swear."

"Wouldn't it be logical for you to tell Carl Abelle?"

"Sweetie, when one of those things is over, it is over all the way. Enough is enough forever."

"Could he have set you up for it?"

"Carl? Definitely no. He's a very sunny type. Very simple needs and very simple habits. Totally transparent, really."

"Usually I gamble expenses, then take them off the top before the fifty-fifty split. But this is a little too chancy for that."

"Expenses guaranteed up to five thousand," she said without hesitation, "and when that's gone we'll talk some more."

"Walt must have said I could be trusted."

"What other choice do I have? That's one thing about this. There hasn't been any trouble making decisions. There's been just one way to go. Will you try? Please? Pretty please?"

"Until it looks hopeless."

She scaled the envelope into my lap. "God knows I'm not the shy type, sweetie, but I don't think I could watch anybody look those over. I'll take a walk. Take your time."

She went to the heavy door and let herself out quietly.

Three

AFTER A LITTLE TIME I put the twelve photographs back
into the envelope. I took a slow turn around the room. I
am too big a boy to be churned up by the explicits of
other people's kicks.

Nor did I feel any compulsion to make moral judgment. These were modern animals caught in black and
white at their silly play. Such sport was not for me, and
very probably not for anyone whose friendship I claimed.
There seemed to be some kind of severe selection involved. An acceptance of that presupposed an inability to
accept or believe in a lot of other things. Personal dignity,
for one.

But something still bothered me, something I could
not quite define. So I took them out and shuffled through
them again. The clue was there. It was the terrible loneliness on their faces. Each one of them, in all that lazy confusion of intimacies, in that lexicon of clinical descrip-
tions, looked utterly, desperately alone.

And they were beautiful people. Lysa Dean was the
featured player in every shot, and her body was as superb
as its promise.

I felt as if I had glimpsed the edge of some great
paradox. The grotesque ultimate of togetherness is the

final loneliness of the human spirit. And once you had been that far out on that barren limb, there was no chance of ever coming all the way back.

I shrugged and looked at them again to see if they told me anything about time lapse. I put them away again.

From the varying lengths of shadow in the pictures, from the changing positions on the sunny terrace, I could tell that they had been taken over a matter of hours, perhaps on separate days.

Soon she returned, coming in with a look half challenge, half calculated demureness. "Well?" she said.

"It doesn't look as if it was a hell of a lot of fun."

That response startled her. She stared at me. "Oh, you are so *right*! You know, it seems to me as if it was all a thousand years ago. I guess I've been trying to fade it out of my mind. Oh, Christ, there's kind of a sickly excitement about it, I guess. But what I remember now is being constantly cross and irritable and impatient. And sleepy. Just terribly sleepy and never being allowed to sleep long enough, and having the feeling that all the rest of them were just one . . . one *thing* somehow. Not like the pictures."

"Are these exactly like the other pictures you got?"

"They are the twelve exact same shots, but not exactly like the others. These are fuzzier and grayer, sort of. Not as sharp. But I didn't save any of the others to compare, of course."

"We have to look through these together so you can give me the names to go with the faces, Lee, and tell me what you know about each one."

"I suppose it has to be done."

"Like a trip to the dentist. I think there's at least one fair picture of every other person in the group."

She made a face. "Those pictures are such a big

boost to my pride, Travis. It does something for a girl to look like a fifty-peso floozy in a back-room circus in Juarez."

I turned a light on and we sat at the desk in the sunken part of the room. I found a pencil and paper. I pointed to the pictures and asked the questions. She answered in a thin small breathy voice, her face half turned away. I took the following notes.

1. Carl Abelle—about 27—six-footer—husky—blond— has left the Valley—try Mohawk Lodge near Speculator, New York.
2. Nancy Abbott—about 22—tall, dark, slender, heavy drinker, good singing voice, believed to have been divorced, perhaps daughter of an architect. Took ski lessons from Abelle at Sun Valley. Believed to be a houseguest of . . .
3. Vance & Patty M'Gruder, perhaps of Carmel, married couple in middle twenties, apparently well-off, Vance a sailboat buff, ocean racing, etc., have house in Hawaii (?), husband very tanned, short, broad, muscular, going prematurely bald, wife lush & fair, very long blond hair, quarrelsome, strong English accent.
4. Cass—could be first name, last name or nickname. Seemed to have known M'Gruders previously. About thirty. Dark, hairy, handsome, very powerful—amusing (?). A painter, perhaps. Friend of . . .
5. Sonny, a little younger than Cass—slender, cold-eyed, flavor of violence, untalkative, occupation unknown, who had brought along . . .
6. Whippy. About nineteen then—copper curls, freckles, perhaps waitress or clerk, scared of Sonny.
7. Two college boys from the East on summer trip—

apparently joined group at bar where Abelle ran into Nancy Abbott. Boys about 20 or 21—Harvey a big blond cheery one, Richie smaller dark nutty one. Cornell.

On the clearest prints of each I had marked the corresponding number from my notes. I could sense Lee's relief when I put the photographs back into the envelope.

"Who got it all started?" I asked her.

She tightened up again. "Why? What do you mean?"

"I don't think a camera gets that lucky. Somebody had to set you up. Or maybe the real target was somebody else, and you turned out to be a bonus."

"It was a long time ago, and I was tight most of the time."

"Tell me what you can remember of how it got started."

She got up slowly and went over and rested her fists on a windowsill, staring out, the fox-pelt hair softly backlighted. I leaned a shoulder against the wall by the window. She talked. Her voice was small. I could not see much of her profile because of the way the hair swung forward. Round of forehead, soft snub tip of nose. I did not press her. I let her find her own words in her own time. Her memory was more acute as regards textures than incident. Six men and four gals that first evening and night. Four places to go—two bedrooms, a long couch in the living room, the leathery sun pads on the terrace. It was a prowling thing then, pursuits and tensions, Lysa Dean a primary target for all but Carl, low lights and ultimate arrangements, and some re-pairings when partners slept.

In phrases and fragments, theatrical sighs and beautifully timed hesitations, she painted the flavor of the hot

40

bright terrace on that first full day of house party. Pitchers of Bloody Marys, vodka haze, arrows of white sunlight through squinting eyes, compulsive beat of the music on the portable radio, oil and aromatics of sun lotion, jokes and tipsy laughter. A game of forfeits, with the rules rigged so that to play was to lose, and to lose was to soon be naked.

In half-sleep, mildly and amiably drunk, after the game had ended, she had fended off the increasing insistence of Cass, whining at him irritably when he became too bold. Finally, propping herself up to drink again, she saw several sound asleep, and saw others who were accepting what she had refused. So, squeezing her eyes hard shut to achieve the illusion of privacy, she had surrendered herself to Cass and her own responses.

She straightened and turned toward me and hooked the fingertips of both hands into my belt, leaned her forehead against my chest. She sighed and said, "Then I guess it stops mattering so much. I don't know. You just seem to learn how to turn one whole part of your mind right off. It's all just something that happens. Everybody is in the same boat. So it doesn't seem to make any difference any more. Nothing does."

She sighed again. In the cold soft light I could see the scalp, clean and white as bone under the coppery spring of hair. "I don't know who started it. Patty was bossy. I can remember people getting mad. Whippy cried sometimes. Cass knocked Carl down once, I don't know why. One of those college kids, the big one, kept getting sick. He couldn't drink. It's all so vague, sweetie. If you watched, and you were all turned off, it was just sort of stupid and boring, and if you'd started to hum a little, you could get into that one or set up something else, or go take a shower, or go make a sandwich, or go build another pitcher of drinks. It just . . . wasn't all that important."

She slid her small hands around my waist, laid her cheek against my chest and held tight. I stroked her hair.

She took the deepest breath of all and said, "Listen to me! God, I know it was important. There are some kinds of poisons, I heard you look as if you got over it, but you never really do. I wish somebody could stick a knife in my head and cut out those four days and nights, Trav. A girl thinks about herself a different way, after that. I have this lousy dream ever since. I've fallen into this empty white swimming pool and the sides are too high to get out. The pool lights are on so it's bright as a stage. And there are six ugly snakes in there on the tile, all after me. I can run and dodge fast enough to keep away from them no matter how they try to hem me in. They all look exactly alike. Then I keep calling for help and suddenly I see that the walls are all kind of coming in. It is getting smaller and smaller. Then I know they are going to get me. As the place gets smaller the snakes get bigger, and I scream and wake up, all sweaty and trembling. Just hold me tight, Trav. Please."

She was trembling and I wondered if it was faked.

After several minutes she quieted down and moved away from me, shoved her hair back with the back of her hand and said, with a funny little shy smile, "You don't want me, do you? I could tell. Just from your hands. Kind of gentle and . . . fatherly and remote. God, I wouldn't blame you for not wanting such a public piece."

"It's not that."

"No? You are certainly not one of those, sweetie."

"No. Well, in all honesty, if that's what you want. I guess the pictures have something to do with it. A man likes the illusion of exclusive option, even on the most

42

temporary basis, I guess. But with or without pictures, let's just say I'm not a trophy hunter."

"What the hell does that mean?"

"Every red-blooded American boy should ride a bike no hands and win some merit badges and go to bed with a household name. Some of them don't get over it, that's all. I had my celebrity innings, but I'm not a locker room historian. I outgrew my bike too, Lee. It's a big scene here. Rich silent house and the closed door and your tight pants and that rostrum-type bed. And mutual attraction. But it isn't worth it. It would be like being taught to dance by your elder sister. She would keep trying to lead, and giving irritable little instructions, and counting out loud and spoiling the music. Then she would give you a patronizing pat and say you did just fine."

For a moment she had the malignant rigidity of a temple demon. Then an urchin grin, seen often in your favorite movie palace, broke it up. "My God, you *are* a strange one, McGee. You wouldn't want me as a gift, eh?"

"Not unless and until it could be more than this for us, Lee."

"You mean like real true love?"

"Affection, understanding, need and respect. You can be sarcastic about that too, if you want. Bed is the simplest thing two people can do. If it goes with a lot of other things, it can be important, and if it goes with nothing else, it isn't worth the time it takes."

She strolled over and curled up in a big chair and pondered me, finger laid against the side of her small nose. "The next time around, Mr. McGee, can you arrange to show up in Dayton about fifteen years ago?"

"I can make a note of it, Miss Dean."

"I've been through too many mills this time."

"Not necessarily."

"But you said respect."

"Once in a while you stop posing for me and remembering lines from old movies, and then I could respect the person that shows through."

"It could be strange to have a friend like you. I have no female friends, really. And just two male friends, fine old guys, both in their early sixties. I love them dearly. Males in your bracket are either studs or competitors, sweetie, or they want to find an angle to get rich off me."

"We might end up friends, Lee. I better go along. I am going to take these pictures along." As I picked them up from the desk she hopped up out of the chair and came running over and grabbed at the envelope. I did not let her pull it out of my hand. I said, "Either you trust me all the way, or I get off right now, Lee. I need them for information and leverage."

After looking at me with a long and searching intensity, she let go. "I never thought I'd let anybody even see those. Trav, will you be terribly careful?"

"Yes."

"I can send Dana over with the expense money tomorrow. Will that be all right?"

"Fine."

"Please be careful with those pictures. If they get out, my career is dead right now. And . . . as you must damn well know, it is the only thing I have left."

Tears balanced on her lower lids, and one broke loose and tracked her cheek. It did not look real. A makeup man had darted onto the set and put them there with an eyedropper. Pure glycerine. Maybe they weren't real. She would have learned to cry almost at will, and cry in a way that would leave her as lovely as before.

"You be careful, Lee. I don't like the sound of that note. Sexually disturbed people try to be the sword of the

Lord, going around slaying the sinful. See that you get pretty good protection this week in Miami."

She walked me to the door. She caught at my arm, gave me a quick kiss, as soft and trusting as a child's, then went down the corridor with me, found Dana Holtzer in a small room, typing, and turned me over to her. Dana got up and took me down the stairs and out to the waiting limousine. I saw the quick and wary way she glanced at the envelope I was carrying, and caught a flavor of total disapproval.

The driver's name was Martin. She told him to take me back, or to wherever I wanted to go. It was after five. I had him stop where I could phone. I phoned Gabe Marchman in Lauderdale and told him I had a problem. He said it was convenient to bring it right over.

On one of those hunches that may save your life, though you can never prove it one way or another, I had Martin drop me off downtown. I went into one end of a big drugstore and out the other and into a cab.

Gabe Marchman was a great combat photographer. You have seen his name on those classic Korea things. A land mine smashed his legs all to hell. While convalescing in Hawaii, he met and married a very rich and very beautiful little Chinese-Hawaiian girl named Doris. Gabe looks like a sawed-off Abraham Lincoln. He is still on crutches. They have six kids. With his mobility gone, he has gotten into another aspect of photography. He has one of the most completely equipped private labs in the South, taking up a wing almost as big as the main house. He does experimental work, and problem assignments for large fees. He is a sour little man, adored by all who get to know him.

Doris, blooming large again with child, sent me on through to the lab. Gabe grunted at me. I said I wanted to know as much as possible about some pictures I had with me. We were in his print room. He turned on more intense lights. He levered himself onto a stool and spread the dozen pictures out in a row on top of the work table.

From his lack of reaction, they could have been pictures of puppies or flower gardens. "Whadaya know about 'em?" he said. "Just technically."

"They were taken a year and a half ago in California on thirty-five-millimeter film. The person involved estimates that the only place from which they could be taken was about a hundred yards away, but that is just an estimate. The person involved saw another set of prints over a year ago, and they were just like these as far as subject matter, but these seem to be fuzzier and grayer."

He grunted and got out a large magnifying glass and began to go over them very carefully, one by one.

I said, "I forgot something. My client saw and destroyed the negatives. The negatives included more than in a lot of these pictures."

He continued his careful examination. Finally he swiveled around. "Okay, we accept the hundred-yard distance. I would say it was probably Plus-X using a very fine telephoto lens, one thousand millimeter. Maybe the f/six-point-three Nikkor, a reflector type with two mirrors. It's only about so long and weighs three or four pounds. It was used with a tripod or some other kind of solid rest. With thirty-five millimeter, a lens that size gives you about a twenty-power magnification, so at a hundred yards it would give the same as a normal lens fifteen feet from the subject. These three are the only ones where he printed the full frame. Now, if he printed about half the frame, it would be like being seven or eight feet away from the subject. And this is the average for most of these. Just this extreme close-up was done from maybe a quarter or less of the negative, showing the woman at a viewing distance of about three feet, with less definition. There's good depth of field and all motion is frozen, so a hundred yards away I'll buy. Okay so far?"

"Yes."

"Assuming the same guy who took the pictures made the original prints, he's a good workman. Excellent exposure, good edge-to-edge definition, and when he masked the negatives and did his printing, he had good quality control. You can tell that he did some burning in and dodging, and he couldn't help using a pretty good sense of composition. I would say he took a hell of a lot of shots, maybe several hundred, and came up with the best ones. Very sharp, very clear, and he made high-gloss prints. I'd say definitely a pro, if that's any help to you. Now then, some clown got hold of a set of the prints. See this little flare here on this one and this one. That's where his lighting kicked back off the gloss. He had a set of copy negatives and a new set of prints. This is crappy paper, and he butchered his developing and butchered his printing solutions and times, but there was enough quality in the prints he copied so that all in all it comes through not too bad. The guy who did the originals would be incapable of doing such cruddy work the second time around, even if he was operating in a motel closet. But, having the copy negatives, he can make any number of these poor prints. Your client destroying the original negatives means nothing now. It is unmistakably her in every one of these. I would guess she's the one you're working for."

"Yes. Now I wonder if you can do something with these."

"I was afraid of that."

"From these can you make another set of negatives, and a set of prints that are a little different than these?"

"McGee, if you start out with crud, you end up with crud. I can't get back to the original print quality. I can print for more contrast and clean up these whites a little, but a close focus on fuzz gives you fuzz."

After an original reluctance, he began to get interested. He used a copy camera, a larger negative size, a copy film with a fine grain. By the time he had developed the negatives, Doris began to howl for a little cooperation, so he hung them up to dry and we went in for drinks. The nursemaid had taken over the bedtime routines. The older ones trudged in to say their well-mannered good nights. Doris cooked and served an old Chinese-Hawaiian specialty—broiled steaks, baked potatoes and tossed green salad. The three of us, in front of the big fireplace with a very small fire, revamped the State Department, simplified all tax legislation, tore down half of Florida and rebuilt it in a more sane and pleasing fashion.

Then we went back to work. He would put a negative in the enlarger and focus it on the base, and I would tell him what I wanted. Then he would go to work. He would cut a piece of masking paper to fit Lysa Dean's projected face. He would use sufficient exposure time to give him opportunity to dodge and burn in so that the face of someone else was emphasized. I ended up with fourteen useful prints, on double-weight paper. Some of those that took in more people were duplicated, altered slightly to highlight one and then another.

Somewhere in the processing they ceased to have any fleshy impact. They became problems in light and shade and emphasis. He put them in his high-speed dryer, and after he had flattened them in a bonding press, I studied them under the bright lights. Lysa Dean's features were white censored patches. Gabe was careful to give me the negatives as well as the test prints which hadn't worked out. We argued price, with me trying to increase it, and agreed on a hundred dollars. Doris had gone to bed.

He crutched his way to the door with me, and came out with me into the cold windy night.

"Taking a little trip, I suppose," he said.

"Yes."

"None of my business. I suppose somebody got too greedy."

"That's usually the way."

"You watch yourself, Trav. A little animal like that, if she'd see a way out by pushing you over the edge, she'd take it. That's an interesting little face, but it isn't a good face."

The taxi slowed, putting his spotlight on the numbers. He turned into the drive. When I looked back I saw Gabe still standing there.

Four

WHEN I GOT BACK to the *Busted Flush* I saw my lights still on. It was a little past eleven. The lounge door was locked. I went in and found Skeeter sound asleep, face down on the yellow couch in her baggy gray coveralls, one frail long-fingered hand trailing on the floor. Drawings of Quimby were propped everywhere. They were wise and funny and good. I admired them. In the middle of the floor was a big stamped brown envelope and a note to me:

"This LOUSY mouse. I am pooped out of my mind. PLEASE would you stuff him in this envelope. He is all weighed in and everything, and PLEASE would you seal him and run him to the P.O. He's an airmail-SPECIAL mouse. Honestly, I had to sleep or DIE!!!!"

I looked down at her. It was typical. God knows how long she'd gone without sleep or when last she had thought of eating. Perfectionists who meet deadlines are usually pretty whipped out.

I went through to the bow of the *Flush* and put my dirty pictures in the hidden safe. It might not take an expert all night to open it, but he'd sure raise hell finding it first. I assembled Quimby and sealed him and turned off one of the lights.

She stirred and raised a sleep-bleared Raggedy Ann face, shoe-button eyes peering, cobweb hair afloat. "Whumya timezit?" she mumbled.

I squatted beside the couch. "You eat anything?"

"Huh? Eat? Uh . . . no."

I knew the problems. I had lived with them. I went into the galley, picked cream of mushroom soup, opened the can, heated it, poured it steaming into a big two-handled mug. She was gone again. I sat her upright and fitted the mug into her hands. When I was sure she was going to keep on sipping at it, I left and took Quimby to the post office and dropped him into an airmail slot.

By the time I got back, the empty mug was on the floor, and she had sagged off to sleep again. I picked her up. The fool girl seemed to have no substance at all. My guest stateroom would have to serve. I carried her in there and then, instead of dropping her into the bed and covering her over, on a strange and lonely impulse I sat on the bed still holding her in my arms. A faintness of marina lights came through the ports. Water slapped and licked at the curve of the barge hull. Mooring lines creaked.

She put her arm around my neck and said, "I thought we gave up on this."

"We did. I thought you were asleep. Go back to sleep."

"I was asleep, damn it. What's this brooding sorrow bit anyway? It's the tenderness keeping me awake."

"I guess I wanted to hold onto you. That's all. Go to sleep."

"Why should you want to hold me? My God, Travis, we ripped each other up pretty good and got over it a long time ago."

"Why do you have to know everything? That's one of your problems."

"I have to know because I can't go back to sleep, that's why."

"Okay. I don't have too many illusions. I just ran into something rotten, that's all. I don't feel shocked. Just sad."

"It was a rotten girl?"

"I don't know. It's a kind of waste, I guess. Go to sleep."

She settled herself more snugly into my lap, arm around me, face in my neck. In a little while she drifted off, and the arm fell away. Her breathing turned deep.

I guess it can be touching. A special kind of trust. Something warm to hold. The way a kitten will drowse in your lap, totally confident.

Holding something alive, warm, sleeping is like handling fresh moist soil under the sun's heat. Restorative.

After a little while I had the idea that it would be an act of good fellowship to peel her out of those coveralls and slip her into the bed. A nice gesture. Sure. This is how McGee kids McGee.

I gave a little shake like a hound coming out of water. During that little time when it had been good, before we had started sawing chunks off each other, I had discovered that narrow little body to be amazingly strong, curiously luxurious. And I had the lonelies.

So I stood her on her feet and held her until she could stand up. "What the hell!" she said.

I stood up and kissed her, gave her a swat on the fanny and told her to sleep tight. I heard the coverall zipper before I got the door entirely closed behind me.

I showered with the strange feeling I was washing

52

off the sweat and sun oil I had acquired on a bright terrace three thousand and more miles away.

I put on a robe and went topside for a nightcap pipe, a load of Irish aromatic in a battered old large apple Comoy. I perched a haunch on the sundeck rail. The wind had died, but the surf still made that endless freight-train sound on the beach. Across the way the Alabama Tiger's perpetual floating house party was muted down to a few girlish squeals and somebody playing bad bongo. Meyer's craft was dark.

Go mention it in the locker room, McGee. There you were with Lysa Dean, and she had on these skin-tight pants, fellas, and there was that big damn bed over there, and her hanging on me, sighing. Go on, McGee. Go *on*, man!

Boys, once when I was riding my bicycle no hands, I hit a stone and removed about one half a square foot of hide from assorted painful places. And once upon a time I won free dancing lessons from Arthur Murray because I knew, right off, what happened in 1776.

When I got up in the morning Skeeter was gone, leaving the bed unmade and no coffee in the pot. But she left a drawing on the sink in the head. A rangy mouse who looked extraordinarily like me sat holding a Skeeter-like girl mouse asleep in his arms. The caption said, "Notorious mouse spares innocent prey. Vitamin deficiency suspected."

After breakfast I phoned her. She said her apartment was smelling much better, thank you.

"McGee," she said. "We might be turning into friends. That's pretty good, don't you think?"

"You're too dangerous on any other basis. What's with this vitamin gag?"

"I guess I was just sort of asleep. You started breathing hard. Then pow! On your feet, girl. And you went off like you used starting blocks."

"Friends play fair, Skeet."

"Well, hell. I don't know. I hadn't decided. You were blue. I practically had a Band-Aid complex. Woman's work or something. I passed the buck by sort of sleeping. Anyway, I was terribly tired."

"Quimby is a fine mouse."

"Trav, dear, I am going to sleep for three days, and then you can take me fishing."

"Deal," I told her. She hung up. It was a sad thing that we had a strange sexual antagonism that made us want to chop each other to bits. We had to cut deep to see how much it would hurt. And it hurt aplenty. You can't live with that. But you can learn to live very nicely without it.

At eleven o'clock Dana Holtzer, as carefully poised as an unfriendly diplomat delivering an ultimatum, arrived with the money. Five thousand in cash. She had a receipt form for my signature, made out in the form of a letter of intent. The money was for "expenses in connection with research for a moving picture as yet untitled, to be purchased in treatment form at a price to be negotiated..."

Apparently I was dealing with something called Ly-Dea Productions. She had a file copy of the letter for me. She sat erect on the cushioned top of one of the stowage lockers along the lounge wall under the ports. She wore no hat. She wore a tailored navy blue suit with pleated skirt over a crisp white blouse. I could see no concession to anything in the set of her heavy mouth, the waiting attentiveness of very vivid dark eyes. Had I not seen her reaction to Skeeter's mouse, I would have given up on her.

"Tax reasons," she said.

"Of course," I said, and signed her copy. She refolded it briskly and tucked it away.

I wondered if anything would dent that efficient calm. I expected her to get up and trot off. But she had something else on her mind, yet wanted me to make a move first. I could guess why she had no particular enthusiasm for me. Her confidence would be given to large organizations with computers in the air-conditioned basement to tell the other machines which cards to drop into the slot. Lysa Dean was in trouble. When you are in trouble, you go to a J. Edgar Hoover, not to an obviously shopworn beach bum, a marina gypsy, a big shambling sharpshooter without an IBM card to his name. To Miss Holtzer I would look like more trouble, not less. My khakis were faded to pale beige, and the toes were out of my topsiders, and the old blue sweatshirt was fringed at the elbows. So I just fell into a chair, hooked a leg over one arm of it and watched her mildly.

She took it well and took it long, and then the pink climbed up her throat. "Miss Dean should be the one to tell you this," she said.

"Tell me what, dear?"

"She could answer any objections better than I could. The agency is sending a competent girl out, to take over for me temporarily with Miss Dean. I'll catch her up to date this evening." She took a deep breath. "Miss Dean has assigned me to work with you on this matter, Mr. McGee."

"That is absolutely ridiculous!"

"Believe me, it wasn't my idea. But in all fairness, it does have some merit. I can get through to her immediately at any time. There may be information about her you might want to have, and information about her friends and associates. Also, I may be able to take some details off your hands: travel arrangements, accommodations, notes, financial records. Miss Dean would feel . . . more at ease about all this if I am with you."

"I work alone, Dana. My God, I don't need any Katie Gibbs-type services, believe me. I wouldn't know how to act with you trudging behind me with a notebook and a ledger. In a thing like this I might have to do a lot of . . . impersonations."

"I am quite flexible and resourceful, Mr. McGee."

I stood up. "But you don't belong in this sort of thing. It looks as if it would be pretty messy, if I have any luck at all."

"I said yes to Miss Dean, but I do have one reservation. I must ask you if . . . if you are employed to kill anyone."

I boggled at her. "What?"

"That's a risk I wouldn't care to accept."

I sat down and I laughed. She let me laugh it out, without a smile, with quiet patience. When I was through she said, "That's answer enough. I had to ask. I have to think of risks."

"Miss Holtzer, I don't know if I could stand the continuous weight of your disapproval."

"What does that mean?"

"I understand you saw those pictures by accident, the ones left at the desk at The Sands, and you wanted to quit then and there. Life is full of a number of things, Miss Holtzer, and many of them get a little grim from time to time."

Her dark eyes flashed. "Do they really?"

"Haven't you noticed?"

With a thoughtful expression she took cigarettes

from her purse, snapped her lighter, huffed a dragon plume of smoke toward me. "What I tell you now is, of course, none of your business. But I think we should understand each other a little bit in the beginning. My personal life is out of bounds for any future discussion. I am in the business of selling skills: tact, great energy, adequate intelligence and total loyalty. I sell this package to Lysa Dean for thirty thousand dollars a year. Assigned to you, you get the same package. When I saw what those pictures were, I went through them to see how damaging they might be. I read the note. To me it meant that Lysa Dean was not as good a gamble for me as she used to be. I worried about that before, when I went through that thirteen-week charade."

I saw her hand tremble slightly as she lifted her cigarette to her lips.

"I am married, Mr. McGee. Or was married. My husband was epileptic. He was a talented writer, with a few very substantial television credits. Marriage was a calculated risk. We had a child, a boy. At first he seemed quite normal. Then we learned gradually that he was so seriously retarded an institution would be the only answer. It had no connection with my husband's difficulty. We had to get away after we put the little boy in. He would never know us, or anyone. Bill had made a good sale. It was a good trip, actually, as good as two emotionally exhausted people could expect. We got well enough to head home. We stopped at a place at night for coffee, along the road. It was a bar. We were not drinking. Bill had a sudden seizure. They never lasted long, but they were quite violent. An off-duty police officer thought he was a murderous drunk and shot him in the head. He did not die. He is permanently comatose, Mr. McGee, with tubes for feeding and elimination, and the alcohol rubs to keep bed sores from rotting him away. It is a medical miracle, of course. That was four years ago. I need that thirty thousand. It is barely enough for me and my family. If Lysa Dean is going down the drain in a messy way, it is my responsibility to leave her before it happens and go where an equivalent job has been offered. The job might not be open if I was in any way connected with scandal. Yes, Mr. McGee, the world can get a little grim from time to time."

"What can I say?"

"Nothing, of course. I thought it would be easier to tell you now before you said more things you might regret later, that's all. You haven't hurt me. I'm not certain anything could hurt me, actually. I am sorry it is all so soap opera. I haven't the . . . self-involvement necessary to make moral judgments. Lee was terribly foolish. The pictures offend me because they are vulgar. And they endanger me. If you can't work things out for her, I will have to leave her. I think she senses that."

"Maybe you could be some help."

"Thank you."

"Drink?"

Her smile was small, and perfectly polite, and totally automatic. "Bourbon, if you have it. Weak, with lots of ice and water."

I do not think she wanted it, but knew I wanted a chance to pull myself together, get the taste of my own foot off my front teeth. I had looked at the empty reserve and guessed repression and disapproval. She was merely burned out. Wires had crossed and a lovely machine had fuzed and quit, become a useless lump for her to carry around the rest of her life. I felt like a jackass adolescent who'd tried to tell a dirty joke in front of real people.

When I went in with the drinks, she was standing

with her back to me, feet apart, sturdy calves braced, fist on a rich curve of Mediterranean hip, head cocked, looking at a painting.

"Like it?"

She turned with a swift grace. "Very much."

"Syd Solomon. He lives over in Sarasota. It's part of a Bahama series he did a few years back."

"It's very rich. Are you a collector?"

"Sometimes. I've got about five things aboard and maybe a dozen in storage. Every so often I switch them around." She sipped her drink. "Is that all right?"

"Yes. Thank you. What do you drink? What is that?"

"Lately Plymouth gin on the rocks with two drops of bitters." I could almost hear the little click as she filed that away. I had acquired a drinkmaker.

She went back to the upholstered locker and sat and said, "By the way, my expenses won't come out of what I brought you. Is there anything I can start doing today? My desk is fairly clean and the girl won't be in until later."

I left her there and went to the safe and took out the envelope. I put Lysa Dean's pictures back in the safe and brought out the ones Gabe had made. I handed them to her. She looked at three of them, and then looked at me with faint surprise and fainter approval. "You had this done, or did it, since you left her yesterday?"

"I had it done."

"It's quite clever. I see, I think, what you have in mind. These are no danger to her. Are the others safe?"

"Yes." I waited until she had glanced through the set and put them aside. "Would you take down a few things?"

A notebook, gold pen and attentive expression appeared with impressive speed. I gave her Gabe's full name and address. "Make out a check for a hundred and mail it to him for the photo work. The checkbook is in the desk drawer over there. See if you can get a line on a Carl Abelle, possibly a ski instructor at the Mohawk Lodge in Speculator, New York, previously at Sun Valley. Phone him and fake it so that he won't be left with a lot of curiosity. If he is there, find the best way to get there, and reserve us through for Tuesday."

"To stay at that lodge?"

"Let's save that until we get a look, if he's there. Next, see what you can dig up about a Mr. and Mrs. Vance M'Gruder. Their home could be in Carmel. Ocean-racing type. It's a small fraternity, so it shouldn't be rough." I went over and sat beside her and handed her my notes. "These are the names and numbers of all the players, as much as she could remember." I identified them in the pictures for her. "All clear?"

"Yes, sir."

"Yes, *Trav*. Can we do it that way, Dana?"

"Of course, Trav."

"When will you get loose?"

"Actually tonight, about midnight. The new girl is taking my accommodations at the Sultana at Miami Beach. Suppose I check in Monday morning with you right here. Nine?"

"Make it ten. Or you can come right here tonight when you're through. There's an extra stateroom. With a lock on the door."

She nodded. "It would be simpler. Lock or no lock, Trav, that's one problem I don't expect to have, and know how to handle if I do."

I went to the desk drawer, tossed the extra key to her. She caught it with a deft twist of the wrist. I explained it was to the lounge door, in case I was asleep when she got in. I took her on the tour. She said it seemed very comfortable. I was glad that with a morning attack of the neats, I had made up the Skeeter-tousled bed afresh. She went to the galley and rinsed her glass and set it out to dry. She went to my desk, wrote Gabe's check, altered my dwindling balance, and presented me the check for signature, saying, "Perhaps you would like me to deposit some of that cash tomorrow? I made a note of the account number."

"Half of it, I guess. Thanks. Remind me tomorrow."

I was asleep when she arrived. The little *bong* of my warning bell alerted me. When anybody comes aboard it rings. Once. That is always enough. I hate unfriendly surprises. I had left a light for her. Gun in hand, I prowled naked to the interior door to the lounge, opened it an inch and looked through, out of darkness, saw her open the door, reach back and get a big suitcase and come in with it, moving quietly. It was ten of one. I went back to my bed, behind the closed door to the master stateroom.

She was a quiet woman. A thread of light appeared under my door. In time I heard water running in the head. The thread of light went out. Soft click of latch of the other stateroom. Night silence. A faint music from some other boat. Grumble of a truck on the drive. Distant whistling scream of a jet.

A woman aboard, quite unlike any I could remember. This was a staunch one. A lot of people can be gutsy when there is a tiny morsel of hope. Damn few keep plugging when there is none. The human animal is basically selfish. Neither the damaged kid nor the lost husband could know what degree of care they were getting. Society could not let them perish if she ceased her support. They could not accuse her. But she had a moral obligation so strong, any other course was inconceivable to her. They were her family. There was no other consideration for her. Life had burned her out, but what was left was considerably more woman than was Lysa Dean.

The night thoughts of Dana Holtzer depressed me. Self-evaluation. It is the skin rash of the emotionally insecure. I felt as if I had spent a lot of years becoming too involved with some monstrously silly people. McGee, the con artist. I would fatten myself off their troubles, and then take the money and coast for a time, taking my retirement in early installments. I was not a very earnest or constructive fellow.

But, I thought, what are the other choices? I am not a nine-to-five animal. I cannot swallow the myths which say that nine to five is a Good Thing because that's the way nearly everybody else gets stuck. I cannot be an orderly consumer, with 2.3 kids and .7 new cars a year, and an after-hours secretarial arrangement. I am not properly acquisitive. I like the *Busted Flush*, the records and paintings, the little accumulations of this and that which stir memories, but I could stand on the shore and watch the whole thing go glug and disappear and feel a mild sardonic regret. No Professional American Wife could stomach that kind of attitude.

I went to sleep feeling critical of the restless animal called Travis McGee and awoke to the sunbrightness of nine in the morning coming through the small shaggy draperies in the stateroom, awoke to a scent of coffee and some furtive clinking sounds from the galley.

After I showered, I went out to find her as full of utterly impersonal morning cheer as a waitress in a good hotel. She said she had slept well, thank you. It's a lovely day. The wind has stopped. It's much warmer.

She said she had taken a chance on the eggs. I said scrambled was just fine. The juice was cold, coffee fragrant, bacon crisp, eggs medium. She served us in the booth. It was a pleasure to watch her move. She gave no impression of haste. Yet each movement was sure, and flowed into the next one without hesitation, and so things got done with a fascinating quickness.

She was wearing gray flannel slacks and a yellow sweater. She looked better in slacks than I would have guessed. She did not look really good. That long-waisted figure was a shade too hearty in the seat and hefty in the thigh to look splendid in slacks. Venus de Milo would have looked like hell in stretch pants. They look just fine on the gangly just-ripening teenagers, or on the calculated slimness of a Lysa Dean. But there is something forlorn and slightly touching about the rump of the mature female who fills them all too well. Dana could not have managed stretch pants, but she did sneak by with the beautifully tailored slacks. They were high-waisted enough to fake a little figure correction, and she was wise enough to wear sandals with about an inch and a half of heel to get her center of gravity a little farther from the deck.

As we sat eating our breakfast, I could see why she was worth a lot of money to a Lysa Dean. She had the deft knack of fitting herself to every situation and operating efficiently with a minimum of fuss. There was no sycophantic flavor about her. She knew her own dignity.

I told her about the *Busted Flush* and how I had acquired it. It is one of my more polished routines. I don't expect people to roll on the floor, but I generally get a little more amusement than I got from her. Her laugh was polite and came in the right places.

Over coffee and cigarettes, the little notebook came out.

"I had a chance to spend quite a bit of time on the

phone, Travis. Carl Abelle is at the Mohawk Lodge. He operates their ski school on some sort of franchise arrangement and runs the ski shop. It would be impossible to stay there. They are booked completely. If you want to go there first, we are reserved out of Miami to Kennedy, arriving at two-fifteen tomorrow. There is a feeder flight which will get us to the Utica-Rome airport at four-ten. It is about a sixty-mile drive from there to Speculator up Route Eight, and the roads are clear."

"What do you mean, *if* I want to go there first?"

"Let me tell you about the others. The M'Gruders are divorced. I couldn't locate her. He has remarried, just a short time ago. They've gone cruising down the Pacific coast to Acapulco, and it is possible they may be on their way back by now. I think I will be able to get a line on his ex-wife. But, having a little extra time, I thought I would see what I could find out about Nancy Abbott. Your notes said her father might be an architect. I checked standard reference sources and found a West Coast architect, Alexander Armitage Abbott in San Francisco. I have a friend in San Francisco, one of Bill's old friends actually, who knows everyone. The architect has a daughter named Nancy, age twenty-four, with matching physical description, so it must be the same one. She has had one annulled marriage. She is a problem drinker. She has been in so many messes, the family has sort of washed their hands of her. He said he would make a couple of calls and phone me back. He did, and said she is in Florida, at some sort of voluntary alcoholic retreat down at Bastion Key. It's called Hope Island. Do you know about it?"

"I took them a customer once. I took her back there three times, but it didn't stick. The same guy may still run it."

"A Mr. Burley? I looked it up."

"That's the one. He gave it a good try with my friend. But she borrowed a car, finally, and drove it into a cypress swamp at about a hundred miles an hour."

"I wondered if . . . as long as she's so nearby . . ."

"Right. We'll go down there tomorrow. Cancel us out on the flight north, and don't set it up again until after we've seen her."

"You have a car?"

"In a manner of speaking. After you left yesterday I was wondering what you think of all this."

"I thought I made that clear."

"I mean what you think of it as a woman."

"Is that pertinent?"

"Perhaps. It might help me in talking to the Abbott girl."

She thought for a moment. It was a long strong face, flat planes in the cheeks, very dark and vivid and lovely eyes, a prominent and forceful nose, broad firm mouth.

"I would say this, I guess. Lee isn't a suggestible child, you know. She's had four marriages. And other relationships, some of them not particularly wholesome. But she's always been pretty cautious. She is very frankly and happily promiscuous, but the situation in those pictures I would say is not her natural style. She was lulled into it somehow, and damned uncomfortable about it later on, and still is. I wouldn't know how those other females reacted to it. But I don't think it is accurate to think of Lee as just another woman getting involved in something messy."

"What do you mean?"

"She is a property, Trav. She has few personal rights and privileges. She's just worth too much money to too many people. They can't afford a blemish on her. I've gotten used to thinking that way about her. So when I look at those pictures, I see them in terms of risk. Like watching a clown juggle priceless glassware. Those men were aware of it, of course. The unattainable goddess suddenly right there within reach, tired and drunk and sweaty and willing. They talk, you know. It spreads like ripples. It has had a lot of time. Little hints and rumors are coming back home to roost. She's scared of that, too. She'll be all right until one picture doesn't pay off. Then there could be some reluctance. Why take a chance?"

"How will this picture do, this *Winds of Chance*?"

"Very well, I think. It's the kind of part she always does well. Coffee?"

"Thanks."

After she poured it she hesitated by the table, empty pot in hand. "You didn't say anything about how you'd like me to dress, Trav. I thought. . . . I imagine women have stayed here with you. I'd be less conspicuous if I . . . stayed with resort clothes."

"You do fine. Use your own judgment."

Five

ON THE WAY DOWN to Bastion Key, Dana was delighted with my stately and ancient pickup truck. It is painted a hideous electric blue and called Miss Agnes by all who know her. It is one of the largest of the old Rolls breed, and some owner of long ago, perhaps after bashing her up, did a backyard job of converting her into a pickup truck. She is high and solid. It takes a long time to move her up through the gears, but when you have a chance to get her up to eighty, she will settle into it all day long in a rushing ghastly silence. She eats gas but holds a little over forty gallons at a time.

I liked Dana's delight. It reminded me of the way she reacted to Skeeter's mouse. I knew I had to watch it, or I would be trapped into the hopeless project of trying to find ways to delight her, to bring out that little spark so deeply buried.

At Bastion Key you turn right off the highway beyond the town and follow a shell road out to a little short causeway that leads over to Hope Island. It is not a luxurious retreat. Stan Burley is the Schweitzer of the gin bottle. The buildings are surplus barracks he brought over by barge long ago. He and all of his small staff are reformed drunks. If he has room, he takes you, at whatever you can afford to pay. He has some theories. They work for him. If you took a seven-foot chimp and shaved every hair off and painted him pink, you'd have a recognizable version of Stan Burley. His graduates who stay dry send contributions regularly.

Before I could turn the motor off, Burley was striding toward us from his little screened office. It was warm and bright, eleven o'clock on Tuesday morning. The Florida bays were blue.

"Ho, McGee," he said, hand outstretched toward me, looking with a keen expectation at Dana, doubtless thinking her a new guest.

I introduced them and said quickly, "We've come down to talk to one of your people, Stan. If possible. Nancy Abbott."

The welcoming light went out of his face. He gnawed his lip. "Miss Holtzer, you go wait in my office a minute, and Jenny will give you a nice glass of iced tea." She nodded and walked away. Burley led me over to a wooden bench in the shade.

"What's it about, Trav?"

"She was involved in something a year and a half ago. I want to ask her some questions about it. Is she all right?"'

He shrugged. "She's dry, if that means very much. Has been since October. I shouldn't tell you a damned thing about that one. But you worked so hard with me that time with Marianne. God help us, we fought hard, but we lost that one, boy. I'll have to tell you, it's on my conscience having her here, this Nancy. It isn't the place for her, but no place is, not any more. Did her father send you?"

"No."

"A retired policewoman brought the child here in

October. Sick drunk and down to ninety pounds. The
D.T.s and the spasms. Pitiful. I got a thousand then, and
I get a thousand a month from a San Francisco bank. I
write the bank a condition report once a month. After
we began to bring her out of it, she puzzled me. I had a
doctor friend look her over. Drunk is only part of it. But
the thousand a month takes care of a lot of other ones.
I'm an evil old man, Trav."

"What's wrong with her?"

"Physically she's as healthy as an ox. She's only
twenty-four. She had nine years of drinking, the last five
of them heavy, not long enough to damage her. Mentally,
you name it, she's got it."

"She's mad?"

"Boy, she isn't sane. What they did, they got too
eager with her long ago. Some people who thought shock
treatments were the answer to all. A cure for anxiety and
depressive symptoms. As far as I can figure, she had over
twenty complete series. That and the alcoholic spasms,
there's degenerative damage. She doesn't track too well.
She can't handle abstract concepts. She's trapped in a
manic-depressive cycle. You hit her at her best. She's on
her way up now, but not up too high yet. This is her
happy time. She could manage in public pretty well if too
much wasn't demanded of her. Pretty soon she'll get real
wild. Violence, compulsive nymphomania, such a craving
for drink she'd kill to get it. Then I put her under restraint. Then she falls all the way down to the bottom.
She won't speak for days. Then she starts to slowly build
again."

"How is her memory?"

"Sometimes good and sometimes gone."

I looked at that tired simian face and remembered

the way he had talked of Marianne. Of love and destruction.

"What did it to her, Stan?"

"Her? The father did it. The adored, talented, mighty father. It was an ugly marriage. The poor child was too much like her mother, so the father couldn't help despising her. He rejected her. So because she couldn't understand why—just like Marianne—she grew up with a conviction of her own worthlessness. Ah, that's where the compulsions start, McGee. People can *not* endure inexplicable worthlessness. So they establish the pattern of proving themselves worthless. For this child it was sex and drink. The guilts made her emotionally unstable. She was after destruction. The shock treatments and the spasms have done the job for her. She's a destroyed personality. Where can she go? Nothing much can be done for her now. Here is as good as anywhere. Sometimes she is very sweet."

"I don't want to upset her."

"What do you want to ask her?"

"If she can remember some names. If she can remember some pictures being taken."

"Pictures?"

I opened the envelope, sorted out two of them and handed them to him. His face puckered with concern and sorrow.

"The poor kid. See what she's saying, in effect? Love me, love me. Rejection by the father, rejection by the young husband, a butchered abortion, a year in an institution when she was seventeen, for hit and run."

"What would showing her these do?"

"Trav, nothing can do her much good or much harm."

"Will she talk to me?"

70

"In this part of the cycle she's very outgoing. She might get agitated. It might strike her as funny. I don't know. It might accelerate this phase of the cycle. I can't see as that would do any harm."

"Should you be there?"

"I think you'd get more out of her alone. When there's two people or more she wants to be entertaining. She reacts too much. She talks better to one. My God, boy, those are some pictures! A year and a half ago? I guess she was bad off then, but it would take a trained man to see it. Now anybody can see it."

"What's the best attitude toward her, Stan?"

"Just natural, friendly. If she says nutty things, just steer her back to what you want to talk about. Don't look shocked and don't laugh. We're used to Nancy around here, and every drunk in the world has heard everything there is to hear. Treat her as if she was . . . a bright, sweet, imaginative child."

"Where is she?"

He took me over to the office and pointed. "Go around the dining hall, and the path to the beach starts on the other side of it. I saw her heading that way about twenty minutes or so ago."

I heard her before I saw her. It was a narrow beach, more shell than sand. It was a lovely contralto voice, very rich and full, singing, with maximum feeling, that cigarette commercial about filter, flavor, flip-top box. She was sitting on a palm log about a hundred feet up the bright beach from where the path exited. As I walked toward her, she heard my steps crunching the shell, stopped singing, turned and stared at me, and then stood up and came toward me with a warm and lovely smile of welcome, teeth very white in her sun-darkened face. *"Hello there!"*

she said. "I'm Nancy. Are you one of the new ones?"

She wore pale blue Bermudas, and a man's white shirt with the tails knotted around her waist. Her dark hair was in braids. She was tall and lithe, and her eyes were a dark clear blue. After a mental hesitation, I realized she made me think of Jane in the very oldest Tarzan movies. She was barefoot, unwincing on the shells.

"I'm just visiting. My name is Trav."

"Are you visiting Jackie? She doesn't throw up as much. Maybe she can go home. Just to visit."

"As a matter of fact, I'm here to visit you."

All the warmth and light went out of her face. "He just sends people. Tell him I don't give a damn. Not now. Not ever. Screw him. Tell him that."

"Nobody sent me. I just know some people who know you. I was down this way. So I stopped in. That's all, Nancy."

"What people?"

"Carl Abelle. Vance and Patty M'Gruder."

Scowling, she turned away from me and went back and sat on the log. I followed and stood near her. She squinted up at me. "I know that Carl. A strong back and a weak mind, believe me. He had that stupid idea. The perfect orgasm. Can you imagine? Maybe he thought it worked me up. Damned coward. Too scared to light a fire in that line shack. My God, it was always cold in there, way up on that ridge, with Auntie thinking I was on the slopes all day. He stole a key from the office. Fifty dollars a day she was paying him for personal instruction. We'd pile everything on that bunk. What was he trying to get? Tell me that? You either come or you don't. Right. And I almost always do, no matter how quick they are the first time. Last week or last year I was trying to remember Carl's name. My God, he was beautiful on skis. When we'd leave that cabin he'd push me down in the snow and rub snow on my face to get me all pink and outdoorsy-looking, and then guide me down the slopes, all the way to the lodge, half stoned on that brandy, like dreaming and floating. But he said some real dumb things. What was I then? He probably told you. Nineteen? I guess so. I'm remembering better. You ask Stan. He'll tell you. But what good is it? I mean, some of the things you remember. Sit by me. But please, I don't want to talk about those puke M'Gruders. I don't have to, do I?"

"No."

"What have you got there?"

"Some pictures."

"May I see them, please?"

She held them in her lap. She looked at them slowly and solemnly, one by one. I watched her face carefully. She sorted one onto the top. She stroked a thumb along the line of Sonny's back. "Burned, burned, burned," she said softly.

"Sunburned?"

"Oh, no. He hit a wall. It was his supercharged Merc with special cams and like that. I wore the big red hat so he could spot me, and I sat on the wall by the pits that day. We towed that car all over everywhere, and it burned him up in Georgia. It bounced and bounced." She stroked her thigh. "Sonny liked me in whore clothes. He bought them all. Tight short skirts and tight bright sweaters, and he said I had to swing it when I walked. Proud as a rooster and mean as a snake, Sonny was."

She ran her thumb across his image on the photograph.

"This one right here. Sonny Catton. He took me along when the party pooped out. I was with him maybe two weeks, and he kept beating me up, for taking another drink, or somebody making a pass at me, or sometimes just from remembering things from the party. Like this picture here, me with this one. What was his name? Cass? Cass something. He drew funny pictures of people. He gave me one of me and I lost it. You know, I've lost every single goddam thing I ever owned? I got sick of him hammering on me and I went home and what do you know, my fa-fa-f-f . . . the man who married my mother, *he* had pictures like this. He said tell my friends it was no sale. They could publish them in the *Chronicle*. Boy, what a smack across the face he gave me! His face was like a stone. I guessed it bugged him to see pictures of his wife laying people. Wife! Did you hear that! I'm his d-d-daugh-daughter. Made it!"

My skin had the cold quivers, just below the nape of my neck. "What did you do then, Nancy?"

"Are you another doctor? For a thousand years I've been up to my hips in doctors. I was a woman when I was fourteen, and when I got caught doing it, that was when they sent me to the first one, and I could tell he would have liked it too, if he could get up the nerve. He used to get sweaty and clean his glasses and walk around. They all make a big thing out of stuttering when I try to say . . . ef ay tee aitch ee are. Are you going to give me tests?"

"My name is Trav. I'm not a doctor."

"Trav. Trav, why did he tell you to bring me these pictures? They aren't even the same. There were more of me. Hey, you know who this was? This one with no face? A very famous movie star. Lysa Dean! Honestly, I'm not kidding. She's just a little thing, but so gorgeous."

"Who took the pictures?"

"How should I know? I didn't know *anybody* took any pictures until I walked into his study and he had them. He gave me money and I caught up with Sonny again. I was with him a long time. Months, I guess. All over. Wherever he raced. I remember the day he died and the next thing I remember is in the hospital in Mexico City. *Somebody* had to take me down there, but who? I couldn't have *wandered* down there, could I? Somebody dumped me in the hospital parking lot in the middle of the night, I found out later. I had bronchial pneumonia and two broken fingers. I was hallucinating and I had a dose of clap. When I could tell them who I was, they wired . . . him. As soon as I could be moved, he sent people to bring me back and put me in . . . Shady Rest? Refuge Mountain? One of those crappy names. How do you expect me to remember. I can't even remember being brought *here*!"

"How did you father get those pictures anyhow?"

"How do I know? He thought I knew all about it. He thought it was friends of mine, and we cooked it up to get money out of him."

"This is a pretty good place to be, Nancy."

"I guess so. I guess I like it. Sometimes I get very very nervous. After that I get sad. I'm sad a long time. I hum sad songs all day without making a single sound."

"Did anybody at that house party say anything about pictures of Lysa Dean?"

She turned toward me with an exasperated look. "You know, you get to be a terrible bore about those pictures. No. Nobody said anything. I didn't see a camera. Let's drop it, shall we?"

I put the pictures away. "Why are you mad at the M'Gruders?"

"I don't want to talk about it."

"Then we won't."

"You know, you are terribly nice, Trav." She smiled

at me, all abeam with innocence. She put her hand on mine.

"Thank you. You're a nice girl."

"I'm a slut, darling. I'm a drunk and a slut. May I ask you a very personal question?"

"Of course."

"Why don't we go over in the bushes a minute, sweetheart?" She tugged at my hand quickly and strongly, trying to press it against herself. I yanked my hand away. "It keeps me from getting nervous," she said. "Please, honey. Please, please, please."

I stood up quickly and she jumped up to try to press herself against me. I held her off with my hands on her shoulders. She dipped her head sharply to the side and licked my hand.

I shook her. "Nancy! Nancy! Cut it out!"

She shuddered, smiled sadly, backed away. "It never makes any difference to a man. Why should you care one way or the other?"

"I have to get back. It was nice to visit with you."

"Thank you," she said politely. "Come and see me again." She squared her shoulders like a child about to recite. "When you get back there, tell my f-f . . . tell him I am being a good girl. Tell him that . . . I am getting good marks."

"Of course."

"Good-by."

I walked the hundred feet to the entrance to the path. When I turned and looked back at her, she shook her fist at me and yelled, "You ask that Patty M'Gruder why she kept locking me up! You just ask that goddam bitch!"

Halfway back to the compound I stopped in the path and leaned against a tree. My knees felt strange. I lit a

76

cigarette, took one drag and threw it away. Stan Burley was in the small office talking to Dana. He got up and brought me some iced tea and said, "How did it go?"

"I don't know. Her memory was pretty good. It damn near broke my heart listening to her trying to call him father. What's the matter with that son of a bitch? He threw her away. He threw away a pretty good person, I think."

"Was she any help?"

"I don't know. I have to check it out. Stan, she made a hell of a direct pass at me."

He raised his ridged monkey brows. "Little early for that. I'll start keeping a close watch on her. Thanks."

"What's the prognosis?"

He wiped his hand across his face. "I don't know. The highs don't seem to get any higher, but the periods of apathy seem deeper and seem to last a little longer. And when she comes up out of them I have the feeling . . . there's a little less of her. She's lost some songs she knew a month ago. She's getting a little more awkward and untidy feeding herself and caring for herself. I . . . I guess we'll keep her here as long as we can. She loves the beach so. She hates to be locked in. This place has the illusion of freedom. Maybe a big institution could arrest it, even improve her a little, but never enough to let her out into the world. She isn't dangerous to anyone. She's a victim. He made her a victim."

"What happened to her mother?"

"She died in a hotel fire when Nancy was seven. She was with a lover at the time. Nancy has a strong body. I am afraid it will keep going long after the brain is gone. Maybe for another forty years or more. There is a brother. Older, and from all reports, extremely righteous. Nice to see you again, Trav. Nice to talk to you, Miss

Holtzer. It's a strange world, you know. We can defend ourselves from our enemies, and even from our friends, but never from our family. That tyke was sent to boarding school at age seven. She had lovers at fourteen, alcoholic dementia in a mild form at fifteen, and her first shock treatments at sixteen. I am off to paint chairs. My cure for depression and indignation. Come by any time, either of you."

We stopped at a fish house in town for lunch. We had the privacy of a corner booth. I told her about the dead one. Sonny Catton. I told her about the eight pictures, the slap, the hostility toward the M'Gruders, her final strange comment.

"From the way you look it was rough, Travis."

"I guess so. I don't know why it rocked me so. I guess because she looks so fresh and clean and bright. I guess a man gets the feeling . . . a lovely mixed-up girl, if you could take her along, love her, treat her well, she'd shape up. But you know you can't. Maybe the last one to be in a position to do anything was Catton, but he wasn't the type for it. I guess she got handed around quite a bit, with none of them doing her much good."

I told her about Carl Abelle. The corners of her strong mouth turned downward in an ironic smile. "The Galahad of the slopes. I met him once. I'd been working for her just a matter of weeks. It was quite a while later they went off to stay in that Chipmann house. He was pretty gorgeous. Dark blond curly hair, huge shoulders, bronzed face, custom sports coat, silk ascot, and a little faky German accent. Hair a little much over the ears. You know. A little wave there too. Lots of huge white teeth, and a very Continental handshake. The almost too typical Hollywood stud."

"Smart enough to rig a blackmail thing on Lee?"

"Oh, I doubt it. I doubt it very much. It couldn't have been his idea in any case. Somebody could have bullied him into it. I think he would shatter quite easily under pressure. Only a damn fool would have tried to use him that way. He would crack too easily. And it wasn't a fool who arranged it all."

"Have any ideas?"

"Who there had money or reputation or something to lose? Lee, and the architect's daughter, and the M'Gruders. Cass apparently, and Sonny and Whippy and the college boys and Carl would be very small fry, not worth the effort compared to the others."

"Agreed. Keep going."

She shrugged. "There's nowhere else to go. We know that two out of the three were contacted. Lee paid off. Mr. Abbott apparently didn't. And we'll know about the M'Gruders later on. We should go to San Francisco, I imagine. After Abelle or before?"

"After."

"Tomorrow?" I nodded. She slid out of the booth. "I'd better do some phoning right now then." She walked to the cashier for change.

When we got back to the boat, Dana checked her copy of Lysa Dean's promo schedule and found that Lysa would be starting a rest hour in about another fifteen minutes. She waited twenty minutes and phoned her on a private line that did not go through the hotel board. They talked together for about fifteen minutes. Then Dana called to me, holding the phone with her palm over the mouthpiece.

"She wants to talk to you. I've caught her up to date on all of it."

When I spoke to her, Lee said in a lazy drawl, "Sweetie, how do you like the little giftie I sent you?"

"I beg your pardon?"

"The highly efficient tragic figger, stupid."

"Oh, fine, just fine."

"She'll keep you honest and keep you scrambling, dear. I miss her already. Little things are starting to get fouled up. So don't keep her too long."

"I didn't make any request, you know."

"Oh, don't be stuffy! And by the way, McGee, don't waste your time in any idle hopes. She's quite something in a sort of swarthy hearty way. The look of banked fires or something. Some of the greatest experts in the industry have taken their Sunday hack at that, dear, and wandered glassily away with icicles forming on their whatsis. It's sort of an in-group joke."

"I'm laughing myself sick."

"You are really a wretched chap, aren't you? Why do I still like you? I understand the Abbott girl is out of the ball park."

"Did she seem odd to you at the time?"

"Not particularly. She kept belting herself pretty good, so who expected too much sense? And she was pretty rowdy now and again. Roughhousing into other people's little games. She kept talking about her dear daddy. And singing that song at very strange moments. 'My heart belongs to' and so forth. When you see Carl, dear, grasp his hand, smile, give him my love, and kick him solidly in the jewels. I would pay a small bonus for that."

"Just one thing. Is that little accent of his genuine?"

"God, no! It's for the ski trade."

"Are you getting good protection?"

"So far it looks fine. Take care of yourself. Dana will keep me informed."

"Want to speak to her again?"

"Good-by and love to you both. Happy hunting."

I hung up and said, "You plan to keep her informed?"

She had taken the checkbook from the desk drawer to post the cash deposit she had made. She looked over at me, one dark eyebrow lifting slightly. "In that business, she's so used to intrigue. Everybody watches everybody. And if you work *for* somebody you have to be at a certain established level, a pecking order. She's just trying to fit you into the ranks, Travis, somewhere between a script writer and an associate producer. She doesn't know it won't work, but there's no point in . . . in making a point of it. I'll tell her what she should know, and enough to keep her happy, and no more or less than that. Okay?"

"Divided loyalty?"

"Not really. You are both after the same thing, aren't you?"

"Should that be a question?"

"Mr. Burley told me about a girl named Marianne. I don't have as many questions about you as I used to."

"I'm reasonably honest, Dana, in my own way. That's about as far as I can go with it. Maybe I have a price. Nobody's come up with just the right amount yet. But maybe next time. Let's see how quick you can get us out of here, Efficient Girl."

Six

SHE MANAGED TO SWITCH IT to earlier arrangements on
Wednesday. By noon, in a gray February world, we had
come down through snow flurries to land at Albany and
had taken off again. When the snow ended the sky was a
luminous gray. I looked down at the winter calligraphy
of upstate New York, white fields marked off by the black
woodlots, an etching without color, superbly restful in
contrast to the smoky, guttering, grinding stink of the
airplane clattering across the sky like an old commuter
bus.

Dana seemed pensive. She had tilted her window
seat and had her face turned toward the window, and I
could not tell whether her eyes were open or closed. I
looked at her still hands resting in her lap, against the
nubbly fabric of her suit skirt. You look at hands long
enough, you can turn them into animal paws. Her hands
were a little larger than perhaps they should have been,
the fingers very long and firm, the nails oval, quite narrow, convex. The pads of fingers and palm were heavy.
The backs of her hands were very smooth and youthful.
You look at hands as animal paws, and you think of the
animal aspects of the human, and suddenly you are back
on that Pacific terrace, seeing that final and most danger-

ous form of gluttony.

Perhaps, I thought, the most absolute way of categorizing people is by what they are capable of and what they are not capable of. Temptation does not deliver most of us into evil, because temptation is a constant and evil is a sometime thing with most of us.

So far I had seen only two people whose pattern of life had led, almost implacably, toward that terrace. One of them had been on exhibition all her adult life, driven by restless greed, emotional instability, a desire to be noticed. Her artificiality had made this just another act, not particularly real to her while it was happening. The younger one had become food for Jack London's Noseless One long before Carl Abelle and the M'Gruders led her onto that terrace. It, like Mexico, like the tour with Sonny Catton, was just another part of the self-destruction.

I would never talk to Catton. Perhaps it had not mattered a damn to him one way or the other. For the soul to be offended it must first exist. Perhaps to snake-mean Sonny, broads were broads were broads, and if they came in a bundle instead of in separate rooms, he could not care less. He had brought one along and discarded it for one that suited him better. Perhaps for him it was like an exchange counter.

I could not be Sonny. I had the old illusions, including the one that maybe I might be gaining a little bit, just a very damn little bit, in wisdom as my time went by. And wisdom says there are no valuable goods on the bargain counter. Wisdom says the only values are the ones you place on yourself. And I have locked myself into this precarious role of the clown-knight in the to-mato-can armor, flailing away at indifferent beasts with my tinfoil sword. A foible of the knight, even the comic ones, is the cherishing of women, and perhaps even my brand of cherishing is quaint in this time and place. Though I have faltered from time to time, I do want the relationship, if it does become intimate, to rest solidly on trust, affection, respect. Not just for taking, or scoring, or using, or proving anything. That knocks out group adventures right there. Not for recreation, not for health rationalizations, not for sociologically constructive contacts. But because she is a woman, and valuable. And you are a man, and equally valuable. There are more than enough girls and boys around. Break down, McGee. Say it. Okay, for love and love alone. They are people, goddam it, not pneumatic, hydraulic, terrace toys. Not necessarily Heloïse and Abelard, Romeo and Miss Capulet, or even Nappi and Jo. But just a crumb of some kind of love there, lad. Love that makes her sweet to hold, warm to murmur to, after no more fireworks are left in the park. And you can't do that with a terrace toy.

Dana rolled her head toward me and smiled and said, "I was almost asleep." She put a fist against her yawn. "You know, when you are thinking of something and then it all turns crazy and then it turns real again, and you know a dream got mixed into it."

"Tell me the crazy part."

"It's just plain dull, Trav, really. I was wondering if the car would be there as I ordered, and then suddenly I was remembering the last time you and I wanted a car—we didn't ever, of course—and we walked out and got into it and it didn't have any wheels. You were furious and you kept saying they always did that to us. And I was thinking that this time I would look for the wheels before signing the slip, and suddenly I realized how nutty that was. I suppose some psychiatrist would have a ball with that."

"I suppose he'd say you were realizing I can't get anyplace with you."

I said it off the top of my mind. She looked at me for another moment and then said, too casually, "I guess you could make it mean almost anything." She turned her face away again, and I saw the redness climb her throat and up her cheek, suffuse her forehead and slowly die away. It had been too logical a guess, and she had for a moment accepted it, and then taken the next step of translating what it meant to dream that this time she'd look for the wheels before signing the slip. I realized I had innocently created the sort of awareness which would keep her doubly on guard against any kind of emotional involvement with me, no matter how minor.

She arranged the car while I claimed the luggage. When she got in beside me, she had a marked map in her hand. She showed it to me and said, "Just the general idea. I'll call the turns." A most valuable gal.

"Food?" I asked.

"Woops," she said, and scrambled out and hustled back into the terminal. She came out with new marks on the map, and we went a few blocks out of our way into North Utica into one of those Italian-Tourist-Close-to-Motels enterprises called the Diplomat. It wasn't going to excite any far-flung gourmet exclamations, but the shots of antifreeze were excellent protection against the 35-degree afternoon, the lowering sky, the chill moistness of the air. Hot Italian sausage with spaghetti *al dente* was a similar precaution.

You know how it is. You wonder. We had drifted into a silence not entirely comfortable. I hadn't seen much lift or life in her. If we were going to spend a lot of time together, it could become a drag. So you wonder, and you think something up. When you say it, you more than half expect a totally blank look and some kind of query like, for example, "Hah! What's that?"

So when she just started to wind a fork of spaghetti, I said to her, "By God, Myra, I bet you forgot to turn the thermostat down."

Her fork clattered on the plate and she said instantly, "*I* forgot to turn it down? Frank, dear, it was on *your* list. Remember?"

"Of course it was on my list. I reminded you and crossed it off."

"I'd think that once, just once, you could . . . what was it set for?"

"Seventy-five. What else? Sixty-eight is enough for normal people. *You* have to have seventy-five."

"Oh, God, all that lovely oil. Darling, maybe we could phone the Hollisbankers."

"So how do they get in?"

She hesitated a moment. "I have it! With Helen's figure, Fred could slip her under the door."

I broke up. A clear victory for her side. You never know until you try. We laughed like a pair of idiots, and then her very next chuckle turned into a strangled howling sob and she jumped up and fled for the ladies' room, nearby lunch customers staring at her and me. She had finished most of her lunch. I finished mine. I would say she was gone a good ten minutes. When she came out her color was not good. Her fine eyes were red-rimmed. She slipped meekly into her chair. She told the waitress she was finished. Just coffee, please.

"I'm sorry," she said to me. "I didn't expect that. It got a little too close. All of a sudden. I'm sorry, it was just a little too much like . . . another game I used to play. Don't look so concerned. It wasn't your fault."

"I won't try it again."

"That's probably better."

The coffee came. The silence was laborious. As we were getting ready to leave, she suddenly gave me a strained and vivid smile and reached a trembling hand across to touch my wrist and said, "Darling, did you remember to mail the cards to Mom and Sis?"

"I mailed them. Your mother got the one of the bucks with their horns locked."

She pursed her lips for a moment, and I knew she was thinking how to cue me so I could win. "I wonder if Mom will think there's some kind of symbolism there, dear, and get upset or anything."

"Baby, fighting over dough is the thing she does best."

She laughed. Acknowledgment of defeat. Bad jokes win. Her eyes glistened, but she laughed. I was proud of her for coming through, but I could not help feeling guilty too. She had her adjustment, her acceptance. It wasn't fair to stir her up. It wasn't fair to her for me to want to see her lift a bit, to see what she looked like behind the iron control. Two games had set a pattern. We were Myra and Frank. If I tried another round, she would feel obligated. So I would leave it up to her to start the next one. And she would know I was leaving it up to her and why. That was the funny thing about us, back in the beginning. I had the absolute confidence in her knowing what I was thinking.

We went north up Route 8 into the hills. We went through a village named Poland. It looked like a Christmas card. The roads were dry, the snow banked high. It was the sort of town that you do not particularly want to live in, but wish you had come from. It looked like a very good place to be from.

Farther up into the Adirondack Forest Preserve, the air was clearer and colder. The heater in the little sedan was comforting. Winding road, winter lakes, blackness of the evergreens against snow, tree-stubbed hills like the humpbacks of old browsing beasts, eating away at eternity. At least we had changed the quality of our silences. Or that lovely land had changed it.

Speculator, at almost four in the afternoon, was about the size of Poland, but with about one-fifth the charm. Progress had begun to clomp down its main drag, whanging at a tin drum, sending off little clusters of neon. The ski kids were roaming the area, hooting their rut cries at each other, speckling the snowbanks with their bright empty beer cans. I parked in front of a big supermarket-type general store called Chas Johns, where all the fluorescence was on in the gray dullness of the overcast afternoon, and Dana called from an outdoor phone booth. She was back in a few moments and said, "They say he went down to Gloversville to pick up a railway express shipment of skis or something, and they expect him back at six."

"So, accommodations, I guess. I want a chance to measure him a little, get the right time and place to break him open."

"Remember, he'll recognize me."

"I know. And I may need you for the finale, after he's gone soft. We'll see."

"It's strange. You make him sound like a locked box."

"That's what they are, Dana. And usually somebody skimped on the design. Bad welds and a dime-store lock."

There was a small and relatively new motel jammed into almost the center of town at a strange angle. I made a try. The gentleman in command said he had one twinbed room only because he had a cancellation, and he could let it go for one night only, because he was reserved from Thursday right through the weekend, and so was everybody else. It was good snow and a good forecast, and it looked like one of the big weeks of the season.

I went back out and got in behind the wheel and said, "Dana, I can't help how this sounds, believe me. It's a high-school routine all the way. You can go in and ask him." I told her what I'd learned, and said, "Suppose I take it and you drive back down to Utica and stay there and come on back out in the morning."

She hesitated for four seconds and then said, "If you'd just do something about that horrible snoring, see a doctor, anything, then we wouldn't have to go through this all the time."

"Myra, I freely admit I do breathe a little heavy."

"A little heavy! When you get going, the neighbors run out into the night screaming 'Lion, Lion.' "

"Only when I get over onto my back, dear."

"Then you have a back on both sides. Anyway, dear, I'll sleep so well in this mountain air, I don't think you'll bother me tonight. But do try to hold it down to a dull roar."

"You act as if I enjoyed it."

"Because, my pet, you *sound* as if you were enjoying it."

A car came in and I was afraid we would lose the room if we waited the game out, so I went in and signed us in as T. McGee and wife. The two three-quarter beds seemed to crowd the room. We did a lot of polite walking around each other, getting organized. An electric wall heater kept the room reasonably comfortable. With one quick trip to the ice machine, and with a considerable magic, she materialized a squat broad silver cup, the right amount of gin on ice, the two drops of bitters.

"The celebrity treatment?" I said ungraciously.

"I wouldn't want to get out of practice."

"Well . . . thanks. It's fine."

"You are so welcome, Travis."

We decided it would be best to leave her right there while I took the first little prod at Carl Abelle. The Mohawk Lodge was seven or eight miles out Indian Lake Road, over some impressively hilly highway. The grounds were aglare with floodlights against snow. The establishment was garishly new, pale varnished pine, A-frames, Swiss-kwaint gables. The sign advertised three tows, eight downhill runs, instruction, beginners' slope, Icelandic bathhouse, prime steaks, cocktails. The whole place was noisy, bursting at the seams, with much coming and going and giggling and hooting.

I worked my way into what seemed to be the main lounge. An ox could have been roasted on a spit in the fieldstone fireplace. The ceiling was low, beams huge. There were a lot of overstuffed couches and chairs, and deep rugs underfoot. There seemed to be a great number of young people sprawled on the floor. I saw several legs in casts, arms in slings. Sweating waiters brought drinks from a corner bar, stepping over and around the people, grimly ignoring the shouts for service. A big stereo juke made loud rock music, and some snow bunnies were energetically trying to revive the Twist, wearing their indoor-fireside-snuggle-pants rather than their outdoor togs.

I angled toward a waiter and stuffed a bill in his shirt pocket. It bought me four seconds of attention. "Carl Abelle," I asked.

He pointed with his head and said, "Red jacket."

Abelle was leaning against a paneled wall. He wore

a red blazer with an Olympic pocket patch, silver buttons, a white silk ascot. He stood with his head bowed, a dainty little snow bunny in each arm. One of them was talking directly into his ear. She writhed and she worked her face in the curious manner of many women telling a dirty joke. I held off until she had made her point. Silvery glissandos from the girls. A hohoho from Abelle. I moved in and the three of them looked up at me with the polite glaze the in-groupers give the outsider. I wasn't wearing the garments.

The girls looked very young, and the out-of-doors had given them both a lovely healthy flush. But their eyes looked wise and old. Carl looked magnificent. The bronzed blond hero, white of tooth, clear of eye. But somehow it all looked like makeup. And in spite of the tailoring, he seemed to be getting a little thick around the middle.

"Abelle?"

"Yesss?"

"I bring you a message from friends."

"Zo?"

"From Cass. From Vance and Patty. From Lee and Sonny and Whippy and Nancy and the whole gang."

"I know zose people?"

"Yes, you know zose people." I didn't say any more. I let him hang there. He added them up. He wasn't very good at it. His face got sulky and wary.

"Oho," he said. "Would you mean Miss Abbott? And the M'Gruders?"

"And the Cornell boys too."

"Giff them all my best regards, ya?"

"That wasn't exactly the message, Carl."

"Zo?"

"If we could take a two-minute walk."

He hugged the bunnies, whispered to them, sent them off toward the fireplace with an identical little stroke at each upholstered little behind.

"Now we can talk here, Mister . . .?"

"It's something in the car I want to show you."

"Bring it in."

"I'm sorry. I have to follow Miss Dean's instructions."

He gained a little confidence. "Zo, you work for her. A very lovely little lady, ya?"

"She sends her very special regards."

He puffed up nicely. But then he remembered the names I had given him. He was not intellectualizing anything. He merely had the animal's awareness of something not quite right. "What could that dear woman send me you could not bring in?"

I winked at him most solemnly. "Herself."

He puffed up and he glowed. "Of courze!" He nudged me. "I understand."

"She isn't exactly waiting out in the car, you understand. She's at a private lodge down by the lake. She heard you were here. She said it was a very pleasant surprise. She's staying with old friends. Incognito."

"She sent you to bring me there?"

"On impulse. You understand."

"Oh, of courze!"

"Shall we go?"

He nibbled at his mouth, an Airedale frown between the hero brows. "I must come back later. Social obligations here. But yes, it would be rude not to go at once."

We went out to the rental car. His red blazer was handsome in the floodlights, between the snowbanks. He strutted. There was a Teutonic wrinkle across the back of his neck. Maybe it had grown there in response to the faked accent. I had two inches in height, and he had at least fifteen pounds in weight. I couldn't risk taking any sporting chance with him. He might know how.

I hurried past him and opened the car door for him. He accepted it with regal satisfaction. As he started to bend to duck into the car, I screwed my feet firmly into the packed snow, pivoted very smartly and, with the best right hook I have, made a very good attempt to drive that middle silver button of the jacket right through to his backbone. These little melodramas always make me feel like a jackass. But you must do them briskly. A sudden, merciless, ugly violence is the great leveler. Men revert to childhood. The night is full of spooks and ghosties, and they are reminded of death. A man whipped in a fair fight retains stubborn remnants of pride and honor. A man rendered helpless without warning is much more suggestible. With a great gassy belch, he doubled. With hands clasped together, I chopped down against the back of his neck, off to one side, just below the mastoid bone. As he crumpled, I body-blocked him into the car, kicked his dangling legs inside and slammed the door. I imagine it took about three and a half seconds.

I got behind the wheel. He was edged partially under the dash. His relaxation was total. I could hear him snore. A few hundred yards down the highway I pulled over, hauled him onto the seat, removed his white silk scarf and tied his wrists together with it. I tied them together in crossed position, under his husky thighs. He toppled over against the door and moaned. Pathos in silver buttons. The world is shiny and the surface is a little too frangible. Something can reach out of the black and grab you at any moment. Everybody wears a different set of compulsions. You can be maimed without warning, in body or in spirit, by a very nice guy. It is the luck of your draw. I did not feel like a nice guy. His red coat was a little too brave and pretty. Now it was a child's toy on the beach after the child drowns. This one was not villainous. He was just a silly stud. A ski-slope, and less reptilian, version of Harry Diadem, a specialist in racing wax and erogenous zones.

I drove on down into Speculator, looking for a place to take him. The snowbanks made it difficult. I turned west on Route 8, and after about a mile I found a darkened structure on the right, some sort of building supply establishment. The drive and parking lot in the rear had been plowed out. Nearby houses were dark. I could see no pedestrians in the glow of the spaced streetlights of the village. No traffic was coming in either direction at the moment. So I turned in quickly, skidding the back end, bumping it off a snowbank, turning off the car lights as I reached the parking lot. I backed it around behind the building, ready to head out. I got out quickly, looking around to see if I had attracted any attention. Snow laid a silence across the land. A dog barked, a comfortable distance away. Night sky speckled with silver. Bare trees in silhouette. Moving flicker of light as cars went by. It was about 20 degrees, I guessed, not too uncomfortable with no wind.

I opened the door on his side. He was coming out of it enough to strain for balance, but he came rolling out, onto the packed soiled snow of the parking area. I bent, braced myself well and picked him up, the two hundred and twenty or so pounds of him, striving to make it seem effortless. The mature male is seldom picked up. It resonates the lost memories of babyhood. It induces a feeling of helplessness. I walked four strides with him and dropped him into the slope of the five-foot bank of bulldozed snow, dropped him butt first, as into an armchair. He chunked down into it, tilted slightly back, feet free, knees up, lashed wrists holding him hunched and about as helpless as a man can be.

He shook his splendid leonine head slowly and said, "Sick. Real sick. Please."

When anything begins to fit their television or movie preconceptions they try to move toward the hero role. So one must give it a flavor they can't comprehend. Cops are good at it. Jocular. You can learn a lot from cop technique.

I stood close and reached to him and rumpled his blond locks with the casual affection you extend toward a small boy. I chuckled. I patted his cheek three times, and on the fourth pat I gave it a little more steam. It was not a blow, yet not a pat. It was a sharp demand for attention. Pay attention to teacher, boy.

My eyes had adjusted. I could see him clearly. Things had moved too quickly for him. He was staring at me with a dumb willingness to ingratiate himself. It was exactly the right attitude. It was a cheap tin box and a joke lock, and it had opened at a touch.

"Carl, baby, Lee is over a thousand miles from here, and she wouldn't say hello if she met you on the street."

"What are you . . .?"

"She's a big investment. The people I work for get very nervous about her. You can understand that, Carl, baby."

"I don't know what you . . ."

"They are very very annoyed with you, sweetie. You've been very stupid and very naughty. And you've gotten their investment very upset. You shouldn't have played ball with the people who wanted to give Lee a hard time. You should have realized we'd come after you sooner or later, baby."

"This is some kind of a mis . . ."

"Don't play dumb. It's too late for that. You have had it. They don't give me much discretion. At the very least, Carl, I have to break you up a little. Like two or three weeks' worth. And at the very most, I get my little shovel out of the truck and stick you under this snow."

The bulge of his eyes tipped me, so when the mouth opened wide for a roar of terror and protest, I packed it swiftly with a handful of snow. After he had coughed and huffed and spat, I used a handkerchief to wipe the snow water off his face. His teeth clittered. He was melting himself wet, but it was fright and cold both.

"Please!" he said. "I don't know what . . ."

I rumpled his hair again. "The *pictures*, sweetie! The photographs, the pics, the way she got set up for it on that terrace. Like this one."

I had it in an inside pocket, folded once. I held it in front of his eyes, a lighter flame off to one side. A Lysa Dean sandwich. I put it away when he closed his eyes.

"Oh," he said weakly. "Oh, God."

I said softly, "Now can you tell me a *good* reason why you shouldn't die young, sweetie?"

Seven

I GOT BACK to the motel room a few minutes before nine. The door was unlocked. As I came in, Dana got up from the room's only armchair and came toward me, silhouetted against the lamplight.

"You were gone so long," she said.

The room was warm. I took my jacket off and stretched out on one of the beds. "A long time and a long way away," I said. "Scratch one ski instructor. We can leave now, if you want."

She looked down at me for a few moments, and then went and fixed another drink in that silver cup. I perched on one elbow and sipped it. "A lot bigger than the last one," I said.

"It seemed like a good idea."

"You've got good instincts." She sat on the foot of the bed. I shifted my feet to make room for her.

"Did . . . you hurt him?"

"I didn't leave a mark on him. I just finished sneaking him to his room up there at the lodge. He didn't want anybody to see him. His legs didn't work very well. I had to help him out of the car. I had to walk him, with my arm around his waist. He was crying like a kid. He had the snuffles. He kept telling me how grateful he was

I didn't kill him. He likes me. It's a quick dependency relationship, something like getting emotionally hooked on your psychiatrist. At his door I patted him on the shoulder and told him to get a good night's rest. No, Dana, I didn't leave any visible marks. But I left the other kind. They last longer."

After a silence she said, "Trav, why do you do this sort of thing if it bothers you so much?"

"Maybe I like it. Maybe that's what bothers me."

"Look at me and tell me you like it."

"Okay. So it was just smart-ass talk. I left him with less. Less assurance, less faith, less confidence. Maybe his mask will start to slip a little from now on. The tone of voice won't be exactly right. The snow bunnies will detect it. And one of them will be a little too knowing, and push the right buttons, and big Carl Abelle will come up impotent just once. Once is all it will take, because that's about all he's got left."

She put her hand on my ankle, a light quick touch, like a pat of assurance. "Travis, if you can feel this way, and keep on feeling this way, isn't it all right for you? What if you should become indifferent to . . . this business of opening people up like little dirty boxes?"

"Maybe I care less now than I did a few years back."

"Is Abelle so valuable?"

"Isn't that the key to it, Dana? This act of judging the value of anyone? Is it something I am entitled to do for money? If we're judging value, why am I working for your boss?"

"Why am I?" We watched each other. Suddenly she grinned. "Don't try to fool me or yourself, McGee. If you'd learned anything important from him, you wouldn't be acting like this."

I admitted it. She fixed me a new drink. I told her

what I had learned. Not very much. He was certain of one thing. No one had followed Lysa Dean to the Chipmann house. None of the playmates could have tipped anybody off that she was there, because he had not said who he was shacked with, and after they all got there, no one left until it was all over, and the phone was disconnected. Cass was Caswell Edgars, a San Francisco artist. Abelle had not known that Nancy Abbott had gone off with Sonny Catton, nor that Sonny was dead. He had confirmed that Nancy had been houseguesting with the M'Gruders in Carmel, and had said that Vance M'Gruder was a friend of Alex Abbott, Nancy's elder brother.

"Nothing else?" she asked.

"Just guesses. But how good are they? A terrorized man tries to please, like a hypnotic subject. Rule out the Cornell boys. Rule out Cass Edgars and the waitress. And, according to Abelle, we can rule out Lysa Dean too. Security was good. So who was the target? Nancy Abbott? Vance M'Gruder? Patty M'Gruder? There's money there. Blackmail targets. Miss Dean was pure profit. The pictures sent Nancy's father were not the same as the ones sent Lee. Okay, so the fellow took perhaps a dozen rolls. Two dozen. Two hundred and fifty to five hundred shots. He could have another set to sell Vance, another to sell Patty, maybe a set for everybody until he could find out which ones had the money. Maybe he started out, for God's sake, after nesting water birds and hit a jackpot on the terrace a hundred yards away."

"But the idea of it being an accident doesn't appeal?"

"No. Before they bought the groceries, they all knew the name of the absentee owners of the house where they were going. If it was set up, either somebody in the group, during the milling around before they took off in the cars, tipped the cameraman off, or they were being followed. Somehow I like the first choice, Dana. It goes with the way the party developed, as if it was being staged that way."

"Could he tell you who started it?"

"He said it just happened. Everybody tight. One of those real swinging parlor games, revised for a sun terrace. Somebody gets blindfolded, crawls around, and the first person they touch has to hold still, not make a sound, and be identified by touch. Guess right and the one identified loses one item they're wearing, and gets the blindfold. Guess wrong and the guesser loses one item and tries again."

"Sounds gaudy."

"He said nobody really started it. They made up the rules as they went along."

"With much jolly laughter."

"It's a funny thing about Abelle. He had absolutely no idea any pictures were taken. But he did have the feeling that something was wrong. And he is not a sensitive guy. He couldn't put it into words. After the group had broken up and he was alone again with Lee, he had the feeling that something was going to work out badly for somebody."

"Wouldn't anyone have that feeling after all that?"

"If it was new to them, I guess so. But Abelle has had that kind of group action before and since, and the other times didn't hit him that way. *Something* gave him that feeling. *Somebody* made him react that way. But he was drunk. I couldn't dig it out. He had the feeling somebody was going to kill somebody sooner or later, because of that house party."

"Where do we go next, Travis?"

"I want to know how Nancy Abbott's father got her pictures, and if there was any more contact."

I put the silver cup aside. It seemed that moments later Dana was gently shaking me awake. There was a delicious aroma in the room. She had walked to a place almost next door called the Log Cabin Restaurant, eaten there and brought me back a huge bowl of homemade clam chowder and a broiled hamburger as thick as her wrist. It tasted as fine as it smelled.

I awoke again. The room was dark. My shoes were off. There was a blanket over me, but the cold had awakened me. A glow of the sign outside came through the blinds, and I could see the sleeping shape of her in the other bed, hair dark against the pillow. I made a silent trip to the bathroom, came back and undressed to my shorts and slipped into the cool sheets and was asleep in an instant. You can seldom guess what will exhaust you emotionally. That hulk of brave muscle had been a weak and pretentious child. In my dreams I heard him sob. Oh, please don't. Oh, please. Oh, please, mister.

She had flight schedules indicating we could do better out of Syracuse. So we got an early start and went down to the Thruway and west to the Syracuse airport, through a cold gray morning and some tentative snow flurries. She found the best way out, through to Chicago and then nonstop to San Francisco. I noticed something about her, in the ticketing and the baggage arrangements and turning in the rental car, and even with the stewardesses. With absolutely no fuss at all, she got the maximum service merely by an attitude—smiling and polite—which seemed to make anything less than perfect service unthinkable. She could raise one eyebrow and bring a porter hustling from eighty feet away. It is a rare gift. I tried to take over some of the chores, but it seemed to make her feel uncomfortable. It was her job and she was used to it, and she knew how to keep everything straight. I had all the benefit of her efficiency. People stared at me as though trying to remember where they had seen me. This knack of getting exactly what you want exactly when you want it is something shared by great ladies, royalty and the very best executive secretaries. Also I must admit that her strong and handsome face and the sparkling intensity of her dark eyes gave the impression that if things did not go her way, all hell would break loose immediately. But it was odd to have someone else taking such efficient care. I began to feel a little like the honeymoon bride of an important widower. Or a boy being taken to camp by one of those supermothers.

She tried to resist being given a window seat. After we'd latched the seat belts, she checked her little notebook and said, "We'll have an hour and fifty minutes in Chicago. I'll make some phone calls from there. Are you perfectly comfortable, Travis? Is there anything you'd like?"

"You'd better hustle up forward and help them with the checklist for takeoff, honey."

Her mouth tightened and her face got slightly red. "I'm not trying to be officious."

"You are a little overwhelming, Dana."

"You could do it all just as well. But why should you?"

"Okay. Thanks. You're very good."

It was not gracious. Most of my women have not been particularly useful outside the home. I looked at her emotionless profile and sighed and said, "Aw, come *on,* Myra."

Reluctantly her mouth softened. "You get these ugly moods, Frank."

"I keep worrying about how things are going back

at the office."

"Honey, I bet they hardly know you're gone."

"Oh, thanks. Thanks a lot. That's a big help." She was laughing with me. Her eyes laughed too. It went deep. That kind of affection is seriously underrated among the hack and grab set. To whom should they give trust? To someone who likes them. When she laughed or smiled broadly I could see that one of the eyeteeth, the one on the left, was set in there aslant, making a little overlap with the tooth in front of it. When an imperfection looks very dear to you, heed the message. Lysa Dean's teeth were mercilessly perfect. No message there. Maybe some of my awareness made a little mark. Dana Holtzer suddenly stopped the real laughter, and went along for a little while on some fake laughter, and then folded herself back into herself, out of sight and out of reach, becoming once again the secretarial presence beside me, smart in wool, laced, girdled, hammocked and erect, her neck severe, eyes distant, seat belt pulled tight for take-off.

Alexander Armitage Abbott, A.I.A., lay dying in room 310 of University Hospital in San Francisco. There was a waiting room at the end of the corridor. A gray rain which was going to continue forever streaked the waiting room windows, obscuring the view of gray hills. It was Friday afternoon. Dana and I sat like dulled passengers in a heavy train sidetracked at the end of noplace. She put a frayed magazine back in the rack and came over to sit beside me on the couch.

"You're doing fine," I told her.

"I don't like that young man. Or his wife."

"It shows a little. It doesn't hurt anything. They're not anxious to be liked."

The young man came back. Not as young as he looked, or perhaps tried to look. Nancy's brother. Alex. Meaty, dark, bland. The kind who have a smell of pine and a perfect manicure. He gave us a smile of measured sadness and sat facing us. "Sorry about the constant interruptions. You know how it is." He shrugged. "One or the other of us should be with him. It seems to help him a little. Elaine is being so good about it. You have no idea."

"I guess he wouldn't want to see Nancy," Dana said innocently.

"God, no!" Alex said. "I believe, I really believe that he might have lived years longer if it wasn't . . . for all the shame and heartbreak she's given him. She's my only sister. But I can't be the least bit sentimental. Some people are just born rotten." He made a helpless gesture. "Nothing we've tried to do for her has done any good. She's made life difficult . . . for all of us."

"You understand our viewpoint in this, Mr. Abbott," I said.

"Of course. Of course. I appreciate the fact you want to handle this on a completely informal basis. I think I understand her present condition, as well as Mr. Burley's concern. And I am perfectly willing to write to him personally guaranteeing the thousand dollars a month for as long as . . . as she can remain there. Frankly, I was responsible for the selection of the retreat. I wanted her just as far from San Francisco as possible. Dad is leaving her nothing, of course. But I can tell you in confidence that the estate is . . . sizable. And I would consider it a moral obligation. I'm very glad you and Miss Holtzer had to come here on another matter. It's good to talk this over."

I sensed that he was trying to brush us off. Thanks and good-by. He was an elusive fellow. "We haven't settled it yet, Mr. Abbott," I told him. "Mr. Burley has certain moral obligations too, and he is aware of them. He is not set up to give her the mental care she needs. Under the present arrangement, he can't afford to bring someone there at regular intervals to treat her there. We are functioning here merely as . . . friends of Hope Island, Mr. Abbott."

"I understand, but . . ."

"If the monthly fee could be doubled . . ."

"That's out of the question," he said with a regretful air. "I guess it would be better if Mr. Burley did arrange commitment to a mental institution, if that's what he thinks she needs."

"There's just one small problem," I said. "At times she seems perfectly healthy and rational. And she has built up a whole structure of conspiracy. We understand that it isn't true, of course, but it does sound very plausible, and if she went to some other place, they might think it necessary to make a complete investigation."

"I don't believe I understand," he said.

I glanced at Dana and nodded and she took over. "Nancy insists that a year and a half ago you put her in the custody of some people in Carmel named M'Gruder."

"In the custody!" he said indignantly. "It wasn't like that at all. They were just helping me out. They knew Nancy, of course. They knew she could be a problem. It was just a case of getting her away from a very unsavory group she was running with, and . . ."

"I am just telling you Nancy's story. We all know she isn't well, Mr. Abbott. She claims that the M'Gruders, as a favor to you, got her drunk and got her into a situation where certain pictures were taken of her under compromising circumstances. These pictures were then sent to your father so you could be certain you would be the sole heir. She claims you and your father then tried to put her away, but she fled and remained at large for quite a while until you caught up to her and sent her to Hope Island."

Dana did beautifully with it. I watched his face. He had a big choice of reactions. He tried for amused indignation, and almost made it. But not quite. You have to watch for the not quites.

"Do you mean to tell me she could make anyone believe such nonsense?"

"Not necessarily," I said. "They might want to check it out."

"But why?"

I nodded to Dana. She took the picture from her big purse. I slipped it out of the envelope and leaned and handed it to Alex Abbott. He held it in two trembling hands and stared at it. He swallowed convulsively. In a small voice he said, "This one wasn't . . ." He caught himself. "She had this? My sister had this?"

"This is one of several. Mr. Burley has them in his safe."

"But where would she get them? She didn't have them when she was taken down there."

"They came to her in the mail," I said. "Mr. Abbott, what was it you started to say? This one wasn't . . . This one wasn't what?"

He opened his eyes very wide. He smiled sadly. "I guess I should be frank with you people."

"We would be most grateful," Dana said.

"I will admit that I made a mistake when I . . . arranged her visit with the M'Gruders. I knew them as a lively couple. I thought they would keep her amused and out of trouble. I had no idea they went in for this sort of thing." He handed it back to me.

"I would think you would act a little more angry," I said.

"To tell you the truth, there were other pictures of Nancy. They were mailed to my father, with a note demanding money. He had a very nasty scene with Nancy. She left. He showed me the pictures. He was wretched. Heartbroken. He asked me to destroy the pictures and I did so, very gladly. Several days later, after Nancy was gone, someone phoned my father about the money. He told them to go to hell, that they could do any damn thing with the pictures they pleased."

"He didn't contact the police?"

"No."

"Did the man on the phone threaten him with anything?"

"No. Dad said the man was quite polite. He seemed to have some sort of lower-class English accent. He said he might phone back later on, but as far as I know he never did. In one of the pictures it was . . . well, it was Vance M'Gruder and my sister. I can tell you that I was furious with him. I went down to see him. He was alone at the house. Patty had left him. I learned later their marriage was being annulled. He didn't seem guilty or ashamed or anything like that. Just terribly indifferent. I couldn't make a dent on him. He said he was not and had never been in the nursemaid business, no matter what impression I may have had. He did not know or care where Nancy was. I actually thought I might find her there with them. I wanted to know who had taken the pictures at that . . . circus."

"Did he know?"

"He said that nobody at the party had taken them. He said it had to be someone with a long lens."

"Did he seem surprised to know pictures had been taken?"

"No. I wondered if he'd been approached for money also."

"Did you ask him?"

"No. He seemed cross and impatient and anxious for me to go."

"Did you know any of the other people in the pictures you saw?"

"Aside from the M'Gruders, just one fellow, an artist I—." He stopped suddenly, frowning at us. "Why are you so curious about the pictures, Mr. McGee?"

I shrugged. "I guess it's only natural. Mr. Burley was curious too. They do have some bearing on the girl's evaluation of herself. I suppose if she feels it was a conspiracy, a trick, she feels better about it."

"Mr. McGee, if Nancy ever had any hopes of inheriting half the estate, she spoiled her chances long before those pictures were taken, believe me. Naturally I'll support her as long as she lives. But what you ask seems . . ."

"Oh, I don't think she could cause you much trouble, Mr. Abbott."

"I don't see how she could cause any."

I smiled and shrugged. "An institution might call in somebody to give her legal advice. You know how it is. Contingency basis. And you say the estate is sizable. She does sound plausible. All it could do, I guess, would be delay the probate."

He studied his thumbnail. He bit a small piece out of the corner of it and got up and went to the steel window and teetered back and forth, heel to toe.

"You say she seems happy there at the island?"

"She has friends there. And the illusion of freedom."

108

Without turning, he said, "And this deterioration you mention. It is progressive?"

"From all indications."

"I imagine that if I footed the bill for additional care for . . . say another six months, by the end of that time she . . ."

"Let's say eighteen months."

"I'll take my chances on a year. No more."

"I will so inform Mr. Burley."

He looked at his watch. "Elaine gets nervous if I leave her in there too long. Uh . . . thanks for the report. Good-by." He walked out without looking directly at either of us.

On the way down in the elevator, Dana looked at me and slowly shook her head. "You are very damn good, Trav. You are better than I realized. You are shameless. You are a bastard, Trav. You know very damn well he thinks you are going to split the increase with Mr. Burley. He thinks you are going to bring suit in her name if he doesn't play. And you sat there, so righteous and kindly. Oh boy, oh boy."

"A man like that can't believe anything that doesn't sound crooked."

"A man like that makes me want to go scrub. They better not leave him alone with dear Dad. He's impatient."

Before I started the car I turned to her and said, "Itemize."

"What? Oh. He didn't have the pictures taken. The man who took them or had them taken has a cheap British accent. M'Gruder knew about the pictures. And something else. Let me think. Oh, the M'Gruder marriage was annulled. Did I miss anything?"

"You are very good too."

"I am afflicted with an orderly mind."

And so we drove back to the heart of the city. San Francisco is the most depressing city in America. The come-latelys might not think so. They may be enchanted by the steep streets up Nob and Russian and Telegraph, by the sea mystery of the Bridge over to redwood country on a foggy night, by the urban compartmentalization of Chinese, Spanish, Greek, Japanese, by the smartness of the women and the city's iron clutch on culture. It might look just fine to the new ones.

But there are too many of us who used to love her. She was like a wild classy kook of a gal, one of those rain-walkers, laughing gray eyes, tousle of dark hair—sea misty, a lithe and lively lady, who could laugh at you or with you, and at herself when needs be. A sayer of strange and lovely things. A girl to be in love with, with love like a heady magic.

But she had lost it, boy. She used to give it away, and now she sells it to the tourists. She imitates herself. Her figure has thickened. The things she says now are mechanical and memorized. She overcharges for cynical services.

Maybe if you are from Dayton or Amarillo or Wheeling or Scranton or Camden she can look like magic to you because you have not had a chance to see what a city can be. This one had her chance to go straight and she lost it somehow, and it has been downhill for her ever since. That's why she is so depressing to those of us who knew her when. We all know what she could have been, and we all know the lousy choice she made. She has driven away the ones who loved her best. A few keep trying. Herb Caen. A few others. But the love words have a hollow tone these days.

Eight

INVESTIGATING A COLD COLD TRAIL can be deadly dull and very discouraging. This one worked pretty well, perhaps because there were two of us, two sets of hunches, two sets of ideas, two methods of approach.

We found Caswell Edgars in Sausalito. He looked twenty pounds heavier than in the pictures. He was living in a pigpen litter in the expensive home of a skinny driftwood blonde on the far side of fifty. She was there too, in extremely tight pants and a high girlish giggle. Any minute now Cassie was going to start working hard getting ready for a one-man show she was going to arrange for him. They had a music system that would have blown the walls out of a less substantial structure. She had soiled ankles, a grubby neck, and a black eye which had faded to saffron. They were hooked on something. From the way they acted, I suspect one of the hypnotics. The house smelled like old laundry. There was a loose and dangerous and desperate flavor about the alliance, and it was easy to imagine that in their blundering they would sooner or later manage to set fire to the place and scream with laughter until they found all exits blocked. She kept talking about poor little ole Henry, who seemed to be a husband, but I could not determine if he was living or dead. If dead, it was conceivable he was buried in the yard, under the weeds. Edgars knew absolutely nothing about any pictures. But he had no difficulty remembering the occasion. He had musician talk which he didn't do too well. "Man, that was a bash. That little movie piece was pure stone fox. The boss fox of all time. Somebody trying to scuffle her with the pics? You never said, man."

"No. I never said."

"Sonny traded the waitress for the tall brunette, and then he burned. It's a harsh way to make bread, man, that chance of burning. I read it someplace."

"Put on my records, Cassie doll baby bug, huh?"

I don't think either of them noticed we'd left, or cared particularly. Though it was warm in the car, Dana shuddered.

"Scratch one more contestant, Dana doll baby bug."

"Please don't," she said in a thin voice.

"Like they say, lives of quiet desperation."

"Trav?"

"Yes?"

"I think that terrace was a damned unlucky place to be. Sonny Catton, Nancy Abbott, Carl Abelle . . . and Caswell Edgars."

"Punishment from on high?"

"I don't know. Maybe. Maybe it can happen, Trav."

She took care of Carmel with some phone calls. The M'Gruder place had been sold almost a year ago. We had less luck with newspaper accounts. I did dig up some background on M'Gruder. There had been an elder brother, killed in a war. M'Gruder's father had invented a little gadget. Every cracking plant in the world had to have one or two of them. Vance M'Gruder had married one Patricia Gedley-Davies some three years ago in California, after apparently importing her from London. She had crewed for him in smaller sailboats. There was no social prominence, nor any attempt apparently to achieve any. But there was money, and so one would think the annulment would be more than a six-line paragraph on page 36. It had happened about two months after the house party.

Dana Holtzer sat in my hotel room with her shoes off and her feet up, frowning thoughtfully after having made a Sunday afternoon call to Lysa Dean.

"This annulment thing," she said. "What you think of, in a state with a community property law, it's the cheap way out."

"Yes, indeed."

"And this was a closed session or closed hearing or whatever you call it, just the judge and them and a lawyer, and everybody agreeing to everything, and a declaration by the judge that the marriage had never existed in fact or something. And this wasn't a humble woman, Trav. Sort of noisy and bossy. Let's say she came from nothing, and she married a rich man. Would she give up without a battle? What made her give up without a battle?"

"And where is she?"

We couldn't answer our questions, but we could look for answers. I decided we would split up on Monday, to save time. I would pursue a small idea of my own. She would use Lloyd's Register as her guidebook and work the boaty people, the ocean-sailing types, with appropriate cover story, and see what she could get in the way of gossip.

It rained all day, matching the mood of the offices I visited. Investigation agencies have very little need for decor. They like to keep the overhead down. Their usual customer does not shop around, looking for better draperies. Most of them are sad, soft, pale, meaty people. They operate with about the same verve as the people who come to spray your home with bug juice.

I had my lines down pat by the time I hit the third one. My name was Jones, said with that emphasis which indicated it was anything but Jones. My employment was "managing my own investment program." That brought a little flicker into tired eyes. My young Italian wife was playing around. I was positive of two men. Perhaps there were three. I wanted somebody who could get some flagrant pictures of her, very quietly and inconspicuously, without her knowing. Then, with the pictures in hand, I could dicker with her and get out of the marriage without too much expense.

No, sir, we don't do that kind of thing.

Who does? Where should I go?

I just wouldn't know, mister.

At four o'clock I hit one who was sufficiently unsavory and hungry. He had the cop look. Not the good cop look, but the apple-stealing look. It was a very good guess that he had been busted for the wrong combination of greed and stupidity, and that he wasn't going to do too well in this line of work either. He had a desk in one of those warehouse offices, the kind where you get the desk, the mail drop, switchboard service and an hourly rate on secretarial help—along with a ragtag collection of phone solicitors, speculators in distressed merchandise, independent jewelry salesmen and so on.

He listened to my story and looked at me with the concealed anguish of a toothless crocodile inspecting a fat brown dog on the riverbank. He wanted to know how to get at me. We hitched chairs close and hunched toward

114

each other. He had that breath which exceptionally bad teeth can create.

"Now, Mr. Jones, maybe I can help and maybe I can't. A thing like this, it would be strictly a cash arrangement. You unnerstand?"

"Of course."

"Now I've got a guy in mind. He's tops. What he goes after, he gets. But he comes high."

"How high?"

"Considering the risks and all I would say this guy couldn't be touched for less than five thousand, but he's a real pro, and he will come up with shots of that little two-timing wop that'll nail her but good. This guy, he's got all the techniques and equipment, but he's funny. He doesn't feel like working, he doesn't work."

"I never heard of such a thing."

"Like an artist, like, he's got temperamental, you know?"

"I guess I know what you mean."

"What would happen, he would work through me. Now I don't want to be wasting my time trying to talk him into anything. What I need, I need a guarantee of good faith on your part, I mean that you want to go ahead at least far enough to take care of the first part of the trouble I'm going to, namely trying to get him on the phone long distance."

I took my wallet out below the desk edge, took a hundred-dollar bill and put it near his elbow. "Is this okay?"

A big paw fell on it and it was gone. With the back of the other paw he wiped his mouth. "Just fine. Now you go wait out in the hall. There's a bench out there to sit on."

I sat for nearly fifteen minutes. Odd-looking people

came and went, tenants and clients and customers. Underside people. The ones that somehow seem to be clinging to the damp underside of reality. The ones that look as if they could truly astonish a psychiatrist or a bacteriologist.

He came out and hunkered in close beside me, to rot my collar with his foul exhalations. "What happened, I can't get him, but the way it looks I got some leads, there's somebody can do a nice job, give me a little time on it."

"Why can't you get the man you were talking about?"

"He's been dead a while. I didn't know that. I didn't hear about it, the ways things are, him out of town."

"What was his name?"

"There are guys around just as good. What I want, you give me how I can get in touch with you, and when I get a good man lined up, one I can guarantee will do this little job, then—"

"I'll give you a ring in a few days."

"On account of I got to do some digging to find the exact right guy for your problem, what about you give me the same figure again as a retainer?"

"We better talk about that if you can find anybody."

After a few more halfhearted attempts, he went shuffling back into his rental bull pen, pants droopy in the seat, hair grizzled gray on the nape of his thick neck.

I made it to the nearest rancid saloon in about eight big bounds, shut myself into a phone booth and called back. I had remembered the name of the switchboard girl on duty. It was posted on her board.

"Miss Ganz, this is Sergeant Zimmerman. Bunco Squad. Within the past twenty minutes you placed a long-distance call for Gannon."

"Who? What?"

"Please give me the name, number and location of the call he placed."

"But I'm not supposed to . . ."

"I can send for you, Miss Ganz, and have you brought down here if you want it that way."

"Did . . . did you say Zimmerman?"

"If you want to play it safe, Miss Ganz, call me back here at headquarters. We have a separate number." I gave her the pay phone number. She had been starting to cool off, and I had to take the chance or get nothing.

In thirty seconds the phone rang. I put my thumb in the side of my mouth, raised my tone level a half octave and said, "Bunco, Halpern."

"Sergeant Zimmerman, please."

"Just a minute." After a ten count, I said, "Zimmerman."

"This is Miss Ganz," she said briskly. "About what you wanted, the call was to a Mr. D. C. Ives, in Santa Rosita. Eight-oh-five, seven-six-five, four-four-three-four. That number had been disconnected. Then he called a Mr. Mendez in Santa Rosita, eight-oh-five, three-eight-four, seven-nine-four-two. They talked for less than three minutes. Is that what you wanted, Sergeant?"

"Thank you very much for your cooperation, Miss Ganz. We'll protect our source in this matter. We may have to ask you for some other favor along the same line in the future."

"You're very welcome," she said.

A nice efficient careful girl. She had to make certain she was really talking to the cops.

Dana got back to the hotel a little after six. She looked pallid and twitchy. Her smile came and went too quickly. She had called me as soon as she got in, and I went down the hallway to her room. A woman in that condition needs to be hugged and held and patted a little. But we weren't on any kind of basis where I could do that.

I lit her trembling cigarette and then she switched around the room and said, "I am now a real drinking buddy of Mrs. T. Madison Devlaney III. I call her Squeakie, as does practically everyone. I poured drinks into her potted plants. Until she passed out. She is twenty-nine. She is two days younger than Vance M'Gruder. She has known him all her life. She has a teeny little voice, ten thousand freckles, ten million dollars, and she's muscled like a circus girl. Swimming every morning, tennis every afternoon, potted every night. No tennis today. Strained ankle."

"What cover story did she buy?"

"Trav, don't be angry, but I couldn't have gotten to her at all without using the best connection I have. Lysa Dean. That opens a lot of doors. And I do have those calling cards."

"I didn't say you shouldn't. I just said don't use her if you don't have to."

"I had to. I told her that Lysa had met Vance. I told her that Lysa was forming a little production company of her own and, as a first picture, was thinking of basing it on one of the ocean races, perhaps the race to Hawaii, and she was asking me to find out just how much cooperation she could get from the people who do own the big boats. It's nonsense, of course, but people know so little about the industry they're ready to believe anything. I made up sort of a plot as I went along."

"So she bought it. That's the important thing. What about M'Gruder?"

"Let me see. Oh, lots of things about M'Gruder. He is a physical fitness nut. He is a fine deep-water sailor. He is fantastically stingy. He gets quarrelsome and violent when he gets drunk. The marriage to Patricia Gedley-Davies was, according to his friends, a grotesque mistake. She said that forty-two times at least. Grotesque mistake. Squeakie and her friends are convinced Patty was a London call girl. I wouldn't say that anyone is particularly fond of Vance, but they are glad to see that marriage ended. They think it was bad form. And so lucky there were no children." She took out her little notebook. "The new wife is supposed to be enchanting. Her name is Ulka Atlund. She turned eighteen a few days before their marriage. Her mother is dead. Her father brought her over here two years ago. He came to lecture for a year at the University of San Francisco and stayed for a second year. He opposed the marriage, then agreed on the basis that, after the honeymoon, she continues her education. They plan to honeymoon for six months. They've been gone two months. Squeakie thinks she heard somewhere that Vance plans to have somebody else bring the boat back from Acapulco. Too much beating into the wind on the way back. She thinks Vance planned to spend that last two months of the honeymoon in his house at Hawaii. Then back to live here while Ulka goes back to college."

"What about the annulment?"

"This is where it gets pretty untidy, Travis."

I got tired of the way she was roving around. I got her wrists and pushed her gently back until the backs of her legs hit the edge of a chair. She sat down and looked up at me, startled.

"Let me tell you something, Miss Holtzer. This whole deal is untidy. The stupendous glamor of Lysa Dean did not suck me into this. You were the item that swayed me."

"What? What?"

"If she'd sent anyone else, the answer would have been no. You looked so staunch and loyal and unyielding and severe. So damned *decent*. You made me feel like an unwashed opportunist. I have emotional reactions to people, Dana, no matter how much I try to deny it. I wanted to prove to you that I am good at what I do."

"But that's absurd!"

I backed away and sat on her bed. "It certainly is. Now, how untidy does this situation get?"

She shrugged. "Squeakie doesn't know for sure. Just second-hand and third-hand gossip. But Nancy Abbott came into it. Apparently, among Squeakie's set, the favorite theory is that Patty M'Gruder had Nancy as a house guest in Carmel, and practically held her a prisoner there, because she . . . Patty . . . had fallen in love with Nancy. The theory is that Vance went along with it because it gave him a chance to get the proof he wanted that Patty had entered into the marriage contract under false pretenses, concealing her real inclinations. Vance used Nancy—Squeakie kept calling her 'that poor poor sick child'—to get the proof, and once he had it, there was no way in the world for Patty to fight his action to annul. It was all handled very quietly."

"That would explain what Nancy yelled at me, about Patty keeping her locked up."

"I suppose so. Patty left. Squeakie's phrase for it was that she slunk away. Somebody saw her several weeks ago, in Las Vegas. Not in one of the big places out on the Strip. Down in town, working at something called the Four Treys. Making change, I think. Some kind of a small job. There certainly wouldn't be many old friends seeing her there. Anyway, Mrs. T. Madison Devlaney didn't know anything about . . . or at least say anything about any pictures. I was lucky to catch her. She and her husband and another couple are flying to Hawaii this week. That whole group seems to be very big for Hawaii. The Devlaneys keep a boat out there."

"You did very well, Dana."

"Thank you. They have a beautiful home. She really got terribly drunk. Did you learn anything at all?"

"I don't know. I traced a man who could have taken the pictures. But he lived three hundred miles away. It looks as if M'Gruder had the pictures taken. I think we can assume that, at least for now. But I can't prove any contact between M'Gruder and the photographer. One thing makes me think I located the right man. He's dead."

"I beg your pardon?"

"Let's say that just for kicks or souvenirs or something he kept one set of prints for himself. He died. Those files got into the hands of somebody who . . ."

"Of course."

"His name was D. C. Ives, possibly. And he lived in Santa Rosita, possibly. We check him out for a vulgar limey accent, and if so it will look a lot more certain."

"Is that what we do next?"

"With one stop on the way, I think."

Nine

ON A BRIGHT CLEAR COLD Tuesday morning, I climbed the back slope of the ridge. Surf tumbled in, making a continuous roar against the rock. I reached and grasped the small trunk of a wind-dwarfed tree and pulled myself up to where I could look over the top. In my surprise I nearly ducked back out of sight. I had not expected the Chipmann sun deck to be so close. I looked down into it at about a thirty-degree angle. Perhaps that made it seem closer. But it was, I judged, three hundred feet away. It was a special irony that there should be a nude woman on the sun terrace. She was prone on a faded blue sun pad. The wall shielded her from some of the west wind, and she had set up an additional wind screen, one of those made of a shining metal to intensify the heat of the sun. She was of heroic dimensions, a redoubtable female, body brown as coffee beans, hair bleached to hemp, thighs like beer kegs, shoulders like Marshall Dillon. I assumed she had to be Mrs. Chipmann, the dear friend who loaned Carl their house for celebrity assignation. It seemed odd to see the sun terrace in such vivid colors after seeing it so many times in black and white. Her face was turned toward me. She wore sunglasses. There was a half glass of tomato juice on the cement next to the sun pad.

There was absolutely no other place from which the terrace could be watched. She had every reason to think herself unobserved. I eased back, out of sight, and turned and looked down. I could see part of the rear end of our pale gray Avis car parked in the cut where I had left it. I looked around at the immediate area. It was nonsensical to expect to find anything, after a year and a half. But find something I did. It was tucked down into a cleft of stone as if someone had wadded it and wedged it there, a small crumpled cardboard container, once yellow, now bleached pulpy white by sun and rain and weather. I could make out ghost writing on it, white on white. Kodak—Plus-X Pan.

I took it down with me and handed it to Dana as I got behind the wheel. She frowned at it, then saw what it was. She looked at me with a strange expression. "Why should this make it more real? God, could anything be more real than those pictures? But this is . . . like archeology, sort of. It's more . . . first hand."

"Don't get hooked on the feeling, Dana. Investigation can be a disease."

"It's a spooky feeling. I don't like it. It's unfair in a way, Travis. People get so exposed. It dwarfs people, doesn't it? By dwarfing them, it makes you feel bigger. Is that the fascination?"

"I don't know."

"But it *does* fulfill you in some way, doesn't it?"

"Let's drop it, shall we?"

"I'm sorry. I didn't realize it was a sore . . ."

"Shall we?"

"All right!"

I drove swiftly southward with the sulks and with a silent woman. Ever since the popularization of the Freud-Fraud, we are all addicted to fingering ourselves to see where it hurts, Mommy. With no one to kiss and make well.

So what if I am hooked on the hunt? All it does is make an orderly life untenable. You trade the kiddies and fireside and regular promotions and appointment to the house committee or the greens committee for a few, a very few, clear clean moments of a savage satisfaction akin to joy. And maybe in the process you keep a little essential privacy. Our dear Uncle owns over 23,000 polygraphs. Lie detectors. God alone knows how many industry owns. Not satisfied any more with giving you the whole series of Multiphasic Personality Inventory tests, they want to make damn well certain you are not merely giving them the answers you think they want. They want to nail you into your permanent box right now, brother. Get in and lie still, and forty years from now we'll bury you.

I get this crazy feeling. Every once in a while I get it. I get the feeling that this is the last time in history when the offbeats like me will have a chance to live free in the nooks and crannies of the huge and rigid structure of an increasingly codified society. Fifty years from now I would be hunted down in the street. They would drill little holes in my skull and make me sensible and reliable and adjusted.

I am, to put it as bitterly as possible, a romantic. I know a windmill when I see one, by God, and I sneer at my white horse. It was appropriate that Lysa Dean should be the damsel in distress. She is such a sweet kid.

"Anyway," I said aloud, "she projects the image of a sweet kid."

Dana was inert for about two seconds, nodding her head, and then she gave a little jump and stared at me. "Don't *do* that!"

124

"Do what?"

"Get inside my head like that! How did you know what I was thinking?"

"I didn't."

She looked dubious. I glanced at her a few times when I could take my eyes off that languorous and lethargic California traffic. And somehow all of a sudden we were closer. Maybe it is like the learning curve, shaped like a profile of a stairway. We both knew something had happened and didn't know what it was. Her face colored and she turned away. I couldn't really *see* her any more. That was another clue. I could remember meeting a dark-haired, strong-featured, composed woman. A stranger. This was not she. This was Dana. Somebody else. Dana's eyes, Dana's mouth, Dana's hair and ears and body. Individual and unique and not related in any way to anyone previously known. Dana of the dear crooked tooth.

Santa Rosita was a stunted version of the Santa Barbara code of existence. Three industries, electronics, plastics and tourists, and squeeze the bejaysus out of all three. It was sharing the big boom-boom. The incomparably dull tract houses, glitteringly new, were marching out across the hills, cluttered with identical station wagons, identical children, identical barbecues, identical tastes in flowers and television. You see, Virginia, there really is a Santa Rosita, full of plastic people, in plastic houses, in areas noduled by the vast basketry of their shopping centers. But do not blame them for being so tiresome and so utterly satisfied with themselves. Because, you see, there is no one left to tell them what they are and what they really should be doing.

The dullest wire services the world has ever seen fill

their little monopoly newspapers with self-congratulatory pap. Their radio is unspeakable. Their television is geared to a minimal approval by thirty million of them. And anything thirty million people like, aside from their more private functions, is bound to be bad. Their schools are group-adjustment centers, fashioned to shame the rebellious. Their churches are weekly votes of confidence in God. Their politicians are enormously likable, never saying a cross word. The goods they buy grow increasingly more shoddy each year, though brighter in color. For those who still read, they make do, for the most part, with the portentous gruntings of Uris, Wouk, Rand and others of that same witless ilk. Their magazine fare is fashioned by nervous committees.

You see, dear, there is no one left to ask them a single troublesome question. Such as: Where have you been and where are you going and is it worth it?

They are the Undisturbed. The Sleep Lovers.

And they fill out an enormous number of forms every year, humbly and sincerely. Each one is given a number to use all his life.

Are they going to be awakened with a kiss? They feel vaguely uneasy about their young. My God, why can't these kids appreciate this best of all possible worlds? What's wrong with these restless punks? These . . . these goddam *dropouts!*

Virginia, dear, through the strange alchemy of the gods, there are a disproportionate number of kids coming along these days with IQs that are soaring toward a level too high to measure. These kids have very cold eyes. They are the ones who, one day, will stop playing with transistors, diodes and microcircuitry and look at Barrentown and start asking the rude questions. Or build a machine that will ask.

126

In the meanwhile, Virginia, Santa Rosita still exists, and it is as if some cynical genius had designed a huge complex penal colony in the sunshine, eliminating the need for guard towers and barbed wire by merely beaming a gigantic electronic message at the inmates, day and night, saying, You are in heaven! Be happy! If you can't be happy here, you can't be happy anywhere! Vote! Consume! Donate! And don't forget to use your number.

We drove in from the north at four in the afternoon of that first Tuesday in March, and I checked us into two singles in a chain motel—architecture: Lubratorium Moderne. She wanted to call Miss Dean, and I wanted to try the number for Mendez. After a small and cautious hesitation, I decided not to put it through the motel switchboard. Caution can be a way of life. Never leave anything which can be traced, when you do have a choice.

A clear-voiced girl said, "Gallagher, Rosen and Mendez. Good afternoon."

"Uh . . . may I speak with Mr. Mendez, please."

"One moment, sir."

"Good afternoon. This is Mr. Mendez' secretary. May I help you?"

"I would like to speak with Mr. Mendez, please."

"He's on another line. May I call you back, or would you like to hold?"

I held. I riffled the phone book with my free hand. They were attorneys.

"Yes? Hello?" Mendez said in an impatient and harried voice.

"Sorry to bother you. We need an address for the next of kin for D. C. Ives."

"Who is we?"

"Keller Photo, sir. We had a lens for repair. It was

under the guarantee, but it took a long time. It had to go back to the factory in Germany, no charge of course, and now we—"

"Miss Trotter? Give this fellow Jocelyn Ives' address."

I heard him hang up. "Hello?" Miss Trotter said. "Just a moment, please." She was back on the line quickly. "Have you a pencil? Miss Jocelyn Ives, Twenty-eight twenty-nine Appleton Way. Phone seven-six-five, three-one-nine-two. Have you got that?"

"Thanks. When did Ives die anyway?"

"Oh, just a few days before Christmas. He held on longer than they thought he could, you know. Days and days, with all that terrible brain damage. It's such a shame. He was *so* talented."

"Well, that's the way it goes."

"I hope they find them some day."

"Don't we all. Thanks, Miss Trotter."

I started out of the phone booth, and then went back in and tried the number she gave me. It rang three times. A woman answered. "Is Georgie around?" I asked.

"You've the wrong number, I expect," she said. I thanked her and hung up. I walked thoughtfully back to the room. I knew that accent. It sounds cockney but isn't. It is Australian.

Dana had just finished talking to Lysa Dean. Miss Dean reported success with the promotion and a good audience response to *Winds of Chance* on premiere night. She was off soon, with group, to New York for additional promo work, panel shows and so on, four days there and then to Chicago.

I reported what I had learned, and added what I could guess. Dana looked more intrigued than shocked. "Killed, eh?"

128

"So it would seem."

"He was in a dangerous line of work."

"The quickest way is to give that sister a try."

"Can I come with you?"

"I might strike out. I'll try it alone. Then you can try from another angle."

Appleton Way was dead end. Truck terminals were edging closer to it. Nearby blocks were being leveled for some unimaginable improvement. But the street still had an illusion of peace. It contained multiple housing, old garden courts of pseudo-Moorish styling, faded citrus-tone paint on old stucco. Number 2829 was one of the larger complexes, and her door was off an arched open corridor along the side. A dark door opening into the gloom of a small apartment with too few windows. She looked at me through the six-inch gap the safety chain allowed, and I saw that she was perhaps daughter rather than sister.

"What do you want?"

You have to have a flair for it, an immediate and unthinking appraisal of the vulnerabilities. This one was wary and haughty. I could see that she was a big pale girl, Alice through a strange looking-glass. A twenty-year-old spinster. There are such. A big awkward fatty body in an unlovely jumper. A child face. Reddened nostrils. Pale heavy lips.

"I want to be sure you are Jocelyn Ives. Is there anything you could show me to prove it?" I kept my voice confidential.

"Why should I bother?"

"You do have the same accent."

"Who are you? What do you want?"

"I was associated with him in a certain venture quite

a long time ago. I came here to make contact, and I just found out he's dead."

She gnawed her lip and then, to my utter astonishment, gave me a huge conspiratorial wink. She closed the door, unlatched the chain and opened it wide. "Please come in," she said heartily. When she had closed the door behind us, she said, "I do understand why you can't give me your name."

"Uh . . . that's good."

"Back through here. The place is a mess. I'm off work today." I followed her along the murky hallway into a small living room. It was crowded with furniture too large and too expensive for the small apartment. Every surface was covered with large photographic prints, and scores of them were on the floor and leaning against the furniture and the walls. Many of them were matted. With clumsy awkward haste she cleared two chairs. "Do sit down. I've been sorting out. Lens Lab . . . that's a local hobby group . . . they want to put on a show of his best work. At the library. There are so *many*. I get quite confused."

"I can see how you would. It looks like fine work."

"Oh, yes! That's my responsibility now, to see that everyone learns how good Father was. I am going to set up a traveling show also. And there is some interest in Rochester, of course."

"Of course."

She sat facing me and knotted her hands together and said, "I have been so hoping that *somebody* would show up. It's been so terribly difficult for me."

"I suppose it has."

"Poor Mr. Mendez has been doing his best to get everything straightened out for tax purposes. But having quite a large amount of cash turn up has sort of complicated things. And, of course, I couldn't explain the cash. Not to him. If it was supposed to be for necessary expenses, I'm sorry. It's all tied up now with courts and tax people and things. I will get it eventually, I imagine, or whatever part of it they don't take. At least the house can be sold. You know, I have been hoping someone would show up. And you look almost exactly like the kind of man I pictured."

"What can I do for you?"

"I kept my mouth shut, as Father would have wished. And I guess I do not really have to have any posthumous glory for him. He said that was the thing none of you could ever expect. He taught me to be very careful and discreet about . . . the contacts and not to ask him questions. I have been wondering if you could go to Mr. Mendez and explain to him the sort of work Father was doing for you. I think it might make the estate work easier."

"I'm sorry. I have no authority to do that."

"I was afraid so," she said. "Oh, dear. And the ridiculous police will have to go right on thinking it was just someone after his pocket money?"

"I'm afraid so."

She studied me. "Really, how do I know you are what I think you are?"

"We don't carry that sort of identification."

"I suppose not. It wouldn't be very safe, I expect." She looked uneasy. "But why wouldn't you have known he was dead?"

"I've been out of touch."

I now had the shape of it all. There was something unwholesome about her, a greasy sheen to her flesh, a soiled smell in the dark little apartment. But she was his loved daughter. Blackmail needed a cover story. Perhaps it had been her guess at first that Father was in some sort of patriotic undercover work, and when she faced him with it, it was easiest to go along. And, of course, the Enemy had slain him.

I had to find the right way to open her up. I leaned toward her and said, "Jocelyn, I think I can promise you that some day it can all be told."

Tear tracks like the sidewalk marks of snails gleamed on the round pale cheeks, and she made a froggy sobbing sound . . .

Ten

I LIKED THE WAY Dana listened. She felt no compulsion to fill a silence with questions. She knew there was more to come. I could not see her distinctly. She sat over by the motel windows in darkness. The light was at my elbow, gleaming on the silver cup.

"Ives liked to live well," I said. "He did free-lance photography in Melbourne. Fashion, news breaks, everything. A Hollywood outfit made a movie over there. He got permission to work on the set. His stills were apparently damned good. The stars liked them. The studio brought him over. That was eight years ago. She was twelve. He had about four years of it and did pretty well. And lived well. Then something went wrong. I guess he got himself on that little blacklist they have. I don't imagine it is important to know what cooked him. The girl says it was jealousy. His work was too good. He moved up here to Santa Rosita. His studio was in his home. Weddings, parties, awards, portraits. A nice cover story. She thinks he had some other base in the city. She's so proud of him. Proud of that cynical son of a bitch with his sports cars and fine house and housekeeper."

I got up and collected both silver cups and fixed us another.

133

"She showed me the clippings. He went on a trip. She doesn't know where. He was gone two days. He came back to the house. He went out again and said he would be back within the hour. That was ten in the evening last December fifth. They found his car, locked, on Verano Street. He was found about a hundred feet away, dragged behind a warehouse, with the top of his skull smashed in, pockets empty, watch gone. They thought he would be dead on arrival, but the heart kept beating for five days. As far as the girl knows, they haven't a clue. Nobody knows what he was doing in that neighborhood. It's mostly industrial small time, empty at night."

After a long silence she said, "Did he leave her anything?"

"Small insurance. The equity in the house. About thirty-eight thousand in cash, already impounded while they check his tax returns. Then a lot of cameras, studio equipment, darkroom equipment, huge stacks of arty photographs."

She asked me if I was certain about Ives. I'd been saving it for her. I told her how I'd wormed it out of the girl.

"So his loving daughter was the one who helped him operate that drop and flashed the green light at you to toss the money out."

Dana shook her head slowly. "And I imagined horrible hoodlums out there . . . and it was that poor simple girl helping Daddy in his spy business. What a total bastard he must have been, to endanger her so!"

And I thought wistfully how easy it would have been for Lysa Dean to have busted it up in the beginning, before it got off the ground. "Ives could trust his daughter," I explained. "And he didn't have to split with her, and she didn't even know what was in the packages. He used her the same way, with variations, on other projects."

"Loyal little helper," Dana said. "Just like me."

"Let's go eat."

She put her sweater on. At the door she stopped me and said, "Trav, you didn't give her any little suspicion that . . . all was not what it seemed?"

"When I left, I told her she could be proud of Daddy. She stood tall and the tears dripped off her fat chin."

She squeezed my arm. In the outside lights, her dark eyes were shiny. "Soft as butter," she said.

"The arm?"

"Idiot, your darn arm is like a slab of redwood. I just meant I'm glad you left her that much."

"I wonder how long she'll keep it."

"What do you mean?"

"Somebody killed him. If they find him, he might have all the right reasons. I think I might talk to a cop."

"Why, dear?" she asked earnestly.

"Dear?"

"Oh, shut up! It was just a . . . reflex."

"You've done it twice today."

"Why will you talk to a cop?"

"Because they very probably know a little more than Miss Ives thinks they know. And we're close to the heart of it now, Dana. Where did D. C. Ives' file copies go?"

My man was Sergeant Starr. Bill Starr. He was a little fellow about forty, very jaunty and bouncy. He was 20 percent nose, and it looked as if that nose had been hit at least once from every possible direction. Under the nose was the abrupt curve of an amiable little smile. He was a clowner, a most happy fellow. He seemed to want you to like him. There was so much nose, there was a danger of misreading the eyes. They were small, cat yellow, and about as soft and mild as cross sections of brass rod.

His tidy little gray office had a rack for cups won in various skills. Several of them were for pistol. He bounced up and perched on the corner of his desk and beamed at me and said, "Why should I play games with anybody, pal? Am I in a buyer's market? Maybe, for residents. If I want to keep a source going. Sure. But I can park your gray tired ass in the tank and keep you there until you get eager to please."

I chuckled as merrily as he and said, "This friend I'm doing the favor for would be terribly upset. No influence here at all, of course. Except the kind of lawyers money will buy. Platoons of them, if need be. I have no record, Sergeant. But careless people have put me in from time to time, here and there. And I have been hit on the head by old-fashioned ones. So it would be an inconvenience for both of us. I'm eager to please right now. And eager to have you please me."

He picked the assorted cards and licenses off his desk and handed them to me. "McGee, there is every identification here except the right one."

"Cards are needed to do a favor for a friend?"

"I'll tell you again. If you have official status then *maybe* you can protect your client. But you have nothing. You *have* to tell me who hired you!"

"But I told you, Sergeant, that we might get around to that, if things go well. Besides, I'm not hired. It's just..."

"Oh, God, yes. A favor for a friend." He reached for his hat. "Let's try some coffee."

He drew a car from the pool and we went ten blocks

to a drive-in. The pretty waitress knew him by name and brought us coffee and raised doughnuts.

"I'll start," I said. "D. C. Ives. Sometimes a man has to be killed before people get the idea of some kind of hanky-panky."

"Hanky-panky. Now isn't that sweet! Put it this way. It isn't a legal requirement a man should have a checking account, but nearly everybody with forty-thousand-dollar homes does. An estimate of his take on a legit basis would be fifty or sixty a week. Living expenses better than a thousand a month. So he could be living off a big score from way back, or making little scores as he goes along."

"He was making it as he went along."

"Thanks a lot. I already figured that."

"Did you figure how?"

"It's your turn again, McGee."

"He had a studio and darkroom in his house, and he also had another setup. I'd guess somewhere near Verano Street. A limited setup. A quality enlarger for thirty-five millimeter, a setup for making and drying eight-by-ten prints, no automation for quantity production—almost what you'd expect of an advanced amateur, a one-man operation."

"To do what?"

"Isn't it your turn, Sergeant?"

"Okay. He would do there something he wouldn't want to do home on account of his daughter. When she wasn't in school, she helped him with the home setup. He did a lot of traveling. Short trips. Assignments, he called them. I say it wasn't just a standard smut shop. The requirements in that field are too low. And the pay is low. What do you say it was, McGee?"

"Discreet, careful, expert blackmail. Plus maybe some industrial espionage. And maybe just the long shots of people with the wrong people—the executive talking to the competition, the banker with the tout. Long-lens stuff, up and down this coast. How would he get the work? Some from legitimate agencies, maybe. Some from the great unwashed. With really juicy negatives, he could wring a lot of money out, if the people were important."

"And eventually make a slip and get his head smashed in."

"Probably."

"McGee, if you are trying to do a favor for a friend by getting hold of prints or negatives, forget it."

"They're gone?"

"If he'd been killed immediately, maybe we'd have moved a little faster. We found his hidey-hole. A warehouse corner with its own entrance. It was an area check that turned it up. His prints were on everything. Not much file space for prints, but it was stone empty. No negatives. The file had been locked, and it was pried open. The door had been unlocked and relocked with a key. A good lock. There was a tin money box in the back of the file. It was busted open too."

"What are you holding back, Starr?"

"Me? Me!"

"So all right. My friend is a sick sad girl. She's at Hope Island on Bastion Key in Florida. Her name is Nancy Abbott. She's a drunk. She's been at that retreat for months. Her rich architect daddy is dying, or dead by now, in San Francisco. Ives sneaked some nasty pictures of her a year and a half ago. Now give me the rest."

"I can check that out. The rest? Okay, I found out beyond any doubt that the break-in wasn't accomplished until the day *after* Ives was clobbered. And in Ives' pocket was a key to his little lab. Ives had an employee. Semi-retarded. Samuel Bogen, age forty-six. On and off welfare for years. Trouble twenty years ago. Peeping Tom and indecent exposure, and about four ninety-day falls for that. From what I can find out, Ives used him for scout work, paying him a dollar an hour for washing trays, drying prints, that sort of thing. By the time we got a line on him, Bogen had dropped off the face of the earth. He could be just a harmless spook. Or he could have flipped and bashed his boss. We think we traced him onto a Los Angeles bus. We've had an alert out on him ever since. Medium height, medium weight, glasses, bad teeth, hair brown turning gray, no special identifying marks or characteristics. No family. Left no lead behind in his furnished room three blocks off Verano Street. There is another thing too that makes me less interested in him. At about the right time, a car left the area at high speed. Bogen apparently never owned a car and doesn't drive."

I couldn't risk pursuing the Bogen matter further. I was afraid the little tiger would check it back and come up with Lysa Dean's name.

"So who was involved in the Abbott girl's pictures?" he demanded.

I was ready for that one. "A stock car driver named Sonny Catton. He was killed last year when he hit a wall."

"Where were the pictures taken?"

"Up around Point Sur someplace, at a private home, I think."

"A year and a half ago, you said? So why the heat to get them back now?"

"She was worried about whether he was using them to blackmail her dying father."

"How did you track it back to this Ives?"

"Sergeant, that's a long long story. Let me ask you one. Suppose somebody had some work for Ives. They couldn't get him. So they called Mendez, of Gallagher, Rosen and Mendez, and found out from Mendez he was dead. Does that mean anything?"

"I wondered about that too. Charlie Mendez is clean. Small services for small fees. Like having mail come there."

"Summation, Sergeant?"

"Who, me? Okay, D. C. Ives was very shifty and clever and careful. But one night he forgot to be careful and one of his pigeons got to him. When Bogen heard his boss was dying, he used his own key to get in. He took the dirty pictures and the money and ran."

"So that makes it a dead end for me, Sergeant."

"Are you sure?"

"It was just a favor for a friend."

Eleven

WE LEFT EARLY Thursday morning and drove down to the city, to Lysa Dean's canyon home, secluded behind an impressive pink wall. The staff was cut down to one Korean couple, maid and gardener. When he recognized Dana, he smiled broadly and unlocked the big metal gates for us. It was a hot day. The wall enclosed about one acre. A Mexican architect had done the house for her and her third husband. I guess you could call it Cuernavaca Aztec.

Dana showed me around. The plantings were splendid. The pool was drained. The dogs had been boarded. Walking through the silence of terrazzo, puffy white rugs, dark paneling removed from ancient churches, I counted five full-length oil portraits of the owner. And not one of an ex-husband.

Dana wanted to get different clothes. She showed me how she was set up. A small functional suite opposite the service area, with a rather stark bedroom, a large and luxurious bath, a small tidy office with a row of large gray filing cabinets, a battleship desk. There was a picture in the bedroom, Dana, younger, glowing, intense—holding the new baby in her arms. A young man with a homely, crooked, likable face was staring down at the child too, his arm around his wife.

She saw me glance at it and said, too imperatively, "Please wait for me out there in the office. This won't take a minute."

On an office shelf I saw bound, gold-lettered scripts for the Lysa Dean movies. *Winds of Chance* was among them. I took it down and opened it at random. It seemed highly improbable to me that anyone, living or dead, had ever said lines like that.

I put the script back on the shelf and paced restlessly. There were loose ends. A lot of them. But I could not see how they were pertinent to what I'd been asked to do. I couldn't recover any of the money Lysa Dean had paid Ives.

It seemed reasonably evident that Bogen had gone into business for himself. His note to Lysa sounded as Starr had described him. He would have picked up a few crude lab techniques from Ives. If the police had been looking for him for three months without success, I didn't have much chance of reaching out and picking him up.

We could fly east and catch Lysa in New York. Make a report. Working a complaint through normal police channels, we could get all there was in the files on Bogen. The people responsible for protecting the star could be alerted to watch for anybody who might be Bogen. If she insisted, maybe we could work out a way to trap him, using her as bait. With a little bit of judgment and a lot of luck, I had pushed it about as far as I could.

I could make a few guesses. Bogen had fled with a good piece of money and a whole stack of unpleasant pictures and holed up, perhaps in Los Angeles. He'd fled on December sixth. Those pictures could seriously upset an already disturbed mind. It was highly unlikely that he could have lifted any neat little list of names and addresses. Maybe the pictures covered quite a few of Ives' quiet ventures. If Bogen wanted to get cute with anyone, he would be restricted to those faces he could recognize. Maybe there were a few more celebrity faces in the stack. What was the time sequence? In early January, a month after he fled Santa Rosita, he was out in Las Vegas leaving off the package for Lysa Dean at the desk at The Sands. The columns would have located her for him. No further contact in two months. Was he busy bugging some other famous people who had been captured by Ives' sneaky lens? Was he waiting for Lysa Dean to come back to the Los Angeles area?

At any rate, it would be a comfort to her to know the kind of nut who was running around with pictures that could ruin her, to know his name and his appearance. She would have to decide what that much was worth. I'd dug a pretty good hole in the expense money.

Ives' murder was none of my business. The list of possibilities would have to be as long as my arm.

But I didn't like the way this one was ending. And I couldn't see Lysa Dean being ecstatic about it either.

Dana came out of her bedroom. She wore a pretty green outfit and carried her repacked suitcase. She said, too cheerfully, "Are we ready?"

She seemed very tense. I went and took the suitcase from her. With a quaver in her cheerful voice, she said, "This place gets on my nerves. It never did before. I don't know why. I feel as if I hardly know the Dana Holtzer who lives here. I expect her to come in and ask me who the hell I am."

"Watch out for her. A very icy broad."

She paused in the doorway to look at me, her expression at once vulnerable and wary. "Travis?"

"Yes, honey."

"I can't take too much change. So please don't. Things that get brittle . . . they break, you know."

"I like you. That's all it is."

She nodded. "But we have laughed too much. Do you understand that?"

"I understand that. And you'll be back in harness tonight."

"That picture you saw in there. Did it explain anything?"

"I could have drawn it from memory before I even saw it. You don't have to be explained to me. I don't have to make adjustments with you and to you. Hell with it. Let's go get on our airplane." I tilted her chin up, kissed the corner of her mouth closest to the crooked tooth. A little peck, like cousins. So she smiled, and one tear spilled, and I followed her in flight, *clackety-whack* across terrazzo, green skirt whipping, powerful calves clenching, back very straight and head held high.

We had twenty minutes before they called the flight. Our gear was checked aboard. Early afternoon. I bought a paper. I was scanning it. The name jumped out at me from a small item on page one of the second section. Casino employee slain in Las Vegas. Patricia Davies bludgeoned at doorstep of trailer last night. Once married to sportsman Vance M'Gruder.

Without a word I pointed it out and handed it to Dana. She looked at me, her eyes wide.

"I can't pass that up," I said. "It could be Sammy."

"But . . . our luggage is . . ."

"Dana, you go on to New York. Take care of my stuff at the other end. I'll check this out and be along."

"But I'm supposed to stay with you."

I took hold of her wrists and gave her a little shake.

144

"You have to go to New York. You're a big girl. I don't have to draw diagrams for you. You and I have . . . run out of time."

She held my gaze and her mouth made the shape of that word. Time. Without making a sound. The strength in her face was softened. And younger. "Thank you," she said solemnly. "Thank you, Travis, for knowing when the time ran out."

I released her, turning away, saying, "Your boss expects you. So go ahead." She murmured something about arranging my ticket and went off into the throng. I watched her go, and for an instant had in my mind the grotesque and unworthy image of the time when you feel the tarpon pick up speed for that last, great, heart-busting leap, and see him go high and see him, right at the peak of it, give that final snap of his head that throws your lure back into your lap. The image wasn't even accurate. I'd turned conservationist. I'd let the line go slack and said good-by.

I waited. And waited. Her flight was called. I went to the gate. I did not see her. I went to the airline desk. They checked the manifest for me. Slowly. Sir, the passenger canceled before flight time. I felt fear, worry, irritation. I had played the whole game too loosely, too confidently, and maybe somebody very fast and bright had moved out of the shadows.

I prowled the martian reaches of the terminal, searching for my girl in green. And found her, saw her through the glass front of a men's shop. I went striding in. A clerk was helping her. She gave me a startled and guilty look, then swung all that vivid force of personality upon me, saying, "Darling, I told you I'd forget the shirt sizes. It's *such* a damn nuisance losing luggage. Are these all right?

Wash-and-wear, so we could make do with two, don't you think? But what size, dear?"

"Seventeen and a half, thirty-six," I said humbly.

"Two of these in that size, please. And you don't really mind stretch socks too much, do you? Size thirty-three shorts, mmm? No, don't wrap them. I can pop them right in here." She lifted the small suitcase up onto the counter, a cheap one of pale blue anodized aluminum. As she put the articles in, I got a glimpse of some feminine things and some drugstore parcels. She latched it and waited for her change.

"We've got a flight in about twenty-five minutes," she said.

I carried the case out of the store into the waiting room area. I carried it to a quiet space and put it down and turned to her and said, "Have you lost your fool mind?"

She locked strong icy fingers onto my wrist and looked up at me and said, "It's all right. Really. It's all right."

"But ..."

"I couldn't get the luggage back. It was stowed aboard. It'll be taken care of in New York. Look. I've been a grownup for a long time."

"It's just that ..."

"Shut up, darling. Shut up, shut up, shut up. Do you want me to draw pictures for you? Stop looking like a spavined moose. Say you're glad. Say something."

I put fingertips on her cheek, ran my thumb along the black gloss of her eyebrow. "Okay. Something."

She closed her eyes and shivered. "Oh, God. No claims, Trav. Nothing like that. Either way."

"Either way."

"Just don't laugh."

"You know better than that."

I read consternation in her expression. "Maybe I'm just not what you . . . maybe you never really . . . you could have been just being polite and now . . ."

"You know better than that too. Shut up, dear."

"I wired New York."

"Kindly excuse delay."

"Dammit, we've never even really kissed. My knees are all wobbly and strange. Please lead me to a drink, darling."

During the flight, in spite of all the persuasive immediate magic of Girl, in spite of scent, closeness, dark eyes to drown in, and the shallow-breathed feeling of expectancy, the workman part of my mind kept moving in old and seamy patterns. We'd made a big swing, and, one by one, we'd been dropping them out of the final count. Carl Abelle, terror of the ski lifts, dangerous as a pratfall on a bunny slope. Sonny Catton, cooked meat in a pretty *whoosh* and bloom of high octane. Nancy Abbott, cooked just as thoroughly but over a lower flame. No point in checking Harvey and Richie, the Cornell kids. Their biggest problem was to find someone, anyone, who would ever believe their story. Caswell Edgars was out of it. And out of just about everything else in the world too. Ives was gone, and violently. So was Patty M'Gruder. If old Abbott, Nancy's father, had any luck left, he was dead by now too. Less violently but less pleasantly. It was narrowing down. To a yacht bum named Vance M'Gruder, to a waitress named Whippy, to a retarded little man named Bogen. It was like going through an empty house, checking the closets. Either it was more complex than I could comprehend, or else it made even less sense. But there was a nastiness somewhere in it that was out of control. I sensed that, and sensed it was aimed at Lysa Dean, and maybe at me, and I couldn't imagine who or how. I knew only two things. I was running out of closets. And I was glad I hadn't been at that house party. So I held the hand of the girl, and told myself it was a fine world, and filed away my doom thoughts.

A bored kid built a shiny little model city with his new kit and when it was finished he gave it one hell of a kick and spewed big hunks of it out across the desert floor. We tilted down across the afternoon, seeing an unreality of blue pools and green fairways against that old lizard-skin brown of the everlasting desert. We came in with a batch of pilgrims—the brand-new ones trying to be cool about their interest in the air terminal slots, about all the hawking and proclaiming and loud instant promotions. All the old pilgrims wore the memory of pain and were impatient to get to that certain table at that certain place, in time for crucifixion. I noticed a pair of appraisers as our group came through the gate, backs against the wall, staring left and right, somnolently vigilant, bouncing the little black glances off the pilgrims like aimed bb shot. They have the index memories of the ten thousand faces in disrepute in Slotsville, plus a feel for new trouble on the way—the ones who have come to get it any way they can, including using a gun on the winners. My lady performed no transit services this time. It was a fine and pleasant distinction related to the absolute silence of the airplane ride, the hand tightly held, the dark eyes hooded. She stood foursquare, still and humble, patient and sensuous, while I, with no bag to retrieve, went off to dicker for a vehicle and, with ironic impulse, took that most typical of game-town cars, a big air-conditioned convertible, this one in metallic blue-green, white leather, ominously silent as Forest Lawn.

There had been a place I liked, way out on the Strip, an utterly gameless and consequently expensive motor house called the Apache, and I knew it would be meaningless and would astonish her should I consult her. At the desk I said I had been there before, knew I wanted a double cabana at the pool, gave the porter a dollar to let me have the key and find my own way.

It was a great long room in gold and green, with two huge beds, all of it too bright in the dazzle of poolside sun. I pulled the cords that creaked the heavy yellow draperies across the acre of window wall, turning the room into a shadowy gloom of gold. The whisper of the hushed cooled air made it an oasis, a thousand years from yesterday and ten thousand years from tomorrow. Every fifth breath she took was very deep, with a little catch, like a hiccup at the high end. I put my hands upon her, at waist and nape of neck, stopping her sleepy sway. The man who sits in the steel office and throws the switches and pushes the buttons can rest his hand on his desk and feel, more like a low-cycle sound than any measurable vibration, the power that thrums in the bowels of the light plant. She felt unyielding and I could not guess how it would be for us. Then she gave a little crooked sigh, turned her mouth upward to me, leaned with heat and softness and purpose.

There is one kind of rightness that is an almost rightness, because it is merciless and total and ends in a death-like lethargy.

Then there is another kind of almost rightness that can never be finished.

Both of these make you strangers to each other. Both

149

of these things make you untidily anxious to give and receive reassurances.

But with Dana it was that rare and selfless rightness which moves with but the gentlest hiatus from one completion to the next, each a growth in knowing and closeness while, unheeded, the deep sweet hours go by. After all the fierceness is gone, it then astonishes by returning in that last time which ends it without question for now, and she is spent and dies there, slumbrous and fond.

I fought sleep. I made myself get up. I covered her over and went and showered and dressed. I turned on a meager light in the room and sat on the bed, pushed black curls aside, kissed the sweet nape of a musky neck. She turned to peer up at me, her face soft and emptied and young. "Yuhraw dress!" she mumbled in accusation.

"I'm going out for a little while. You sleep, honey."

She tried to frown. "Y'be careful, d'ling."

"Love you," I said. It doesn't cost a thing. Not when you do. I kissed a soft and smiling mouth, and I think she was asleep before I stood up. I left the low light on and let myself out.

I walked toward the main buildings feeling all that strange ambivalence of the conquering male. Goaty self-esteem, slight melancholy, a mildly pleasant and unfocused guilt, a tin-soldier strut.

But something more than that with her. A feeling of achieving and establishing identities, hers and mine.

There had been no dishonesties. And so, in all that total giving and taking, I had been aware of her as Dana, so vital and so enduring. The slight physical strangeness of the very beginning of it had lasted but a very short time. Then she was all known and dear. As if we had been apart for a very long time and found each other again, quickly getting over the awkwardness of separation.

After that it was a knowing and re-knowing in a profound way which has no words. It became a symbolic dialogue. I give thee. I take thee. I prize thee.

And there was also the fatuous feeling of enormous luck. It is such a damned blind chance, after all.

I worked my way through two bemused gin and bitters while they seared my steak. Over coffee I stopped marveling at myself and got a local paper and read the more detailed account of the murder of Patty M'Gruder.

Then I drove downtown and parked and wandered through that strange area of cut-rate stores, pastel marriage chapels, open-sided casinos bathed in a garish fluorescence. Spooks trudged amid the tourists, and the cops kept a close sharp watch. Old ladies yanked at the handles, playing their dimes out of paper cups. Music bashed across the dry night air, in conflict with itself, and in the noisier alcoves one could buy anything from a dream book to a plastic bird turd.

The Four Treys was a long bright narrow jungle of machinery. What happened to the old-fashioned slot machine? Now you can pull two handles, hit three space ships and an astronaut and get a moon pot, which is one and a half jackpots. The change girls sat behind wire, popping open the paper cylinders of silver, dumping it into paper cups for the people. At regular intervals came the clash of money into the scoop and a shrillness of joy.

I had just wanted a look. I need no directions. Presently I got back behind the wheel of the luxury device afforded me by a famous movie star and drove off again through the neoned light.

Twelve

THE TRAILER PARK was called Desert Gate. I had to go down through town and out the far side to get to it. It was a little after ten o'clock when I got there. Some orderly soul had set it up with the requirement that all trailers be parked in herringbone array on either side of a broad strip of asphalt going nowhere. The entrance was an aluminum arch, tall and skinny, with a pink flood-light on it.

The trailers were large, all snugged down off their wheels, with little patios and screened porches added. About half of them were dark. Patricia had lived in—and died in front of—the sixth one on the left. It was lighted. I parked and went to the porch door. As I raised a hand to bang on the aluminum frame, a big woman appeared, silhouetted in the inner doorway.

"Whatya want?"

"I want to talk to Martha Whippler."

"Who are you?"

"The name is McGee. I was a friend of Patty's."

"Look, why don't you go away? The kid has had a hard day. She's pooped. Okay?"

"It's all right, Bobby," a frail voice said. "Let him in."

As I went in, the big woman stood back out of the way. When I saw her in the light I realized she was younger than I had thought. She wore jeans and a blue work shirt, sleeves rolled high over brown heavy forearms. Her hair was brown and cropped short and she wore no makeup. The interior was all pale plywood paneling, vinyl tile, glass curtains, plastic upholstery, stainless steel. A slight girl lay on a daybed, propped up on pillows, long coppery hair tousled around her sad wan face. Her eyes were red. Her lipstick was smeared. She had a drink in her hand. She wore a very frilly nylon robe. Though she was a lot slimmer, I knew her at once.

"Whippy!" I said, and then felt like a damn fool for not having figured it out.

It startled her. She stared at me with disapproval. "I don't know you. I don't remember you from anyplace. People call me Martha now. Pat wouldn't let them call me by my old name." There was something quite solemn and childlike about her. And vulnerable.

"I'm sorry. I'll call you Martha."

"What's your name?"

"Travis McGee."

"I never heard Pat say your name."

"I didn't know her well, Martha. I know a few other people you might know. Vance. Cass. Carl. Nancy Abbott. Harvey. Richie. Sonny."

She sipped her drink, frowning at me over the rim of the glass. "Sonny is dead. I heard that. I heard that he burned up, and it didn't mean a thing to me."

"Nancy saw him burn."

She looked incredulous. "How could that happen?"

"She was traveling with him then."

She shook her head in slow wonder. "Her traveling with him. Oh, boy. Who could imagine that. Me, sure.

153

But her? Gee, it doesn't seem possible, believe you me."

"Martha, I want to talk to you alone."

"I bet you do," the big girl behind me said.

"Mr. McGee, this is my friend Bobby Blessing. Bobby, whyn't you go away awhile, okay?"

Bobby studied me. It is the traditional look they reserve for the authentic male, a challenging contempt, a bully-boy antagonism. There seem to be more of them around these days. Or perhaps they are merely bolder. The word is butch. Having not the penis nor the beard, they damn well try to have everything else. One of the secondary sex characteristics they seem to be able to acquire is the ballsy manner, the taut-shouldered swagger, the roostery go-to-hell attitude. They have a menacing habit of running in packs lately. And the unwary chap who tries to make off with one of their brides can get himself a stomping that stevedores would admire. These are a subculture, long extant but recently emerged from hiding. In their new boldness they do a frightening job of recruiting, having their major successes among the vulnerable platoons of those meek girls who, like Martha Whippler, are abused by men, by the Catton kind of man, used, abused, sickened, shared, frightened and . . . at last, driven into the camp of the butch.

"I'll be where I can hear you call me," Bobby said without taking her stony stare from my face. She went out, rolling her shoulders, hitching at her jeans.

I moved closer to Martha and sat in a skeletal plastic chair half facing her. She looked down into her half of a drink and said, "You named the people that were there that time."

"And left one out?"

"That movie actress," she whispered.

"Have you told people about her being there?"

"Oh, nothing like that ever happened to me before. I couldn't *tell* anybody about it. I mean, I could talk to Pat about it sometimes. You know. I used to have nightmares. She took me back home with her from there. I knew . . . I always knew she would rather it was Nancy."

She looked wistful. She had a cheap, empty, pretty little face, eyebrows plucked to fine lines, mouth made larger with lipstick.

"Did you ever get to see the pictures?" I asked her.

Even the most vapid ones have an urchin shrewdness about them, the wariness of the consistently defensive posture.

"What pictures?"

"The ones Vance had taken."

"For hours and hours today they kept asking me questions, questions. How do I know you just aren't another smart guy?"

"I can't prove I'm not." I hesitated. She was suggestible. I wanted the right approach, without fuss. Grief made an additional vulnerability. Kindly ol' McGee seemed the best bet. I shook my head sadly. "I'm just a fellow who thinks Patricia got a very bad deal from Vance M'Gruder, very bad indeed."

Tears welled. She snuffled into her fist. "Oh, God. Oh, God, yes. That bastard. That total bastard!"

"Some of us have never understood why Pat didn't fight it a little harder."

"Gee, you don't know what she had stacked against her. That rotten Vance had been planning it a long time. He got some kind of morality report on her from the London police from way before they were married, I guess to show that she knew she shouldn't get married. And then he had the tape recorder things of her and Nancy at their house, and her and me at their house, and the pictures he hired that man to get, following them around. It must have cost an awful lot, the whole thing, but as Pat said, it was a hell of a lot cheaper than California divorce. She couldn't get a lawyer to agree to fight it. I mean, after all, there wasn't any question about the way she was."

"Did you get to see those pictures, Martha?"

"Oh, sure. The funny thing, they made it look like nobody else was around at all. I don't know how that man got those pictures so close, Pat with me and with Nancy and with Lysa Dean, just one with Lysa Dean, one where you couldn't tell it was Lysa Dean unless you knew."

"So by the time you saw those pictures, you and Pat were together?"

"Yes. The rotten thing he did, we went up to the city to see some friends of hers, and we came back to Carmel, he was gone and the locks were changed, and our personal stuff was piled in a carport, and there was a man there to keep anybody from breaking in or anything. The way it was, she was still trying to get over being in love with Nancy, and maybe she never did. I guess maybe she never did get over it. But I did try to make her happy, I really did."

"Why would somebody want to kill her, Martha?"

She sobbed again and blew her nose. "I don't *know!* I just don't *know.* That's what they kept asking me. Gee, we lived real quiet here, over a year now, and for a long time we've been working the same shift at the Four Treys, me as a drink waitress and her on a change booth. Just a few friends. She hadn't got interested in any other girl or anything, and nobody was after me like that. There was just one thing."

"What do you mean?"

She frowned and shook her head. "I don't know. It started weeks ago. Before that, whenever she'd think of Vance she'd go into a terrible rage, and sometimes she'd cry. Weeks ago she got a letter from somebody. She didn't let me see it and I can't find it so I guess she destroyed it. She was kind of . . . far away for a few days after she got it and she wouldn't tell me anything. Then one day when I was out, she made long-distance phone calls. She really ran up a terrible bill. Forty dollars and something. And later she made a few more calls. Then she got very pleased about something. She'd be grinning and humming around and I'd ask her why she felt so good and she'd say never mind. Sometimes she would grab me and dance me around and she'd tell me everything was going to be just fine, and we were going to be rich. It didn't matter so much to me. I mean, we were doing all right here. We didn't *have* to be rich. I don't know if it had anything to do with her being murdered last night."

"Where were you when it happened?"

"I *heard* it! My God, I was in bed half asleep. I was sort of worrying about her. I've got a virus and I was off work. She was supposed to be finished at eleven and home by quarter past, but it was a little after midnight when I heard the car motor. I could tell it was ours, it's such a noisy little car. I'd left one light on for her. I wondered what she'd bring me. She'd bring me a little present if I was sick. Some kind of joke, sort of. The car stopped out there and I heard the car door, and then just outside that screen door, she yelled 'What are you . . .' Just those words. There was a kind of a terrible crunching sound. And a falling sound. And steps running. I turned on the lights and put my robe on and ran

157

out and she was just outside the door on the ground, and her head ..."

I waited several minutes while she slowly and painfully pulled herself back together.

"She was so alive," Martha moaned.

"But several weeks ago she stopped being mad at Vance?"

"Yes. But I don't know what it means."

"After she was locked out of the house, she did have a chance to talk to her husband?"

"Oh, several times. She begged and pleaded."

"But it didn't do any good."

"He wouldn't even let her have her car. He said she was lucky to keep the clothes she'd bought. Finally he gave her five hundred dollars so she could afford to go away. I had about seventy-five dollars. We came here on a bus and got jobs. He was nasty to her."

"Martha, does the name Ives mean anything to you? D. C. Ives?"

She looked blank. "No."

"Santa Rosita?"

She tilted her empty little head. "That's strange!"

"What do you mean?"

"Just a couple of days ago she was singing that old song. 'Santa Lucia.' But she was saying Rosita instead of Lucia, and I said she had it wrong and she laughed and said she knew she did. Why did you ask about that? I don't understand."

"Maybe it doesn't mean anything."

"But if it has anything to do with who killed her ..."

"Did she have any kind of appointment coming up?"

"Appointment? Oh, I'd forgotten. Just the other day she said she might have to take a little trip. Alone. Just for a day or two. It made me jealous. She teased me and let me get real jealous, and then she said it was a kind of a business trip, and she'd tell me all about it later."

"Where was she going to go?"

"Phoenix. Gee, we don't know a soul in Phoenix."

"How soon was she going?"

"I don't know. It sounded as if she meant real soon."

I couldn't shake loose anything else of interest. She was worn out. But she was still alert enough to ask again who I was and what I wanted. I had to answer a question with a question.

"What are you going to do now, Martha?"

"I haven't thought about it."

"It's your chance to get out of . . . this kind of situation."

Her little mouth firmed up. "I don't know what you think you mean by that. Listen, Pat got me out of a lousy situation. I don't want anything like that again ever. What do you know about anything?"

"Don't get sore."

"Why shouldn't I? Jesus Christ! Anything you people don't understand, it has to be lousy. Pat always said that. The world doesn't have to be your way. We never asked anybody to approve or disapprove. It's our own business. Who did we hurt?"

"You?"

"Me! That's some joke. That really is. Honest to God, when I remember the way it used to have to be, when I thought that was the only thing there was, boy, it makes my stomach turn right over. I've got friends who want to take care of me."

"I bet you have."

She stared at me, narrowed her eyes, threw her head back and yelled, "Bobby! Bobby!"

I left without any particular haste, but without delay either. Even so, they were between me and my car. Bobby had a friend, equally sizable. In the angle of the light the friend looked like the young Joe DiMaggio, but with a black dutch bob, and wearing desert rat khakis. Joe carried a putter. The gold head and chrome shaft glittered.

They separated and moved in from either side.

"Don't make any stupid mistakes," I said, coming to a halt.

Joe had managed to train herself down to a good imitation of a baritone. "You bassars got to get a lesson not to come around here bothering the brides."

"What have you got here?" I asked. "A colony?"

"Smart-ass," Bobby said as they moved in.

They generally do very well against the undoctrinated male. There is a chivalrous reluctance to hit a woman. Martha had come to the trailer doorway to watch the sport. I had learned a painful lesson long ago when reluctance had slowed reaction time, and I had spent the next several days walking around like an eighty-eight-year-old man. It is the type of mistake you are not likely to make twice in one lifetime. And these two were more dangerous than male thugs because their aberrations fired their hatred of the authentic male. They might not know when to stop hitting.

The light was tricky and the putter made me nervous. If I tried sweet reason, she was going to try to sink it into my skull. So I moved with no regard for chivalry. I feinted toward Bobby and lunged at Joe. I got a hand on the putter shaft before she could build up any momentum with it. I wrested it out of her hand, reversed it, sidestepped her and laid the limber end of it across the seat of those khakis. It made a little whirring in the air and a mighty crack on impact. Joe leaped high and, probably much to her own disgust, gave a high girlish scream of anguish. I turned in time to see Bobby hurl a rock at my head. It tickled the hair on the crown of my head, and the fright lent considerable enthusiasm to my pursuit. Bobby turned in flight. I welted her three hearty times across tight denim, and she joined her yelps to those of her buddy. Joe grappled with me, trying to trip me. She was sobbing in frustration, and she smelled like a mule skinner. I spun her away and whacked her another beauty. She screamed and gave up and started running toward the trailer.

Bobby made the mistake of running right along beside her, about five feet away from her. I sped into the gap with forehand and backhand. Martha Whippler had come to the doorway to watch them brutalize me. They nearly trampled her in their haste to get out of range. They sounded as if they were trying to yodel. I laughed, hurled the putter well out of the colony and drove away from there.

Back in the muted silence of the big room at the Apache, Dana slept on. Remembering that the Apache food service would be closed, I had stopped at an implausible delicatessen in town. I turned more lights on. I unsacked my purchases, pried the top off the beef stew with noodles. It was still steaming. I carried it over and sat on the floor beside the bed and wafted it back and forth in front of her face. Her nose twitched, twitched again. Suddenly her eyes opened wide. She focused on me. She gave a great start.

"Hey!" she said. "Hey now!" She gave a great creaking, stretching, shuddering yawn and then reached for the container. She hitched herself up, arranged the pillows, tucked the sheet around her, under her arms, and lifted a huge plastic forkful into the greedy waiting

161 ·

mouth. "Oh!" she said. "Oh, my God, Trav, nothing has ever tasted like this."

I moved a small table close to her elbow, brought over the garlic dills, the hot tea and the strawberry cheesecake. I sat on the foot of the bed, admiring her. When the edge of hunger began to be eased, she began to be uncomfortable.

"Did you eat?" she asked.

"Like a wolf."

She poked at her tangled hair. "I'm a mess, I bet."

Her dark vital eyes were puffy, shadowed with fatigue. Her lips were swollen, pale without lipstick. There was a long scratch on her throat, three oval blue smudges on the front of her left shoulder, where my fingers had bruised her.

"You look just fine, Dana."

Her face got pink. She would not look directly at me. "I bet. Uh . . . what time is it?"

"Twenty of one."

She said she would finish the cheesecake later. She asked me to please turn my back. She lugged our suitcase into the bathroom. I heard her take a quick shower. In a little while after the water stopped, she came shyly out, hair brushed, mouth made up, and she was wearing a little blue hip-length nightgown, diaphanous, with lace at throat and hem. Rather than making any attempt to model it, she scuttled for the bed in a knock-kneed half run, slightly hunched over. She piled in, covered herself and said, blushing furiously, "It isn't exactly what I thought I was buying."

I laughed at her. She frowned part way through the cheesecake and then managed a timid smile, a direct but fleeting glance. "I'm not used to this sort of situation, Trav. I'm sorry."

162

"Don't be. Nobody else is."

She swallowed and looked pained. "I was so . . . I don't know what you must th . . . . I never . . . oh, *hell*, anyway!"

"Stop fussing. So it's a new relationship. We are something to each other we weren't before. And took a risk. You know that. Somebody, Hemingway maybe, had a definition of a moral act. It's something you feel good after. And coming back here to you after where I've been makes us seem like the innocence of angels."

She showed her concern. "What happened, dear?"

The cheesecake and tea were long gone by the time I finished with the facts and the speculations.

She looked dubious. "It seems like an *awful* lot of guessing."

I went through it once more, in précis form. "What do we know about M'Gruder? He is feisty, rich, ruthless and stingy. And, with no occupation, he is highly mobile. He's brown and fit and damned callous. Okay, as the purchaser of a service, he got into direct contact with Ives. Ives, seeing a golden opportunity, recognizing Lysa, took all the pictures he could get, hundreds of them, knowing he could crop and enlarge to exhibit every relationship that went on during those four days. Assume that when M'Gruder learned where the party was going to be, he got to a phone and alerted his hired photographer. We know one thing about Ives. He was greedy. He did his job for M'Gruder and got his fee. He collected big from Lysa Dean. He took a hack at the Abbott money and struck out, because Nancy was past protecting.

"Now we have to guess. M'Gruder was hot to marry the young Atlund girl. Her professor father disapproved. M'Gruder won him over. I think that with a Swedish girl's traditional respect for parental authority, the professor had to be won over or there would have been no marriage. I think Ives made the mistake of trying to blackmail a previous client, someone who knew who he was and where to find him. The timing fits. Ives threatened to show Professor Atlund the terrace pictures featuring M'Gruder. Anything that rancid would have bitched the marriage forever. The professor would not have his dear girl marrying a libertine like that. Ives did not think M'Gruder dangerous. Maybe he underestimated his stinginess. M'Gruder followed him, saw a good opportunity and smashed the top of his head in. A couple of weeks later he married his Ulka.

"Take it a step further. We have to assume that Patty M'Gruder learned the name of the photographer from Vance. He would delight in telling her how smart he had been, how cleverly he had cut her loose from the M'Gruder money. He would want to rub her nose in it. He would *have* to hate her. He is a very virile type, and it would be an outrage to his pride to realize his English wife had merely pretended pleasure with him and actually preferred girls. Patty got a letter from somebody. Gossip, perhaps. Vance's child bride and the problem with the professor. It started her thinking. She had known of Ives' death. She knew Vance. She knew him damned well, and how his mind operated, and his capacity for violence. Somehow, checking this out by phone, she became convinced Vance had done in Ives. So she sent a letter to Vance. It would be a very veiled hint. Come through with the money you cheated me out of, boy, or the Santa Rosita police are going to take an interest in you. Words to that effect. He couldn't risk that. I'd say he'd write back something about planning to be in Phoenix and be willing to discuss her financial situation at that time. She would realize she had struck gold. Now he could not risk being publicly in Las Vegas. When women die, they check out their ex-husbands. I say he set up a good solid alibi in Phoenix and came over here last night and killed her. He smashed the top of her head in. He would imagine he had no other choice. She hated him as much as he hated her. She would show no mercy. She would bleed him forever."

She thought it over. "I guess it does make sense. But, Trav, is it our problem? Isn't Samuel Bogen our problem, really?"

"At this moment, my darling Dana, some very shrewd cop may be checking out some small slip M'Gruder made. The death of Patricia *has* to require he be checked out. So they grab him for murder first. Do you think he would maintain a chivalrous silence? He would want to lay all the facts on the line, with little distortions here and there, to try to show justification or at least a plausible excuse for murder. Once they round up Cass and Carl and Martha Whippler and start questioning them one at a time, how long do you think Lysa Dean would stay in the clear? Make up a headline, honey. Star Implicated in Orgy Murder. She'd be even worse off. I have to find out how good these guesses are. If she's going to be in the soup, the best I can do is warn her. Maybe she can take some steps. Long-term contracts. Public relations advice. Something."

Dana frowned. "I see what you mean. But he could have just *said* Phoenix."

"I think he's there. It's close. I want to check it out."

"All right, dear."

I patted her on the foot. "I like obedient women."

She yawned. "I just feel terribly passive, I guess."

"Entirely, completely passive?"

She pursed her lips. She tilted her head. She laid a finger alongside her nose. "Well . . . I wouldn't go so far as to say *that*."

Thirteen

I HAD THE RANDOM IDEA of poking around the Four Treys to see if I could find a small hint of a visit from Vance M'Gruder the night of Patty's death, but my few small memories of the hard-nosed vigilance of the Las Vegas cops outweighed the impulse. They deal, day and night, with every kind of spook and hustler in the world, and they would be focused very intently on this murder, and I did not relish the prospect of being bounced up and down while trying to explain my passing interest.

Besides, if M'Gruder was as bright as I imagined, he would not have put in an appearance in the stage lighting of any of the downtown casinos. He would have her Desert Gate address. Once he got to town it would be no great feat to find out when her shift ended. As I shaved I tried to guess his most plausible mode of transportation. It was just about three hundred miles to Phoenix. I decided that if I were doing it, I'd settle for a good fast car. With enough muscle under the hood, and the right kind of springing for the mountain curves, you could safely call it a five-hour run. Leave Phoenix at six and arrive at eleven. Spend an hour hunting her down and killing her. Back by five-thirty in the morning. Sneak into the bridal bed. A private car was safer than a bus, a scheduled flight or a private plane. Cash for gas. No records, no fellow passengers. Properly done, casually done, he could have people convinced he had never left at all. If he had the cold nerve necessary to make that earlier run to Santa Rosita . . .

We walked to the dining room for breakfast, my lady wearing that green which was all she happened to have. My drowsy lady walked close at my side, without haste, her smile as inward and bemused as that of the Mona Lisa. She hugged my arm and beamed up at me and gave me a sleepy wink. And then she yawned.

Between us we ate a mountain of wheat cakes, a bale of bacon.

I found a Phoenix paper in the lobby rack, checked through it and found a society editor by-line. I coached Dana and put her into a phone booth with a fake name and a reasonably plausible cover story. I stood outside the booth and saw her eyes go fierce and bright. She gave me a savage little nod. When she came out, she said, "What a sweet woman! The M'Gruders are staying with a couple named Glenn and Joanne Barnweather. She spake their names with social awe. Old friends of his, apparently. They flew in from Mexico City about five days ago, she thinks. She had an item on it. They're staying at the Barnweather ranch out beyond Scottsdale. You were sure, weren't you?"

"Not completely. But I'm beginning to be. So let's go take a look at them."

We went back to the room and packed. A tremendous chore. She made a housewifely ceremony of it, trotting around the room in a charade of seeing that no meager possession was overlooked, earnest frown between her eyes, white teeth biting into the fullness of underlip.

I caught her as she went by, planted a kiss upon the

frown lines and told her that she was a fine girl. She said she was glad I thought she was a fine girl, but it might be a pretty good idea to just leggo of the fine girl or maybe we wouldn't be out of there by noon, which she had happened to notice was checkout time.

We were on our way with the top down heading toward Boulder City by noon, after one quick stop at a department store for a stretch denim skirt and halter top and bright yellow scarf for her, white sport shirt for the driver.

The car was heavy and agile. The day had a honeymoon flavor. The sun and the dry wind baked us. We laughed. We made bad jokes. She slanted dark eyes at me, lively with her mischief. This was the way I had wanted her to be. Totally alive and free, not tucked back into her own darkness.

But, totally alive, she was an impressive handful. This was not some pretty little girl, coyly flirtatious, delicately stimulated. This was the mature female of the species, vivid, handsome and strong, demanding that all the life and need within her be matched. Her instinct would immediately detect any hedging, any dishonesty, any less than complete response to her—and then she would be gone for good. Wholeness was all she could comprehend or accept. For now there were no shadows in her eyes, no hesitations as a bad edge of memory stung her. Even in this pursuit of murder, it was a fine fine world.

When we stopped for lunch in an outdoor patio in heavy shade, I looked at her and said, "Why?"

She knew what I meant. She scowled into her iced coffee. "I guess way back after you came back to the room after seeing Carl Abelle. I don't know. You could have stomped around, the hard-guy grin and all that. But you felt bad about hurting and humiliating him. And he isn't much, certainly. So I figured out you don't go around proving you are a man because you are already sure you are. It isn't all faked up. And in the same way you didn't have to try to use me to prove what a hell of a fellow you are. Even though we were both . . . being attracted in a physical way. I know this sounds as if I'm some kind of an egomaniac, but I just thought well . . . heck, if being a man is a good and valid thing, then there should be like an award of merit or something, an offering. In Abnertalk, namely me. As if I'm so great."

"Don't do that to yourself, Dana. You are implausibly . . . astoundingly, unforgettably great. And I don't mean just in a . . ."

"I know. It isn't me, and it isn't you. Let's not talk about it. It's the total of us, the crazy total. I'm not going to talk about it, or think of what comes after. Okay? Okay, darling?"

"No talk. No analysis."

"We are kind of beautiful," she said. "It's enough to know that, I guess. Alone I'm just . . . sort of efficient and severe and a little heavy-handed. Defensive. Alone you're just sort of a rough, wry opportunist, a little bit cold and shrewd and watchful. Cruel, maybe. You and your sybarite boat and your damned beach girls. But we add up to beautiful in some crazy way. For now."

"For now, Dana?"

"I'm no kid, Travis. I know hurt is inevitable always."

"Shut up."

"I talk too much?"

"Only sometimes."

So off we went, to Kingman, to Wikieup, to Congress—up into cold places, down into heats—to Wickenburg, to Wittman, and down into the richness of the old

Salt River Valley where Phoenix presides over the boom that threatens never to quit. It has become a big fast rough grasping town, where both the irrigation heiresses and the B girls wear the same brand of ranch pants.

The sun was low behind us as we came in, breasting the outgoing traffic of the close of Friday business. I cruised and settled for a glassy sprawl called the Hallmark, a big U of stone, teak and thermo-windows enclosing a great green of lawn and gardens, a blue of water in a marbled pool in the shape of a painter's pallette. In a nearby specialty shop, still open, we let Lysa Dean refurbish our dwindled wardrobes to the extent of swim trunks for me and a swimsuit for the lady. We fixed ourselves tall ones of gin and bitter lemon. Dana swam with utmost earnestness, chin held very high, using a stroke I told her was early sheep dog. In the bathroom, in fading light of day, her body bore the halter marks of the long sunny ride, her broad flat breasts pale, responsive to soapy ablutions cooperatively offered. In a predictable haste, I toted the untoweled seal shape of her, dripping, to bed, a firm, lithe, gleaming, chuckling burden which seemed to have no weight at all. Ceremonial celebration of our twenty-fourth hour.

Eased and complete, in mild and affectionate embrace, we took up the duty of talking about M'Gruder, weighing the merits of the possible methods of contact.

I could not tell her precisely what I hoped to accomplish. If M'Gruder was the man, I wanted to stir him up. I didn't want him to believe he had any chance at all. A man running is a dead man. A trial would finish Lysa Dean as well. And when you take someone's money for expenses, there is a morality involved. He would have some confidence he had gotten away with it. I had to blast that out of him and set him running. And arrange a chase.

The Barnweather number was listed. We went over it carefully. I coached her. She added a few ideas. There was a phone extension in the bath. I went in there and listened.

A servant said the M'Gruders were in the guest house. He gave Dana another number to call.

A man answered. A cultivated baritone, loosened slightly by drink, admitting that he, indeed, was Mister M'Gruder himself.

"You don't know me, Mr. M'Gruder."

"From your charming voice, that is my loss, my dear. What is your name?"

"I've just picked a new name for myself. I wondered if you'd like it. Patty Ives. Do you like that name?"

It was a slow five-count before he spoke. His voice was under careful control. "You sound as if you thought you were telling me something. But I am afraid I don't follow."

"I guess I do have you at a disadvantage. I know so *much* more about you than you know about me."

"I don't wish to be rude, but I don't like guessing games, whoever you are. So if you don't mind . . ."

"I thought we might make a date for a quiet talk, if you would like to sneak away from your little bride, Vance. We have mutual friends. Carl Abelle. Lysa Dean. Cass Edgars. Nancy Abbott. Martha Whippler. Of course Sonny Catton is dead. Poor Sonny."

Again I could have counted to five. "I think you might be a very foolish girl."

"Foolish, but not very greedy. And very, very careful, Vance."

"Let me put it this way. You might have something you think is valuable. But suppose it is only an annoyance?"

"Oh wouldn't it have to be a *lot* more than that!"

"You are talking in circles, my dear. I am quite certain I can be forgiven for old indiscretions. Life with my ex often became very unwholesome. Mrs. M'Gruder is aware of that. I've reformed. The police were here yesterday afternoon, cooperating with the Las Vegas police, I imagine. To make certain I hadn't killed Patty. I'm not sorry she's dead. I'm not that much of a hypocrite. She was a horrid woman. I had to get free of her in any way I could. All this is none of your business, of course. But I didn't want you to think you've alarmed me. You just make me feel . . . irritable. Please don't phone me again." Click.

I reached and put the phone on the hook and then sat back on the wide yellow rim of the little triangular tub. In a few moments Dana appeared in the bathroom doorway. She had put on my sport shirt. She leaned against the doorframe and said, "Well?"

"I don't know. I just don't know. Either we're dead wrong, or he's got the nerve of a headwaiter. So much points his way. Damn it, it *has* to be him. We're going out there."

"Just like that?"

"We're going to be invited out, I hope."

There is one theory that there are but a hundred thousand people in the United States, and the rest of the 189,900,000 is a faceless mob. The theory further states that any person in the hundred thousand can be linked to any other by no more than a three-step process. Example: Ron knew Carol's brother at Princeton; Carol's husband worked with Vern at the Ford Foundation; Vern's cousin met Lucy at the film festival. Thus when Ron and Lucy met as strangers, and sense that they are each members of the hundred thousand, they can play a warm and heartening and satisfying game of who-do-you-know and, with little cries of delight, trace the relationship.

By dint of past endeavors I had acquired provisional membership in the group, and it seemed likely to me that Glenn and Joanne Barnweather would be solid members. So I had to tap other members most likely to know them. I tried Tulio in Oklahoma City and drew a dead blank. I remembered Mary West in Tucson. She knew them, but not well. But she did know Paul and Betty Diver in Flagstaff who knew them intimately, and she was certain she could get Betty to play along. If there was any hitch, she would phone back. If not, I would hear from Joanne Barnweather directly. She briefed me on what I'd have to know about the Divers.

We had a twenty-minute wait before the phone rang. "Trav McGee?" a woman asked. "This is Joanne Barnweather. I just got a call from our very dear mutual friend, Paul Diver, saying you're in town. Could you come out to the place? Are you free?"

"If I can bring along a gal."

"Of *course* you can, dear. Glenn and I will be delighted. We've got some people in to meet our house-guests and we're just churning around here, very informal, drinking up a small storm and waiting for time to throw a steak on. Do come as you are. We'll be delighted to see you." She gave me directions.

Dana had been nestled close to me, listening. When I hung up she gave me a look of mock admiration. "You are a scoundrel, McGee."

"Darling, go put on your green."

"She said to come as we are."

"Then at least button my shirt."

Fourteen

ON THE WAY OUT, under a chilly spangle of stars, I had
briefed Dana on how we'd handle it. She was to stay away
from M'Gruder, target on his young Swede bride if possible. I would do what I could with M'Gruder.

The Barnweather place was a simple little quarter-
million-dollar ranch house a few hundred yards into a
lot of rocky acreage, with fifteen cars glinting in the star-
light, music and festive sounds coming from the floodlighted pool area.

I sensed that Dana took a deep breath and braced
herself as we walked toward the party jabber. There
were infrared heaters focused on the broad terrace area
at the house end of the pool. A gleaming, beaming little
fellow in a red coat tended bar. These were a pack of
the young marrieds, the success-prone ones. The tense
and girlish mothers of three and five and seven young,
their beefier husbands, expansive with bourbon and land
deals. About thirty-five people in all, forming and re-
forming their little conversational groups. Dress was
varied, all the way from shorts and slacks to some of
those fanciful ranch coats on the men, the pale whipcord
jobs with the pearl buttons and pocket flaps. The audible
talk had that Southwest flavor so quickly acquired by the

people who move there from Indiana and Pennsylvania.

When we hesitated, a slender pretty woman came smiling toward us, holding one hand out to each of us. "Trav? I'm Joanne."

"And this is Diana Hollis." We had decided it was possible Lysa Dean had spoken of her girl Friday to M'Gruder, and the name was just unusual enough to stick in his mind.

"So glad you could come, dears. Come meet the group."

She steered us over for a drink first and then swung us through the throng, rattling off the names and identifications. Glenn was one of the burly ones in whipcord. Joanne made a little more special thing of the introduction to their houseguests. Vance M'Gruder was a little balder, a little browner, a little taller than he had seemed in the pictures. He was a type. The totally muscled sportsman—muscles upon muscles so that even his face looked like a leather bag of walnuts. Polo muscles, tennis muscles, sail-handling muscles, fencing muscles—the type who does handstands every morning of his life, works out with professionals whenever possible, and has a savage and singleminded desire to whip you at anything you're willing to play with him, from squash racquets to tetherball. He had the personality to go with the body—a flavor of remote, knowing, arrogant amusement.

His young bride was one of the most striking females I have ever seen in my life. You had a tendency to speak to her in a hushed voice, an awed voice. The Swedes grow some of the finest specimens of our times. This Ulka Atlund M'Gruder was big enough for M'Gruder to keep her in flat heels at all times. She wore a woolly tangerine-colored shift. Her arms were bare. The others were bundled in jackets, sweaters, tunics, shawls, stoles.

She looked as if she had enough animal heat to keep her entirely comfortable at 30 below. Her body, under the touch of the fabric, was ripe, leggy and entirely perfect. Without makeup, her features were almost those of some heroic, dedicated young boy, a page from the time of King Arthur. Or an idealized Joan of Arc. Her tilted gray-green-blue Icelandic eyes were the cold of northern seas. Her hair was a rich, ripe, heavy spill of pale pale gold, curved across the high and placid brow. She had little to say, and a sleepy and disinterested way of saying it. Her eyes kept seeking out her husband. Over all that stalwart Viking loveliness there was such a haze of sensuality it was perceptible, like a strange matte finish. It was stamped into the slow and heavy curve of her smile, marked by the delicate violet shadows under her eyes, expressed by the cant of her high round hips in the way she stood. Though by far the youngest person there, she at the same time seemed far older. She had been bolted to the bowsprit of an ancient ship for a thousand years. And every woman there hated her and feared her. The look of her confirmed my guesses about Vance M'Gruder. Wearing this one like a banner or a medal was the ultimate cachet of competitive masculinity. She had a strange primitive flavor of sexual docility. She was indentured to M'Gruder, totally focused upon him, yet were she taken from him by someone with more strength and force and purpose, she would shift loyalty without question or hesitation. A man like M'Gruder would go to any length to acquire her. And he had. I was certain of that. I thought of M'Gruder's past habits and inclinations, and I wondered if, when his physical resources began to flag, he would stimulate himself by corrupting her. A woman to him would be something owned, to use as he wished.

176

Later, standing in a group with M'Gruder, I looked over and saw Dana alone with Ulka, talking quietly to her. Ulka nodded. She was watching Vance. I could not get anywhere with Vance. I tried to play do-you-know with him, bringing up the names of some of the Florida sailboat bums I know. Yes, he knew them. Sure. So what. I guessed he could not become interested in trivia. He had taken two horrible risks to acquire and keep the Viking princess. Maybe somebody was getting set to drop the noose on him and end it. Apprehension could make small talk almost impossible. I could not comprehend M'Gruder's promise to put this creature back into college. I found it hard to believe that a professorial type had spawned her. In days of old whenever one of these rarities appeared, one of the king's agents would run to the castle with the news, and the girl child would disappear forever into one of the royal suites, and her family would get a little sack of gold coins in exchange. In these more random times they are grabbed off by oil men, celebrity athletes, television moguls and M'Gruders. But the man who has one stays nervous because, unless you are a king, you don't really get to own it. It is on temporary loan from providence.

Later I sat near Ulka in a big game room in the house while she carved and chewed her way through a huge rare steak, knife and teeth flashing, jaw muscles and throat working, her eyes made blank by a total concentration on this physical gratification. The effort made a sweaty highlight on her pale brow, and at last she picked up the sirloin bone and gnawed it bare, putting a slick of grease on lips and fingertips. There was no vulgarity in this hunger, any more than when a tiger cracks the hip socket to suck the marrow.

The party fragmented, and there was room enough

for them to roam all the house and grounds, various degrees of alcohol dividing them more positively than social class or business interest. I had lost track of Dana, and I went night-walking in unhurried search. Skirting a tall cactus garden, floodlighted in eerie blue, I heard, off to my right, a conspiratorial rasp of female venom. "Bastard! Bastard! Bastard!" It was more contemptuous than indignant. I sought to move quietly out of range. I did not care how husbands were gutted in this desert paradise. I imagined it was done the same as elsewhere.

But the male voice stopped me. "All I want to know is where you . . ." The rest of the sentence was lost. He had raised his voice to cut her off and lowered it as she fell silent. But it was Vance M'Gruder.

"You are so smart! You are *soooooo* smart! Oh, *God,* what a brilliant mind I married!"

"Sssh, Ullie. Don't shout!"

"Maybe it was one of my Mexican boyfriends. How about that? Hah? How about that? And just what would you do about it?" Sweet voice of Ulka Atlund M'Gruder, bride of two months. And where was the sleepy remote smile? The placid acceptance? This was the malignancy of a taunting woman, an emasculating woman. He shushed her again and they moved off, out of range. I circled and discovered I had been near the path that probably led over to the guest house.

I admit feeling a certain dirty little satisfaction. It was as if the fox had made one leap just high enough and found out the grapes actually *were* sour. Here was this brown hard bundle of sport muscles trying to kid the calendar by wedding the glorious child bride, and now all his game skills and all his money and his social standing were no defense at all against that killer instinct which could launch her right at his most vulnerable point, his aging masculinity. Seeking paradise, he had embraced a sweet disaster.

The party dwindled. Laughter was drunken. A group sang "The Yellow Rose of Texas."

I stood with Dana, saying good night, and Joanne Barnweather swayed against us, and said, "You all come riding tomorrow morning, you hear? Got lovely horses. Jus' lovely. Diana, sweetie, like I said, I got stuff'll fit you. Don' worry 'bout it. Jus' you all and us and the M'Gruders. You know what, Diana? Ulka liked you. She wants you 'long. How about that anyhow? To find out she likes anybody. Crissake, we've known Vance forever and we love the sweet ol' son of a bitch, and it was great he got loose from that limey dyke, believe me, but hones' I can't figure this Ulka. Sheese! A zombie, thass what she is. I shouldn't talk like this, but I'm a wee little bit stoned, sweeties. What you do, you get here like nine in the morning, okay?"

On the way home Dana said, "Horses scare me."

"How did you make out?"

"Didn't you hear? She likes me. But I never would have been able to tell. Trav, that child has very limited reactions, really. I had a friend who got like that once. They said finally it was a hypothyroid condition. She sort of drifted, slept fourteen hours a night and couldn't keep track of conversations. Believe me, dear, I tried. I really tried. I had about forty minutes alone with her. I tried to drop key words into it to get some kind of a reaction. After a long struggle I did find out that her husband played poker last Wednesday night. He loves a good poker session, she said. She said he didn't come back until Thursday just before noon. I practically had to shake her to get that much out of her."

I did not tell Dana I felt uneasy. I had the feeling the play was being taken away from us. I had made a move. Now either this was all in innocence, or M'Gruder was making one. I resolved to handle myself as though he were making a move. Violence is the stepchild of desperation.

We both had to borrow gear. Glenn Barnweather's pants were too short in the leg and big in the waist for me. Dana had a slightly different problem with Joanne's twill britches. The waist was fine and the length was good, but in thigh and bottom Dana filled them to bursting. The stable hands saddled the mounts while a rather shaky Joanne doled out therapeutic rum sours. Joanne assigned the mounts. Dana, as a novice, got a rather plump and amiable mare. I was given a hammer-head buckskin with a rolling eye. He sensed a certain incompetence and tried simultaneously to nibble my leg and bash me into a post. I sawed him and kicked him into a dubious docility. By all odds, as we went clattering and snorting up a long baked slope, Joanne and Vance were the best of the group. Elbows in, heels correct, moving like a part of the animal. Glenn on a big red stallion was a close second. Ulka and I were about on a level. She looked glorious in pale blue denim with a white cowgirl hat on the back of her fair head, laced under her chin. Ulka seemed much merrier than on the night before. But Vance looked wretched. He had a greenish look under his tan. His eyes were bloodshot. With the air of a man under great tension he had knocked down three sours in rapid order before mounting.

Joanne chattered about the ranch and what they

were eventually going to do with it. She pointed out where things would be. My damned horse kept trying to stumble to see if he could loosen me a little bit, then hurl me the rest of the way. For a time I rode beside Ulka. She dipped into a pale leather pouchpurse she wore looped around one wrist and got out cigarettes, leaned and gave me one, then leaned and after several near misses, managed to give me a light. We smiled in wordless idiocy at each other. Her big breasts bounced very firmly under the denim. Her classic nose was shiny. I lost her when my horse moved up from a canter into a full run. He didn't seem to like a canter. He tended to drop back into a spine-shattering trot or suddenly go like hell. He kept me busy. Suddenly everybody, at Glenn's suggestion, went careening across rocky flats toward a distant stand of trees. My horse was beginning to take me a little more seriously. We were spread out. Dana was up with Glenn, hunched toward the horse's neck, perhaps grasping at the saddle horn, pale pants bouncing. Joanne was at my left and a half a length ahead of me.

That was when Ulka Atlund M'Gruder gave her terrible, piercing scream. The horses had violent reactions. I went up with mine and came down with mine, then spurred him forward and caught at Dana just as she began to slip off the side of her mare's neck, hauled her back toward the saddle. Glenn had taken off to the left. I looked and saw M'Gruder's horse running wildly in that direction, with a terrible ragdoll figure bounding along the rocks beside the rear hooves. It slipped free and lay still, wet-shiny with some patches of red. Ulka dismounted and, screaming again, ran stumbling across the rocks to drop beside the figure. I dropped off and knotted my barbarous steed to a dwarfed bush. Dana's mare suddenly took off, heading for home. Joanne reined around and set out after Dana. I ran over to the body. It took one look to identify it forever as such. I pulled Ulka to her feet and walked her away from it. She was shuddering, over and over.

"He just leaned forward and slipped off," she said in her thin little voice with just a trace of accent. "He slipped off but his foot was caught. He just leaned forward and slipped off. Oh, my God." She dropped onto her knees and haunches, face in her hands.

They brought the body back in a jeep and transferred it into an ambulance near the Barnweather house. The necessary red tape was handled with dispatch. We all agreed that M'Gruder had not seemed well. Ulka said that he'd had a stomach upset and had not slept. She rested in Joanne's bedroom. Joanne and Dana were with her. Her father was notified. He would arrive in Phoenix Sunday morning to take her back to San Francisco. The funeral would be there. M'Gruder's lawyer was notified. Reporters hovered around, sitting in cars, looking irritable.

I sat in the terrace shade with Glenn Barnweather. He kept shaking his head and saying, "Hell of a thing, hell of a thing," and then fixing himself another stiff bourbon.

"He certainly had everything to live for," I said.

"Christ, you ought to see his place in Hawaii. Her place now, I guess. You know why it hits her so damned hard having it happen right now? I got woozy last night. If I'd gone to bed, I'd have been sick. I took a little walk. Sounds carry in the night. They were having one hell of a battle last night. Screaming at each other. I couldn't hear the words. It went on a long time. You wouldn't think she could get that worked up, would you? Maybe it was their first fight. I had the idea he was in charge.

Maybe he thought so too. A man married two months and he can stay out all night for poker when there's that item home in bed, you *know* he has to be boss."

"Poker?"

"Down in town at the club last Wednesday. It's a regular thing. All-night session once a month. He dropped about two thousand. I got some of it. I would have had more, but he came back pretty good toward the end."

When you sell yourself something, and all the parts fit, you resent the hell out of having somebody kick the foundation out from under it. You want to grab the structure to keep it from falling down.

"He played all night long?" I said, looking at that big red earnest face, looking in vain for any hint of lie or evasion.

His fleeting grin was mildly lewd. "Well into the bright cruel light of day, McGee. I can understand anybody being startled, after a good look at that Swede bride. Maybe poor Vance had to take a breather. She looks like one hell of a project."

My pretty tower fell down. Fallacious suppositions make a hell of a jangle when they hit the dirt, particularly when you dislike the person you've nominated. I'd heard one little piece of that quarrel too, a piece that could be related to the previous Wednesday night. Maybe I'd heard him asking her where she'd gone that night. And she taunted him about Mexican boyfriends . . .

"Did Ulka have a night on the town too?" I asked him.

"She was going to, but not what you'd call a real swinging situation. One of Joanne's concert things. I miss every one I can. Cocktails and a dinner party and a concert party. It was all set up, and Ulka decided not to go, and Joanne went alone."

"Maybe Ulka went out later. Did they have a rental car?"

"I loaned them the Corvette I bought Jo. It's the three-sixty, and it's just too much car for her. It scares her. Vance was wondering about buying it and they could drive it to San Francisco and have the rest of their stuff shipped. Okay with me, but we didn't get around to making the deal. It's new. About fifteen hundred miles on it. It scares Jo. She gets absentminded and gooses it and it scares her."

"Was that Wednesday night the only time they've been apart?"

"He stuck pretty close to her."

"They drive around in that car much?"

"We were keeping them too busy. What's this all about?"

I shrugged. "Nothing. Idle chatter." After some small talk, he fixed himself another drink and ambled off into the house. I went down the path to the guest house. The Sting Ray was in the carport, top down. I looked at the speedometer and then walked slowly and thoughtfully back to the main house. I couldn't tell Glenn what was on my mind. The toppled pieces of my theory suddenly looked good again. I was putting it back together, with a new name on it. The problem was motive. A weird guess stopped me in my tracks. I took long strides the rest of the way to the main house.

I whispered to Dana in the hallway. "Honey, just keep anybody from going into that bedroom. Make any excuse you can think of."

"You look so strange, darling."

"I feel strange."

"Can you tell me?"

"When I'm sure. Then I can tell you."

I went into Joanne's bedroom and closed the door behind me. It was a long room. The draperies were drawn. It was early afternoon. Ulka reclined on a quilted yellow chaise with a fuzzy yellow blanket over her lap. Her slanted eyes were reddened. She was still in her stretch denim, and drifting on the air-conditioned chill was the faint effluvium of saddle horse. She watched me with apparent unconcern as, without greeting, I pulled a hassock over close to the chaise and sat facing her. She had so much presence I had to remind myself she was, after all, just an eighteen-year-old girl, with the very last diminishing hint of a childish roundness in her cheeks.

Silence is a useful gambit, but I could not tell if it was having any effect at all upon her.

"Well, Ullie," I said.

"I will never let anyone else ever call me that, all my life."

"That's very sentimental, Ullie. Very tenderhearted. I guess you are a very tenderhearted girl. You didn't want your father upset, did you? Those pictures Ives took of your husband-to-be would have upset the professor. He would have forbidden the marriage. And you are a dutiful daughter. Ives was a very greedy fellow. He knew how badly Vance wanted you. He must have asked for a great deal of money. You know, it wasn't smart of Ives to blackmail his previous client with the pictures he took, because Vance knew him. Ives must have decided Vance was incapable of violence."

She frowned and shook her pretty head. "Ives? Pictures? Blackmail? Why do you come in here with this crazy talk?"

"Ives had to get it in one big chunk because as soon as you were married to Vance, there was no more leverage Ives could use. I guess Vance must have confessed the problem to you and showed you the pictures, perhaps to see if you would marry without Daddy's permission, so he could save a bundle. It's pretty sad and funny, Ullie. Your great respect for your father, and no respect for life."

"You should not call me Ullie. I will not permit it."

"Vance must have thought it was just a marvelous accident when Ives got killed. All he cared was that it got him off the hook, and when no confederate appeared to pick up where Ives had left off, he knew he was home free. He was going to have the girl, the gold ring and everything. His tragedy was in slowly finding out what a psychotic bitch you really are."

"Who are you? You must be mad, entirely."

"Let's check it out together, Ullie. No one suspected Vance. Patty, his ex-wife, was the only one in the world in a position to brood about it and begin to add two and two. And finally she got an answer and checked it out as closely as she could, and knew she had Vance right where she wanted him. She had every reason to want to get back at him. Believing Vance had killed Ives, and knowing that he could be a good big source of income to her for the rest of her life, she got in touch with him. I think we can figure out how that went wrong, Ullie. Vance could prove where he was on the night of December fifth. But where was his darling girl? Quite a husky girl. And someone who could get close to Ives and close to Patty at night, in lonely places, whereas Vance couldn't have managed it. After you'd bashed Ives, Patty was a necessity. Clumsy murder is like housework, dear. Once you begin, you're never really finished."

"All this is so absurd, and so boring."

186

"Patty would have persisted, and sooner or later Vance would have had to face the idea that you killed Ives. Maybe he couldn't stomach that. Maybe he would have turned you in. He was finding out that his marriage wasn't what he had counted on."

"We couldn't have been happier!"

"Ullie! Ullie! What about the Mexican boyfriends? Just little flirtations, I imagine. Just enough to keep him off balance, make him sweat."

"How could you—" She stopped. I could guess she remembered how he had tried to shush her. Her breathing had gone slightly shallow and there were spots of color in flawless cheeks. I saw her recover herself with an effort, slowing and deepening her breathing.

"I don't imagine Vance really wanted to play poker. You left unobserved, you got back unobserved. Home free. But all it would take would be legwork, Ullie. One of those plodding methodical checks of every gas station along the way. You didn't have the range. Some little joker is probably still dreaming about you—the most beautiful girl he ever saw, coming in out of the night in that Sting Ray."

"So? I got very restless. I took a drive. I drive very fast. Can I help it if Vance got very suspicious of me, if he got very foolish ideas? You don't know how it is . . . how it was. He wanted to be . . . so very young and lively and fun, to be like boys I know. But really he wanted things quieter. I could see strangers laughing at him. He should have had *dignity!* Certainly I wanted all that money and travel and clothes and fun. A professor has a shabby little life. All my life I knew the husband I would have, older and very rich and strong, to buy me everything and adore me, to sit and smile at me and admire me when I danced with all the young men, and trust me. When I'd found him I could not lose him. But every day was a contest to see . . . which one of us was younger. He did not understand how love should be a perfection. All he cared was how many times he could take me. He thought that was another way to be young. Why did he have to prove so much? I can tell about you. You would understand. You are older too, but not as old as he was. You are stronger, Travis McGee. There is the money now. I listened when you told Joanne about your funny little boat with the funny name." She closed her eyes for a moment, opened them wide and looked at me. "You see, I have always . . . felt like a special person. As if my life would be . . . beautiful and important. Things happen in strange ways. Vance was not the one. But suddenly you are here. It is strange. It is so strange the way we both have that little feeling it would be . . . what was planned for us all along."

It was such a fabulous con job, I could feel the dirty dreams seeping into my mind. Help her cover up the mistakes she'd made. That was the unspoken offer. And you get the girl on a platter. Mmmm . . . trade the *Busted Flush* for a really good motor sailer, crew of three—captain, steward, deckhand—and see how many sheltered coves in the world's oceans had really top-grade moonlight. And, of course, remember never to turn your back to her . . .

"Ullie, dear, we can't get onto a new subject until we finish the first one. I repeat your interesting statement. 'When I'd found him I could not lose him.' But he finally worked himself into a position where you had to lose him. I knew he was prying at you to find out where you'd gone, and I wondered why he thought you'd gone anywhere. Then Glenn told me about Vance thinking he might buy the car. Men who think of buying cars kick the tires and slam the doors and check the mileage. So he checked the mileage, and then he checked it again and found a great big inexplicable addition, taking it up to past two thousand. He hadn't put it on, so you had, and Patty was dead in the same way Ives was dead, and he found himself in a pretty eerie marriage. I'll make a little guess, Ullie. From the way he acted this morning, I don't think he got much sleep. I think he kept digging at you until you opened up and told him the whole thing. Then after you told him, you realized he couldn't exactly forgive and forget. He couldn't handle it. It was too much. Maybe he felt so wretched he didn't want to take any morning ride, but you knew that sooner or later you could maneuver it so that all the rest of us would be ahead of you two."

"Could I be such a monster, darling? Could you believe that of me, really?"

That narrow leather pouchpurse was in the chaise beside her hip. She made a futile grab for it as I took it quickly. It was new. I examined it and found a little area still moist near the bottom seam. The leather thongs were long and sturdy. Holding it by the thongs, I felt the deadly heft and balance of it. It was like a sock with a rock in the toe. It was a skull smasher, wicked as a medieval flail. I opened the pouch top, reached in and fumbled past lipstick, little comb, cigarettes and matches, and pulled out a rabbit. It was carved of some dense gray stone, sitting hunched, ears laid back, crude, a lump about two-thirds the size of a baseball.

"There is the legwork with the gas stations, and there are the miracles of modern chemistry, Ullie. The tiny little blotch of blood on this, with maybe a sweet little tuft of hubby's hair stuck thereon, scrubbed off nicely right there in Joanne's bathroom. But a police lab can prove it was human blood hereon, though they can't type it. And they can dismantle the plumbing and find traces in the drain in there. I imagine that after Ives and Patty you disposed of the bags. They'd have been a lot messier."

"That's a very old bunny," she said. "It's primitive folk art from Iceland."

"Ullie, a good enough lawyer might be able to plead you sick and buy the experts to back him up. Age would be a consideration, of course. And beauty. Maybe you are sick. I don't know. Perhaps it is just an egoism so intense other people don't seem quite real to you. Murder wouldn't seem real then either, I suppose."

She tilted her head. "Vance cried and cried. He hugged me and said he would get me the best—" She stopped, gnawed her thumb knuckle, looked at me in a speculative way. The admission had been made, and I could not tell if it was inadvertent or meant to look inadvertent. "You can understand, Travis. There's such a thing as thinking of the best for everybody concerned. I'd very much like to have you take me home to Father. I know you would like each other, very much. He is very old-fashioned, you know. He would want me to wait a year. Waiting isn't too hard, is it, when you're sure?"

I bounced the bunny in the palm of my hand, dropped it back into the lethal sack, yanked the drawstring tight. I could not even tell if she knew what a desperate game she was playing. She sat up, reached and closed her warm strong hand around my wrist. I was planning the words to tell her I was blowing the whistle when I heard the door behind me open slowly. I realized, as I turned, I had spent a long time with the bereaved widow, and Dana might be having problems keeping people out.

Dana stared in at us from the doorway. "Joanne has to . . ."

190

"I'm through here, honey," I said. "Tell Glenn to phone the law. This eerie child killed all three of them, and she made so many mistakes it won't be hard to . . ."

I had made the elementary mistake of taking my eyes off Ulka. When the pouch bag was ripped out of my hand, I did not bother to turn around and see what she was going to do with it. I dived to my left, away from the chaise, but bunny rabbit still glanced off my skull and came down onto my shoulder, smashing the collarbone. I sprawled on the floor, with my ears roaring and with lights spangling my vision, absolutely unable to avoid a second and mortal crunching if she had taken time. But a vagueness moved past me with tiger pace, and I made a stifled whimper which was supposed to be a roar of warning to Dana. As vision cleared, as I got onto my knees, I saw Dana go down flat and heavy and hopelessly limp, onto her face. I heard a distant shout of query and alarm. I began the slow crawl toward my woman.

Fifteen

I HAD A PRETTY FAIR CONCUSSION, just enough so that I had blackouts, and they kept shining lights into my eyes, testing my reflexes and giving me mental arithmetic to solve. My right arm, taped across my chest, felt leaden, and the smashed bone caused enough pain to keep them sticking needles into me. It made me groggy, and I kept asking about Dana. Miss Holtzer is in surgery. Miss Holtzer is still in surgery. Miss Holtzer is in the recovery room.

Then it was Sunday morning and I was told that Miss Holtzer was doing as well as could be expected. It is a dim phrase. Who sets up the expectations?

Glenn Barnweather arrived with a big solemn face, a hundred sighs, a sad shaking of the head, a rich smell of bourbon to tell me Ulka was dead. I already knew that, but I didn't know how.

"She took off in the Corvette, northeast out Sixty-five like a goddam road race, and they still can't figure how she got past as many curves as she did. They put a roadblock up there in the straight, way beyond Sunflower, one car blocking the road, and she came down on it at, they estimate, a hundred and thirty or better. Tried to cut around it. Hit the gravel, skidded, hit a rock, went two hundred and fifty feet through the air, hit and bounced and went over a rim and down a thousand-foot slope, bouncing all the way, and the final couple hundred feet on fire. Like you told the cops, McGee, she must have been crazed with grief. That's right, isn't it? Crazed with grief."

"Out of her head completely. Maniacal strength. You've heard of that."

"I've heard of that. And Diana Hollis turns into Dana Holtzer. What goes on, old buddy?"

"We have to try to protect a lady's reputation, don't we?"

"Oh, sure. Hell, what you do is your own business, I guess, but Jo is going to come in here and really blow her stack."

"I guess she checked with the Divers."

"And Mary West, who wouldn't tell her a damned thing. So she's steaming."

"Glenn, how about you finding out just how Dana is. I would appreciate it very much. "

"Glad to do anything for an old buddy who tells me every little thing," he said.

He came back in a half hour. "She's one sick gal, Trav. They spent six hours picking little bits of bone out of the front of her brain, right here. And I find out she works for Lysa Dean. That's going to intrigue hell out of Jo. They say Dana's going to be okay." He stood up. "You'll be able to see her by tomorrow."

More officials visited me. I told my tale of hysterical violence again, the young bride crazed by her terrible loss.

Joanne came in. She was furious. After fifteen minutes she was merely resentful, reluctantly accepting the fact there must be some good reason why she'd never find out all she wanted to know. She was decent enough to do some errands for me, like telling the Hallmark to save the room for me, like getting a phone put in, like getting a resident neurosurgeon to come in and give me some straight answers on Dana. He said she should take two months' rest and recuperation before going back to work. I had passed my tests and would be released Monday, unless I acquired some new symptoms. He said not to worry about how she'd act on Monday when I could see her for a few minutes. She would be dazed and semiconscious still and might not know me.

After he left I was planning to try to locate Lysa Dean, but she phoned me, putting one very nervous quaver in the switchboard operator's voice. Lysa was terribly dramatic and terribly concerned about everything, full of elaborate assurances about hospital bills—but shrewd enough to play the whole thing as though I was Dana's dear friend who had accompanied her on her little vacation. She said she and her whole entourage would stop off on the way back to the Coast, but she couldn't be sure exactly when they could manage it.

On Monday I got dressed and paid my bill and had five minutes with Dana. She was in an adhesive turban, face bloated, shiny, streaked with bruise marks, slits revealing dazed eyes, mouth cracked and puffy. She seemed to know me. She squeezed my hand. I could not understand her mumblings. The nurse stood by and called time on me and sent me away. I moved back into the Hallmark. On Tuesday I saw her three times, morning, afternoon, evening, ten minutes each time. She knew me, and her diction was better, but she was unaware of what had happened to her and seemed in no hurry to find out. She had a tendency to drop off and start snoring in the middle of a vague remark, but she did like her hand held.

At midnight on Tuesday I was awakened by a phone call from an abjectly apologetic fellow telling me that

194

Lysa Dean was in residence at the best hotel in town and wanted to see me right away. I told him to tell Lysa Dean to go emote up a rope and hung up. I picked up my phone and told the Hallmark switchboard to leave me in peace until nine the next morning. The pinned bone made dressing too much of a problem. If she wanted me, she knew where I was.

Just as I got back to sleep, forty minutes later, there was a brisk knock at my door. Muttering various Anglo-Saxon expressions, I got up and adjusted my sling and went in my shorts to the door. A portly chap in a black suit entered, followed by a Hallmark porter carrying the luggage which Dana and I had checked on to New York and couldn't retrieve in time.

"I'm Herm Louker," he said with an air of imparting information any fool would know. When I looked blank he said, "From the agency." It was supposed to explain everything.

He dipped two fingers into a breast pocket, pulled out two crisp dollars, crackled them very loudly as he handed them to the porter.

Herm looked somewhat like a penguin. He had the same walk. He wore a hairpiece, with a deep wave. His eyes were cigar holes in a hotel towel. He had gold jewelry. He settled himself into a chair, sliced the end off a cigar with a gold knife, lit it with a gold lighter.

"Let me make myself entirely clear, Mr. McGee. The client's interest is my interest. Aside from loving that little woman personally, because she is all doll, through and through, what I got in my mind is a maximum protection of her interests and mine and the industry's." He held up a fat warning hand. "In addition to that, before we go further, I've got also a nervous stomach, and I want to know no more than I already know. I have been with her in Miami, New York and Chicago, and she was a great little trouper, performing in every way. They love that girl all over America. She is all star."

"So I'd better know how much you know."

"Merely that there has been, we shall say, an indiscretion. Show business people, Mr. McGee, are high-spirited and hot-blooded, and some people can take advantage. What we have going is an unfortunate situation where some character wants to give her a rough time. What the little lady feels is that after you started to perform, then you went off on a tangent. Time has been wasted. We got certain information from you in New York. One Samuel Bogen wanted already by the cops. There is no picture. Fingerprints only. A complete description which could be ninety-five thousand guys including me, almost. So we laid on special guards with that description in mind. Nothing in New York. Nothing in Chicago. No contact. As I get it, certain financial inducements were offered. Our star gets nervous, Mr. McGee. What we need now is some way to bring this to a head. If you can solve that, the little lady says she will live up to her end of your deal. I do not want to know your deal, believe me."

"I had one idea worked out."

"So?"

"I wanted to be part of it. I'm not in top shape at the moment."

"So I see."

"It depends on several things. Could you set up a time for her arrival at Los Angeles by air and give it a lot of publicity around Los Angeles?"

"But naturally. It's done every day."

"The man who is after her is disturbed. I think that except for one trip to Vegas, he's stayed in the Los Angeles area. He might come to the airport. He might be waiting at her house. He may want money. He may want to kill her. He might not even know which he wants."

"Please. It gives me cramps."

"You have to know a few things, Mr. Louker. We don't want to endanger your star. You could arrange a reasonably good facsimile?"

"The right size, right dye job, right clothes, dark glasses, makeup, a quick study in the way she waves and walks. Sure. Ten minutes on the phone I've got one, believe me."

"But she gets maximum protection too."

"I would insist."

"Now here is the delicate point, Mr. Louker. If this Bogen is picked up, the cops are going to know the name he is using and the address he is using in about three minutes. Somebody has to be ready to move very quickly. At that address are going to be some things which should be destroyed, or maybe your star's career goes down the drain. Somebody has to be smart and quick."

"Are you going to give me more cramps?"

"Photographs, Herm. Of your star in a circus. A mob scene. If they got out it might not dent her too badly as long as she stays big at the box office. But two dog pictures in a row could cook her."

He got up and tiptoed about, patting his stomach, moaning softly. There was a lot of stomach. It started under his chin and descended in a long penguin curve to his knees.

"How can we get the pictures?" he demanded, more of himself than of me.

"Get a very nimble lawyer, and charge Bogen with stealing them from her. Get them impounded for her identification, then returned to her for destruction, and give him some impressive pieces of cash to hand out if he has to. Hell, you people have given out little gifts other times."

He studied me. "I know you from someplace, maybe? Like in Rome with Manny?"

"No."

"It will come to me. We'll work it out somehow." He took a wad of currency out and counted out a thousand dollars. "She said expenses. You can sign the receipt okay?"

I managed. He wished me well and left, looking gastric.

Dana wasn't very responsive the next morning. After I left her room the head nurse on the floor intercepted me. She was wearing a curious expression, as if she had just discovered that if she flapped her arms hard enough she could fly.

"Lysa Dean came to see her."

"Was she conscious then?"

"Oh, no. Miss Dean was very shocked. She was very upset. I think she must have a very warm heart."

"She must have."

"She left this for you, sir."

I opened it with one hand on my way down the hall. Heavy blue paper, scented. Sprawling backhand in blue ink. "I must see you. Please. L."

The cab took me there. The desk said sorry, she isn't registered here, sir. I gave them my name. Oh. Go right up, sir. She has the west wing on the fourth floor. A cop type guarded the wing. He glanced at the sling and spoke my last name with a question mark after it. Last door on the right, he said.

She sat on a dressing table bench in a white robe. A

man was saying rude words over a phone. A thin man was fixing her hair. A girl in glasses was reading her a script aloud in a nasal monotonous voice. She shooed them all out.

"Dear McGee," she said. "Your poor arm, dear. Oh, my God, the way Dana looked. It broke my heart. It really did. I actually wept."

"That's nice."

"Please don't be sullen. We're going to do what you suggested to Herm. They're going to fly a girl in. I'm going to hide out here like a thief, dear. God, things are going to get into the damnedest mess without Dana. They're going to pot already. How could she?"

"I guess it was just thoughtlessness."

She studied me, head cocked on the side. Then she laughed aloud. "Oh, *no!* Really? But when I kidded you in Miami, I never *really* thought you could actually *get* her. You must be very damned . . ."

"You would be doing me one of the world's greatest favors to please shut your mouth, Lee. There's been a lot of dying done. My shoulder aches. Dana is worth ten of you."

She went back and sat on the bench. "At least I know why you two were futzing around out here on my expense money. Making the fun last, eh?"

"That's right."

"Damn you, tell me the real reason."

"The man who took you for a hundred and twenty thousand was murdered. It looked as if M'Gruder might have done it and could be arrested for it sooner or later. Then that house party would have figured in the trial. I wanted to check it out."

The quick red fox stared at me with foxy eyes, instantly aware of the implications. She fingered her throat. "'Off the hook on that, eh?"

"Yes. And I have a hunch you'll be in the clear on the other too. I wonder about you, Lee. Take a look at that house party list. Nancy Abbott is beyond hope. Vance and Patty and Sonny Catton are dead. The photographer is dead. Poor little Whippy is trade for the butch."

"Really? What is all this? The hand of God? Punishment? Don't be an ass, McGee. Sometimes the swingers go quicker. Maybe because they don't have their feet braced. If that kind of little fun party could kill, honey, lower California would be shrinking. You know, you do drag a little. Have you noticed it? Oh, hell, I don't want to fight you. It's going to be weeks and weeks before Dana can get back on the ball. That's what they told me. I'll keep her on salary, of course. And there's a sick benefit thing she's entitled to. Scotty will check that all out for her and take care of it. I think . . ."

Herm came to the door and beckoned to her. She excused herself and went to him. They talked a few moments in low tones. He left and she came slowly back to me. "There's a meeting I don't dare miss. Damn it. I did want to see Dana, at least once more. Herm is going to have to smuggle me into town and bring the stand-in along later. McGee, my darling, I've got a thousand things to do . . ."

"You sent for me. Remember?"

She snapped her fingers. "Of course. Darling, you got the thousand expenses? You understand that our deal was to get me completely free and clear. Right? It's all or nothing, you understand. If your plan works, you come to see me and we'll settle up. All right? Darling, I do love Dana like a sister, but sick people depress me so. Could you find some nice little dude ranch or something for her, and a woman to take care. I'll have Victor Scott work out the money end with you. Would you mind terribly? After all, you *must* find each other attractive. I'm entirely clear publicity-wise on this end because, thank God, there isn't a shred to link me to Vance in any way." She patted my face. "Be a dear and take care of our girl. Give her my love, and bring her back to me when she's truly healthy again."

On Thursday afternoon the improvement in Dana was astonishing. The puffiness was gone, but there were saffron marks of the bruises. She wore lipstick. She was propped up. Her smile of greeting was shy.

They let me have an hour with her. She was anxious to know what had happened. I knew it might tire her, but I had to brief her before some official visited her and asked questions. I caught her up to date, including the plan to trap Bogen.

When I got back to the Hallmark at four that afternoon, there was a message to call a Los Angeles operator. When it went through, Lysa came on the phone, yapping with glee and relief. "McGee, darling? It worked, you shrewd, shrewd man! Our own people got him, and took away the nasty little gun he was going to shoot me with. Shoot the stand-in, I mean. And they went to his nasty little rooms and got all the photographs, and then they turned him and his nasty little gun over to the law. My God, I didn't even know the terrible tension I was under. It's *such* a relief."

"Wouldn't it be nice if you asked about Dana?"

"Give me *time*, for God's sake! All right. How is she?"

"Much, much better."

"That's fine. That's good to hear."

"You and I have a little accounting to do."

"I *know* that. Damn it, what makes you so sour? Give me a chance. What's today? Thursday. Let me look at my book." I waited five minutes and she came back on the line. "Darling, I'll be home Monday afternoon. You fly in and come talk to me about it."

"Talk to you about it?"

"Darling, you don't exactly have a contract, you know. And a frightened person can make some *very* rash promises. Technically, you really weren't in at the kill, were you?"

"Monday afternoon," I said and hung up. I did not know why I had been sour with her. Something was wrong, and I did not know what it was.

On Sunday afternoon I found out what my instincts had been trying to tell me. The nurse and I helped Dana into the wheelchair and I rolled her to the big sun-room, to a private corner.

"Here's the way I have it lined up," I told her. I sat holding her hand. "Ten days before they spring you, then say a week or so more before you can travel, honey. So I tote you east, get you settled aboard, and after a few days we can go cruising. How does that sound?"

She gently, firmly pulled her hand away from mine. She looked away from me. "Travis, you have been very good to me."

"What's the matter?"

"It was all . . . mixed up and crazy. It wasn't me, really. I don't know how to tell you. I'm not like that. I'm married. I don't even know how I could have been so . . . so silly. I think it was because of working for her, maybe. I'm not going back to her."

I put my fingertips under her chin and turned her

head and made her look at me. I looked at her until she flushed and twisted her head away. She meant it. A new conception. You could get a hit on the head that could knock love out of you for good and all. When their eyes go that dead for you, there's no way to ever get back. I knew what my instincts had been trying to tell me.

"You don't have to stay around," she said. "I mean, I'm used to looking after myself. I'll be fine, really. I do want to thank you for everything. I feel so sorry about . . . giving you the wrong idea and a lot of false hopes and . . ."

"You can still be honest, can't you?"

"Of course."

"How do you feel about my coming to see you here, Dana?"

She hesitated, then lifted her chin a half inch. "I d-dread it, Travis. I'm terribly sorry. It just keeps reminding me of something I'd rather forget."

Then all that was left us was the good-by ritual, which was, after the details of what to do with her belongings, and my promise to send a nurse to wheel her back to her room, a handshake. McGee, the great lover. This was one I wanted to keep. No, not this one. I didn't even know this one. The one I wanted to keep was the one Ullie had bashed on her way to go kill herself. This Dana wanted to forget that Dana. And damn well soon would. So shake hands with your darling and say good-by and try not to see the evident relief she tries to hide.

The cab deposited me in front of Lysa Dean's iron gates on Monday afternoon. The Korean let me through the gates. The maid let me into the house and then disappeared. The house was as silent as when I had been there with Dana. The big oil portraits of Lysa Dean stared emotionally at me through the half gloom of draperied sunlight.

I roamed and plinked two notes out of the gold and white piano. Lysa Dean came swiftly into the room, in black knit pants and a white silk overblouse, an effective combination to go with gold-red hair in a room of whites and blacks and golds. She wore woolly white slippers and carried a white envelope in her hand. She hurried to me, stretched up to kiss me with the faked sweet shyness of a welcoming child, and took me by my good hand to a vast couch in a shadowed alcove.

"How is dear Dana?" she asked.

"Marvelously improved."

"When can she come back to work, dear? I really need her, desperately."

"She'll have to take it easy for a while."

"McGee, darling, *do* use your influence on her. Tell her Lysa needs her *sooooo* much."

"I'll tell her that the very first chance I get."

"You *are* a huge old sweetie. Now what about the photos I gave you in Miami?"

"I've destroyed the ones I had made, with your face blanked out. When I get back, I'll destroy the other ones . . . unless you want them."

"God, I don't ever want to see them again. Darling, they say that little Bogen is way way off. If he'd tried to fire his rusty little gun, it would have blown his hand off. They are going to put him away."

"So now your life is all neatened up, Miss Dean. And you'll get to marry your dear friend. Congratulations. Is that my money you keep hanging onto?"

She handed me the envelope. I fumbled it open, and saw that it was light, and found that it counted up to ten thousand. It wouldn't count one inch past that. Before I could get the first word out, she was hanging onto me, laughing and teasing, saying, "Now darling, *do* be realistic, after all! I gave you all that nice travel money, and sent you off with quite a handsome and exciting gal, and you had some exciting and delicious adventures, all on the house. I'm really not *made* of money, darling. Taxes are fantastic. Really, when you think of it, I think you are doing terribly well out of this, and some of my advisers would think I was out of my head to give you all this." As she was talking she got the money out of my hand and slipped it into the inside pocket of my jacket, and was going quite directly and efficiently to work on me, with the quickness of a lot of little kissings, and an arching and presentation of all the celebrity curves and fragrances, a lot of cleverness of little hands, and a convincing steaminess of breath and growing excitement, worming her way astride my lap. This was the artist at work, at the work she knew best, operating from a lifelong knowledge of the male animal and quite convinced, apparently, that a good quick solid bang would send the man away too happy to care about being shorted, too dazed to object. Already she was beginning to work her way out of those soft knit pants and simultaneously beginning the little pressures which were supposed to topple me over onto my back on the big couch under a picture of the lady herself.

I got my good left arm in between us and my palm flat against her wishbone, then abruptly straightened my arm, sending her catapulting back, scrambling, slipping on the smooth hard terrazzo, sitting hard on a white furry rug and riding it back like a sled to end up under another picture so soulful the artist had indicated a halo effect.

She bounded up, hair masking one eye, yanking the knit pants up over the white behind. "What the hell!" she squalled. "Jesus Christ, McGee, you could have bust my tailbone!"

I was standing up, fixing my sling, starting toward the door.

"It's okay, Lee baby," I said. "I'll take the short count. You don't have to try to sweeten it. It wouldn't mean one damn thing to you, and it would mean just a little less than that to me."

I left amid a shrieking of ten-letter words, and I was hastened on my way by a hail of elephants. She had a collection. She threw fast, but not well.

I crunched down the finest grade of brown gravel, past sprinkler water pattering on fat green leaves. The Korean let me out. I could feel the meager money weight in my jacket pocket. I stopped and took my arm out of the sling and stuffed the sling in a pocket. The arm did not feel good swinging, so I tucked a thumb in my belt.

I walked and thought of what a weird way to lose a good woman. I saw old men carefully driving lookalike cars with names like Fury and Tempest and Dart. Through a fence I saw a quintet of little girls dashing in and out of the silvery spray of a sprinkler, shrilling. A dog smiled at me.

What a ridiculous way to lose a woman. They do not like pedestrians in that neighborhood. Polite cops stopped, asked polite questions and politely drove me to the nearest taxi stand. I got into the cab and the only place to go was my hotel room, and I didn't want to go there, but I couldn't think of anything else.

When we stopped for a light I saw a magic store, and I asked the driver if he thought they might sell love potions in there. He said that if I was looking for action, just say the word. I went back to the hotel, and seventy minutes later I was on the Miami jet.